Who You Might Be

Who You Might Be

A NOVEL

Leigh N. Gallagher

Henry Holt and Company
NEW YORK

Henry Holt and Company
Publishers since 1866
120 Broadway
New York, New York 10271
www.henryholt.com

Henry Holt® and Ⓗ® are registered trademarks
of Macmillan Publishing Group, LLC.

Library of Congress Cataloging-in-Publication Data

Names: Gallagher, Leigh N., author.
Title: Who you might be : a novel / Leigh N. Gallagher.
Description: First edition. | New York : Henry Holt and Company, 2022.
Identifiers: LCCN 2021047380 (print) | LCCN 2021047381 (ebook) |
  ISBN 9781250817846 (hardcover) | ISBN 9781250817853 (ebook)
Subjects: LCGFT: Bildungsromans. | Novels.
Classification: LCC PS3607.A4154414 W48 2022 (print) |
  LCC PS3607.A4154414 (ebook) | DDC 813/.6—dc23
LC record available at https://lccn.loc.gov/2021047380
LC ebook record available at https://lccn.loc.gov/2021047381

Our books may be purchased in bulk for promotional, educational,
or business use. Please contact your local bookseller or the Macmillan
Corporate and Premium Sales Department at (800) 221-7945, extension 5442,
or by e-mail at MacmillanSpecialMarkets@macmillan.com.

First Edition 2022

Designed by Karen Minster

Printed in the United States of America

1 3 5 7 9 10 8 6 4 2

Who You Might Be

I.

NIGHT SHIPS

1997

An uneasy child, all scratched up, somewhat disgusting, without a precise body or image, having lost his specificity, an alien in a world of desire and power, he longs only to reinvent love.

Julia Kristeva,
"Extraterrestrials Suffering for Want of Love"

1.

TWO FOURTEEN-YEAR-OLD GIRLS, ONE BEAUTIFUL AND ONE just okay, are running away from home on a northbound Amtrak. A Friday in August: California is all dried out, ready to catch fire beneath a bad-mood sun. Miniature navy window curtains recall the pressed and pleated skirts girls wear on television but which Judy and Meghan have never worn. They are publicly schooled and more or less poor. A plastic table between them accommodates their homey mess. Seatback veils—*dandruff absorbers*—wisp up, then lower, all by themselves.

The girls chew their cuticles and turn their heads fast to remember their ponytails. They scoff at the name of the train line, the Coastal Quest.

"Courtney is totally mental."

"Courtney S. or Courtney N.?"

"Duh."

"Mental *and* crazy."

"She's kind of a mental slut."

"She kind of has a mustache."

"I heard she sleeps with a *stuffed animal*."

"She probably practices stuff on it."

"I bet she practices stuff on her dog."

"Melissa *definitely* practices stuff on her dog."

"Ew, her dog's name is *Cootie*."

"Ew, more like Coochy."

"*Coochy cooties*."

"Ew!"

Meghan, the pretty one, starts it, but Judy, anxious today, has the compulsion to keep it going. They talk until it's painful, until their subjects are obliterated and the babble blends with the train's manic engine, its determined, rattling charge, though they perform cool indifference. *Whatever, who cares,* eye contact—less. Meghan, as in most things, is better at the act than Judy. Judy has a tendency to slip into earnestness.

"Is it weird, though? To do a blow job? How do people *breathe*?" A change in her vocal register—a mix of doubt and hope, wanting to believe what she thinks she believes.

"If a guy really wants it, you just . . . Like, when I did it with that Mexican guy last year at day camp, it's not like I didn't *want to*, but . . ." Meghan shakes her head. She's discovered this way of cutting herself off, enviable to Judy, right at the edge of disgrace. Her long fingers are lost in French-braiding her thick blond hair, adroit as weaving spiders. There's a disconnect between them, an imbalance of experience that makes Meghan a kind of mentor and Judy an involuntary test taker. In addition to Bacardi, pot cookies, hangovers, and cigarettes, Meghan has been through all the bases except the last one and is already armed with descriptions and advice (finger-banging is *like a tampon left in too long*; if a guy eats a lot of pineapple *his sperm will taste sweeter*), while Judy, besides two back-to-back Zimas, her own experimental finger, and a parking lot make-out with Jessie M.'s twin brother, has done almost nothing. She wants to more for the advance of it—the awkward but necessary stepping forward—than for anything like physical pleasure, which she suspects is mostly a myth.

"Josh B. probably, like, dreams of you blow j-ing him." Meghan holds the finished braid, waiting for a hair tie. Judy is, among other roles, the keeper of the friendship's hair ties.

"God, barf," Judy says, raising her pelvis to get into her pocket. Last week, Josh called Meghan's house to say that he and Jared were going to the pool. *Tell Judy to wear her two-piece*, he'd requested, *that blue one*, and Meghan's eyes went huge. Had Judy buzzed with excitement, with something like *pride*? She had, before it bottomed out despondently. When they arrived at the Van Nuys rec park in their bikini tops and shorts (Judy's blue two-piece was the only suit she had) and waved to the boys in the water, her stomach swarmed—a hive of anticipation, as Josh, whom she'd spent most of middle school coveting at a distance, emerged from the ladder streaming wet. But his pale skin looked thick as mozzarella, purple bacne splayed across his shoulders, and there was something tumorous and alive about the pouch beneath his belly button. Judy tensed in a different way. He grinned at her—right *at* her—then trotted over and wagged his head so water sprayed and his hair spiked. Treading in the deep end, Jared called Josh a fucktard for the girls' benefit, which Josh rejoined with a wet armpit fart, a casual mooning. *No Fear!* his board shorts announced on the thigh, wet and clinging, as he settled behind Judy and set to rubbing her shoulders. His cold legs gripped her, and his hands squeezed and pinched. *You're tight—relax. Damn, girl. Glad you wore this thing*, toying with the knot at her neck. Pulling not hard enough to untie it, just hard enough to show that he could. *Oh my god, you guys, get a room!* Meghan sang.

Last year, Josh had been the best skater in school. Judy had drunk in the sight of his body, waiting for his smile when Meghan hollered something funny. How had he become repulsive? The change made her feel apart from herself, not today who she had been yesterday. She wanted only to wriggle away from his touch. Obscurely, Rick, her mother's new husband, seemed to be to blame.

"I don't know, he used to be fine but, like, something *happened*," Judy says now, handing over the rubber band.

"You just don't like guys once they start liking you."

What *guys*? Judy wants to know. Meghan is always making a precedent of things that have happened only once. "At least Jared is, like, sort of *nice*."

Meghan pipes an aria of laughter—"Judy and Jared, b-l-o-w-i-n-g!"—and looks around to see if any of the other passengers (men in baseball caps, mothers in sandals, children in pajamas, and a homeless-looking couple) are as titillated as she is.

The braid, fixed and symmetrical when Meghan turns, is a perfect, glowing cord—a spinal, fairy-tale thing, the density of which Judy will never feel on her own head. "You're perverted," she says, but something churns in her, that familiar Meghan-jealousy. Her own hair is unspectacularly brown, cowlicked and staticky and frizzing at the temples in heat and during rain.

The train runs inland just enough that everything is ugly. Withered palms tick by—dead-body dumpsters, stock-still pit bulls, the junky rears of strip malls no one is supposed to see. Judy has the backward-facing carnival seat, the one that makes you feel not propelled forward so much as dragged from behind, into the future against your will. *Simi* and *Oxnard* crackle through the intercom—kiddie pools and broken fences, graffiti on fast-forward. It's hardly different from the setting of their lives (they're only twenty, thirty miles from home) but everything is tweaked strange by this sudden autonomy—the fear that comes with acting out the illicit—a heart-fluttering sensation like hands let go.

Last week, the girls spent a whole afternoon at the twenty-four-hour Kinkos to cut, paste, and ditto, serial-killer style, old permission slips and various sign-up sheets imprinted with the school logo to make elaborately fake dossiers outlining an elaborately fake two-night field trip to Yonderwild Cabins and Outdoor Center at Lake Arrowhead. They nailed the verisimilitude right down to the mint-green paper, used their most adult handwriting to address the envelopes to their own houses, mailed them from the post office nearest Ulysses S. Grant High School, then flung their ripped-open contents at their stupid respective mothers. *WHAT, Mom, you didn't even know that the ninth-grade summer trip was next week? Child neglect! Jesus H. Christ! I need forty-six dollars, cash.* It was exactly the sort of project to fill the late-vacation days, when their eyes were numb to the television and their beds gummy with so much shed sunburnt skin. So pleased were they by their own thorough craftiness that they almost wished Bonnie or Rita would squint into the fine print, detecting something fishy, something *off*, if only for the chance to make up even more. But neither Bonnie nor Rita were that kind of mother.

"Do you think they'll figure it out, though?" Judy asks. "What if they're at, like, Vons, and they run into Stephanie? Or Melissa's mom? Or Mrs. Lombardi?" These worries, vague all along, are solidifying now as she says them. What *would* her mother think? What, if she discovered Judy missing, would she feel?

Meghan sighs. She has one hand on a doorstop copy of Stephen King's *It*, which she's been adamantly opening and closing for so many months the book has become a kind of permanent, spooky accessory to her otherwise beachy beauty. "Yeah, like your mom is going to run into anyone *anywhere*," Meghan says. "Except maybe the bar."

It stings because it's true, and because Meghan knows enough to say it. Meghan's mother, Rita, won't uncover the girls' lie because she works sixty-hour weeks catering sets in Studio City. Every morning and every night she's at the gym, training for one of her competitions. (Judy knows Rita best tornadoing through the front door after a 5:00 a.m. power-pump session, slick-faced and yapping, hardly able to complete a sentence before she's grinding a shake and running the shower. A 1994 calendar features Rita as April: a look on her face like childbirth, her calves and quads as orange and greased as a Thanksgiving turkey on a grocery-store coupon.) But Bonnie's hobbies have no place on a wall calendar. Judy's mother follows an inverse regimen (sleep, drink, sex, repeat) when she isn't working at Sunset Dialysis, hooking real kidneys up to fake kidneys. Whiskey, tequila, the antiseptic sting of vodka when you think you're reaching for a glass of water—red wine that leaves stains on the granite, the coffee table, Judy's open social studies textbook. The Trail of Tears, ringed maroon. Judy wishes she could say that this is all the fault of Rick, her mother's new husband—something that started with *him*—but it's been this way forever, and if anything, Rick's presence has made Bonnie's drinking more of a party, at least, and less of a sad movie.

Judy looks deliberately out the window and makes her voice blasé. "What are you going to say if Cassie asks you how *It* is and you have to admit you can't read?"

When she looks back at Meghan she can't help but grin. But Meghan affects a vampy, open-mouthed stare and mumbles, "Juvenile." She shoves the book back into her pack, swapping it for her Discman, the slipped-on headphones a signal that they're done talking. Judy doesn't have a Discman yet, only a Walkman still, which she decided to bring, then put back, then decided to bring, but finally put back again while packing this morning. Now she wishes she had it: Tom Petty singing in sweet agreement—*You don't know how it feels . . . to be meeeee*—a song she and Meghan played on repeat and crooned a cappella, walking arm in arm down Magnolia, every single afternoon of eighth grade. But Meghan says they are over that song now (*It's old*) and over Tom Petty altogether (*He's old*). With high school in sight, they like *this* now—the boppy horns and nasty lyrics fuzzing out of Meghan's headphones, a chunky-guy band Judy has listened to begrudgingly but hasn't yet "gotten into," even as she knows that, next year, if she wants to be one of the girls who loiter in the parking lot of Tribal Expressions after school, who wear purple lipstick and burn patchouli sticks and date skaters—if she wants to be one of the girls that Meghan will effortlessly become, she'd better give this music a more generous chance. If the CD is on at the party tonight, Judy decides, she'll dance.

Instead of the Walkman, Judy opted to haul along her beading caddy with the broken latch, which she wiggles open now. She'd asked for a Caboodle last Christmas but got this cheapo generic instead. Through the tangle of begun and abandoned projects, of fishing line and crimp beads, she hunts for the spool of stretch cord, thinking she'll start something new. A bracelet appears in her mind like a holy vision: alternating green and pink groupings culminating in a tarnished silver fleur-de-lis. Or green and black and then a pewter skull and crossbones. She'll pretend to stumble across the bracelet casually, then present it to Cassie in some offhand moment—*Oh, I made this thing I don't want; do you, like, want it?*—handing over one or the other, the flowers or the bones, depending on who Cassie turns out to be. And maybe Cassie, whoever she is, will wear it to the party that night and say to everyone, *Isn't it cool? My friend Judy made it!*

Meghan and Judy—but mostly Meghan—met Cassie last month, because Judy now has a computer: Rick's living-room Hewlett Packard, which Judy is allowed to use as long as no one is expecting a phone call, or when Rick and her mother are upstairs (which is often—they lug up cartons of orange juice and handles of vodka and don't emerge for hours, playing something the girls have termed *screwdriver motel*), is just one of many treasures in the paradisal new house. At Rick's, a liquidy TV evokes the screen at the AMC, a second refrigerator in the garage holds back-stocked soda and frozen egg rolls, and sprinklers come on automatically each evening, ensuring a flush green border of uniform, unspotty lawn. Judy has, at long last, her own room—aqua walled, light filled, with a ceiling fan decaled with glow-in-the-dark stars and a mattress and box spring all to herself (in the old apartment at the Valley Arms, she and Bonnie had shared, to her growing shame, a water bed in the single, cramped bedroom). All of this is possible because Rick is rich-ish, she's training herself to remember: to focus on the positives of this new life and leave the one big negative—Rick himself—way-down submerged, like a floaty stepped on underwater. Never mind that Judy locks and relocks her door each night. Has woken more than once in a cold sweat, hallucinating hands on the knob. That Rick's hands—at first just regular—now strike her as too full of cartilage, too big and too powerful, something in their mass implying lies and an unfair advantage, even as he lint-rolls, harmlessly, fastidiously, the polos and sport coats he wears to coach junior varsity volleyball. That his smell—mayonnaise and rubber, warm beer and the Black Ice car fresheners that hang five deep from the rearview mirrors of the Camrys and Corollas at Rick B's E-Z Driving School—is sharp in her nose the moment she enters the front door and then, eerily, fades. The smell doesn't *really* go away—she only acclimates to it, she knows; the subtlest betrayal by her senses.

After they moved in with Rick in June, it was hardly a question that Judy's new house would become the girls' default hangout (Meghan's own apartment, a moldy garden-level at the Sandpiper, was only a small step up from the dark hovel at the Valley Arms). On dazed, soggy-butted, chlorinated afternoons, the HP entirely their own, the girls dragged an extra chair over to the desk, dialed up, listened to the modem's crunch, waited, waited, and— online! They clicked and watched, hesitant at first, explorers in an abstract territory teeming with glitchy life. Each new screen led to another screen, each underlined link led to another choice of links. There was a burrowing quality about it all, more like an ant farm than a web.

W, w, w, dot, Meghan typed. She'd discovered the website last spring in Ms. Olicky's computer class. A purple screen constructed itself inch by inch, with the words *Through Thick N Thin* loaded in a *Chicken Soup for the Soul* font. Clip-art flowers on the left and a graphic of a woman's waist, encircled by a measuring tape that cinched and uncinched in jerky stop-motion. At first the site seemed to promote some churchy brand of health advice—something for old ladies—and Judy had thought Meghan was joking or misled. But if you scrolled down to the chat window's babble, it became clear that the cryptic screen names were as living and messed up as real people, real girls, and just as united by common enemies: muffin tops and cellulite, double chins and stretch marks, bikinis and calories and unvanquishable feelings of helplessness. *Look, look, look*, Meghan would point to Judy, whenever the screen names swapped tips. Ipecac, salt water, mustard seeds. Toothbrushes down the throat, of course, cabbage soup, and laxatives. If anyone you knew had Ritalin, try to get some Ritalin. Text after text appeared, a conversation you had to elbow—keystroke—your way into, and before Judy knew it, Natural_ blondie was born, a two-dimensional Meghan existent mostly in exclamation marks and misspellings, desperate questions tossed one after another into the stream of other desperate questions. That summer, Rick's computer went from novelty to necessity; for hours at a time, Meghan hunted and pecked, her face bowed to the keyboard, oblivious to anything else. When Judy suggested maybe they should tan in the backyard? Or walk to the gas station for chips?—a lost look clouded Natural_blondie's eyes; the glazed vacancy of the newly addicted. Judy, having no idea what to think, ventured into the kitchen to eat handfuls of Froot Loops from the box.

Cassie_freakme_81 appeared again and again—a being Judy thought of as existing solely in the chat realm but who was, Meghan argued, her *good friend now and super nice*, only a few years older than they were but with the top-tier stats Natural_blondie aspired to. Cassie weighed 116 at five foot nine, bragged of a thigh gap large enough to fit a pool noodle through, and had recently been discovered by Wet n Wild cosmetics—she'd done some *shoots* and her photographer was *a-maze-ing*. Meghan summarized, "Cassie lives in San Luis Obispo. Her boyfriend is a basketball player at the college. She wants us to *visit*."

"Both of us?" Judy asked.

Meghan rolled her eyes. "Of *course*. Of course she wants to meet my best friend in the entire freaking universe."

"Yeah, but who *is* she?"

Meghan blew air through her lips. "I've lost four pounds in five days. I *trust* her. She wants us to come to this party next week."

It was true; Meghan was looking skeletal and ecstatic, her hipbones flaring like wings where her cutoffs sagged, her casual eighth-grade eating disorder evolving, to Judy's alarm, into something full-blown—*serious*. Meghan had decided on a number, ninety-nine (as in pounds), arbitrary but magic, that she'd convinced herself was the secret to becoming a model—a dream she claimed she'd had since she was five years old but which Judy suspected she'd formulated more recently. Tall, projected to be but not yet Cassie's reported height, Meghan stepped on the scale every time she visited the bathroom, tracking the numbers in a sophisticated notebook filched from Rita. *7/27 9:36 a.m.: 106 lbs., 7/27 1:42 p.m.: 106 lbs., 7/28 9:40 a.m.: 105 lbs., 7/29 10:02 a.m.: 103 lbs!*, and so on, stars and frowny faces in the margins. But that August at Judy's, not long before the party invite, she had a sort of breakthrough, when Cassie_freakme_81 typed, *Try eating only expired food it really wrks!*—and Meghan, steeling herself against the challenge, systematically scoured Rick's kitchen. She sampled bluing bread, cheese growing hairstyles, salsa not meant to be effervescent but which now, lid off, effervesced. Judy tried to talk her down, but her eyes burned with determination: she was a suicide hanging from the ledge. Poor already-skinny, already-beautiful Meghan tasted and choked on her feast—then spewed her brains out all over the downstairs bathroom.

Beyond the immediate consequences (benefits?) of eating mold, the method had, too, a Pavlovian conditioning effect. A week later, Natural_blondie wrote, *Food is totally over for me now! I don't even want it anymore*, and detailed her gross success. They'd switched to instant messaging, and Freakme's response burbled up. *U HAVE to come celibrate with me and my bf this wknd! Were having a party.*

Meghan turned to Judy, the sockets of her eyes too lavender, Halloween looking, even as she smiled sweetly. "Judy? Can we? I *want to*."

What could Judy do? She said, "Our moms, though?" knowing they weren't the real problem; the real problem was that Cassie_whoever was a name without a face, a blurry Someone, maybe not a teen model at all but a lonely basement murderer straight off *Dateline*. And yet Judy knew how easily disappointment could become wrath when Meghan did not get her way. At the end of sixth grade, she'd ousted Melissa from their threesome while Judy stood by mute, and the best friendship became theirs alone, poised meanly against anyone who threatened. Meghan was powerful like that; capable of *doing things* before the thought had even occurred to Judy. Obliquely Judy felt that, if she wanted to learn the secret to life's entry, she'd better stick with someone like this: braver than herself, and savvier, who knew, among other things, how to convincingly lie to train conductors.

When Judy agreed to the trip, Meghan sprang up and hugged her. But the embrace was perfunctory, impersonal, already moving on. Back at the keyboard, Meghan said dreamily, "I think we should change our names."

"What?" Judy asked. Her attention was focused on Meghan's hands, on what Meghan would type and how Cassie would respond.

"We should change them to something cool. I like Cassie's name. Her full name is *Cassidy*."

"Like Butch Cassidy?" Judy asked absently. The screen stayed static.

"Who's that?"

"A cowboy or something. A man."

A gargling sound came from Meghan's throat as she pecked out *Were in!!!* "It's not a *man*'s name. It's *unisex*."

Cassie's reply appeared instantly: *!!!!!* and an address in, yes, San Luis.

"How is *Cassie* short for *Cassidy*? They're almost the same number of letters."

Meghan closed her eyes and puffed her cheeks—a riff she was developing on eye rolling—then let the air seep out. "This isn't English class, Judy. It's real life."

Judy's full name was actually Judith, though she never thought of herself as Judith; for a long time, she'd harbored the secret decision that when she was an adult, she'd go by *Jude*—a name she associated with black turtlenecks and sleek, sophisticated hairstyles, with poetry and gourmet food. She wondered momentarily if Meghan even knew her full, real name, even though they'd been friends since kindergarten. They still kept spare underwear in one another's drawers, shared toothbrushes without a thought. And two years ago, when Bonnie had come home late and a thud like a sack dropping had come from the bathroom, it was Meghan who clicked into action, dragging Bonnie into the shower, directing Judy to help heft her over the metal lip, jeans and all, and turning on the cold water. It was Meghan who thought to hold Bonnie's head up like a baby's so she wouldn't choke or drown—Judy was shaking too hard, too bent on the tiny purpose of removing her mother's favorite pumps, because water would ruin the suede and it was better to look at the shoes than at the pale, unmoving face. *My mother is dying my mother is dying*, Judy thought, but out loud she asked, *Should we call nine one one? Should we call nine one one?* Later, guilt rose like bile in her throat. She was at fault somehow; she and Meghan had passed the evening happily enough, choreographing a dance to Mariah Carey's "Fantasy," bugging out on the everyday reality that Bonnie wasn't home (*No moms!*), and yet here was the result. In her selfishness, Judy had failed to keep her mother safe.

Later, when Bonnie's face at last scrunched and blinked, and they got her clothes off and dried her and covered her up in bed, it was Meghan who offered that she wouldn't tell about the episode. *Anyone*, she repeated, by which Judy knew she meant Rita. And it was Meghan who suggested Judy shouldn't tell, either. *They might try to take you away or something.*

That was at the beginning of seventh grade, before Meghan was a B cup, when she still had a tie-dyed retainer she tongued out for pizza and had not yet mastered sarcasm. But where, exactly, was *that* Meghan in *this* Meghan? Something is changing and will continue to change, Judy knows. The surface of their time together has already taken on the oddly grainy quality of last year's photos.

The train bores through a tunnel somewhere around Santa Barbara, and then the teal, sun-reflecting Pacific opens up on Judy's right. In the books she reads, the authors are always making the sea so sparkling and glass-bottle blue, but the ocean strikes her now as more like plastic, generic, tiring to watch. The waves do their California thing, unceasing and forever. Meghan falls asleep curled against the window, and Judy does the same, her head in her arms on the table. When she wakes, she's pained by hunger. The ocean is gone; they're turning now, carving like a blade around peroxide-yellow hills. Despite the pact they made that morning (no eating until they get to Cassie: they'll arrive with their stomachs flat and their eyeballs white, and then at the party they'll hazard melon chunks on toothpicks, or something Meghan calls *canapés*), Judy edges from her seat, then returns from the café car with a bag of Cheetos, lowering her teeth as crunchlessly as possible. Meghan's eyes flutter open, and she frowns. "What are you doing? You pinky-swore." Too groggy to be angry. Judy merely shrugs, returning her eyes to the hillside shadows. Oak trees and some lazy cows. To be a routine irritation, a constant work in progress, is another one of Judy's roles.

And yet later, coming back from the bathroom, balancing in the noisy vestibule between cars, Judy spies Meghan through the lozenge-shaped window: her jaw working rabbit-fast, a frantic swallow as the door hushes open. Meghan doesn't see Judy, but Judy has seen her, and the neon trace of chip dust powdering one corner of her mouth.

2.

THEY STEP OFF THE TRAIN INTO THE BLAZING AFTERNOON and move dizzily through the San Luis station, the journey still swaying in their bodies. The broken latch on Judy's beading caddy means she has to carry it from the cumbersome bottom; it seems suddenly insane to have brought it. Shadows crisscross under the vaulted ceiling. Vending machines echo. Hardly anyone is around.

In the waiting area, Meghan approaches a man leaning to spit seed shells into an institutional trash can. She has *It* open, where she's written Freakme's address on the inside cover. "Excuse me, sir . . ."

He is grandfatherly, loose in the face and wearing a railroad-branded cap, which does little to ease the knot in Judy's stomach. Why did Meghan not think to get this Cassie person's phone number? And why, in all their cyber exchanges, didn't Cassie herself ever offer it? In a foreign California city now, their fate rests on four handwritten numbers and a street name Meghan can't pronounce.

Shell debris sticks to the old man's lips. "Bu*chon*," he corrects Frenchly. "781, you'll wanna go down this a-way. Take a left off Leff—that's easy to remember! And . . ." He swerves his hand and spouts proper nouns Judy does her best to memorize. "Mind yourselves around the park. Creeps out there sometimes, 'specially by the playground. Pretty gals like you, you mind yourselves."

Meghan raises one eyebrow. "Sure," she says, then turns away, removing from her backpack sunglasses Judy hasn't seen before. When she puts them on, two sets of red plastic lips frame dark, oval lenses; Meghan's real eyes float inside cartoon mouths. The old man looks them over then, scanning their separate torsos and faces, his smile like a bent wire, and Judy can read his mind: *Isn't it strange that girls can be so different—some so pretty and others drab as drapes?*

Judy lifts the caddy to shield her middle. On the far wall of the station, above the bulletproof alcoves of the ticket counter, a marquee shows the Coastal Quest in the opposite direction, due in at 3:20 but delayed. There are other buses and trains with Los Angeles showing as the DESTINATION. Judy makes a mental note and pinches Meghan's elbow. Before they turn to go, Meghan gives the old man the gift of her modeling smile: the smallest tip of tongue clamped between semi-straightened teeth. "Son of a gun," he calls after them. "Y'all be careful now."

They follow an uphill sidewalk buckled by the San Andreas. It's a cute neighborhood; every dollhouse Victorian and stucco apartment building seem to suggest its inhabitants are all friends, friends who've decided to take a synchronized afternoon nap. Trellised walkways drip bougainvillea, swings creak on porches, potted cacti and propped bicycles languish with a southern sort of appeal. Through one fence the girls glimpse a luxurious backyard pool fed by a pump-operated waterfall. Minivans and station wagons galvanize in the sun, while cypress trees and stubby palms and overfertile figs litter their harvests of pods and fronds and fallen black testes in a mess across the sidewalk. They pass a market with wide green awnings, Labor Day sales advertised in the windows. From the side alley comes the too-ripe smell of pot, weed, grass, skunk, Mary Jane, Mary J. Blige. Meghan and Judy know all the names.

When they reach the park, they see what the train guy meant—several encampments are scattered around a central gazebo, shopping carts draped with sleeping bags and tarps, the black-bottomed feet of sleeping figures. Homelessness is nothing new to them; in fact, to Judy, it is the frightening reality she'd so often considered they might be heading toward—she and her mother—before Rick appeared, for better or for worse. The thought, like a roach scurrying across her brain, makes Judy shiver now and change the mental subject. She focuses her eyes on the house numbers. 885, 861, 847.

On Buchon, every bungalow seems to have put forth special effort to be better than the last by way of wrought iron details, or avocado saplings, or new roofs made of tin. But 781 has a decidedly given-up look, a throwing-in-the-towel stubbornness to its elemental beauty. The curving porch slants to the left as if under invisible weight. The glass diamonds in the latticed windows look greasy. Its hedges are more thorns than roses, and groupings of turds decorate the bleached lawn, buzzing with little fly parties. It is nothing short of a miracle to see the brass numbers there, descending by the screen door—a real building matching up with the written address—but Judy's relief passes quickly into a whole new set of worries, moving up the walk a step behind Meghan. Meghan turns briefly and raises her sunglasses: *I told you so.*

Too late, now, to retreat. On the shaded porch, Meghan has reached her finger forward, touched the buzzer, pressed. Muffled chimes ring inside.

The girls don't look at each other. The moment is too potent to share.

When the door opens, the woman standing there is not Cassie at all. She is old. Her hair has that corn-silk texture of the long hospitalized, and her skin is so pale it's bluish. Lipstick off its mark gives her a playing-dress-up look. And yet she's the opposite of dressed-up: her pale-green blouse hangs crooked, its buttons missing their corresponding holes, and Judy is alarmed to see that she's without pants. Two bird-skinny legs flash before the woman closes and knots her bathrobe, cinching it up very tight. Crusty spots on the terrycloth lapel look like weeks' worth of breakfast spillage.

She stares at them out of big, green, shocked-looking eyes. "Yes?" she says. As if there might be dire news.

"Hi," Meghan starts, drawing a loose strand of hair from her mouth. "Does Cassie—Cassidy—live here? We're friends of hers."

The woman raises an ineffectual hand and turns, trembling, toward the cave of the house. When she turns back, her hand is quivering even worse. There's something unbearable, Judy feels, about old people shaking. Just barely hanging on to aliveness.

"Cassie is my niece," she says finally. "Sarah and I had an agreement. That I would . . . Sarah and I agreed."

Judy looks to Meghan, hoping she might translate, but Meghan's eyebrows arch up in a *cuckoo* signal. Judy takes *It* from her hand and holds open the front cover. "This is Seven Eighty-one, right?"

The old woman's face crinkles as if the numbers spell a curse word. She waves her hand floppily. "I'm a reporter for the *Morro Bay Minute,*" she says. "I've read my fair share of books."

And yet when she gestures them inside, Judy and Meghan are met with neither bookshelves nor books: just a front room dark as a movie theater, an upright piano covered in newspapers, a muted television casting its glow, and a pretty brown dog perched upright in a recliner, sagging an ill-fitting diaper. The dog whines and tamps the seat at the sight of the visitors. Between the figures on TV and Meghan and Judy, he swivels his head back and forth, as if wondering who is more real.

"Cassie knows we're coming," Meghan says, preparing to argue. The air in the room, furiously conditioned, smells urinated on. "She invited us for a sleepover. Is she—is she here?"

They're following the old woman up the carpeted stairs now. She doesn't turn when she tells them, "My name is Linda. You can call me Linda, or Aunt Linda, like Cassie does."

Meghan bulges her eyes at Judy, and Judy feels suddenly that she isn't doing her part. "Linda, is—is Cassie home?" she tries. When something wet touches her calf, she gasps. It's only the dog's nose—the dog who limps along behind them, front legs first, then hoisting up his rickety back half.

"Cassie!" the aunt sings down the hall. "Cassieeeee! You have company!"

But when they reach the open door at the end of the hall, the room is entirely vacant. The three stand there, looking in, as if Cassie might jump out from behind the bed. It is not a model's room. It is not a sixteen-year-old's room. And yet they must have the right place. A familiar smell, like used underwear and fake vanilla, hangs out here, where it's warmer than downstairs and not unpleasant. Faded cutout letters spell *CASSIDY*, strung on yarn and crooked above the double windows. The bed is unmade: a heaping peach-colored comforter, silky and threadbare. Wilting ribbons make bows around the spindles of a white chair matching a messy desk. A shelf overflows with picture books and trinkets, stuffed animals and jewelry boxes, and a plastic snow globe with Snoopy inside, wearing a scarf and driving a taxi. The snow globe reads, THE BIG APPLE! NY, NY.

"She must have slipped out," the aunt says uncertainly. And then she looks very concerned. "Do your mothers know where you are?"

Surveying the scene, Meghan steps into the room. "Oh yes, of course," she says, taking it all in. Judy hears the distraction in her voice—how hard she's working to make sense of what doesn't. "My mom drove us here. Do you know when she'll be back? Or where she went? Maybe we could . . . catch up with her somewhere?"

Let's go, let's go, let's go, Judy's brain surges as she steps in after Meghan. She's thinking they can hustle straight back to the station (maybe the return train is still delayed? Maybe, by some miracle, it will wait for them?) and go home as easily as they've come. But the beacon of escape is a fast-fading hope. Linda is saying, "She only went out for a minute. You'd better just wait in here. Until it's safe."

There in the doorway, with the dog at her heels, the aunt's eyes seem to light and spin, otherworldly discs of sudden decision. She pulls the door toward her, shutting it fast as Meghan lunges. Judy hears the tiniest click. The sound is so small it might be fake: a fake lock—it must be. But Meghan is twisting the handle and nothing is happening—*Hey! Hey!*—the knob sticking uselessly in its socket. When Judy grabs too—nothing. "Hey!" she shrieks, as every prescient, half-formed fear begins to rise to her surface, hot as blood, wrongly coming true. Meghan slaps the door in rapid time. "What are you *doing*?! It's *locked*!"

Through the barrier, the aunt's voice drops an octave. "It's only for your safety." She is a headmistress now, metallic and soulless. "The girls in this house must be kept safe. Heaven forbid the police get involved."

"*Police?!* What's she talking about? Did Cassie mention an—"

Despite their questions, despite *Wait!* becoming a wail—the aunt's steps move off down the hall.

Sh-sh-sh. They stop, straining to hear over their own desperate heartbeats. But there is no indication of doubling back, of mercy or understanding on the old lady's part—just the creak of the stairs and the jaunty rattle of the dog's descending collar.

Their foreheads are slick, on the verge of instant breakouts. At the bottom of the door, a hole splinters where a heavy boot might've once kicked.

They drop to this space and call *Let us out! We don't want to wait!* like prisoners through bars. Judy pushes her arm into the hallway, feeling along the floor as if she might land on some dropped key. In the middle of the room, Meghan stomps hard—she might kick through the ceiling. *We know you hear us!* But the television volume goes up and up—*What is she thinking? What is she* doing?—before Meghan drops to all fours and screams "*Hello?!*" straight down, into the thick, impenetrable carpet.

The four-paned window, they discover, has been painted shut—decades of coats. The phone on the nightstand is just for play; disconnected, no jack in the wall. From door to windows to phone they move in desperate triangulation, even as some part of them denies this locking-in has happened—is happening—at all. It can't be. And yet Judy's pulse begs to differ as she bends her knees and pushes up, straining against the sill. She thinks her temples might pop, but nothing gives. She can smell herself—her own rotten armpits—and smell Meghan, too, who whimpers across the room, fiddling with a bobby pin in the lock. Through the glass, the barren yard, the heat-warped sidewalk, a lone squirrel with a pipe-cleaner tail—the world outside, so effortlessly occupied just a moment ago, is somehow no longer accessible. She shrieks for the sheer insanity of it.

"What is *happening*," she moans at last to Meghan. Meghan's face, when she straightens and turns, is more frightened than Judy's ever seen it, a look that throws the situation scarily out of bounds—beyond the reaches, even, of her best friend's confidence.

"I don't know," Meghan says. "I don't *know*."

They pant. In the nothing-feeling of standing there, in the cloud of their own heavy breath, Judy senses how suddenly plans can collapse: the wrong Jenga block pushed out, the map read upside down . . . the big eeriness of not-knowing, embedded in the otherwise known. It's like she's being punished for some transgression she hardly remembers, a wrong committed in another life.

3.

ON A VEGAS-BOUND BUS ALIVE WITH THE PRE-KENO TITTER-
ing of two dozen old ladies, a rather unpretty girl—a girl who knows she is
more or less unpretty but has decided to live anyway—is running away from
home.

If anyone could call it that—a *home*. The question is of no small debate to
Cassie. Doesn't a home mean a mother and father and brother and/or sister,
and bright conversations spanning rooms? A schedule of domestic events like
Sunday-morning pancakes and Friday-night Scrabble, vacations in July and
Christmas trees at Christmas? What Cassie has instead is a recently demented
aunt and her aunt's demented dog, Moose, who humps her awake most mornings and sometimes pees in her shoes. What Cassie has is a substitute parent,
talking to herself and putting her pants on backwards, lining the bathtub with
newspaper and hiding money in the freezer. What Cassie has are constipat-
ing meals she prepares for herself and her aunt, dinners like grilled Velveeta
sandwiches and lunches like bananas con peanut butter. After school and on
weekends, Cassie eats Ritz crackers in front of the television or upstairs in
bed with a book, knowing the consequences of those grainy night crumbs
but unable to give up this small pleasure. By a similar habit, she's been living
recently with a painful snarl hidden in the depths of her hair, a tangle that
formed mysteriously last spring and has been growing ever since, metastasiz-
ing with each shower and toweling, becoming unbrushably complex. The way
other girls watch for their reflections in mirrored surfaces, Cassie checks for
the mass often, just to make sure it's there. A recurring premonition: someday,
some future hairdresser will uncover the nested pet and gasp.

It didn't use to be like this. Aunt Linda used to brush and headband
Cassie's hair, used to play Mozart on the downstairs piano, roast chicken
and potatoes, drive her to school promptly at 7:50 each morning and be
there again every afternoon—reliably reading *Time* behind the Volvo's

wheel, Moose in the backseat not peeing anywhere, just a regular dog loll-
ing his tongue, his head raised in simultaneous anxiety and patience. In
that era (from as far back as Cassie can remember until fifth grade), Cassie's
lunchbox was packed snugly with turkey-sandwich-no-mayo-no-crust, carrot sticks she threw away, homemade persimmon cookies tradable for rolls
of fruity tape. The other kids used to look at Cassie's floral-print culottes
and gingham parachute pants and especially her purple velvet jumper with
the abalone buttons and say, *Where did you get that?* in tones she chose to
interpret as admiration. *My aunt made it*—so casually. She knew that the
classmates who noticed her clothes were more accurately noticing the novelty
of Cassie's home life itself: orphans in the nineties were curiously admired,
Cassie had picked up on, and all through elementary school, whenever her
class was sent home with forms requiring signatures, the other kids whined,
I wish I *had a legal guardian!*

And yet for Cassie orphanhood is not exactly thrilling. When she thinks
of *family*, it's with a psychic lopsidedness that leaves her wanting to lie down.
"I want to meet my mother," she announced last month, walking straight into
Aunt Linda's room while the old woman sat rearranging ancient cosmetics on
the vanity, tubes and bottles and crystal swan-shaped perfumes that no one
in the world cared whether or not she wore.

Aunt Linda made a *hmm* sound—a melodious question lacking the question.

"I've been talking to her on the telephone. She wants to meet me, too,"
Cassie tried. It wasn't exactly true. She *did* have her mother's phone number
and she *did* call almost nightly, secreting the downstairs cordless into her
bedroom, but it was almost never that anyone picked up. There was no answering machine, and even if there had been, Cassie's mother was not the type to
call back. About once a month, Bill, the man her mother lived with, would
inevitably demand *Who's there?* after twenty-five or so rings. *Just a minute*, Bill
would say, followed by a very long pause—an eternity of waiting—in which
Cassie was left to assume the message had been forgotten on its way to delivery, or worse, her mother had refused the call altogether. *Hello?* Cassie would
ask into the silence, her own voice and all her hopes left there on a kitchen

counter she could not for the life of her picture, in a house somewhere in Nevada.

Usually she hung up. But occasionally her mother did finally, miraculously, come on the line. In these cases, Cassie had only a handful of shaking, ecstatic seconds to convince her mother of . . . what? *I'm sorry, and why are you contacting me?* Sarah Waller would ask. A series of confusing exchanges would ensue, in which Cassie explained the obvious, and her mother seemed to spend a lot of time mulling over the obvious, but to no avail, before she rushed off the phone to attend to some emergency. Something was on fire out across the desert. Bill needed her help. Or there was an echo through the receiver—*I have to get off now. I don't trust this connection.*

On that July afternoon, Aunt Linda turned fully in the dim bedroom. "Oh? And what has that been like?" She pawed into a tub of moisturizer, then rubbed the ancient goop into the webs between her fingers.

"She wants me to come visit," Cassie fibbed. She ventured further, "To ride the bus there and stay with her and Bill."

Aunt Linda turned back to her bottles. In the mirror, her face was paper pale, but her eyes were as intensely green as ever—like the sea glass shards they used to hunt for at Pismo. "Daryl and I—we wanted a child *so* badly. But Doctor Rees told me I was *broken*, somehow . . ." she drifted bitterly, staring into the cream. Cassie waited. Saying her aunt's name used to help wrench her back, repeating it three times fast—*Aunt Linda! Aunt Linda! Aunt Linda!*— but this time her aunt only turned with the same muddled lack of urgency that enraged Cassie, and smiled.

"What were we talking about then?" she asked.

"My mother!" Cassie said. "Sarah Waller! Your niece! Daryl's niece! Remember?"

"Sarah? She had a little baby."

"Yes!" Cassie exclaimed. She stamped her foot. "*I'm* that baby. Earth to Aunt Linda!"

The smile remained. "I hate to tell you this, darling, but she's crazy, you should know"—shaking her head as if this were nothing. "Just like *her* mother, that whole side of Daryl's is cra—"

"*You're* crazy! *You're* the crazy one! You're *demented*!" Cassie cried and ran down the hall, slamming her bedroom door so that the whole house shook.

In the stunted conversations with her mother, Cassie had never mentioned the possibility of a visit before; usually there wasn't time or opportunity or the slightest glimmer of hope that Sarah would say yes. But last week, Cassie must've called at precisely the right time; perhaps her mother had just emerged from a long, deep nap, the kind where you wake to find everything around you a little sadder than it had been when you fell asleep. She sounded depressed, uncharacteristically defenseless—closer, Cassie thought, than she'd ever been before.

"Do you get lonely?" Cassie asked, seizing the moment. "I've never been to the desert, but it seems lonely."

"Not really," her mother said in a lonely voice. "No. I have Bill. We have the animals. And our work."

"What sort of work?" Because Cassie really had no idea. She imagined a diminutive woman with frizzy auburn hair, bandaging the paw of an injured coyote. In the only picture of Sarah Cassie had ever seen, her mother stood in a modest garden, holding up for the camera a bunch of unimpressive carrots, a look of resigned disappointment directed at the ground.

"I'm not at liberty to discuss it."

Cassie's face grew hot. "But what about me? Don't you ever want to see me?" She felt around, where her hair met her neck, and hooked a finger inside the tangle.

"It's difficult . . . of course you *seem* normal right now, but . . ." A sound on the line, of a far-off, mechanical whirring, made Cassie think of appliances. Perhaps her mother was running a mixer, like Aunt Linda used to, for a cake. "It's difficult for me to . . . the conflict around your birth . . . there's trauma there, you know."

You know was a statement, not a question, but Cassie didn't, in fact, know. Vaguely she knew *trauma*, but around her birth . . . more than *twelve years ago*? How long did it take for trauma to pass? Twelve years was, to Cassie, a lifetime.

Afraid she was losing her—afraid she would chicken out—Cassie rushed bravely in, reciting her rehearsed argument. "Actually, the real reason I'm calling, Mom, is about this boy here who won't leave me alone. An older boy. He drives a car already." She began to say his name, but *Brandon* clung to the inside of her mouth. "I met him at Gus's Grocery, but now he comes by every day and does things like paint graffiti on the house and torture Moose. The dog. He—sometimes he sleeps in his car and just waits for me. He's *stalking* me."

A long second passed, as if her mother might be writing these things down on a legal pad. Finally, she asked, "Does he—how much does he know about you? Is he affiliated with anyone?"

Cassie thought it wise to say *I think a lot*, and that yes, she was pretty sure he was. Bad people, who might try to hurt her. "School starts in a week, but I'm afraid to walk there. I thought, if I could go away for a few days—come to Nevada—maybe he'd think I moved or something and leave me alone."

She could hear her mother's deliberate breathing atop the machine sound. The voice was small and slow when it came back. "I'll admit your asking isn't a surprise. Bill and I have discussed it, actually. Often. And I *would* like to know the truth about you, once and for all." She went on like this, cryptically, until at last she agreed to what Cassie had been yearning for. *This weekend, then. We'll collect you at the stop.* It'd be a long day of travel, and Cassie would have to transfer in Las Vegas, from the Orange bus to the Greyhound, the one toward Reno. "Can you remember that? Orange to gray?"

"I can!" Cassie said. "Orange to gray."

"But Cassidy?" her mother asked.

She was breathless with happiness—with the full sound of her name, like a *yes* in her mother's voice. "Yes?" she asked back.

"Make sure this boy doesn't follow you. We don't stand for anything funny out here."

It *was* true that Brandon had come around a few times in his amphibious Ford Taurus, the garbage bag that stood in for the passenger-side window billowing in its duct-tape frame as Cassie watched through a gap in the front blinds. And it was true that when the car appeared, her heart raced with real panic, *No, no, no*, and that she'd grown wary of walking alone down the street.

But Brandon's drive-bys were the opposite of stalking, fast in a way that left her curiously depressed in their dust. He'd idle on Buchon for less than a minute, ashing his cigarette out the window, then peel out angrily, leaving black parallel arcs on the pavement. It made everything that had passed between them seem so insignificant, hardly worth his time, as if he had only limited interest in revisiting his victim, swinging by on his way to band practice or home from work, noncommittal even in his cruelty.

Was it cheap to gamble with real threats? To use Brandon to weasel toward her mother? In the end, she reasoned that her lie was nothing compared to whatever exactly it was that Brandon and the other boys had done to her.

COMING OUT of the bathroom at the Las Vegas transfer, a terrible realization: Cassie's forgotten to pack her diary. Her pulse goes spastic as she whips her backpack around, unpacks it right there on the paisley carpet amid the wild music of a thousand jangly slots. No, no, *no*! It's not that she's afraid of the diary's discovery (the book is locked, and anyway, Aunt Linda's reading-comprehension skills are low these days) but without it she feels keenly naked. It's become so regular, to tell the diary what she cannot tell another person, that without the comfort of *writing it down*, Cassie gets all clogged up—robbed of a crucial valve, abandoned to the raw, mucky tumult of herself. The voice on the intercom announces her next bus. She joins the line of questionable people but manages to find a seat alone, at least, slightly damp and near the back, where she sorts through the backpack again.

She forgot the diary but not her current favorite book, the hardcover library copy of Swedish folktales she takes out now, back in the bright highway sunlight. The stories exhilarate her with their leafy woods and magic common objects (could a flip-flop have powers, then? A hair clip?) and their serpent-bodied women, the watery illustrations of milky, moonlit snow, despite her knowing she's too old for picture books. Snow has become something of a fascination for Cassie. She's only seen it once in real life, in New York City, where Aunt Linda took her the Christmas Cassie was nine. On the sidewalk and on hat brims, on tree branches and car hoods, the snow fell and gathered like movie glitter shaken from a giant canister in the sky. She'd seen the all-at-once lighting of the enormous tree, the ice skaters carving and spinning in its gold reflection, the towering buildings like a fortress all around her. The big frozen park, the clopping horses pulling buggies, the hot, sweet nuts they bought from a cart, the car horns and shouting, the saxophones echoing underground. How amazed she'd been by the train—the subway!— burrowing and shrieking, crammed with passengers, so many coats and umbrellas and reading materials it was incredible everyone wasn't always losing things or mixing them up. Out on the street, pedestrians gestured *after you*, then rushed out into the presence of their lives with a funny, on-foot confidence Cassie certainly didn't recognize from a place as boring and collegiate as San Luis. In New York, young people and old people, babies and businessmen, Chinese-looking people and Black people and brown-skinned people and freckled people, people with legs and canes and in wheelchairs and pushing strollers, all seemed to share one huge, civilized brain: they knew when to cross against the light and when it was best to wait; they knew how to use revolving doors and talk to doormen and how to dip off the curb around slowpokes, how to tap-dance down staircases, how to drink coffee, smoke, yell, beg for money, and argue all at the same time; how to wear hair and position hats. How to eat bagels, hot dogs, or bubbling slices of pizza, folded in half and without burning the roof of your mouth.

On a busy street, at a restaurant, or in a museum—having so many people around had felt instinctually right to Cassie. Inside a pedestrian press, she forgot her own face; she couldn't hear, all the time, her own annoying voice ricocheting around in her thick-sided head.

Perhaps because it's the hot, exhausting tail end of summer, and because Cassie is nervous to meet her mother, and because what happened to her body still rattles and seizes and stabs her to consider—she finds herself returning to this remembered place often: yearning to be back there, her warm, mittened hand inside her aunt's gloved one, before Aunt Linda's brain slipped away from them like a pet lost in the night. And Aunt Linda had been happy, too— wearing old cold-weather clothes pulled from deep within her closet, cashmere hats and a scarf made of fur she'd never worn in California; comparing certain architecture to other buildings, ones she'd loved and even worked in in Detroit, where she'd grown up; putting two fingers in her mouth and whis-tling (!) so loudly, as Cassie had never before seen her do, for a taxi. They'd sat in a dome-ceilinged theater, on springy purple seats, watching actors charge across the stage in old-fashioned clothes, throwing up their hands, elated or angry under the lights. Cassie, herself, was elated just to be there, peering down from the dizzying balcony. At intermission Aunt Linda bought her a squat bottle of Martinelli's, which she sipped from a plastic champagne flute.

Why is it that you can't just walk back into memories? Why *isn't* it pos-sible, when you can still see and smell and feel it all, exactly as sweet as it was? And yet, if it's impossible to relive memories, how is it *also* impossible to ever totally forget them? Life is cruel like that, Cassie is beginning to know. A cruelness she's trying hard not to look straight at, lest it blind her like the sun. The bus pulls off the freeway on a wide, tilting curve, then up in front of a big stucco hotel. A woman gets on and totters down the aisle, peering into every available seat as if checking for poop or ghosts, until she spots the emptiness beside Cassie and smiles. Despite the deterring mantra Cassie chants in her head, the woman plops down.

"*Ahhhhhh*," she says. She holds on her lap a big canvas bag that dou-bles her girth. Her earrings are two dangling pairs of white dice. Cassie has already seen several pairs of earrings like this in Nevada.

Because Cassie doesn't say anything the first time, again the woman goes, *Ahhhhhh*. When she looks over to Cassie, the dice show snake eyes. "Whatcha readin', cutie?"

She must be the sort of person who's always declaring how good she is with "kids" but who really doesn't know any. Something in her shiny, tarp-like blouse gives an electric charge to Cassie's arm hairs. She pulls herself inward, away from the woman's spreading aura. "Nothing," she says. "A book."

The woman is moderately fat, thick-neck fat, which makes Cassie suspicious—not the sort of fat that spells jolly smiles and treats pulled out of drawers, people so slow they couldn't chase you if they had to. "Well what's it *about*, honey?"

Cassie lies. "I don't know, I haven't read it yet. I just got it as a birthday gift. My mother mailed it to me." She moves her hand to cover up the sticker along the spine: *SLO Pub. Lib.*

"Can I see?" the woman bubbles. "It looks like a very fun read."

Cassie is done being nice. In one swift motion, she tucks the book between herself and the bus wall. "I'm sorry, but it's a very special book."

The woman raises her eyebrows and flashes a look that says, *What a girl! I like your pluck.* But on the exhale she affects disappointment. "Well. I guess I'll have to settle for my own boring old book. It doesn't have any pictures, unfortunately."

Cassie couldn't care less. There are more interesting things to care about, outside the window, than this lady and her dumb book. The Jurassic plane of desert, for example, thirsty-looking and thirsty-making, the rock formations making faces, and the occasional, urgent message on a passing billboard.

4.

WHEN CASSIE OPENS HER EYES, THE BUS IS STOPPED, AND someone is giving her a shake. She thinks she is in New York—but no, she is awake now.

"This's you, little miss." It's the driver, who looks exactly the way a bus driver should look.

She wipes her mouth of drool, gathers her backpack and her book, and steps over the unhelpful mass of the woman, whose cheek twitches against some treacherous dream.

"I hope you got some good people out here," the driver says as the door whispers open. "'Cause you are in the dead middle of nowhere."

Cassie mimics a smile. "Thank you, sir," like the always polite, unexpectedly brave heroine of her own haphazard adventure. "I'm pretty sure I do."

After the bus, outside is an oven. The groove down her back sweats instantly. The driver was not a liar: there is nothing but brown horizon in four directions, a few clouds tacked up in the big blue sky, one leaning turquoise portajohn across the gravel lot, and a crude wooden frame built solely to hold a map of Nevada, an austere, triangular terrain bolted and bleached under Plexi. YOU ARE HERE. A handful of carlike things are parked at random angles, rust-bitten, deflated vehicles bound together with bungee cords that look like they might snap at any moment. *Jalopy* is a word Cassie has recently learned, and she is pleased for the chance to apply it, to mull the syllables like the first chews of a very delicious cheeseburger. *Jalopy, jalopy.* Her stomach folds and cramps. That morning she packed a banana and two buttered slices of bread, but the banana is black now, and she ate the bread in Vegas. It seems correct enough, Cassie reasons, to present herself to her mother in a hungry, sorry, truly orphaned-looking state. To learn whether or not this mother of hers is capable, as mothers are supposed to be, of worry and fuss, of care and love.

Two figures emerge from a weighed-down Jeep at the far end of the lot—a short man and a shorter woman. Cassie swells with relief and something like pride. There she is, as real as anyone, if a different, older, more living version of the single picture. The person beside her must be Bill, who Aunt Linda once described as *a man who seems to share your mother's interests.*

A big wiry ball—oh! A tumbleweed!—appropriately tumbles by, bounces into a ditch, springs over the bank, then bounds across the highway in the path of the departing bus.

Cassie galumphs forward under her load. "Hi!" she calls, striding fast. "Hi! Hello, Mom! Hello, Bill!"

When they close the distance, she realizes she's panting. Her pulse presses like a frog in her neck. Face-to-face in the smoke-dry heat, the semblance of family takes their found parts in.

Sarah Waller has Cassie's same rusty-colored hair and the same pushed-deep eyes, tinged green and tired underneath. But her nose is bonier, beakier, and her hair, where Cassie's is more or less straight, is kinked into small, crunchy-looking curls, combed up and bound in a tight sprout atop her head, bringing the corners of her eyebrows with it. This gives her mother a look of sharp hyperattention, the sense that she can see in all directions without turning her head. Her shoulders bend toward a narrow chest, bagging with something (breasts?) low inside her T-shirt. Cassie cannot help but feel a pang of disappointment: Sarah isn't *ugly*, per se, but she's somewhere out in the vast territory of beauty's opposite. This, then, is Cassie's source.

An oddity Cassie is noticing: her mother and Bill wear identical T-shirts, as if maybe they've just come from some sort of club or team event where this is the official uniform. But it certainly doesn't *look* like a uniform. From the center of a mottled sky peers the big illustrated face of a wolf, staring Cassie dead in the eye. In the background another wolf, or maybe the same wolf, in full-body profile, howls up at something unseen. They match in other ways, too—in almost every other way, actually—the same brown multipocket shorts, shoes that look good for stomping snakes and scorpions, and jewelry . . . *strange* jewelry: chunky crystals and soft leather pouches tied around their necks, chains and turquoise pendants and, perhaps most confusingly, thick black chokers studded with fake-looking metal spikes. Similarly spikey bracelets cuff their wrists. When her mother sticks out a rigid hand, Cassie is cautious as she reaches forward.

It is a weak, chalky shake. "It's nice to see you again," her mother says.

As if there's been only a casual lapse in their acquaintance. As if her mother had not signed her over, more than twelve years before, to her great-aunt, childless and widowed, with plenty of money and a house all to herself. *You were my next chapter*, Aunt Linda used to tell Cassie, snugging the covers around her, while Moose lay at her feet regal as a sphinx and Cassie begged for her origin story. *Just when I thought there might be nothing left. My new day. My sea change.* Cassie's mother, the story had always gone, was too alone and too poor and too, well, *unstable* to raise a child, and so that had been that—reasons that Cassie is only recently suspecting might've been simplified, altered, *abridged* for Cassie's sake, like certain cheating books.

"And it's nice to meet you," Bill says. His grip is plump to match the rest of him. White hair encircles his face in a lighting-struck disaster, but his eyes are calm and his wrinkles inspire trust. He reminds Cassie of Santa Claus, a movie Santa who abandons Christmas and the North Pole for a different kind of life in the desert.

Bill helps her out of her backpack, and Cassie steps up into the Jeep, which has only a bar for a roof. She climbs over piles of miscellany, careful not to snag her socks or twist an ankle. In the backseat, cardboard boxes overflow with paperbacks, file folders, notepads and laminated booklets, videocassettes melting in the heat. There are tools and rags in milk crates, hiking boots and empty water jugs, binoculars, maps wrongly refolded, a first-aid kit marked with bloody handprints, a dozen cans of kidney beans shrink-wrapped in a cardboard flat, sacks of rice, sawdust, and birdseed, torn in one spot and spilling. Everything smells like oil and puke and the down-and-dirty work of never-ending maintenance. Cassie settles herself in a small space between a diagonal-leaning crutch and a chainsaw that won't quite fit. When Bill hoists over her bag, he says, "Boy oh boy! That's a mighty load you brought!"

"Last year my teacher, Ms. Murphy, said I have an accumulation problem. Because of how my desk got." She searches for a seat belt, which has been swallowed by the surrounding junk. "But it seems like you have . . . a lot of stuff, too."

Bill scowls good-naturedly. "Well. We don't think of it as a *problem*. Lehr—your mother and I—we aim foremost for preparedness."

"That's right," Cassie's mother says from the front. She is adjusting the drawstring on a khaki hat with flaps that hang like dog ears. In the rearview mirror, her eyes focus on Cassie's. "I don't know what nonsense these teachers spout all day in the public schools, but you can bet your ass it's mostly bull. They're paid to say things, you know."

Cassie is puzzled—puzzlement bordering on concern. Of course Cassie knows that people say *ass*, but she doesn't like her mother saying it, so easily and meanly. And *of course* she knows that Ms. Murphy gets paid; teachers aren't just volunteers, like the old ladies at Hospice Thrift.

"What things?" she asks.

Bill starts the engine, and the jalopy rumbles to life. He is a certain kind of driver (she is stabbed by the thought of Brandon), revving hard already over the road the bus drove in on, except they're heading the opposite way now. Cassie wedges a folding canvas chair between her bouncing leg and the chainsaw and uses the crutch as a sort of waist brace, as if this were a ride with a height requirement—*cla-clank*—a suggestion of safety but not a guarantee.

She calls, "It's like Indiana Jones!" in an effort to stay excited, to prevent this slippage into fear, but no one in the front seat turns. Her heart is racing. "What things?" she says again, louder.

Bill swivels his head back in a glance. "Name, for example, just a few of the facts you learned last year in school," he yells over the engine. On the word *facts*, he takes his hands off the wheel to pump his index fingers in quotes. The road is straight enough that it doesn't matter. "In—what was it—fourth grade?"

Cassie nearly chokes. *Fourth!*—like she's some little baby who's just learned her ABCs. "In *sixth* grade," she yells, "we learned about the Fertile Crescent, in Mesopotamia, and the birth of agriculture." They learned ancient Egypt,

Queen Hatshepsut, Amun-Ra, Isis and the jackals. Plate tectonics, photosyn-
thesis, ratios and how these are like fractions. "But I'm not really much of a
math person, I don't think."

All the time she speaks, the back of Bill's head moves up and down in
patient nods, his eyes smiling on the road. When Cassie finishes, her mother
turns, gripping the seat back. "See, now, the reason Hamilton was asking?
Everything you just said? Consider it all baloney."

Who, Cassie wants to know, is Hamilton? And that other name, *Lehr*,
that Bill had said before? There's no time to ask—Bill is clearing his throat,
and when he speaks, his voice quivers with seriousness. "Or—or—consider it
about one *millionth*"—and he holds up his right hand to show a gap of space
between thumb and forefinger—"consider all those things you know to be
about one *millionth* of the *actual* story."

It is an extreme ride after that. Extremely hot and loud and rough. The
road leads to another highway, two lanes of potholed, seething blacktop that
end in a perfect vanishing point Cassie knows how to draw with a ruler and
three straight lines. Every few minutes a wavering square appears in the distance, a time traveler shimmering through the warp, until the image solidi-
fies and an ordinary semi roars past, its brands all a blur. The wind makes a
tempest of her hair, except for the snarl, which is heavy enough to command
gravity. Cassie puts her hand there and fondles.

Questions are brewing and brimming—questions the noise and commotion of the engine make impossible to ask. From the highway they turn onto
a rutted dirt road. In their wake, powder-light plumes rise up and hang, and
frightened rabbits dart out of their rooms to race risky zigzags in front of
the Jeep. Cassie's heart leaps—*Bunnies!*—at the bobbing tails, gray on top
but pure white on the bottom, cute as glued-on pom-poms, but Bill charges
steadily forward, the tires mere yards behind their lucky, terrified feet, and
Cassie's mother makes not so much as a gesture.

At last they reach the house—or, rather, a compound of low buildings
behind a patchwork fence of weathered wood, stucco pilings, and chain link
run through with green plastic. After the deafening noise of the car, the air is
so quiet it hurts. When Bill swings open the door and Cassie steps onto the

caked ground, she begins to sense how open things are here—an emptiness and visibility that frighten her. The land is just as moony and characterless, sage- and scrub-furred and unfriendly as it was back at the bus stop, as if challenging the point of all that distance they just covered. Crickets chirp, near and far at the same time. Smalling. Stilling.

She puts a nail to her teeth and tears off a crescent. "Who is Hamilton?" she asks. "And that other person you said?"

Bill is hoisting out her bag and rummaging in one of the backseat boxes. "We have our . . . I'm not sure what you're aware of here and what you're not, of course, but there are names we're . . . comfortable with the shadow government knowing . . . and then names we're not."

Her pack is tiny and ridiculous on his shoulder. She squints up at him. "But your real name is—what's the name on your driver's license, I mean?"

He exhales, steering her toward a gate. "It's not that one is *real* and one is fake—that's a false dichotomy, of course. It's that one name they know— Bill and Sarah, here—and the other they don't. Or, they might *know* it, but it's not linked to Bill and Sarah, see? We've simply borrowed names from . . . others in our field, people who've done the same work before us, just to make it . . . confusing, I suppose, for anyone who might have a vested interest in— and what I mean here is a variety of factions of the EMIC that—"

"Hamilton," Cassie's mother interrupts. She is looking for something in her reedy shoulder bag. "Let's get this girl in the house, shall we?"

Bill offers Cassie a wink as they walk. "To conclude," he begins, and repeats the explanation a second time, but in different words and to no greater clarity. "You're young, of course, but it's important to understand as soon as possible: the less they know about you, the less power they have. And the *more* they know about you . . ."

He has a talking problem, too, Cassie gathers; is a motormouth like herself. Pre-dementing Aunt Linda had once made this phenomenon plain: the things that bug us most in others are also our own worst traits, flung back at us.

"The less they know about you, the less power they have," Bill says again. "But the *more* they know about you . . ." and he dips his head in Cassie's direction.

Begrudgingly, she finishes: "The more power they have?" Though she has no clue what she's saying, and *they* is uncomfortable on her tongue. Her knees itch suddenly; when she looks down past her shorts, her legs seem like pale producers of their own dust.

"See there? A very smart girl," Bill says. "I expected nothing less."

"A girl I know changed her name," Cassie offers.

Beginning to huff, she goes on to tell the brief anecdote of how Lindsey Clowe one day demanded that everyone call her Amethyst, even the teacher, around the time that Amber had chosen Lindsey as her new best friend.

"She only changed it to match Amber's, though, to be more popular," Cassie explains. "An amethyst is a gem that's sort of like a purple crystal. You can buy them at the rock shop downtown where I live; they have ones already with hooks in them for hanging on necklaces or in your window or whatever and others that are loose, just for keeping, that are cheaper. They only cost about four dollars. Are your necklaces from a rock shop?"

But Bill is no longer listening; he only halfway turns and says *smart girl* again, like he's reading off a piece of paper.

I am boring already, she thinks. *I am boring even to myself. Motormouth, dumbass.* No matter the passage of time—what birthdays come, what changes endured, what people braved, experiences survived, no matter having come all this way, so courageously and alone—still Cassie's voice, nasal and annoying, never ceases to be just the same today as it was the day before, and the day before, and probably will be forever.

Her mother is at the gate with a whole janitor's ring of keys, unlocking the first of three padlocks on three heavy chains.

5.

AN HOUR—AN HOUR OF LOCK PICKING AND WINDOW trying—and Meghan is a resigned lump, head in hands, in the center of Cassie's sagging bed. *We should have told* someone, *at least, where we were going*, Judy says, sitting at last on the carpet, though what she really means is *You're to blame* and something more desperate, a new clog in her heart—*I want my mother*. But when Meghan lifts her face again she looks casual and blithe—and entirely delusional. "She probably just went to the party early," she says, her eyes off toward the window.

"Maybe," Judy tries. "Or we got tricked or something . . ." Stuck on *or something*. "But did you even see a computer downstairs? I didn't see . . ."

"Maybe she uses her boyfriend's computer?"

"Maybe the aunt is a kidnapper?"

"Or maybe . . ." but Meghan's voice trails to nowhere.

Whoever Cassie_freakme_81 is is not actually, Judy's thinking, the inhabitant of this room. And yet the Cassie who lives here, whoever *that* is, is fast becoming real despite her absence. Cassie is here in the whirligig, ghost-turning in the pencil jar. She's here in the origami animals in various stages of dimension resting on the window ledge, and in the view of the mountain out the window, symmetrically peaked. She's here in the mirrored closet and the overflowing hamper, the carnival bottles filled with colored sand. And she's here in a photograph on the shelf, which Judy crawls over to now.

Judy knows it in her palms—this is, of course, their girl: eight or nine in big pink earmuffs and a jacket that gives her a Michelin Man look, her pink cotton leggings bunchy where her legs meet (there is no thigh gap; there is the opposite of a thigh gap). A younger version of the aunt stands with her hands on maybe-Cassie's shoulders, distinctly uncrazy in a long beige coat and a black scarf, capable of normal eye contact. They're outside in a cold-looking park—the Statue of Liberty is like a tiny figurine pegged on the ocean behind them. It might be one of those fake photo backdrops people stand in front of and then tell their relatives *I was at the Grand Canyon!* except that several real people fuzz in the margins, and the wind pushes all their hair in the same direction.

Cassie's smile, aiming for the same degree of enthusiasm her aunt's achieves, is a wonky, hand-drawn oval.

The realization settles: the stupidity of their faith in some computer person . . . who may or may not be this little girl. Afraid she might start to cry, Judy tries, "She looks nice, though."

Meghan leaps off the bed and tears the picture away. "No way, no way is this her . . ." and her face, in concentration, belies a forking of thoughts. Down one road, Judy sees, she turns against Cassidy just like that: considers what barrage of insults might transform their wasted time into a self-empowering dweeb torch. But this route will call on Meghan to admit that she's been duped in the first place by her cyber friend, and doubly duped by a total nerd. The other option is to give Cassie the generous benefit of the doubt—to argue that the girl in the photo must be some anonymous cousin or dead baby sister, or to understand the photo as an ancient personal artifact: that Cassie *had* been this girl, six or seven years ago, but that she's *totally changed*, redeemed herself through cigarettes and a nose piercing and getting skinny.

Hedging this way, Judy says, "It's probably old."

But Meghan's face is already scrunching and darkening in draconian judgment. "No *way* is she a model," she says, her eyes all over the picture. Disgust stretches out her vowels. "She looks like *Melissa*. She's so . . . *lame*."

"Yeah, obviously," Judy says, grabbing the picture back, anxious to replace it on its shelf, to protect it from further scrutiny. Meghan is right; the girl in the photograph *does* look like Melissa (rule-following, clean-mouthed, lunch-in-the-library Melissa). But Judy also thinks—a thing she won't say—that if you took away the bulky winter clothes, the girl in the photo looks like Judy, too, a few years back.

Meghan moves around the room now, a sudden Sherlock, opening a cigar box that holds rubber stamps, digging through a sock drawer that turns up nothing more interesting than potpourri sachets and a pack of mermaid-themed temporary tattoos. She lifts a plate off the dresser for close inspection—the kind of naturally brown-speckled plate that looks dirty by design and makes you wonder why anyone making plates would speckle them brown. "Peanut butter is totally dry," she says. "She hasn't been here in days"—like a forensics person on television.

"Or she hasn't eaten peanut butter in days," Judy says.

Meghan sets down the plate, rolling her eyes with such circumference her whole head rotates, then opens the closet to rifle. With each sliding hanger the look on her face turns ever more appalled. Pastel blouses with Peter Pan collars, rumpled plaid prairie frocks, holiday sweaters and Hammer pants and stirrup leggings with shot elastic. "If this chick's a model then I'm the goddamned president of America," Meghan says. She flashes a leering orange vest, appliquéd to look like a jack-o'-lantern, and reads from the tag, "*Made by Linda, with Love.* Homemade! Her closet is like a frickin' Salvation Army!" Judy knows for a fact that most of Meghan's clothes are secondhand, just as Judy's are, but her best friend is resolute on her warpath. Her modus operandi is to hold up a garment and speculate how immature/boyish/fat Cassie must look in it, then toss the item into a gathering pile for one of them to try on.

Meghan strips down to her underwear, then steps into a pair of corduroy shorts, guffawing when they're inches too loose, holding out the waistband like a former fatso in a diet commercial. She catwalks across the room, then whips around fast to strike a pose in the mirror—adjusts the cups of her bra, which Judy knows is half padding but can't help but be impressed by anyway. Judy has yet to graduate from a training bra, though she's already a 5 in juniors, vs. Meghan's 0. Meghan has taken to repeating, *It's just baby fat*, anytime Judy risks a gripe. *You'll even out eventually.*

"Maybe she'll come back soon, though?" Judy tries. "Maybe she'll turn out to be cool anyway?" stepping, still in her shorts, into an ugly velvet jumper with shiny shell buttons. Spotting a disposable camera on the desk, she gestures her chin, adds weakly, "She might still know a photographer?"

Meghan grabs the camera in a huff and studies it. "Ten left." She snaps

Judy's picture as she's buttoning the jumper. "The whole reason I came up here," Meghan pouts, winding forward the next exposure, "and all I get is this fake-ass Kodak from Longs."

Over maroon sweatpants Meghan layers a leopard-print leotard so that the crotch bunches absurdly. "Oh my *god*," Judy laughs. Meghan can't help but giggle too now, and Judy is happy, at least, to have this glimmer of the old Meghan, the *good* Meghan, back. She drapes on Mardi Gras beads from a hook by the dresser, and Judy retrieves a straw hat from the top shelf of the closet. Her pose on the bed is adult-sexy, *Sports Illustrated*–inspired—she kneels, shoulders pulled back, pelvis forward, fingering the beads with one hand while the other touches the hat brim. "Are there shadows? Can you see my philtrum?"

Through the viewfinder, Judy, dutiful friend, finds her unshadowed, philtrum-first face. "It's good," she says. "Say Cassie!"

"Freak me!" Meghan sings, her most Valley-inflected mimic.

Last April at the Sherman Oaks Galleria, as Meghan and Judy sat on a bench slurping Orange Juliuses and scanning the dallying high school cliques for hot guys, a man approached them across the atrium, squelching in his shoes. When the stranger was three feet before them, he stopped, cocked his head thoughtfully, looked hard at Meghan, and said, "Excuse me, Miss, I don't mean no disrespect, but you have the most exceptional philtrum I've ever seen."

They'd been shopping at the Limited for school-appropriate tank tops with two-inch or thicker straps, had found nothing they could afford, and so spent their moms' tens on miniature butterfly clips, now roosting in their hair. The weird man drew out the word *exceptional* like someone from another era. The compliment was unmistakably for Meghan, though he glanced at Judy occasionally, as though she were Meghan's translator.

"Can I ask you: How long have you been modeling? And are you happy with your current representation?"

When, flustered and flattered, uncrossing and recrossing her legs in her flaring jeans, Meghan said that no, she wasn't *represented*, the man drew his moony face into a deep, doubling chin, then launched into a car salesman's monologue. He was a scout and an agent, he said, always on the lookout for stunning young *discoveries* like Meghan. How would she like to have a career as a "professional knockout?" Make hundreds, thousands, millions? He used his hands to flick flashing lights in her face. Magazines, billboards, runways, he said. How does Paris sound? London? *Mee-lawn?*

The man knelt right there on the tile floor and opened his official-looking briefcase. They watched as he rummaged—through folded newsprint, stapled packets, fine-print Xeroxes, pink Chinese takeout menus, business cards, playing cards.

There were plenty of suspect things about him, Judy reflects now (brown corduroys with the knees rubbed flat, stains on his tie like paper-plate grease, an infantile haircut, and Velcroed, marshmallowy shoes), but at the time it did not occur to her (and certainly not to Meghan, who didn't take her wide eyes off him—*something big was happening*) that he was probably a fraud, a nut job, or a perv. At the time, she thought, Maybe he's just an unorthodox sort of modeling-world person? A genius savant with his own slapdash style, the kind who's later portrayed in movies about famous models' lives by Jack Nicholson in the right costume? Finally, he looked up from the spilling papers, raised his hands, and lowered them with a sigh. He couldn't find what he was looking for. In the end, still squatting, he wrote his name (JIM CAUL) and a phone number with a mystery area code along the edge of a brake-pad coupon, which he proffered to Meghan.

"You go ahead and call me now after you lose a few," he told her. Then he whispered out the side of his mouth, "Pounds," moving his eyes toward her midriff, bare and creased beneath her crop top.

Meghan moved an arm to shield her skin. Her whole body scrunched, stunned, as he stood up laboriously, picked up the briefcase, and walked away.

After he'd gone, Meghan stormed to the nearest trash can to drop her drink, bawled in the restroom, and vowed, red-eyed, to get herself down to ninety-nine before ninth grade if it killed her. She carried the brake-pad coupon in the smallest pocket of her purse until Rita caught wind of it— Meghan spilled the beans in the midst of a screaming argument—and ripped the purse open and found it. *Some pedophile? I swear to god, you're dense as shit*

on a stick! A familiar threat was made: she'd ship Meghan off to the waste-
lands of Utah to live with her born-again Mormon father, his bevy of wives
and brainwashed progeny, where she would wear a bonnet and be forbidden
even ChapStick—to which Meghan wailed and begged, *No! Don't make me!*
as Rita twisted Jim Caul down the sink, ran the water, and flipped on the
disposal.

They'd believed Jim Caul, Judy thinks now, in part because of *philtrum*,
a word unknown to them, and yet Meghan's *was* exceptional. Wasn't this the
definition of discovery? Someone showing you what's spectacular about you
that you can't see for yourself? Later the girls looked the word up in an anatomy
book at the library. Chapter 4, "The Human Face," page 159. *In utero, the two
halves of the face develop separately, meeting in the center at a final seam between
upper lip and septum, called the philtrum.* In Judy's imagination, a fleshy sheet,
a skin nebula, began at the ears and grew forward, became cheeks, forehead,
nose, a magic mask inching philtrumward, covering the gore of whatever lay
beneath. *The Romans considered the philtrum an erotic site, calling it "Cupid's
bow."*

Meghan didn't share Judy's level of interest; she'd wandered off that day
for the magazine rack, leafing through the newest *Seventeen*. Her philtrum
had already been signed and sealed; why did she need its cultural history? But
Judy experienced a small epiphany, reading the book, seeing the illustration,
touching her own average lip-dent. How did the body do all that, without
your permission? It wasn't erotic like sex but because of the miracle of it: that
anyone's face ever came together at all, let alone with any symmetry.

The dress-up game exhausted, the room a disaster of wrong-side-out fab-
rics, the girls set to scouring Cassie's desk drawer by drawer, pencil pouch
by gum pack. Judy is as hopeful to discover some tool with which to better
attack the door lock as Meghan is to further reveal the sham of Cassie-the-
model—no contracts, no lifetime lip gloss supply or Polaroids of her chiseled
boyfriend's pelvic V, just more little-girly accouterments. They learn that,
according to her June report card, Cassie has just finished sixth grade, excels
in language arts and social studies, sucks at math, and *should continue to
practice raising her hand, allowing other students time to problem-solve, before*

shouting out an answer. She saves her birthday postcards from the dentist, chews the aluminum rings that connect eraser to pencil, has a baby's taste in music (Disney soundtracks and Michael Jackson CDs, with the single strange exception of a group called Cat Stank, whose members' faces have all been scribbled out on the ink-jet-printed cover—by Cassie or by someone else?), and got the same sex ed starter pack Meghan and Judy received three years in a row at their own school. The mini deodorant stick is gone, but the tampons and pads remain, secure in their wrappers as disappointing candies.

Rooting in a lower drawer, wrist-deep in a bushel of static-electric Easter grass, Meghan shrieks, "Oh my *god*," and shows Judy her find: a small, pink canvas book embossed DIARY. A dinky gold lock—a lock that could be bitten off or yanked—is built into the strap and snapped officially shut.

In the hour they've been here, Judy hasn't thought much about the possibility of Cassie suddenly walking into the room, the room that is quickly becoming all theirs. But as Meghan hunts for the key, feverishly emptying the drawers now, then slamming them shut again, strewing the fake grass and pulling whole stacks of books off Cassie's shelf—now Judy imagines it—Cassie walking in on this invasion, this trashing. When Meghan raises the Snoopy snow globe and brings its base down on the lock, Judy lets slip, "Don't!"

Meghan looks at Judy like she's a dog pooping on her shoe. Again she bangs with the globe, and again. The lock doesn't spring, but there are now several obvious dents—evidence of tampering. She gets up and flops back on the bed with a groan, her feathery body bouncing once with unchecked irritation. "You were right," she says to the ceiling. "We're probably being kidnapped. This is probably what kidnapping feels like. Hopefully she's not a murderer. A cannibal or something . . ."

"A *cannibal*?" Judy asks. She strains to hear downstairs, but there is no decipherable sound of cannibalism . . . only the fluctuating *wah-wah* of the television. A bad-dream feeling rushes at her dizzyingly, and she senses Meghan must feel it, too. What she wants in the room now is optimism, hope, lies even; something. On the carpet, she picks at a glossy pink crust where a manicure went off the rails. *Off the nails.* "It looks like someone's manicure went off the nails," Judy hears herself say.

Meghan sits up and glares. "What are you *talking* about?" and Judy feels familiarly stung.

A noise—an engine slowing, a radio—draws them to the window. Across the street, a car, bronze in the seven o'clock sun, noses into the driveway of one of the shadier, fancier houses. A family straggles out of a sleek black station wagon, a bootlegged peace sign ornamenting its hood. The neighbors have been to the beach: four sun-soaked, healthy people, a kind of born-with satisfaction in their expressions, their smiles. Two shirtless little boys traipse toward the porch eating from a white paper bag. "*French fries!*" Judy gasps, and saliva pools in her cheeks. Someone's stomach (her own, or Meghan's, or both in unison?) churns, and even Meghan whines pitifully.

The man—the husband, the *father*, the sort of dreamy, easy, immune-to-shark-attack-and-cancer husband/father that California advertises but whom the girls never encounter in real life—takes off his hat and shakes out a blond shag. "He's like a blond Keanu Reeves," Meghan whispers.

"Or that one Australian guy," Judy says.

"What the hell did she do to get *that* . . ."

But she is just as gorgeous as he is. A wet knot of hair hangs down her back, and she has a way of gesturing, of moving her head as she speaks, that strikes Judy as French or Italian, exotically refined. When a strap of her black dress slips down, she returns it to her shoulder absently. Judy wants a dress like that, and to be a woman, someday, who returns a fallen strap to its place while speaking French to a gorgeous husband. One of the boys drops his sack, fries scatter, and the woman hurries to him. Judy is stunned by another thought: a woman like *that* is also a mother.

Bonnie—the morning Bonnie announced that she and Rick had gotten married, Judy focused all her attention on the large mole, growing raisinlike between Bonnie's breasts, where her kimono hung open as she sipped coffee. This was a Sunday back in June, a mere week after Judy and her mother had moved in, when Judy returned from two nights at Meghan's to find the lovebirds wearing matching gold wedding bands, her mother's too loose and Rick's too tight, and a single cardboard-framed photograph propped on the counter. The frame read in gold letters, *Last Love Chapel, Mesquite, Nevada*, and the couple held hands beneath a white balloon arch, like kids Judy's age at a school dance. Her mother wore the coral-colored pantsuit Judy had seen many times, but the red, gauzy scarf knotted flamboyantly around her neck was new and made her look like someone else—someone who'd arrived, finally, at a hard-won place on the other side of a chintzy rainbow. Someone with money to spend in a hotel gift shop.

On the table beside the coffee stood a bottle of Johnnie Walker. They'd gone to hit the slots, and then—*We just thought, the hell with it!* Rick said. *A whim!* her mother said, scooting closer to him. *I won the jackpot, didn't I?* Her eyes gleamed wetly in their having-drinks way, holding nothing of the bashful apology, the embarrassed explanation, Judy thought should be there. No one had asked *her*, her mother seemed not to have considered. No one had thought to ask *Judy*, it occurred to her helplessly, whether or not she wanted a stepfather. Her father father—her real father—that had been *a whim*, too, Judy thought, a sick feeling—anger—burning into her cheeks. *A Bakersfield fling named Tom*, was all her mother would ever say, and Judy was left to infer: one in a string of them. *We're better off*, Bonnie liked to cap the questions. But how could she know that, and who was this *we*? How dare she lump Judy, a person all her own, in with *this*—the dangling raisin mole, the string of one-night stands, the spiked coffee, the stupid, watermelon-gutted Rick?

But they won't, she comforts herself now, last. *Bonnie, you go through men faster than I go through aspirin*, Rita liked to say. Bonnie will get bored, or too drunk, or she'll cheat, or he will—they'll ruin it any number of ways. And Judy and Meghan agree: to get married is also to begin the process of divorce.

Across the street, the front door is open, the boys are gone, the mother and father are hauling straw bags and towels and buckets from the car. Meghan and Judy smack the glass and shout. "Hey! Hey! Up here!" slapping and waving, standing and flailing. But they are a thick pane, a wide yard, a street, and a driveway away. The woman goes inside (*Get* her *out of the picture, anyway*, Meghan huffs), but the man—he's unraveling a hose now, spraying down shrubs in big cobalt planters as if nothing in the world could ever be wrong. Judy's palms sting, but still she hits. "Look up! Look *up*!" she screams.

Until at last he does—raises his chin and looks right at them. The girls gasp. Caught voyeurs, they freeze instinctively, then wave and jump, all emergency. He watches, amused, and waves back—a beautiful, smiling *Hi there*, before he turns, dragging the hose behind him, and disappears around the side of the house.

No, no, no! they wail. *Come back!*

Meghan sprints over to Cassie's desk, urgent with purpose. When she finds a pad of construction paper, she tears off the first yellow sheet and grabs a marker. Judy watches her friend, studious when an idea is her own, hunch over the desk and draw the first big letters. "Are you even going to *help*?" she screams.

Judy is generally thought of as *a bright girl, despite her home life. As an independent thinker in the classroom but impressionable in social situations.* "Well give me a piece!" Judy says. Meghan rips off several sheets and tosses her a marker, and Judy sets to work writing on the floor, using a world atlas for support.

TEENS TRAPPED! SEND HELP! Meghan's first sign reads. Judy does the same but with cute curlicues at the ends of her Ss. "Like this?"

Meghan flaps her hands, seething. "It's not a coloring contest, Judy! We have to hurry!"

The sting, deep in the sockets of Judy's eyes, returns from before, the result of having been spotted, then ignored, and of Meghan's voice, acerbic and mean, on top of everything else. She chews the pen cap for a moment and then rushes out on the sort of redemptive limb that will make Meghan remember why they're friends. She scrawls *HORNY* above *TEENS*. Then whips out a second sign: *S.O.S.* across the top and, reading down, acrostic-style, *SAVE OUR SLUTS!* on pale-pink paper. When Judy peeks up to see Meghan's reaction, Meghan's eyes are wide and her mouth is ajar. Judy grins—how satisfying, to shock the shocker—but Meghan's face twists into a grimace. "You're—" She has no word for Judy, just a furious, back-of-throat growl. "This is basically, like, do we have to pee in a jar or not. It's *life or death*." Purple ink has made spots on her fingers, stains that recall kindergarten, and Judy shrinks with regret.

After long minutes of work, only Meghan's signs make it to the glass, Scotch-taped and crooked:

TEENS TRAPPED! SEND HELP!

KIDNAPPED!

CALL 9–1–1!

But the sky is dimming from pink to purple, and their pleas are likely already illegible, just dark squares in the darkening window. *Teens trapped! Send help!* they chant, desperate cheerleaders, slapping the glass in time.

Blond Keanu must've gone inside through another door. Or snuck past while they were drawing. The hose has been left out, leaking a long, shaggy stain down the driveway. Inside the house, the lights come on in the downstairs windows. A silhouette occasionally passes, but the family is as sealed up in their world now as Snoopy in the New York snow globe.

Look! Help! Look! Help! Their words boomerang instantly back, rejected, silenced. No one hears, and no one to hear. A bird chirps its head off at the wrong time of day. A dog barks in another yard. A squirrel on a tree branch sees the girls and freezes, but no creature appears that cares.

6.

BEHIND THE FORTRESSING WALL, IT'S LIKE . . . CASSIE HARDLY
knows. A paradoxical aura of neglect and love. A homemade oasis, camouflaged and protected. A series of low-roofed stucco buildings connect in an O
around a weedy central courtyard. On the left side, the structure looks almost
houselike, with a number of mismatched doors and doormats, random plants
poking out of plastic and terra-cotta pots, wind chimes and stained-glass
trinkets, mobiles of bent forks and broken seashells, empty gas cans and five-
gallon buckets and splayed lawn chairs and a silver satellite dish that cups the
air and casts shade. The eastern half of the O is comprised of ramshackle sheds
and lean-tos with tarps for doors and corrugated roofs, plastic and aluminum.
A dozen speckled chickens peck around a coop, and a rooster, miserable and
diseased behind meaty face growths, eyes their arrival suspiciously. Farther
back, what Bill calls *the farm* hums invisibly with mammalian heartbeats;
Cassie hears treading hoof falls and smells the fetid bake of manure. Across
the dirt square, a peacock drags craft-store feathers through the dust, then
cranes toward an empty fountain scooped into the ground. The peacock's
breast seems to absorb and release all the heat of the sun. "Who is *that*?"
Cassie asks. She's never seen a peacock in real life.

The fountain where the bird gazes doesn't hold more than a layer of toxic-
looking slime and a few yellow leaves, shed from the property's single tree.

"That's Sergeant," Bill says. "Handsome, but dumb as a rock. You'll meet
the other critters later. We got a milk cow back there, too. Priscilla."

"I love animals," Cassie says. But does she really? The only animal she's ever
really known is Moose. What she loves is the notion of animal consciousness—
the possibility of animal understanding, animal intuition, their harboring of
silent intelligence. When Cassie imagines her future self, walking down a New
York City sidewalk, she is, among other things, a vegetarian.

Off the same ring of keys, her mother unlocks one of the doors in the house-looking part of the square. Inside, something woody and spicy burns in the air. "Casa de los Forasteros," Bill says behind her. "You have arrived."

Her mother and Bill remove their boots in the tiled entry, and Cassie follows their lead, unties her Reeboks and airs her damp, hot feet. With her backpack slung over his shoulder, dangling its beaded baubles and stubbed lanyards, Bill looks like a weird old man who's gotten mixed up in life and wandered back to school. He leads Cassie from room to room on a sort of tour, her mother trailing a few feet behind, so quiet in her socks that Cassie can't even hear her footsteps.

Each room has its own color. The orange entryway becomes a more-or-less-regular green living room, with a television and sofas and all sorts of metal lizards and brightly painted skulls and dried chili-pepper bundles fixed to the wall. They pass through a similarly decorated purple kitchen, the counters busy with pottery and chopsticks and Dr. Seuss plants growing in clear jars without soil, and then down a hall past a bathroom under construction, a trough-like concrete tub holding buckets and trowels and bound tiles. The laundry room is lined with metal shelves containing enough bagged and boxed and canned nonperishables to feed a summer camp. Crackers, chili, Chicken of the Sea, split peas. Beyond this is a bright-yellow dining room Bill explains they've never once dined in, and Cassie can see why: its long table is stacked with brown-lidded file boxes, manila folders, and other stacks of paper, loose and towering. The pages Cassie can see are crammed with word-processed type. Perhaps someone's writing a book? The idea excites her. She stores the question away for later.

In the hallway beyond the dining room, Cassie peeks her head through a door ajar and spies a clutter of coffee mugs around a bulky computer, several more of the file boxes, a bookshelf bowing with hand-labeled videotapes, a small television that appears to broadcast a black-and-white picture of the desert and, pinned to the wall, a number of illustrations (semihuman figures with balloon-shaped heads atop cartoonish bodies: distended limbs, genitalia-less groins) and grainy photographs of aerial landscapes, a smudge in the sky, a telescopic view of a rainbow formation Cassie knows is called a *nebula*—another of those words she loves.

Bill hurries up behind her. "Oops, oops, not so fast," and swings the door closed, locks it. "My office. Off-limits." On the back of the door is a simple poster tacked at eye level: a flying saucer hovering over silhouetted hills, the words WE BELIEVE printed across the sky assertively. Bill moves along ahead of her and nods toward a second door, this one closed already and with no poster. "And Lehr's office. Equally off-limits."

Remembering her mother (did her mother see her see the office?), Cassie turns. The woman's appearance jars her—Cassie can't help but compare this real-life mother to the one she's kept for so long in her heart, whose default expression is one of smiling, placid contentment. Instead, Sarah's mouth is firmly drawn, twitching occasionally with some upper-lip impulse Cassie can't quite decipher. She holds her left arm perfectly straight, clutching it with her right hand as if she's injured. Cassie smiles shyly, but her mother looks down: she's found a chip in the tile to toe at, more interesting than her daughter.

Past the offices is another closed door, this one wooden, with carved designs of flowers and birds and other flourishes gathering dust. "Our love nest," Bill says. "Believe me, you have no interest in that"—but before Cassie can blush, they're rounding another corner, to the closet-sized add-on where Cassie will be staying. "It's hot now but it'll cool off soon," Bill says, pulling on the ceiling fan. "Hope you don't mind a roommate."

Inside, Cassie sees immediately what he means. "Cassie, meet Gertrude. Gertie, Cassie." Gertrude's cage takes up a whole corner. "Cockatoo," Bill says. "Not to be confused with the diminutive and much less impressive *cockatiel*—a mere cousin."

Upon hearing its name, the bird sidles down the big branch, then stops to shift in place, moving from foot to foot like an exaggeration of nervousness. Its eyes look pasted on, googly.

Bill slings Cassie's backpack off onto the plaid sleeper couch that's already been pulled out. There's a single flat pillow and several layers of blankets not quite smooth; a bed Bill has made up, Cassie thinks, not her mother. "You got your light switch here, bathroom down the hall, and the top drawer of that file cabinet is spare for your things, if you'd like."

From the doorway, her mother says to Bill, "She won't be here long enough for all that," and turns to go.

"Well," is all Bill says. He moves across the room to a large picture window and pulleys back the blinds. "And out here is your whole backyard." Cassie sees on Bill's digital watch that it's after six, but you wouldn't know it from the landscape, which stretches sun-bright and vast, marked only here and there by a tree like a person in arms-up surrender, or a bush shaking in the wind. It strikes Cassie as a terrain where anything could happen, with only the sky as witness. And there's nothing between her and that anything except a thin sheet of glass.

Bill moves his finger, pointing. "Prickly pear there, Joshua tree there, 'nother Joshua, piñon, Joshua."

Cassie points, too. "Sky, sky, sky."

Bill emits a hacking sort of laugh and squeezes her shoulder. Once, fast, friendly.

In the kitchen her mother is filling three glasses of water from a free-standing cooler Cassie knows from the teachers' lounge but has never seen in someone's house. "Would anyone like some water?" her mother asks. She looks uncomfortable and worried: like maybe she read about offering water in a manual on how to have guests.

"I would," Cassie hurries to say.

"I would, too," Bill says.

"So would I," her mother says.

Sipping, watching her mother and Bill sip, Cassie is suddenly afraid. Who are these people? Who are they, and where *is* she? It's the same kind of fear that caught her breath at the sound of the laundry-room door locking, the light pinging off, and laughter—*No one wants to see this*. A jitter in her heart and then, thank goodness, it dulls and lengthens to something manageable, low-key. With her free hand, Cassie pretends to scratch her neck but instead touches the knot. Still there. All this time, waiting to meet her mother, and now . . . How do people, real people, get to know other people?

Bill excuses himself—some duty with the animals—and then they are alone. They drink one and then two and then three glasses of water, to keep the silence from overtaking them—from swallowing up their very fragile arrangement, of stranger-daughter visiting stranger-mother.

At last, to say something—and because she is, actually, very hungry, Cassie ventures, "Are there any—do you and Bill have any crackers, Mother? Or anything to snack on?"

Her mother eyes her over the rim of her glass like she's asked for money or drugs. "Hamilton and I don't *snack*," she says. "And we don't run a restaurant, either. Didn't you bring food?"

"Well—" Cassie starts, but now she doesn't know how to finish. Her mother's eyes travel down, to the tight waist of her shorts and the stomach chub at her sides, and Cassie flushes, tugging down her shirt, which has ridden embarrassingly up. "I brought food," she says weakly, "but I ate most of it already."

Her mother is skinny by comparison—*bony*, even, under so much jewelry. "Well. It sounds like you'd be wise to eat what's left," she says. "You need to be adaptable. I'm sorry."

And yet she doesn't *sound* particularly sorry. She's looking Cassie right in the eye now, her own intrepid stare scanning Cassie's face. But her expression isn't of wonder or curiosity; it is of evaluation, skepticism, *distrust*. Cassie shifts from one socked foot to the other, feeling the pain of direct observation. She wonders suddenly: Why was she so rude to that fat woman on the bus?

Finally, her mother takes the glass from her and turns to the sink. "I suppose you've come here with a lot of questions," she begins over the tap. "You want to know why I got rid of you and things like that. Am I right?" She glances at Cassie over her shoulder, and her voice rises to a disturbing pitch. "*Why did you leave me, Mummy? Mummy, who is my daddy?*" It is a shocking, phony whine, but it only lasts an instant, and then she's normal again. "Etcetera, etcetera. Am I right?" She turns the water off and looks at Cassie again. "I'll tell you right now: I'm prepared to talk about these things. You're old enough; I suppose you have a right to know. Bill believes you do. But I'm warning you: Don't open that can of worms if you're not ready for the answers. They might be—difficult to hear."

She turns back to the sink to wash the cups a second time, soaping the sponge and scrubbing as if they might've contained poison.

In her temporary room, Cassie sits on the pullout and looks around. Gertrude is in her cage, gnawing at her own leg; office chairs and floor lamps and a crooked recliner, crammed against the opposite wall, give an unsettling sense of audience. Cassie takes her time unpacking, knowing nothing else to do. Better to be in here than out there, exposed to her mother's hostility. The questions she mentioned have not been, actually, at the forefront of Cassie's brain today (precisely because they're *always there*, growing cobwebs in the corners), but now she wonders anew: Why *did* she give me up? Who *is* my father? And what kind of tangled beginning might constitute what her mother calls a *can of worms*? The suggested drama thrills her a little—that she might have anything to do with a *can of worms*.

She eases open the zipper of her backpack, and its tight contents expand. The dreaded black banana is there on top, staining the paper bag and smelling up everything with its rotten fruitiness. There is no wastebasket in the room, but Cassie is *adaptable*: she slides open the big picture window and drops the sack outside, thinking a coyote or a big lizard will come and snatch it away. Then she sets to removing each item from her pack and placing it carefully on the bed. The three books she's brought (no diary! and again the loneliness its absence brings), her sandals, two sets of weekend clothes, pajamas, toothbrush, hairbrush, and Batty, her old stuffed bat she's had since forever, his wings worn to drooping and his body unraveling at vital seams. From the bottom of the pack, rolled and crumpled, she pulls out her favorite dress-up dress and gives it a good shake.

The dress, of midnight-blue crushed velvet, is from a store and not Aunt Linda's sewing room, with a rhinestone neck closure and matching rhinestone barrette Cassie keeps clipped, for safe storage, against the dress's tag. She wore this to the school Christmas gala last year and the year before, but recently it's tightened against her chest and bottom, and she knows that soon, soon, sadly, she'll have to give it up. When Brandon had still been just the distant, magnetic boy behind the deli counter, before she knew who Brandon really was, she had put on this very dress in her bedroom and conducted whole imaginary conversations with him, mutated movie scripts, fantasies she now shames to have conjured. But because he never saw the dress in real life, Cassie has deemed it safe, still on limits, protected from Brandon distinctly the way that, say, the bike shorts and Monterey Bay Aquarium T-shirt and strawberry-printed underpants she wore That Night were not—have long since been stuffed into a plastic Safeway bag and deposited in the garbage. An outfit ruined by what it had been through, the way the smell of campfire is now ruined for Cassie. The bitter burn of alcohol. Beef jerky and most cold cuts.

The crush had begun benignly enough, when Cassie visited Gus's Grocery one weekend last spring to buy Coke and Red Vines with a twenty snuck from Aunt Linda's jewelry box, spotted the new boy behind the deli counter, and went watery in the mouth: she suddenly wanted a sandwich. It was another, uglier boy she ordered from (the boy who would turn out to be Travis), but it was Brandon who looked up from the meat slicer, powered down the whirling saw, and hollered, *I got this one*. He took his sweet time constructing her lunch, banging spoons on the cutting board and jutting his chin in fast jerks to the music screaming from the boom box in a way that all felt for Cassie's benefit, a little show he was putting on just for her.

Saturday after Saturday, she found reasons to go to Gus's. She sipped Coke at the fiberglass tables on the patio, sunning her pale shins and pretending to read her most advanced-looking books, until the moment he might appear, smoking by the dumpsters. Then a game of playing dumb, of eye contact and looking away ensued: He'd remove his baseball hat and whip his brownish, chin-length hair forward and then back like a woman in a shampoo commercial, while Cassie would move her head frenetically between her book page and the sun and Brandon's direction, waiting for him to notice her. If she was feeling especially bold, she'd lope back into the store through the back door, pretending to have forgotten a spork, right past Brandon's flick-flicking lighter.

How's the sandwich?

It's really good; thank you.

You eat a lot of sandwiches, huh?

Only, like, once a week.

Saturday, Saturday, and Saturday. Roast beef, pastrami, and slippery tricolored pasta salad. She could walk there from home. Whenever she arrived, Damien or Travis would explode in laughter and cover his face with his shirt. More than once, Damien announced, *Hey man, your stalker's here—* teases she chose to ignore. May came, and the weather got warmer. Behind the counter Brandon swatted flies, mixed industrial amounts of ranch, pulled on baggy plastic gloves. He had a habit of giving her back the wrong change, of fake-stuttering, and of adding mayonnaise even though she requested none. *With extra mayo. For Cass-ass-ass-assie. Don't let it get all over you.* Finally, one day, punching in the numbers on the register, he asked her how old she was. It was the first non–sandwich related exchange they'd had.

I'm in sixth, she told him, the heat rising to her cheeks.

Sixth grade? No fuckin' way. You look sixteen. Whadja do, get held back a bunch?

He swiped his tongue in an oval around his gums and grinned. *This is flirting. He is flirting with me.* She was conscious of a twitch in her underwear, just one but meaning business. He looked down only to seal the bright-orange PAID sticker over her pasta salad. It was dangerous and incredible. The pocked skin on his cheeks was the blushing color of baloney, but his jaw was mannish, his cheekbones nice. Beneath the curled upper lip, one of his teeth was brown at the top but pristine and pointed at the bottom. She thought distinctly, *He's strange, but I will love him.*

His olderness seemed not so much a complication as supporting evidence of the mysteries of fate. It was fated because she was drawn to him, like all the examples in all of the songs, and because he, she could hardly believe, seemed drawn to her, too.

Some days she waited on the patio but his break never came (or maybe he'd already taken it? She wasn't brave enough to ask), so that eventually, crushed by disappointment but with no other option, she summoned the courage to leave before she embarrassed herself further. *See ya, Brandon—* popping inside under the pretense of dumping her trash, though there were plenty of trash cans outside. He smirked and flopped a gloved hand up like he hardly remembered her name.

One day, though (at last! One day!), finishing his cigarette in the sun while Cassie tried to look busy biting her nails, he called over to her, *You wanna walk the train tracks? I'm getting off.* Before she knew it, she was inches from her love in the flickering spring dusk, the shadows long and the plants fragrant, balancing in her sneakers on the smooth metal rails while he smoked and coughed. With the green apron off he was like a new person—a real person, a real boy, in a real T-shirt and jeans and backward hat, with a real interest in her. She never had to think of what to say with Brandon, because he did all of the talking. He cycled through the same list of topics in breathless, curious monologues, as if he had only just learned to speak and Cassie were a consciousnessless alien he could try out talking on. His band, his mom, his job, his friends, his car trouble, and his ex-girlfriend—he spoke, and all she had to do was say, *Hmm.* Or, *Really?* Or, *Wow, she sounds mean.* He didn't ask why she only came to the deli alone, or where she lived, or what her interests were, but Cassie didn't mind. She liked being this version of herself: quiet, demure, sweet.

Hey, you wanna go drink beer in the park?

Hey, you wanna sit in my car and listen to CDs?

Hey, you wanna come to Damien's and see our band?

You're kind of cute, he said once, driving Cassie home after two blistering hours of Cat Stank practice. *Like, you don't look like most girls. But you're cute in a different way.* His hand touched her bare knee, which she had especially shaved, this knee and the attached leg, for the first time this morning, in the hope that Brandon would do just this. The clammy coolness of his fingers made her shiver in the dark of the car. She wasn't used to being noticed, let alone touched. His touch seemed to know something in her, some interesting new thing that she herself had only ever guessed at.

Around the same time, Cassie was learning a technique in the world religions unit of Ms. Murphy's class. Those last weeks of school, Ms. Murphy brought in twenty-four porcelain teacups, each with its own painted design, a purple iris or a blue bridge and a willow tree, and the class sipped tea bitter as grass while Ms. Murphy talked them through meditation. Someone giggled. Someone hissed, *Shut up!* But Cassie shut her eyes and felt her chest expand, contract, expand. Her arms and legs seemed to lose their nerves and meld with the classroom chair. *Picture a garden; now picture a lake; now picture a bird and a boat—then wipe the picture away like you're painting over it with white.* What was left was a clean, blank nothingness. *Now look at that white wall for as long as you can. Just look at the white, and breathe, and any other thoughts that come in, paint over those, too.* Long seconds passed. It was like giving your brain a little nap. When Cassie opened her eyes, everything looked brighter, more vivid somehow, as if cleaned by a hard rain.

In the days and weeks after the basement, it was this blessed technique that made it possible to go on living. To wipe what had transpired away for whole minutes at a time; to feel at least kinda sorta free. Now when the fear rushes back at her, paralyzing (especially at night, especially in the dark), she tells herself to watch for as long as she can bear—and then she paints it white.

She whites out B and D and T and then herself and holds it, holds it, clings to the white until the walls of her brain burn with blankness. Sometimes, the meditation works long enough to calm her and make her feel she has been cured. But other times, the memories reemerge with such palpable, menacing force that her heart speeds up, her spine tingles, and it's a wonder other people can't read the past all over Cassie's face. Sometimes, a part of her wishes they could.

From the bottom of the backpack she removes the last item, a pair of white patent-leather shoes that go with the dress, in case she ends up staying for a while, or if her mother and Bill decide to take her out to a tablecloths-and-bread-basket type of restaurant—hopes fading fast into total impossibilities. Cassie can feel her armpits dampening. What was she thinking? Long-sleeved velvet in August, in the desert, for a family who doesn't want her? She looks over at the big white bird, perched now on a silver ring, its dumb black eyes watching her but knowing nothing, and all at once, Cassie is filled with malice.

She inches toward the cage, clutching Batty to her chest. "What a stupid old hat," she whispers at the bird. Gertrude's plume *is* stupid, like something some fuddy-duddy would wear in a black-and-white movie, and her petrified beak curves in a snobby, stuck-up way. "Stupid hat, stupid bird," Cassie whispers. "Ugly hat, ugly bird."

Just because she can, Cassie leaps forward, plunging Batty right into

Gertrude's walnut-sized face. "Gah!" she cries, shaking. The face retracts and the beak opens, revealing a tough black tongue. The screech is prehistoric. Each feather on Gertrude's breast expands as if alive, and her wings rise ominously into forms as powerful and wide as arms.

Cassie gasps and stumbles backward. "I'm sorry," she whispers, trembling, pressing Batty against her cheek. She was only playing, but her nose stings on the inside and her heartbeat fills her ears. "I didn't mean to," she says to the bird, who is moving side to side again, ready for another round. "I didn't mean to," she says to Batty.

7.

WHY IS CASSIE HERE AGAIN? ALL OF THE BRAVE RESOLVE she'd felt that morning, hurrying down the dark sidewalk, is breaking up now like a stale cracker. "Batty, why are we here?" she asks, crouched on the pullout, away from Gertrude.

The sound of a door closing far off in the house tells Cassie her mother is gone from the kitchen. She brushes her hair, careful to leave the snarl untouched (they have a kind of agreement), tucks Batty into the waistband of her shorts, and creeps out. Something salty is bubbling in a slow cooker, and both of the office doors are closed. *My mother is making dinner and working,* Cassie communicates to Batty, and everything seems a little better.

Out in the courtyard, the sky is just beginning to turn cantaloupe, and the clouds are stretching in long, linty formations—a scene so pretty that Cassie's heart swells. The peacock is gone, but the chickens still *bock-bock* around their little house. Bill is there, with one arm in the coop's trapdoor, removing two fragile beige orbs. "Howdy!" he calls, on the other side of the low wire fence. "You ready to be put to work?"

She follows him under a tarp that leads to a sort of barn, if barns could be low-ceilinged and this stupefyingly hot, a dark animal quarters of breath and stench. It takes a second for her eyes to adjust. When she can see again, Bill is several feet in front of her, running a hose into a trough behind a wide, oblong corral. He points to a bucket on the dirt floor. "You ever fed goats before?"

"I don't think so," Cassie says.

"It's most fun by hand, I think."

Behind the wooden fence, the goats are piled in a white, hairy pack up against the wall, looking captured and hopeless. "Don't be afraid; they want potato peels, not fingers," Bill says. When he clicks his tongue, the layered bodies shake free of their collective—there are four—and when Cassie reaches in for the first zucchini stump, they surge toward her, weaving their heads in her direction, lobotomized. They sniff and lick—lap up the garbage from her palm, tickling her, the biggest one butting the smaller ones out of the way, so that, to feed them equally, Cassie has to keep shifting her angle and position.

"No! Not you again!" she scolds the big one. "Give the others their turn!" Fairness matters, Cassie knows; if the world won't keep track of who deserves what, it's up to people to stay extra alert, to pay attention to all the excesses and lacks. When the bucket is empty, every cornhusk and carrot stem inhaled and digesting, the goats bleat and rise up on their hind legs, twist their tubular necks skyward, looking even more feverishly insane than before. The slits of their pupils appear blinded by confusion. They are all Aunt Lindas, Cassie sees, on her very worst days, when she's so muddled by strangeness that she doesn't even know where to look.

On her worst days, Aunt Linda sees no problem with locking Cassie in her bedroom. (It will be years—it will be adulthood, really, before Cassie fully comprehends the backward bizarreness of a lock on the *outside* of a bedroom.) More than once, her aunt bore silent witness to Cassie coming in after dark, her now too-small I ♥ NY T-shirt smelling of cigarettes and spring night—*Hi, Auntie*. And more than once, she trailed up the stairs after Cassie, asking questions about Daryl and a band of crooks; *I know where you've been; you've been with your uncle*—then turned the lock on the door and shouted something on loop about *safety*. This was after hours of Cassie listening to Cat Stank practice in Damien's garage on a milk crate that hurt her butt, the sound storm like a punishment she had to endure in order to get to the prize at the end: the car ride home, a hand on her knee, his eyes meeting hers, and the promise of more to come—*Well, see ya later*. On those nights, she entered the house floating on the understanding that, even if she wasn't his girlfriend, *she might be his girlfriend soon!*—and hardly cared about Aunt Linda's lock. Eventually she learned to pick it using a paperclip at just the right angle, like she'd read about in Nancy Drew. And when she reappeared downstairs to make herself a sandwich, as if nothing had happened, Aunt Linda, absorbed in one of her shows or some new confusion, merely said, "I thought I put you away up there"—but feebly, as if she couldn't really be sure and certainly didn't have the energy to trek upstairs all over again.

After the basement, though—when crickets screamed in the yard and the moon was way up high when Brandon dropped her off—she looked forward to the lock. Leaving his car, walking across the yard to a house that now looked different, she did not stumble. She didn't walk like someone whose body had been roughly borrowed and then returned. He hollered, *Hey, sleep tight*, as Cassie pictured her own entrapment with something approaching gladness. She wouldn't leave her room tomorrow, or the next day, or the next day, she thought. Her aunt was there, looking faithfully loony at the foot of the stairs, following Cassie up. In the morning, she brought her already-cold oatmeal, wrongly served on a plate.

For a minute, Cassie feels a pang of fondness for her old aunt. She hopes that today is a solidly senile day; it troubles her to think how Aunt Linda's brain might run wild with possibility, of snatchers and murderers and accidents or injuries, exhausting her last stores of sanity, if today happened to be (unlikely but not impossible) clear. When clear Aunt Linda worries, she rubs and rubs her hands until her knuckles chafe and leaves bright-red marks on the white bathroom towels.

With her forearm, Cassie can feel the plush lump of Batty beneath her shirt as she follows Bill back to the house. Her mother has made soup. A big, diarrhea-brown pot of it steams on the kitchen table, lentils and carrots and stuff, with scoops of chewy rice to go along, and more glasses of water. Bill unfolds his napkin eagerly as they sit. "And afterward, there's special cake. Macrobiotic, no sugar—you've never had anything like it. You'll be *astounded* by how clean food can taste."

Cassie taps the back of her spoon against the rice in dull percussion. The food is not what she wishes they were eating, but it isn't so terrible, either, to sit here with her mother and Bill, smelling the salty liquid, trying out something new. Bill has turned on the CD player with a remote control, and he bobs his head in time. She's been dimly afraid of music in the wake of Cat Stank (as if an angry wail of guitar could summon him out of thin air), so it's a relief to genuinely like this song. It jangles with a familiar, groovy optimism, and her shoulders move without her brain moving them. Just listening, dancing modestly in her seat, her happiness is like the smallest thimble-sized doll nested among other, more complicated dolls. She looks at her mother and smiles, hoping to catch her eye, but her mother is busy stirring and stirring a tub of cottage cheese.

"Who plays this song?" Cassie asks. "I think I know it." And she hums along, off-key but not too off.

Bill blows on a spoonful. "Well I should *hope* you do. That's Mr. Bob Marley."

They sit in silence for a minute as Mr. Bob Marley sings, *Is this love is this love is this love is this love that I'm feelin?*—and then a breath, and then again: *Is this love is this love is this love is this love that I'm feelin?* When the next verse begins, the melody goes up, then down, in a heart-sinking way, before he croons his modest wants all over again.

"He was murdered, you know," her mother says. Instead of eating her soup, she's spooning it up and tipping the liquid back into the bowl. Spooning it and tipping it.

"Mr. Bob Marley?" Cassie asks.

"By Dracs," her mother says. "Verifiable."

Cassie looks to Bill, who nods in sad agreement. He sighs. "Poor young Bob."

"Dracs?" Cassie asks. "What's Dracs?" She imagines a rare disease; a blood problem.

When Cassie looks to her mother, there is the smallest suggestion of a smile on her lips. She gestures toward Bill with her spoon.

Bill dabs his mouth with the cloth napkin. "Dracs—without getting too far afield here—well, originating in the Alpha Draconis star system you have a hierarchical caste species of what are known as Draco Reptilians—warriors at the top, followed by the royal Ciakars, and then all the way down the line to the Earth-seeded species—native Terrans, or Reptoids, more commonly called, who're responsible for everything from Easter Island, of course, to the Kennedy assassination, the rise in Saudi oil, and the first Macintosh systems . . . but back to our topic, Bob M. and roots reggae—well, Rastafarianism of course has its origins in Ethiopianism, and deified the emperor Selassie, better known as the first Sirian amphibious interdimensional time traveler from Sirius B, in control of entire hybrid Sirian-Vega-human populations—Bob being one—by Selassie's use of an olfactory code emitted through his sweat." Bill holds up his palms, which are not sweating but could be, before he continues.

"And of course once ACIO—excuse me, the Advanced Contact Intelligence Organization—realized Selassie's influence, all of Jamaica was under heavy surveillance beginning around, oh, the midsixties, for evidence of Blank Slate Technology or other clandestine agendas out of the Extraterrestrial Military Industrial Complex—I mean, we're talking covert human-rights abuses in the name of genetic testing, experiments in cognitive manipulation, technological theft, the spread of divisive religious dogma, the altering of human history by infliction of radiation-induced amnesia on the mass populace, and the physical interjection of fabricated events into files, databases, and memories. But did they find anything? Did they find *anything*?"

Cassie looks to her mother, who is looking at Bill. The knowing semismile is still fixed to her face. Her mother shakes her head *no*.

"Did they find anything?" he asks Cassie again.

"No," Cassie says.

"No!" Bill slaps the tabletop with both palms and everything jumps. "They found *nothing*! Because, of course, the Sirian-Vegans are more or less a benevolent race, as anyone familiar with the Assessment knows. But—and this is the complication—the ACIO is so obviously in cahoots with the CIA and the NSA—well, at that point the mad have taken over the madhouse, because the CIA is full-blown Reptilian, starting with the Eisenhower agreements, and even Tall Grays and Anunnaki are in there in the lower ranks—I saw a report once proving that the goddamned *janitors* at Langley are mostly Short Grays—anyhoo—anyway—it's still debatable if Bob was Vega or only working alongside them; some theorize he could've even been Tau Cetian—if you listen closely to certain lyrics, they're *mantras* almost, starseed language-tactics for subverting manipulation and promoting multidimensional consciousness—covert Tau Cetianesque strategies. Whatever he was, the Dracs and the feds agreed he was a threat. Offed—injected, infected, and covered up—just because, really, he spread messages of peace and optimism and interstellar brotherhood to so many people through the power of song."

Abruptly, Bill returns his attention to his soup. For a long moment, the music and their slurping are the only sounds in the room. Cassie feels she's supposed to say something—something to prove she has understood the gist of Bill's monologue—but his words feel like a junk drawer she must sort through blindfolded. She concentrates on the music—listens hard for some clue, some potential meaning—but all she hears is a plucky guitar interlude in the next song and the cheers of an audience when Bob's voice comes back in. Finally, she ventures, "Is Michael Jackson one, too?"

Bill laughs then, though Cassie hasn't meant to be funny. But her mother turns to her and says sharply, "One what?"

It is a kind of test. The blood is hot in Cassie's cheeks. "An—an alien?" she tries. This much she has gathered, but the word still feels risky—stupid and plain—in her mouth.

Bill clears his throat. When he looks at Cassie again, his eyes are small with disappointment, as if Cassie has said a very bad word. She's failed somewhere, she sees; her mother looks at Bill with a certain satisfaction. "An—extraterrestrial?" she tries again. "Like E.T.?"

"If she's only playing dumb she's very good," her mother says to Bill, as if Cassie isn't in the room at all. Then she looks to Cassie herself and says, to a blemish on Cassie's chin, "Are you only playing dumb?"

When Bill stands, his chair makes a desperate scrape. He stacks Cassie's bowl in his own, and her mother's bowl—nearly full still—on top of that. "Who wants cake?" he says. "Cake? Cake?" And then he's in the kitchen, clanking silverware out of sight. Even with Bill one room away, Cassie feels the vacancy of sudden abandonment.

She looks at the Mexican-type weave of the tablecloth and runs her dirty thumbnail against the intersecting rainbow threads. Her mother's stare, her mother's thoughts, bore into her, drill-like, like whoever it was Bill had talked about—the emperor who controlled people, impossibly, through his sweat. A thought occurs to Cassie: a question to magically break this spell. She'll ask her mother if she's ever been to New York City, back before Cassie was born; Aunt Linda said her mother had lived many different places, and many different lives, before Cassie was born. She prepares the question in her mouth. It will go, *Mom? Mom, have you ever?*

But when she looks up, all of her mother's attention is funneled into an empty space on her right. Her eyes pulse in that direction and she moves her head in quick little nods. A nod, a pause—and then a vigorous shaking, *No.* It seems she's listening to a message only she can hear.

Beneath the table, Cassie clutches Batty close against her stomach. Before Aunt Linda's descent, before the kids turned mean at school, before Brandon and his friends and a new perceived dirtiness coating Cassie's interior, this silent dialogue between her mother and whatever invisible or imagined presence would've terrified Cassie. She would've screamed, or whimpered into her T-shirt, or run into the kitchen for Bill's protection. But Cassie now, so recently pushed into the strange mud of life, now-Cassie only grips Batty tighter and watches her mother with detached curiosity. Whisper, whisper, and Cassie watches: another display of the kaleidoscopic mystery of human beings.

8.

MORE DIRE THAN HUNGER, MORE INSISTENT THAN THIRST, is the need to pee.

It is down to doing it in a jar. "I can't hold it anymore," Judy says, picking up a juice can sided with popsicle sticks and dumping its pens and pencils and latch-key creations across the desk. She takes the can into the closet where the door sticks on the runner, pulls down her shorts, and squats. In the long, graceless seconds it takes her nervous stream to begin, the fear that Meghan might turn on her and fling something—a cruel word or a physical object—only makes her body work slower. Meghan doesn't, though. Still human, her need is the same. She waits with her eyes down until Judy finishes, zipping up boyishly, and then Meghan takes a peach-scented candle, its wax burned down to the quick, and enters the same makeshift powder room in their fast-forming civilization of two.

When their brimming receptacles sit safely on a closet shelf, Meghan closes the door to contain the smell. Outside, the sky is the color of a fresh bruise behind the mountain, obscured by the rectangular signs. When they switch on the overhead light, they know the signs will go totally black—but relieved of their bladders and with the night descending, something almost like comfort befalls them.

On the desk, Judy spots a gleam among the contents of her repurposed toilet. Under pencil shavings and gum wrappers is a key: thin and tiny and cheap.

Meghan, following Judy's stare, lunges for it. "The diary!" she screams. She flings the desk drawer open and fishes out the book. When the key fits and the lock yields, Meghan *oooohs* evilly.

Judy tries, "Wait, don't"—meek protests, silenced before they're formed by the power of Meghan's excitement.

Pages and pages flip by: handwriting adolescent-bubbly, overflowing its lines, purple gel pen and graphite, pressed hard enough to leave textured indents. "Holy *moly*!" Meghan exclaims, climbing onto the bed. "This girl is . . . what's a word for it, Judy? Someone who has, like, a lot to say?"

"Loquacious?" Judy says. It was a vocab word last year.

"*Low-quay-she-ous!*" Meghan straightens her posture, clears her throat, and rests an oratory hand on her clavicle. In a whiny falsetto, she begins. "*Dear Diary, Ms. Murphy is my favorite teacher of all time, as you know. But yesterday she didn't even notice when Amethyst*—like the crystal?"

Judy perches beside Meghan, her back against the wall and her knees tented. She looks over at the word. "Yeah. The purple one."

"*Didn't even notice when Amethyst kept faking like she would light my hair with the bunson burner. If no one had been there she probably would have, too. She probably has dreams about my whole head catching on fire.*" Meghan raises her eyebrows. "Whoa, freak!" she says, turning the page. "Amethyst again, and someone named Amber. *They prank-called the house again last night. Aunt Linda answered in her room, but I got on the kitchen line. Amber pretended to be the school nurse and said that I had AIDS. When I told them to shut up, to stop calling and confusing my aunt, they just barked and barked like dogs.*" Meghan has the book shielded enough that Judy can read only the occasional word, but not the jumbled sentences they form. She glances at underlines, all caps, scribbled-out curses, and quadruple exclamation marks. There is a not-great drawing of a dog's face in the margin. Teardrops fall from its big, egg-shaped eyes.

"Amethyst *again*, and Amber, Ms. Murphy, Amber, someone from the public library named Denise . . . a *librarian*? Chick, chick, chick." Meghan notes. "Cassie's a total lesbo."

"Go to the end. What's the most recent one?" Judy leans toward the book, but Meghan rotates away. "Hold up, wow"—on to juicier entries many pages back, describing a boy who works someplace called Gus's Grocery. "*He is sooo cute, his hair is like Jared Leto's. He has a tattoo of hieroglyphics on his arm and almost a mustache. He's eighteen but he doesn't go to the high school, he's taking the GED and waiting for his band to get famous. I think I'm in love with him. I think about marrying him about 100 times a day.*" The name *BRANDON* is written large at the bottom, floating on clouds, surrounded by hearts, filigree, explosion signs.

"*Gus's Grocery?* Or you could lay off the Lay's, Cassie," Meghan says, and turns several pages ahead, her eyes hungry. "Here's a good one. *I just like being next to him, it doesn't even matter what he's saying or what we're doing. Today he asked me why I didn't wear a bra yet since I have a chest (!) which I guess I haven't really noticed? They still look like mosquito bites to me.*" Meghan sighs heavily. "Jesus *Christ*," she says. "She knows *nothing*, huh?"

Against Judy's pleas to see the diary herself, Meghan reads on silently, rubbing it in, reciting only choice passages. "*Brandon brought me to band practice at his friend's house by the airport. Brandon is the drummer, he is really good, but he gets mad and cusses whenever they mess up, even though Cat Stank only has four songs. I don't care. His face is so cute when he plays. There were some high school girls there (A & A types), and one of them asked who his little sister was, but Brandon just ignored it.*" ("Amber and Amethyst," Judy decodes.) "*On a scale of 1–10 I think he likes me about a 4.*"

Annoyed, caring but not wanting to care, Judy gets up to make a nest for herself, of an afghan, a pillow, and a number of Cassie's discarded garments beneath the window. It is story time. Meghan's tone fluctuates and mocks. The entries stray away from Brandon, then return to him again. She comes to a page titled *Qs for MOM* followed by a numbered list of questions like *Do you bite your fingernails too? Does your hair get tangly? When I was inside you did I kick a lot? When you were twelve did you wear a bra yet?* (Meghan: "What, is her mom, like, in prison?")

Cassie complains about Aunt Linda—*She forgets to take showers and never takes out the trash and she doesn't even really grocery shop anymore. I have to get money out of her jewelry box and buy us things at Gus's*—and wonders why she can't *go back to be being NORMAL again!* In another entry, Brandon's breath smells bad, but Cassie decides to *work around it.* In another, she laments how she's called and called and called her mother but her mother hasn't called back. And Brandon hasn't yet kissed her; he'll only squeeze her thigh or tease-grab her stomach: *Maybe I should just give him up? Diary, please tell me what to do!* The librarian has special-ordered a new Roald Dahl boxed set Cassie can't wait to check out (Meghan: *Oh, wow, better bring those books to band practice!*). She imagines living in New York City someday, which she describes as full of *so many people! So many sounds! I miss riding on the subway and the old, tall buildings. When we were there, it snowed. In San Luis, it never snows*, and Judy can picture something of this sensory magic, cinematic, a place of seasons and history and elegance, everything the exact opposite of Van Nuys. (How wonderful it would be if a *place* was capable of changing your life: a feeling she experienced those first days in Rick's house. A feeling she doesn't want to give up on.) Also, Cassie confesses, someday she wants to be an author of books. New York—more than anywhere else Cassie knows of—seems like the place to be that.

"Let me see it," Judy begs. "Look at the last entry. Maybe it will say where she is."

Meghan flips, scans, frowns. *"I'm not sure how long to pack for. It could be one night or it could be the rest of my life, if my mother asks me to stay! I've never been to the desert, but Bill says it can get chilly at night."*

A trip, her mother, the desert. Judy is puzzling the story together. "What date is that? So maybe she's there?"

But Meghan is uninterested in this revelation. "She doesn't even mention Thick N Thin." Still stuck in the chat room. "Or me. It's so *weird*."

Through the floor, Judy can hear the vibrato laughter of the television, low now, and the sound of air moving through vents. "Those girls she's talking about? Amber and Amethyst? I wonder if they were, like, pretending to be her. I mean online."

Meghan is silent for a minute. "What do you mean, pretending?"

Judy sighs and rolls onto her side. "I mean, maybe it was *them* typing in Thick N Thin. Like, from their own computer. Like, totally making up Cassie_freakme." From this vantage, all Judy can see of Meghan is her pale, blank face, working its way through the word problem of this theory. "Get it? And they gave us the real Cassie's address just to prank her?"

Meghan's mouth twists. "Wait." Her eyes move, disturbed, to the door. "Wait. You're saying that this, like . . . you're saying that it wasn't even . . . that we're in some total *stranger's* room?" Anorexia, Judy thinks, must be rotting her brain, dissolving its cells. "You're saying this room . . . all the stuff in this room . . . it isn't . . . it's not . . . who we were chatting with?"

Judy looks at her knee, where an ingrown hair has made a small pimple. She squeezes, but the spot only gets redder. "Ding, ding, ding," she says quietly. "Now can I see it? The diary?"

But Meghan is within her puzzled self now, looking down at the book like it's changing colors in her hands. She flips the pages with a different sort of interest, though Judy can tell she's not sure, anymore, what she's reading for. "July twenty-eighth," she begins. "*Dear Diary, Something bad happened. Something really bad. It was three days ago but I'm only just now writing.*"

She looks to Judy. Judy sits up. "Keep going," she says.

Meghan's expression is quizzical verging on scared. "*I went to a party,*" she begins. "*Like a real high school party, with B and some other boys whose names I don't even want to write down that's how much I hate them now.*"

She looks at Judy again, and Judy motions with her hand: *Keep going.*

The original Cassie-whine is gone from Meghan's voice. "*It was full of people I didn't know (obviously), smoking and drinking stuff around the fire and they got me to do it too. It tasted horrible and made me feel dizzy. I will never even sip alcohol ever again as long as I'm alive.*"

As Meghan reads on, Judy can see the backyard full of high schoolers, smoking cigarettes and laughing. Dust clouds and smoke clouds against the California sunset. She can see the naïve little face of Cassie from the New York photo, at sternum height beside the older boys, orange flames painting her cheeks, her hands on a red cup and one of them tipping it, laughing. "*They said let's go downstairs to the basement and I don't know why, but I went. They said they wanted to show me something. But I should have left and walked home.*" She can see the way the boys steer her along the hall, herding her, their big hands on her small shoulders, boisterous with the thought of what they have, what they've caught, what they'll do. She sees them weave down a staircase, then move through a doorway, drunk, bumping the sides of the frame, a laundry room. She can see Cassie looking to Brandon for reassurance or love.

His denim jacket with the sleeves cut off. His unwashed hair and waxy skin. Closing the door behind them. The smile he gives Cassie, crooked toothed, when she turns around and asks what's down here. What they're doing down here.

"*When it was just me and them alone I knew it wasn't good. I couldn't see because they turned the light off but I knew it was Brandon holding me down. When the other boys started to do stuff he just let them. I couldn't breathe.*" Judy can feel Cassie's body in her own: a hand smothering her face, the tightening of every nerve, your own self, smaller and more injurable than you'd ever known you could be, and no help, no help, no help from anyone. The runaway momentum of fear and pain and the unfortunate resolution—the only way—to simply bear it. "*I couldn't tell what was Brandon and what was D and T. They were laughing at first but then they weren't. If I screamed they were going to kill me.*" The telling begins to dissipate; to spangle into vagueness. "*It kept going. It hurt so bad, I didn't know what.*" And Judy senses the effort here: to make sense of something by shoving it into words, except the words can't hold much; they rip and tear like cheap plastic bags.

"*I knew this was a thing that happened but I didn't know it was like this. I didn't know your friends could be there and do it too.*"

Meghan's voice is compulsive and whispery. Picking up speed, becoming dramatic in a way that makes Judy nervous. But what *is* the right voice, for what she is reading? Can there be a right voice for this sort of story?

"*He said he knew I wanted it otherwise why was I stalking him at Gus's? I never stalked him. I only liked him.*"

Cassie's words in Meghan's voice, Meghan's voice in Judy's prickling skin.

"*His breath smelled like beef jerky. Why did they do this to me?*"

Judy feels like a spy or a thief, queasy with complicity. As if Cassie, wherever she is, can hear and see everything, every detail of their terrible discovery, through time and space and the walls of the old house. *Why did they do this to me?*

Meghan inhales through her nose and lets it out long. She's scanning the last pages over, as if to double-check she's read it all right, grimacing. When she looks up at Judy, her voice is hard again, skeptical and cruel. "Beef jerky. Beef *jerky*? What is she *talking* about?" A dramatic pause. "Can you *believe* this?"

Judy is aware of her arms around her knees. Her closeness to herself, her shell-like posture. Quietly—she doesn't mean to be so quiet, but that's how her voice comes out—she asks, "Did they, like, *rape* her?" Her mouth is dry, cottony and thick, a sick-tasting, slept-in lemonyness. Whatever sperm tastes like—whatever aftertaste it leaves behind—Judy guesses it's akin, somehow, to the bitterness she's experiencing now.

But Meghan puffs her cheeks and exhales. "Riddle me this, Judy. If you got *raped*, would you put *freakme* in your screen name?"

Judy stares at the nightstand, where issues of *Highlights* are piled, because she can't bear to look Meghan's meanness in the eye. "But she didn't make up the name, remember? If Amber and Am—"

"If you got *raped*, Judy, would you write about it in your diary for every-one to read? Wouldn't you be so *traumatized* you couldn't even *write*? And last time I checked, it isn't *rape* if you dream about *marrying* the guy."

Judy doesn't like this. She fears they're entering an argument she doesn't have the dexterity to win right now. But she says it anyway. "Checked *what*, exactly, Meghan?"

"Checked, like, *the way the world works*." She coughs in the back of her throat, gathering a loogie so robust it's difficult to talk around. "Cassie-*whatever*. More like Cassie-a-loser-who-wants-attention-because-she's-freakin-*fugly*," Meghan garbles. Then she does what Judy knows she'll do—spits the wad of mucus right onto the page, snaps the heartbroken book shut, and flings it across the room.

Judy hears herself say, without any obvious feeling, "That was unneces-sary," but Meghan only rolls her eyes. She falls back against the bed, thrashes without screaming in a minor, silent tantrum, and again the room is still.

Meghan's callousness is so average, so totally not surprising, that Judy dully wonders how this person ever came to be her best friend. Why she gave up Melissa's genuine niceness for *this*. Regret, then self-pity, settles on her like those X-ray blankets they lay over you at the dentist's. She is trapped by the feeling and by Meghan's cruelty, trapped by Cassie's story, just as Brandon had trapped Cassie, just as the crazy aunt has trapped the girls. *Between a rock and a hard place.* A phrase Rick is fond of. Between a present and a past and a future—and Judy shudders.

Each time Judy recalls the episode, she feels she is still experiencing it, caught in the middle of a looping action/inaction even now, two hundred miles and two months removed. It's as if that moment from June is happening and always happening, somewhere, and all Judy has to do is open another door to see it.

Rick had opened the door to the downstairs bathroom without her realizing. Her mother was on the early shift that week, and Rick had been out somewhere, at the gym or the bar or the driving school, who knew. The air in the house was peaceful with the adults' absence, and Judy took her time in the shower, shaving, moisturizing, turning this way and that in the wide sink mirror as steam framed the edges of the glass. The slope of her stomach, the pudge on her hips. She poked at the sides of her small, gathering breasts. They were mostly all nipple, but when she pinched them they became rounder, less tulip-shaped. Judy was frowning at her reflection, waiting for it to change, when someone in the doorway said, "Don't worry. They're coming along."

There was enough steam left in the air that it could have been a mistake. A room walked into by accident. A sound bite meant to apply to something else. But she saw the dark gap of his mouth in the mirror first, relaxed and open, and then his eyes. His gaze moved lazily around Judy's body, everywhere at once, an airborne grope she couldn't manage to obstruct. It was like free-falling off a building, like trying to run with feet glued in the sand. She turned then; what else could she do? Time had stopped, and so Judy turned. The impulse to cover herself with her towel warred with that to shut the door. The door was closer. Judy lunged forward and pushed.

He's drunk, he's drunk, he's just drunk, her logic stuttered, turning the lock. How long had he been watching her, before Judy had seen?

She hurried into her two-piece, her shorts and tank top, and rushed out of the bathroom, acutely aware, in a different way now, that her mother was not home. That Judy was shaking around in a dream, with no one else but Rick.

Once, not long ago, he'd stood staring into the fridge in just his boxers, and Judy had glimpsed through the flap in the shorts (accidentally!) his frizzled, fleshy groin, a rodent in hiding. "I'm out now," she hollered, but her voice didn't sound like her own. It trembled and was six years old. He had made an honest, drunk mistake; there was no other way. A cupboard banged shut in the kitchen. The arctic sound of the freezer opening.

"You and that cute friend of yours—what's her name?" Rick's voice snaked down the hall. "What are you two up to today? Swimsuit competition?" She heard the twist of the ice tray, cubes dislodged, dropping into a glass, and the faucet turning on. Everything felt extra loud; time stretched out and froze. She stood in the hall, her heart a living thing.

She had to cross the kitchen to get to the front door. Moving in that direction, fixed to the goal of the knob, but Rick stepped forward. He grabbed her arm and gripped it.

His voice was a gravelly whisper, as if they shared some secret. "You're gonna be trouble for me," he said. "You know that? You better watch it now. You know what you're doing." She smelled nothing on his breath but stale coffee.

You, you, you. Incantatory. But what had Judy done? It was an accusation so insane that she actually laughed, just to kill the words. She yanked her arm away. Laughing—laughing weirdly, some other girl's laugh, she flung open the door and sprinted out into the freedom of the day. The thing in her chest wailed; her face was so full of hot, impossible blood she thought it might leak out her eyes. All seven blocks to Meghan's, Judy ran, thinking, *I'll live with Meghan, I'll live with Meghan, I'll move in with Meghan.*

And yet when Judy reached the Sandpiper and burst into apartment 4, she found Meghan mid–phone call with one of her admirers from day camp, saying, *You wish,* and making a gun gesture at her temple. By the time she hung up, twenty minutes had passed, and Judy had lost herself in the vexing thought that it wasn't impossible that Rick might, actually, be right. Maybe Judy *had* done something, or was always doing something, unintentionally, to flaunt and tease. In general she followed Meghan's lead and practiced revealing her best angles, laughing at just the right pitch, flirting openly with boys in line at Taco Bell or clustered in posses by the bleachers—but where Meghan excelled effortlessly, Judy fumbled, said the wrong thing or the right thing too quietly, so that these boys were always leaning forward with narrowed eyes, looking at her like she was half-retarded or spoke no English, and asked Meghan, *Whud she say?* She was more comfortable attempting hotness in all the silent, nonverbal, distant ways (certain techniques with eye-shimmer, certain ways of affecting disinterest above all things, and supremely deliberate postures while leaning, standing, walking, sitting—every nanosecond of girlhood, Judy was beginning to realize, could be choreographed for maximum effect, if only Judy could remember to remember). And yet, while none of these tactics were meant to attract a person like *Rick*, Judy couldn't help but worry that some of her skills were maybe better than she knew—that she'd practiced allure too artfully in Rick's watchful presence. Or maybe Judy exuded more sexiness than she realized, of a brand different from Alicia Silverstone's or Liv Tyler's—girls with whole words in their names. Maybe—Judy's brain burrowed deeper—there was some *other* kind of appeal she'd never quite seen articulated, in movies or magazines, but which nonetheless existed, and which she'd somehow channeled unknowingly or had even *been born with*. The theory both excited and terrified her.

When Meghan finally hung up the receiver and asked, *God, what's wrong with you?* Judy swallowed as if on trial. *Rick is gross, I think. He*—but she couldn't say it. Instead, she told Meghan she'd found a stash of dirty videotapes in her mother and Rick's closet. She had, the week before, but it wasn't the truth she'd meant to confess. Meghan had rolled her eyes and said she wasn't surprised. *I am a coward*, Judy thought.

That night, Judy watched her mother at the sink, her hands soapy in the dishwater, her new wedding band resting on the counter and her yellow hair fried and withering against her shoulders. Bonnie hummed a Fleetwood Mac song she'd been humming all Judy's life. She had a good voice; every time she sang anything, Judy was reminded of this oddity, how tuneful and lovely a voice could be, issuing from an otherwise defective person. When her mother turned around and dried her hands, replacing the ring, she was smiling.

Happiness made Bonnie beautiful. To tell would be to spoil all this—all her mother had longed for, a house and a husband and *love*—and it would be, also, to risk not being believed.

Disbelieved and sided against, Bonnie and Rick a unit against Judy. Disbelieved and then sided against and then, maybe, hated, abandoned, as a ruiner of at-last happiness. Judy said nothing.

9.

YOU JUST MAKE YOURSELF COMFORTABLE, BILL SUGGESTED, gesturing toward the couch, when the cake was eaten, when the plates were cleared, when the CD started skipping and had to be switched for something fluty and ancient. Cassie makes a game of it—there are enough throw pillows and cushions to prop together a little fort, a close hideout for her and Batty while the grown-ups sit at the table and do something Cassie thinks she probably shouldn't be seeing—pass between them a cigarette she knows is really drugs. The grassy, mildewed smell stirs up a confusion of memories—the inside of Brandon's car but also her own comfortable neighborhood, invisible odors drifting out of windows, around corners, across the park, familiar as roses and bay trees.

In pretending to sleep Cassie falls, actually, asleep. When she opens her eyes, she has no idea how much time has passed. The cushion blocking her face has fallen down, and the pillow covering her head is gone. The windows and the walls are black. A lion's mane, a human body, crouches before her, silhouetted by a light left on somewhere else.

Bill—it's only Bill, whoever he is. In his hand is something mango-sized, which he waggles toward Cassie's face. Batty's stuffed wings flap absurdly in a way Batty finds insulting. "Hello there, Miss Cassie." His voice is uncomfortably goofy, ambiguously accented. "Miss Cassie, are you asleep?"

Cassie says nothing. She stares, blinking, knowing the power of silence. Then she snatches Batty back and snuggles her face, not gently, in his fur.

"Cassie, is it time for bed?"

Not wanting to agree with anything, she shakes her head.

"Look," Bill says after a minute, grown-up to grown-up. "Sarah—your mother—I hope she's not too much of a"—he clears his throat—"surprise to you. She hasn't been much of a mother, I know that. I knew that from the beginning, when we met, and she told me how she'd just . . . handed you over. Like it was nothing. Like she was giving that woman a loaf of bread."

Cassie doesn't like this. "My aunt," she says. Her voice is weak. "Aunt Linda."

"Yes. Your aunt. Your mother is a good woman. You have to trust me on this. And she loves you. You might not understand this exactly, but she does love you. She's only—she's afraid of you, if you can believe it."

Each time Bill says *love*, a knuckle in Cassie's heart cracks. She wants so badly to know it—she is certain she had loved Brandon, before, but love's fickle capacity to spoil and rot, to become fear and disgust and even hate, is a lesson she never anticipated. Her want, now, is tempered by love's broken contract. And yet.

"She *loves* me?" she asks. "My mother told you that?"

"I trust that you have no secrets. Is that correct?" Bill asks. "Cassie? Truthfully?"

Cassie swallows, but there is no spit in her mouth. Does Bill know? How can Bill know? "I don't have any secrets," she says, offended, annoyed, guilty. Her secret is nothing Bill will understand, and nothing her mother will, either. The fact hits Cassie like a wall run up against: her real reason for coming here, a reason buried inside other, easier reasons. For her mother to ask, and for Cassie to tell, and for her mother to say, *You didn't do anything wrong.*

Bill groans as he stands. "Why don't you go up and have a talk with her? She's on the viewing platform. You'll need something warm."

From the hall closet he pulls out a red wool coat. He helps her bend her arms into it, and the jacket settles heavily around her shoulders, a sort of itchy armor. She has to roll the sleeves until they're four cuffs thick to free her tiny-feeling hands.

The courtyard is rigged with motion-detecting lights, but beyond the front gate the landscape is dark beneath the swirling, fanatical sky. Past the parked Jeep, the trail Bill leads her down is really a kind of ditch, an empty runnel that rushes with water during rainstorms, Bill explains, but otherwise stays bone-dry. "It's an all-or-nothing place out here. I do hope you can come back sometime for a storm." His voice moves with a gentle cadence. "When it rains—boy oh boy! It's a deluge, a flood, a totally wild thing. Buckets and rivers falling on the roof. The animals go insane. It's like the entire desert could become an ocean at any minute, and you'd just be stranded and floating in the middle of it. But also, there's an incredible *warmth* to just sitting inside with the lights on. Have you ever been on a boat? Out in the middle of the ocean? The way there's just nothing but water in all directions, but somehow you feel safe? Of course you haven't! You're young, you're young still. You will someday, though. Someday, Cassie, you'll be out in the middle of something huge and you'll know exactly the feeling I'm describing."

Cassie has her eyes down on the blue sand, careful not to step on a cactus or a coiled snake, listening to the rhythm of Bill's voice, when they stop. "You're on your own now," he says, pointing ahead to a sort of deck, attached to no structure and raised up on posts. Up there is the dark shape of her mother, and beside her mother an empty chair.

Bill pats her on the shoulder and turns back without a word. When Cassie climbs the ladder, she's sweating inside the coat but her legs, still in shorts, prickle in the cold. The open chair is still warm from Bill, a blanket abandoned in its seat. Cassie sits, wraps this around her, and unsnaps the coat enough to let Batty breathe. This close to her mother's silence, her mother's barely-breathing breath, Cassie's pulse bangs in her ears.

No welcome, no objection, though it seems her mother's been expecting her. She's looking dead ahead at the horizon through black, oversized binoculars. A menacing-looking tool.

"See anything interesting?" Cassie asks. Her voice has hardly any volume at all.

"Not yet," her mother says. "It's early still."

Cassie clears her throat. "But what can you see in the dark?"

Her mother lowers the binoculars and looks at Cassie as if Cassie is very dense. Her face is pale beneath her curly hair, her eyes beady in the moonlight. "Would you confirm under oath who you are? You have no visible implants, but to lie now would be to break interstellar law."

It feels like a joke, but her mother isn't laughing. Stellar means *super . . .*

law means police . . . *implants* means . . . something under the skin? Cassie's stomach cramps. She needs to pass gas, but she holds it in. Her tangle is there, protective as ever, and when she moves her hand to her neck, the skin is hot but smooth.

Her mother clears her throat fakely. "I'll ask you once more. What do you purport to be?"

"What do I—" Cassie stammers. "I don't know what *purport* is. Is it like *purpose*?"

Her mother, leaning forward in her chair, is silent for a long moment, waiting. When she smiles, Cassie realizes she hasn't seen this yet. Her mother's smile. It's lopsided; the plump bottom lip pulls lower on one side than the other, and the top stretches too taut and thin. Froggy and badly designed. Just like Cassie's own.

"You're just an ordinary little girl," she says. Not meanly. Gently, factually. "Aren't you."

It isn't a question, but Cassie says, "I guess so."

"An ordinary girl, wanting things, like all girls do. From me. From Bill. From everyone." She sighs, leaning back, and hands the binoculars to Cassie then. They are just as heavy as they look. "Lights," she says. Her voice is tired. "You're looking for lights."

Through the lenses, Cassie sees the landscape change from charcoals and slate to an eerie spectrum of greens. The darkness takes on shades of hot, toxic-looking neon; bushes glow, rock clumps have outlines now, and distant mountains appear etched in light, as in the shiny brown negative strips that come with photographs from Longs. In the green desert, something trots low, moving its snout along the ground. A dog, she thinks at first, but its tail is too full, too dragging and wild.

It raises its head and howls. It is a cry of sheer mourning.

"Coyote," her mother says. Two syllables, without the long E on the end, as Cassie has never heard it.

"Cai-ote," Cassie repeats. The animal slinks off. Cassie lowers the goggles and hands them back. "Bill told me to come out here," she begins.

After a silence, her mother says, "It was mostly his idea, you know. To let you visit. It's his nature to try to mend things."

"Is Bill my father?" Cassie asks, before she loses the courage. Does she want it to be true?

"How old are you again?"

Her mother—her own *mother*, asking her this question. "Twelve," Cassie says stonily. "Thirteen in February. February sixth," she says. "In case you forgot."

"February sixth strikes me as unlucky," her mother says. "You have to understand, my brain was like a washing machine on spin cycle for a good two years after it happened. All those memories are . . . cloudy." She raises the binoculars again, and for a moment her voice is almost normal, even trusting. "That's why it's been so hard, in part, to write my book."

Cassie fidgets, excited. "You're—you're writing a book? Really? I sort of thought you might be, or Bill, when I saw all those papers on the—"

"What papers?" her mother asks sharply.

"On the table in the dining room—"

"It's not on paper yet. But it's all in my head. I have to wait for the right time."

"Wow, a book!"

"I'll give you one, when it's done. I'll sign it for you," she says. Cassie wells with new hope. While no good with kindness or soup, her mother is, at least, a writer. And Cassie, all on her own, had guessed it.

"What's it—what's it going to be about?" she asks, thinking that soon, when the moment is right, she'll tell her mother that she, too, dreams of writing books. She'll tell her about the library, and Ms. Murphy, and perhaps when they return to the house, Cassie can show her mother the fairy-tale book, and maybe they'll sit in bed, even, and read together.

But at the question, her mother's face changes again, and once more, she appears annoyed, put-upon. "What it's *about* is my abduction."

Cassie swallows. "Your—your what?"

Sarah Waller says *abduction* again and again, a blur between *suction* and *adoption*. Her mother's is a body story, too, Cassie understands from the very beginning, told in this even, factual voice that betrays how many times it's been told before, to other people or to herself—a stone worn smooth by so much worrying. Deep in the pockets of Bill's coat, Cassie's fingers feel loose strings, grains of dirt.

Sarah Waller and her dog were driving across the country in a little pickup truck, from Bloomington, Indiana, to Northern California. *I was leaving behind a very bad person and I'd been driving straight for many hours. I had some friends on this farm where they grew apricots and pistachios. I was wrecked. I just kept thinking, get to the apricots, get to the apricots.* In Bloomington she'd lived not on a farm but at a *camp*, she called it, where everyone worked together and lived together and shared things. But then this man she was with went wacko and tried to—*but that's a different story for a different time.* Well, Sarah got very tired, so tired she couldn't keep her eyes open. She pulled off the highway in the mesalands of Wyoming, somewhere that was nowhere, and unfurled her bedroll in the back of the truck, the moon in the sky almost full. She was asleep when she felt the force in her chest. Heard a buzz like electricity through live wires, thought at first that she was dreaming. *It was just like a magnet— like how one magnet hovering above another magnet snaps the two together.* The dog heard it, too; his ears had sharpened into points. The ground dropped out beneath her. She felt herself lift. The dog barking. An empty night not unlike this one. Rising chest-forward toward a hovering shape, an enormous, blimp-like craft, so large as she approached that it blocked out half the sky, like a storm cloud made solid. Dreaming except not dreaming. She was twenty-four years old. Beneath her, her sleeping bag, the dog, her truck, shrank to dots.

The huge, dark ornament hung suspended, illuminated down its center seam as if secreting a vast incinerator. The beam pulled her into the glowing split, which parted wide as a boulevard. In the bordering quadrants rose hundreds of portholes, covered not by glass but by some living, translucent membrane, and inside, long faces watched (imagine a skyscraper, she says, a very tall apartment building, where every single inhabitant is called to the window by some spectacle outside) until Cassie's mother, paralyzed in body but fully awake, lost consciousness.

"They squeezed something in my eyes, some sort of cream that made everything blurry. I couldn't move; they'd tranquilized me from my forehead to my toes. The same pressure I'd felt against my chest glued me to the operating table. I was naked. I could see them cutting me open, I could feel the cold of the blade on my stomach, but I didn't feel any pain. You think you know terror, as a human on this earth, but you don't . . . let me tell you, you don't . . ."

It was like watching everything through a fogged-up window, she goes on. They were tall, with something powdery about their skin, hairless, stretched-flat noses and bulbous skulls, seed-shaped nostrils and black, reflective eyes, perfectly smooth, obsidian, like human pupils dilated to the point of inhumanity. The worst thing, her mother says, was the fingers: eight, ten inches long, knobbed, multijointed. One—the one in charge—used its bare, branchy fingers to open her up at the cut. Her insides steamed like torn bread. A living sac was placed inside her. An egg sac or embryo—she only saw the quivering translucence of it, held in two long-fingered hands, some organism or potential, no bigger than a grape. They sealed her closed with a kind of glowing wand. She saw her own flesh melt together again, painlessly. And two minutes or two days or two weeks later (she'd never know how the Tall Grays could bend and crumple time), Cassie's mother woke up with her cheek pressed into the sleeping bag, right back in the truck bed, a light rain beginning to fall. The car keys still in her pocket. It was just after five in the morning. The dog was gone; she never knew what happened to the dog. What all it knew or saw.

Sarah moves the binoculars and pulls back the blanket, lifts up her sweater and tugs down the waistband of her pants, just enough that Cassie can see the top of a scar. A white, puckered line, beginning at the navel and running down.

Eight and a half months later, the baby that came out was not gray skinned and bug-eyed but red, shriveled, ugly as a living prune. *I thought I might die when the labor came. That they might've—whatever they put in me—that it might be a sacrifice-the-host–type situation.* But Cassie, apparently, delivered easily, as if she knew what was expected of her. *On the farm, like all the women*—and she can't help but imagine the goats in the pen, her mother in the dirt. *I couldn't hold you. I couldn't even—one of the other mothers had to look after you until Linda came—if that hadn't been arranged, I don't know what I'd have done. Just dropped you, maybe, in the pond.*

Cassie's voice is so tiny. How can she ask it? "But—"

"You looked so—I thought, they've really got this down. Right down to the genetics. You looked like any other baby."

"But you thought I was an *alien*?"

"I thought, whatever she is, she isn't mine."

You thought I wasn't yours. But now that—but now that I'm here. "But now . . ."

A quizzical smile hooks Sarah Waller's lips. "Now?" She pauses long and sighs. "I suppose I have an ending for my book."

10.

THE SQUARE-EDGED NUMBERS ON THE BEDSIDE CLOCK SAY 9:58, then 10:01, then 10:06. Sunk in their private dazes, Meghan lies across the bed picking at her nail polish while Judy sits on the floor, drawing a checkerboard design down the sole of her Airwalks. These are her new, back-to-school shoes—a brand-name splurge she and her mother fought over for two long weeks until Bonnie relented and took her to Journeys, swiped Rick's brass-colored AmEx with a newfound authority that bewildered her. Now Judy regrets the choice, hates that she's wearing what is, in a roundabout way, a gift from *him*—and anyway, on her the sneakers look big and clunky, not the way they do in the advertisements, on models with bodies like Meghan's. She messes up the pattern: colors two black squares right on top of each other. Everything is ruined, anyway. She throws the shoe across the room, where it hits the dresser and falls.

One of their signs comes unstuck from the window; its lazy drift rouses Meghan, who watches with a purity of despair. Another follows, and then, insultingly, the third. With a growl she rises from the bed, picks up the third sign, rolls it into a tube, and shoots it through the splintered door hole. Then she drops to the carpet and screams, "We're starving! We have to pee again! You'll go to jail!" When she pushes her arm through, too, her impotent flailing is a sad sight: a captive reaching for whatever she can get.

As if reading Judy's pity, Meghan whips her head around and glares. Tears streak gray mascara down her cheeks, reminiscent of the ink-wash portraits they painted last year in art. "We have to *do* something!" she wails. "We can't just spend the *night* in here!"

Has Judy ever seen her friend like this, so indelicately unhinged? She goes over to Cassie's desk and finds a paper clip in the detritus, straightens it and pokes the knob, waiting for something to click. "Where would we go, anyway?" Judy asks, testing the handle again. She imagines them huddled in the park they passed, halogen shadows and rapey psychos, Brandons and Ricks in the bushes.

Meghan is picking splinters from the hole now, though it is endlessly laminated and the opening widens only one millimeter at a time, and on their side. "Anywhere," she says. "Maybe there's a twenty-four-hour McDonald's. Maybe there's another party we could find. There's a college here, right? There are probably parties."

It is the hope of a deranged person. "Are you—I don't know if that's such a good idea"—meaning both Meghan's picking and the party, after Cassie's diary entry. But Meghan continues, lifting the wood strips with her fingertips, animal-bent on her task, picking and then sucking on her own red fingers. "Meg? You're hurting yourself."

Meghan's face, when she looks at Judy again, is as pure and open as a wound. In a flash, Judy sees that, despite the philtrum, Meghan will never be a model. She will be pretty, of course, always, but she's too spiritually empty–looking, too pitifully unhappy in the middle of her eyes to ever have her image airbrushed and saturated in full-color print, projected enormously on celluloid. Judy feels helpless just to witness it: this clear vision of failure. How strange, to see more of someone else than they can see of themselves.

There's a sound in the hall—a creak on the stairs, and the gentle feeling of weight, just perceptibly moving the floor. Someone is approaching. The faint, universal smell of the unwashed coming near. Through the hole, Judy sees a trollish foot, cracked-calloused and multicolored, the sort of casualty of time that makes her fear getting old as much as anything else. The girls shrink back, clutching each other. Meghan's nails dig into Judy's skin. They're not thinking now—they're watching the handle, waiting for its slightest turn, for the door to creak open, the moment they will rush and topple—and run and run and run. But the knob stays frozen. The foot disappears. They can hear the aunt's breathing—she is kneeling, and as Meghan's grip tightens, so does Judy's on Meghan's arm—the same current of fear cycling between them. A hand enters the hole bearing a quivering half of sandwich. Tuna fish, white bread, crustless . . . the fingers bone white, dead looking. The girls gasp and hold it in. Goopy chunks of runoff fall to the carpet.

"*Ew, ew, ew, ew, ew, ew, ew,*" Meghan cannot stop chanting.

Judy cups her hands to yell, as if yelling might penetrate this insanity once and for all, "No thank you! No thanks! Can you let us out now please? *Please?!* We need to go home! *We have to go home now!*"

But the body rises silently again, a flash of bathrobe and the slow retreat. The reeking sandwich sits on the carpet like something dropped. An offering of horror. Boys in their grade equate tuna smell with vaginas, vaginas they haven't smelled yet. Judy sees their point but will never, in a million years, admit it.

Back on the bed Meghan curls up and cries, not even bothering to palm away the tears. "Aren't you even *upset* by this?" she wails. "You don't even seem upset." She clutches one of Cassie's stuffed animals, a giraffe with eyes as morose as her own, and releases loud sobs.

"Maybe we can make the phone work," Judy tries. "Like, if there's a plug somewhere else . . . we can call our moms. Or nine one one," because she's groping in the dark for any solution, any thought that might return Meghan to calm.

But Meghan unfurls herself, reaches for the phone, her face streaming and furious. "Are you *moronic*?! You think it's going to *magically*"—she picks up the whole thing, the dead receiver and the heavy rotary base, and heaves it to the floor, where it crashes and pings like a broken instrument. "Anyway, our moms would *kill us* if they knew where we were." Her crying stops abruptly. Theater tears, summoned and then abandoned. "Not like they would even answer. My mom's probably at the gym," she says, in the direction of the phone. But then Meghan turns toward Judy, daring her with her eyes. "And your mom's probably getting face-fucked by Rick."

The moment is a staring contest. Meghan's pupils are like thumbtacks or the heads of nails, pinning Judy to the challenge, waiting, Judy sees, for a flicker of disturbance. All Meghan's anger—over Cassie and the aunt and her own dumb, believing self—she's channeling toward Judy now, who, despite the picture forming in her brain, of Rick and her mother groin to mouth (perhaps the most terrible thing she's ever conjured with her own imagination), will not let Meghan win. Meghan has caused the picture, and now Judy will never forget it.

She tries to swallow, but there's no spit in her throat. "No she's not," is all she manages.

But Meghan is boiling. "No she's not *what*?" She sits up to kneeling, arching her chest grotesquely, and still her eyes are glued to Judy's. "No she's not *what*?!" She pushes. "God, you can't even say *fuck*! You're such a little baby. You're just like *Melissa. Say* it! Grow *up*! *Little baby Judy!*"

But Judy can boil, too. "*Fuck!*" she screams. "*Fuck!* Yes I can!"

Meghan runs the giraffe up her chest, up her neck and back down, caressing her torso. "He's like, *Ooh, ooh, yes*, that feels good, Judy. I mean Bonnie! I mean suck me, *Bonnie!*"

A devilish clown, she is grinning through the disaster of her face. Her cheeks are pink and splotchy, and the smeared makeup does something masklike, primal, to her bloodshot eyes. She's like the worst part of everything; Judy wants nothing more than to destroy her. They burn eye to eye, grin to fury, for one more second of mislaid hate before Judy rushes the bed.

She rips the giraffe out of Meghan's hand and whaps her across the face. Meghan wails—more from shock than hurt, shielding her head with her arms, falling over on her side. But Judy is on her, fast and full throttle, thwacking at her fetal crouch, wielding the giraffe by the legs and clubbing every available opening between Meghan's thrashes. Again and again she hits, hoping that the toy's plastic nose will do real damage. Annihilate something. Her teeth are gritted, doglike and wild. "Get off me! You're insane!" Meghan screams.

"You're totally evil!" Judy screams back, at a pitch she doesn't know. Meghan's French braid whips like the tail of a dying horse, and Judy opens her jaw to catch a segment. She yanks her head back in a savage tear and the hair gives; releases like blades of grass. Meghan screams murder. Her hands cover the injured spot. A not insubstantial clutch, strands glossy and perfect, hangs from Judy's teeth. She spits.

This sudden fury—it is a distant but related cousin of what she was left with that day with Rick, when Judy had not told, had not been *able* to tell, her best and truest friend what, exactly, had happened. Not her friend and not her mother. That night, Judy lay in bed and felt the pain of the kept secret morph into a second, scarier pain . . . a dread . . . a fear that mingled her future, once personal, with the bigger, uncharitable world . . . a fear she now must live with. That it would happen again, except worse. Her heart raced, waiting for Rick to knock. Waiting for Rick to come in, somehow, despite the lock. But the knock never came, his entrance was not forced, and in the days that followed, he hardly let his eyes land on hers—took even greater pains to avoid her, it seemed, than she took to avoid him. Just last week at Sizzler, while her mother was in the restroom, her heart raced to be alone with him in the sticky red booth. But he only asked her about the fraudulent class trip, then sipped his beer and told a boring story about some preseason scrimmage in Anaheim. Asked Judy why she didn't try out for volleyball herself next year—a question he'd asked, already, a dozen times before. *I don't care about sports*, she'd said, as coldly as possible. Statue-still, her legs twined and tensed beneath the table, concentrating on the pile of discarded shrimp tails on her plate. When he ran out of stuff to say, he hummed along to the oldies song, canned and tinny, on the speakers. Humming like that, while he sawed his steak, somehow made him harmless—the interaction was so normal Judy wondered if she'd imagined that day, or if enough time had passed that now she should just forget it.

Maybe she really *is* just as silly and babyish as Meghan says she is, for making *such a big deal*. Maybe it's Judy herself that Judy imagines hitting. What happened to her is nothing, after all, compared to what happened to Cassie.

Drained of rage and suddenly exhausted, her blows are merely rhythmic, her heart no longer in it. Her arms ache. Meghan is a whimpering huddle of hair and limbs, a sort of punching bag fallen off the chain. To any observer, entering the room just then, the attack would pass as a pillow fight—two girls playing games. Judy slumps off the bed and feels her pulse slow, her breath return. The only sound in the room is Meghan's juicy sniffles.

Judy goes over to the door and picks up the sandwich. She takes the biggest bite her mouth will allow. *Mmmm*, she goes, smiling, because there is nothing left to lose. The canned fish is cold and salty and delicious, and when she's done, she licks the oil off her fingers.

"You're insane," Meghan breathes, high-pitched, a victim of biblical proportion. "If you ever touch me again, I'll have my mom kill you."

Judy smiles. The threat is dust. She's immune to fear, to have raged like that.

She flips off the overhead light. The reading lamp still glows on the nightstand, but Meghan is too in-character to move. Cassie's diary is there on the floor by Judy's makeshift bed, the spat-in page still soggy; she wipes it facedown, as best she can, across the carpet. Then she folds her pillow in half, tucks herself into her self-made nest, and turns to the beginning to read.

Dear Diary, It is Thursday and Christmas in 1996. Aunt Linda bought you for me and I found you in my stocking with also a book of Lifesavers, a scrunchy, and some oranges. Aunt Linda was pretty good today. We had chicken chow main for dinner yum. Cassie's voice lands naturally in Judy's head; it is the earnest, clever, annoying, self-hating, unlucky voice Judy already knows . . . a friend of Judy's own self. *Moose had an accident in the hall and I almost stepped on it going to brush my teeth. Goodnight diary.* She reads in anticipation of the Brandon sections—she wants to see for herself, to see what Cassie has discovered that maybe Judy hasn't yet. *If this isn't love than what is it? Where is it? How do you know it?* Past the entries Meghan shared there is little mention of him, of the terrible event. The pages turn to anxieties over the coming school year, excitements for new library books, heartbreaking manifestos for random self-improvement (*Goals: 1. Be nicer to strangers. 2. To talk less! 3. Learn to fix broccoli and eat more broccoli*). The plan to visit her mother (*Finally!*) in an entry from last week, followed by a list of bus times and brainstorms for conversation starters. Something in Judy swells with hope. If Cassie isn't here, then she must be there. *I hope you're in Nevada, Cassie. I hope you're there right now, snug as a bug in a rug, reading with your mother.*

Meghan stirs loudly on the bed, forcing Judy to hear. She sits up and makes a traumatized expression. Her nose is dripping bright, thin blood. It is most definitely from the air-conditioning, Judy thinks. But still she feels a wave of guilt.

Meghan touches the blood, looks at her red finger, looks at Judy with the same sustained shock. "Look what—"

There's a box of Kleenex on the dresser, which Judy tosses, though gently, careful not to hit Meghan's shin (now that everything has changed, what parameters govern the gestures of ex-friends?). Meghan pulls out half a dozen tissues and twists these up one nostril until it bulges. The tourniquet will stay there, lodged and turning vermilion, all through their restless night and into the next morning, when they'll find the door incredibly cracked (as if it had never been locked at all) and tear from the room, pound down the stairs, past Aunt Linda in the kitchen as she watches, dumbly, the coffee drip. Out into the freedom of the sunshine, running, unspeaking but keeping pace, Judy's beading caddy springing open and its tiny, plastic baubles spilling and rolling all over the sidewalk so that she'll have no choice but to fling it, in the recklessness of her ecstasy, out into the street, where an oncoming SUV will smash it to a billion bits. They'll run all the way to the station, where the 8:20 Coastal Quest is already waiting on the track, so silver and perfect in its open-door patience, like a promise actually kept. They'll ride in seats at opposite ends of the same car, and when Judy passes her en route to the bathroom, Meghan will keep her profile mummy-fixed to the seatback in front of her. The bedraggled tissue will remain as if the nose still bled, as if the nose will go on bleeding forever. "Hello?" Judy will try, but Meghan won't answer. It is the last word that will ever pass between them.

Judy lies back down and stares up at a ceiling stain in the shape of a head. "I'm sorry," she says to the shape. She *does* mean the apology, though maybe not to Meghan.

Meghan sniffles. "Sometimes sorry doesn't cut it."

From the final entry: *When I see her, at least I'll know who she is. At least I'll know something instead of guessing forever and ever.*

Judy waits. A car hushes past outside. Across the street, the lights in the happy house are off. *Where are you, Cassie? Are you all right? Where are you, Cassie? Are you all right?*

The bedside lamp burns. Meghan's breathing is steady and far away. There is one page left to read, and then Judy will have only herself.

11.

ONE OF THE MORE REASSURING PARTS FROM BOB MARLEY—
Everything's gonna be all right. Everything's gonna be all right. Everything is gonna be all right—runs through Cassie's head like a counterpoint to the cumulative unknowns. In the hall bathroom, a pink-crystal night-light glows above the sink. Internally, some part of her seems to have loosened—she aches in her lower abdomen, a cramp that began around dinner and then doubled on the walk back to the house with her mother, during which nothing was said except *Good night.* A rotten stomachache. On the toilet, in the crotch of her underwear, she touches something brown and sticky, like blood contaminated, a snail's trail of mucus. Alien slime. *What do you purport to be?* Again her insides lurch, and a wormy rope plops out of her, into the water, where it sinks substantially.

What is worse—to discover she might be an alien, or to discover that her mother does not want her?

In a panic, trying not to breathe, she struggles to recall the lessons from the school nurse. The diagrams on the board and the girls, even Amber and Amethyst, hesitant and shy with their raised hands. They were given little kits with the necessary accessories. How feminine and teenaged Cassie had felt, uncapping the stick that night at home, applying the chalky Secret, but she forgot the technical things quickly and had not read the pamphlets.

She unspools half the roll of toilet paper, wraps it around her underwear, and tucks in the tail to make a sort of diaper, lumpy when she pulls up her shorts. Batty rides in the deep pocket of the wool coat now, where she reaches in to check—to feel his soft, nut-sized head. *Everything's gonna be all right,* Cassie whisper-sings toward the pocket. She laughs—once, a tiny tittering giggle—at how out-in-the-open she has become. *Egg sac,* she remembers, the phrase like a skin-wrapped sack itself. Can Cassie imagine her own beginning, condensed as a bath bead, a glimmering pulse of life? She tries; she squeezes her eyes shut and tries, but the feeling does not take. *You're just an ordinary girl.* But she doesn't think she's that, either.

The house is so dark. In the passages untouched by moonlight, she runs her hand along the cool wall that leads to the kitchen. On the counter, the keys of the cordless phone glow with green light. She removes the receiver from the cradle, then sneaks back down the hall, past Bill and Sarah's closed bedroom door; it's possible they're in there, pressed up and listening, watching her through spy holes. It's possible, Cassie thinks, that cameras, other night-vision devices, might be recording her—all the more reason to escape now, while she still can.

Cassie huddles on the sofa bed with the phone, staring at the numbers. Her fingers hurt where she's chewed the nails away. Someone—Bill—has covered the birdcage with a sheet. It looms there like a pale, raised cube, silent and still, but Cassie is keenly aware of the beating life inside. If she whisks the sheet away, what might be revealed? Again, something dangerous spills from her body. She's shivering, even in the coat. She'll have to steal Bill's coat. Stealing isn't right; everyone knows that, but suddenly *doing the right thing* doesn't seem all that important.

SOMEWHERE, a bell is ringing.

It jingles and leaps and pauses and then begins again. Linda crawls, pushes up, through the surface of mud and blindness to make it stop. It is the phone, on the end table, and she is there, in the living room, in her chair.

"Yes?"

"Aunt Linda?" A small, far-off voice.

"Yes?"

"Aunt Linda?"

"Cassie?"

"It's me. Are you there?"

Hazing in her periphery, somewhere in the recent past, is a vision of two girl strangers, sunlight blasting through the doorway. She'd taken them upstairs to see Cassie. But here is Cassie calling now. The vision precipitates into something surer: Cassie is not in the house. She is somewhere not at home, and it is late, in the middle of the night.

"Cassie?" she says again. Her own voice clicks into being as it doesn't always. "Honey, where are you?"

There's silence on the end of the line, and something in the static makes Linda sit up fast, push down the footrest. "Cassie? Where are you? Are you in trouble?"

"Are you clear right now, Aunt Linda?"

Is Linda clear? She looks around, at a picture moving on the muted television, and the big front window yellowy and grainy behind the blinds, the streetlight outside, Moose asleep and cat-curled in his chair, the milk-glass pitcher and basin in its stand that are only for decoration. She's been retired fifteen years now from the newspaper. She used to live in this house with Daryl, who put in the upstairs carpet and always kept the yard going, but now she lives here with Cassie, the yard is disgraceful, and Daryl's been dead a long time. Her mother is dead, too. Comatose, then lifeless, in a hospital in Pontiac. The big house in Detroit long ago went to seed, when they'd moved her mother out and couldn't find a buyer, probably razed by now in one of those awful fires. Her chest hurts for an instant. Facts so sadly familiar, and yet nothing will change before she dies, Linda thinks despondently—nothing will reverse. But Cassie, Linda's own precious Cassie, is here, now, on the phone.

"Yes, Cassie, I'm clear as day. Except my god—what time is it? Tell me where you are. I'm coming for you."

Something muffled comes through the receiver, and Linda knows that Cassie is crying. The sound destroys her. It is the sound of her own failure. "Cassie," she is saying, "Cassie, Cassie, tell me"—standing now, stepping into her slippers.

She speaks through tunnels of distance. "I'm in the desert," she whispers. "I'm safe, but I'm . . . I'm far away." There is a pause then, and when her voice returns it is stronger. "I was abducted," she says.

"*Abducted?*" Linda repeats. Insane, impossible. "Who on earth—" That boy, she thinks. The no-good teenager who comes around here with the music blaring, smogging up the block, looking ghoulish. His dirty hair reminds Linda too much of where Cassie is from—the conditions Linda rescued her from. She never knew which of those commune bums it was (Sarah refused to say), but it didn't exactly matter, they were all of the same stock, irreverent and dumb, stoned and selfish, unfit to be fathers. "Tell me exactly where you are. I'm coming for you now."

But Cassie says, "It's okay; I'm safe. They're going to let me go. They're driving me to the bus."

Linda is wondering about her car keys. *Where are the keys?* They're not in the pocket of her robe. She's wondering where the Volvo is when it occurs to her it's been gone for some time now—at least a year, maybe longer. That boy has a car, but Linda has no car. She is seventy-four years old. She stands there looking at her long, misshapen feet, waiting for another fact to come. Another thing she can be sure of.

"I'll be home tomorrow. I'll just go back the way I came. But Aunt Linda?" Cassie's voice is a whisper inside a whisper, and the pain—the Daryl pain— clenches her again. "Can you try to stay clear until I get home? There are a lot of things I want to tell you about."

What has become of those girls upstairs? She took them into Cassie's room, and then . . . when did her life become a dark, wild forest?

"Yes, I'll stay clear. I'll do my best. I'll make a big pot of coffee, Cassie, and I won't sleep until you're home."

"Okay," Cassie says. "I love you, Aunt Linda. Everything's going to be all right."

She is seventy-four. Linda knows this much. She is seventy-four, and she hasn't had the Volvo for at least a year now, but she has her Cassie.

QUIETLY, QUICKLY, Cassie packs her things. Her books make a hard, flat panel against her back. Batty is snug between her armpit in the coat and the front strap. The diaper is wetting and twisting, uncomfortable between her legs, but there are much bigger things to worry about. She unlatches the window and hoists a leg up onto the ledge. Gravity stalls her for a moment, but then she shifts, and the weight of her backpack pulls her over. She's down on the ground, free.

In the thick of the moony desert, the dirt road runs limestone-pale. Warm currents hover at her ankles. The brush smells freshly clean and dusty at the same time, tinged at the bottom with the spice of baked vegetation. Later she'll learn that this is sage, a thing girls will burn in bundles in the musty corners of their first apartments to clean out spirits and start fresh, but which will always bring Cassie back to this endless moment, the surreal walk, the distant memory of a little girl's will, suddenly brought forth, with a brightness almost impossible to believe. Yet it was her, it *is* her. The road splits, and Cassie turns left. *My fear is my only carriage*, she thinks the song goes. Another thing she'll learn when she grows up—*Oh, it's not fear, it's feet!* but it will be too late, the two words forever linked in her mind's heart.

She will tell Aunt Linda the story; she will tell her diary. She composes the story as she walks. It is a way to pass the time. *I walked and walked. I saw a long pink line where the sun was coming up.*

What feels like hours later, Cassie sees movement in the distance. Relief is so sweet she could cry. With her right hand, she clutches and releases Batty, clutches and releases—and with her left she feels the snarl. The desert ends at the highway. Lights—not of flying saucers, but the earthly, human, ground-skimming beacons of headlights—approach and then zoom past, in steady pairs.

II.

TRESPASSING

1996

Does the body rule the mind
or does the mind rule the body?

I don't know.

MORRISSEY,
"Still Ill"

1.

"YOU'RE COMING OVER, RIGHT?" CHRIS CHEN HAD A WAY OF asking Miles that spring. On the 1 California they rode arm against arm, prim and quiet as girls, their JanSports heavy in their laps. Behind them echoed the shouts and whines of their classmates, and farther back, the profanities of Hilltop Prep high schoolers, wide-legged boys whose duffels swung pendulously close to the faces of older, more monastic passengers. Kids too short to reach the overhead bars surfed the bus's accordion middle until their nannies snatched them back to sitting. At fourteen, Miles was too old, now, for a nanny, and Chris had never had one. They were allowed to ride to and from school alone because, as Miles vaguely understood it, his parents were liberal and trusting, and Chris's were immigrants and poor. Also, compared to their older siblings, the two seemed incorruptible.

That Chris still *asked* Miles found funny, since the two were by now undeniably linked and their hanging out had become, over the course of that year, a matter of after-school routine. Chris blinked twice: he was a blinker.

"Sure," Miles said. "Yeah," and turned away, his neck hot with awareness.

They passed apartment buildings and houses in yellow, gray, ivory, poop green; the faded signage of familiar businesses and glossy-leafed trees that grew streetward, toward the electric lines. By Arguello the bus had mostly emptied and refilled with sadder riders, the school day entering the slipstream of the world. A ragged, mud-flecked creature dragged behind him a netted bag of onions and did not pay the fare. An ancient woman in latex gloves ate a pastry from a Kleenex. It was one of those buns with bean filling, Miles saw, the kind that tricked him at the bakery when he expected chocolate.

At Eighth Avenue they got off and walked west. Both looked, as they always did, at the new concrete square where they'd scratched their names last month (looked without acknowledging), then swung north. Chris's family occupied both levels of a stucco duplex: upstairs, he lived with his mother and father and older sister, Kimber, a sophomore at George Washington, and his two little brothers, one with a cleft palate, in their identical *Space Jam* sweat sets. Downstairs lived Chris's grandmother and uncle and aunt and three girl cousins, whose Chinese names Miles never remembered and didn't seem to be expected to. At any given time, various familial arrangements could be found crammed on the couch in Chris's living room, watching cable and eating out of bright plastic bowls. Today it was the brothers and two of the cousins, slumped in front of *Power Rangers*. When Chris and Miles walked in, no eyes left the screen. Chris's mother had once said (in English, and so probably for Miles's benefit) that if a pack of thieves broke in and robbed the place, no one would even notice until they unplugged the TV.

From the kitchen came the radio, utensils clattering in the sink, and a specter of steam. Chris hollered hello and a voice—the grandmother, who frightened Miles in her foreignness and age, her overt spryness—said something back in the language that Miles had come to associate with this apartment, with Chris-at-home, with another, realer Chris inside the best friend he had come to know.

No matter how many times he'd been there, the same nervousness descended, almost pleasant in its familiarity. It was the sense that he both absolutely should and absolutely shouldn't be there. The boys slipped off their shoes and left them by the door. Inevitably, on the way down the hall, a hard kernel of something would catch Miles's sock.

At the back of the apartment, Chris had a room smaller than most of the closets in Miles's house. Between his twin bed and the three-drawer dresser, a narrow swath of floor led to the single window and the fire escape, the room's sole luxury, onto which the boys climbed now. From up here they could see the alley, the backs of other apartments with cheap, single-paned windows and droopy, faulty-looking phone lines, the neighbor's carport, and the dumpster behind the corner store. The air was bright, damp, indecisive, and marine, a kind of everything weather that pulled the smell out of trees and gave his mother headaches.

Chris studied the liner notes of a Joy Division CD while, across the ladder gap, Miles opened his sketchbook to his current drawing and its source image, taped to the facing page. A handbag ad showed a white woman's face in close-up, beautiful and unsmiling beneath a headband, her chin perched atop a complicated arrangement of hands (he was trying to master certain basics of the human face before he'd allow himself to render the parts he found more fun—the contours of the bag and its symmetrical print, small in the background; the skinny, round simplicity of the letters that made *Gucci*). But the portrait he'd initiated was nothing like the face in the clipping. He sank, remembering its problems: the muddled area between eyes and brow, the too-heavy jaw and fingers that appeared broken, like talons in their forced gesture. Last Sunday afternoon, while Miles was drawing at the dining room table, Caleb had emerged, heavy footed, from his bedroom, poured himself a cold mug of coffee, and leaned close over Miles's work. He gave off the same brand of fumes that emanated from the back doors of the bars on Geary, alcohol and something pukey, souvenirs of whatever party he'd been at the night before. His voice came out fluty and British, close to Miles's ear: *Well it's not bad, exactly, but your lady's looking rather . . . well, she's looking a bit* mannish, *wouldn't you say, like she might grow a mustache any second now?* He waved a hand dandily over the face—*And the eyes are floating up in her forehead, you see, so unless it's a Picasso thing you're going for . . .*

Caleb couldn't look at Miles's drawings—couldn't, actually, make *any* comment pertaining to art—without affecting the persona of Ms. Burns, his painting teacher at the arts high school since sophomore year, whom he and his friends seemed to equally loathe and revere, ridicule and desire. Frequently these imitations answered a need to distort or tamp what might otherwise be perceived as earnestness in their voices, or to exaggerate some already perverted aside . . . and yet looking at the drawing, Miles saw that Caleb was right, in whatever voice he said it. Miles snorted and edged away, but his brother had the page pinned beneath his elbow. He plucked the pencil from Miles's hand (Caleb was left-handed, like their father—a trait Miles envied), then reached across to sketch, in four fast motions in the page's corner, an egg-shaped diagram, a faint line through at the center where the eyes should go. The accent dropped. *It makes sense when you look in the mirror. Your eyes are actually in the center of your head.*

They *were*, Miles conceded silently, studying the photo with these new proportions in mind. In the privacy of his room, he'd furiously erased, the gum shedding in thick rolls. Unable to ever simply *ask* Caleb for a lesson (in art, in clothes, in what to like, in how to be cool—there was some law, almost physical in Miles's heart, against just *asking*), he'd long ago learned to settle for these random wisdoms, or whatever could be gleaned from looking and listening—intuitive modes that made him feel desperate, young, like no one at all. Be funny, Miles learned. Be sarcastic. Girls, not boys. Become an artist.

Now, looking down at the portrait, two pairs of eyes looked back. The newly rendered set implored him, correctish in their placement, but the original gaze still hovered, trace lashes and residual irises, a half inch higher. The effect was of eerie superimposition; a portrait of possession. Miles detached the clipping by its scuzzy tape and flipped to a fresh page. Here he arced out a large, faint oval, and then a bisecting line, just as Caleb had.

Chris's humming broke off. He craned his neck to see. "Why'd you start over?"

"I messed up," Miles said and moved his arm an inch. Enough to say, *Don't look.*

"I thought it was good," Chris said.

"I suck at this."

"Come on. You're, like, the best drawer in the school."

"Whatever," Miles said. Though the compliment, even as he expected it, had its intended effect.

They were still in the short sleeves of their school shirts, but the fog was thickening, and Miles shivered. Chris moved his eyes to Miles's bare arm. "You have goose bumps," he declared. Cold was often their signal to move inside. "Does your family call it *goose bumps* or *goose pimples? Goose pimples* sounds disgusting."

Chris climbed in first, lithe and easy, while Miles returned his pencil to its case, closed the sketchbook, and crouched through the window, hopped, and hit the floor with a thud. Sometimes his body fit him naturally enough, but at other times it moved around him with a will of its own, awkward as a suit of flesh. Chris was already sitting on the bed, his back against the wall and the comforter pulled up over him. There was nowhere else in the room to sit. "Give me some," Miles mumbled, scooting in beside him. Beneath the blanket, the gentle weight of Chris's leg folded on top of his own.

It was not, of course, their first time touching—that border had been crossed months before—and yet still, each time they were alone on this bed, their caution refreshed itself all over again, as if, without these almost proce-dural measures, they might rush headlong into something dangerous, losing everything in the process. Chris asked questions, and Miles answered, mono-syllabic and automatic, their brains already on to other things.

"Is it weird to be, like, rich?" A favorite of Chris's.

Miles paused. He knew to say *wealthy* or *well-off—upper-middle-class*. "I don't know." Rich was butlers in your house and Ferraris in the driveway; his father drove a Lexus, but they also had a Honda.

"But is it weird to have white parents?"

Something in Miles flinched. "I'm pretty much white."

"But if your real mom and your adopted mom were both hanging off the ledge of a hundred-story building, and you could only save one, which one would you pick?"

He pictured his mother stopped at a red light, singing along to the radio, an almost-invisible whisker sprouting from the mole on her cheek, dancing in her seat. *Don't know much about his-tor-y. Don't know much bio-lo-gy! But I do knooow that I love you*—pointing to Miles with every *you*.

"I—my adopted mom *is* my real mom."

"I know," Chris said. He was picking tiny pills off the comforter and roll-ing these together into a larger wad of fuzz when Kimber's door slammed shut and music blared through the cardboard wall. Chris placed the fuzz on the web of skin between Miles's thumb and forefinger, on his own knee above the blanket. Then he looked at Miles's face, as if to see if he'd seen, and blinked three times rapidly.

Time, suddenly, seemed in short supply, their talk an unnecessary stall-ing. Miles tipped the fuzz off his hand and into a fold, and, now that the hand was in motion anyway, shifted it under the blanket to Chris's cool knee, hard and living.

Chris slumped down so that his head was still against the wall but his torso was flat, and Miles scooted down, too, pivoted to lie against the pillow and stretched his legs out. In this position, they couldn't see each other's faces. Their hands reached and landed, as if by accident, then migrated with minds of their own. There was always this discomfiting threshold, where their wills and body parts split away, disassociated, before cohering again to make something whole: to overwhelm. Miles stared at the poster tacked and sagging on Chris's ceiling, the perfect-as-a-drawing black-and-white face of Morrissey, head cocked, receiving sunlight.

THEIR SCHOOL was actually an enormous converted mansion, pre-1906, with postcard views of the Golden Gate, marble in the foyer, and plaster lions flanking the doors. Even architecturally, the place seemed to demand uniforms. The boys wore white polos and navy slacks with black belts and white socks and foamy black shoes the cooler boys called *dingus shoes*, often violating dress code for Jordans instead. The girls wore white knee socks and baggy pleated skirts, which grazed their legs at the most unflattering lengths, neither long nor short, and made even the prettiest ones appear wrongly proportioned, like centaurs or T. rexes. The dress code, the way it distorted and costumed, was one of many minor oppressions Miles perceived daily: also the burning, antiseptic smell of the cafeteria tables; the piercing cry of the bells in certain classrooms; the randomness with which Mr. Larson ordered unsuspecting students to race algebra problems on the board and Mr. Felix forced you to climb the rope (to *try* to climb it) in front of your whole spectating class (struggling up a mere three feet, Miles thought of himself as a fat koala who wouldn't survive natural selection); the dirty names André G.'s group hissed at the girls, even the defenseless and exhausted-looking ones, like Anna T. and Kathryn S., even Tammy McNichols, who wore a plastic scoliosis brace and was exceptionally nice to everyone. Miles entered the institution each morning with a blockage between his throat and chest, stuck as a bite of toast, a polyp of opaque anxiety that warned *Be careful!* but which Chris's presence helped shape into something he could live with. Together they practiced the same strategy: slip through the day quietly, politely, eyes down, and no harm can come. Together but not *too* together.

Miles had transferred to Saint Delphine in sixth grade because his elementary school (where they'd done a lot of singing and dipping their hands in paint, acting out the seasons and field trips to the redwoods) wasn't *adequately preparing him for high school or college*: his test scores, illustrated by bars on a graph, fell short of the dotted line they should have reached, the line that meant only *average*, but that his parents insisted was a gross misrepresentation. He needed a *more structured learning environment, higher expectations*, and *incentives to cultivate his own initiative*. (In his private mind he argued that artists were allowed to be misunderstood—they were people who could fail again and again but were still, at the end of the day, geniuses. It was his defense against another descriptor that caught and echoed in his heart: *Slow, slow*, a word no one had said but Miles suspected they thought.) Caleb explained, *Basically it's because Dad knows the principal. Just don't let them brainwash you.* They weren't religious as a family—his parents found it necessary to reiterate this whenever reminders came home on fancy letterhead about Confirmation preparation or Thursday-night liturgy. *It's totally your own choice, you know, to decide how or even if spirituality will fit into your life, baby*, his mother said. *You're just there for the quality of education*, his father added. During Mass, a blanched wooden effigy floated above the altar like a clue to some lesson kept just beyond Miles's grasp. Christ's eyes were closed in agony, the divot of his stomach looked starved, the blood on his face was a red-black dribble—but what did the suffering mean, and why? Chris told Miles that the real-life Jesus hadn't looked like that. The real-life Jesus had black hair, brown eyes, dark skin. "Like yours," he said.

Although the kids at his school were almost all from families similar to Miles's, most of them were white—*extra* white, with natural blondness and delicate, pink lips, slender, pinched noses, and regular blue or brown eyes, not the goldish-yellow of Miles's—*cat's-eyes* or *tigereyes* or *dragon eyes*, as he'd heard them variously described, *beautiful* or *evil* or *spooky* by turns. Girls in his class looked at him and said, *Miles, ohmygod, your eyes are so pretty!* The Black girls (there were three at Saint Delphine) asked if they were contacts. These were the same girls who complimented his sketchbook, mooning over his shoulder, *Doood, that's so good, draw me one!* and asked unabashedly, *So are you, like, Hispanic or Black? Theresa wants to know.* His mother used the term *multiracial* and told him to do the same—on documents, or *when it comes up.* But if a stranger questioned Miles's "ethnicity" (a nosey store clerk once, bagging their groceries, asked: *So what is he? You're the nanny?*) Mom's jaw would clench and her eyes would flatten (*My* son *is . . .*) even as she did the inquirer the courtesy of patiently outlining, in her lecturing tone, the specifics of Miles's ancestry: his Dominican-Bajan birth mother and Dutch-English-Sinhalese–Sri Lankan birth father. It was a way to *educate them*, Mom said, even as Miles felt himself overheating, a person-made-pie-chart suddenly, sections of him lighting up with percentages and colors. When Mom returned the question to the clerk, he stuttered, *Hell, I'm German and some Irish—just your average American mutt!*

Sometimes, examining his reflection, Miles tried to parse out that regurgitated inheritance, a history he couldn't have located on a map. It had been explained to him from the very beginning that the adoption was *closed*—handled, they meant, behind the closed doors of a lawyer's office, one face-to-face meeting between his parents and his birth mother (she was young and very shy) and that had been that; Miles a bundle retrieved six months later from the Oakland Kaiser, and her name reduced to a blacked-out line on the carbon-copied file he'd been free to flip through for as long as he could remember. But where he'd really *come from* was not to be found in the file—it was not to be found anywhere. Caleb used the word *mixed*, and this felt closer to the truth: not exactly *this* but also not just *that*, not all orphan but not all son, not exactly part of something but not entirely alone, either. In the privacy of the downstairs bathroom, he forced himself to look in the mirror. From head to thighs, a heavy, gel-like layer covered him, circling the deep cranny of his belly button and making two tiny boy-breasts, like spills waiting to be scraped up. Beneath the stomach, inside a sparse nest of hair, a diminutive creature lived, exposed as a thumb and just as dumb. Lacking the confidence of *dick* or the power of *cock*, day and night the little thing carried instead an air of patient waiting, infuriating and sad. It was not so much smaller than Chris's, he reminded himself, but even still, its image in the mirror burned him up with shame. To consider that anyone would hazard to touch it.

It made sense that Chris and Miles had found each other. Both belonged to a marginal nongroup othered for various reasons: speech impediments or birthmarks, bad skin or bad breath. Miles by his chub and unnamable race, and Chris by his scholarship status, his bok choy in Tupperware, his high-water pants, and the faded blues of what were still, obvious to everyone, last year's uniforms. Chris's father, Roger, was Saint Delphine's head gardener, a job that meant free tuition for one child. But if the beat-up Nissan mainte-nance truck was backed into the central courtyard and the boys' class hap-pened to pass by on the way to the library, father and son acknowledged one another with nothing more than brief eye contact, covert as spies. The popular girls would holler, *Hi, Roger! Hello, Roger!* having made some curious decision that the gardener was their friend, to which Roger would smile up from where he knelt in the dirt and generously wave a spade.

"Why don't you ever say hi to your dad?" Miles asked once. Since Chris never greeted Roger, Miles thought he shouldn't either, which felt wrong, given the daily hours Miles spent in his home and Roger's steady politeness, on the occasions the boys exited Chris's room and he was there at the kitchen table, his hat in his lap and his hand in his thick, black hair. Not saying hello only verified Miles's guilt. "It's weird," he told Chris.

"Yeah, so what?" Chris said. The boys were on their way to the lunchroom, edging along the wall to avoid the rush in the corridor. "How would you feel if your dad was the gardener at your school instead of a doctor?"

Miles shrugged. "He's not, like, a *regular* doctor. Being a gynecologist is gross." In truth, Miles wasn't sure how he should feel about his father's pro-fession. Many times, he'd heard Caleb refer to *Doc Poonani* or *Sir Speculum*, their dad as a *pussy specialist*, laughing for his friends in the stilted, high-pitched chuckle Miles knew wasn't his real laugh. His real laugh was giddy and giggly, a thing that bubbled up like sparkling cider and strained Caleb's face red, pushing out tears and sliding him from his chair.

"You don't get it," Chris said. "You have a perfect family."

Heat came into Miles's face. "Not even!" He looked at Chris's ear, which Chris badly wanted to pierce. Through the ear, into the tube, Miles could read his thoughts: *Rich, rich, rich.* "But don't you think it—"

He was going to say, *Don't you think it hurts your dad's feelings?* but Chris interrupted. "He barely speaks English. I wish *I* was adopted." He dropped his backpack on the lunch table and tore open the zipper.

"Dude," Miles said, the way that Caleb might.

"What?" Chris asked, exasperated.

"Nothing," Miles said. "Don't be—"

"It's fine," Chris said. The ear was pink now.

In moments like these, Miles envied the girls, who could pull each other into hard, close hugs whenever the want struck them. As it was, Miles and Chris had been spared suspicion—*somehow*—though Miles lay awake many nights spiraling into paranoia, worrying over the likelihood that *maybe everyone knew*—all of the kids at school, and also the teachers, and the lunch ladies, and the principal, and Roger, and therefore Chris's whole family and therefore his own family, including Caleb. Maybe all of them knew and were just waiting for the right moment, like the commencement of a surprise party, to jump out and exclaim, *Gay!*

And then one day, it happened. Or a version of it. As they exited Chris's room, Kimber stopped them from where she was slumped on the couch. The window in the kitchen was slate-blue, which meant Miles should've been home already. "Hey," she said. "What's your name again?"

Kimber chewed idly on the end of one of the tiny, bleached braids she wore on either side of her part. Chris's CD collection came from her, borrowed but at a price; sometimes she pounded on the door and yelled *If you scratch that I'll slit your throat in your sleep!*—threats that clashed scarily with her smallness. A boy he'd never seen before sat beside her with his hand on her leg. His eyelids looked extra droopy. The room smelled like cigarettes.

"It's Miles," Chris said for him.

"I'm talking to *him*," Kimber said. She spat out the braid and looked at Miles. Her eyes were circled dark with makeup and her lips were black, as if she'd eaten a whole pack of licorice. "So, Miles, are you gay, too?"

Standing there in his socks, his erection ebbing in his school pants and sweat gathering in his armpits, Miles felt as if he were watching himself on film—waiting to see himself respond. His pulse filled his ears. "What?" he heard.

The boy next to Kimber leaned forward and snorted.

"I *asked* if you're gay. Or are you one of those people who isn't sure?"

Miles swallowed. He was aware of Chris's body, perfectly still, two inches away.

"Chris, shut your eyes!" Kimber snapped. Then she scooted forward on the couch and lifted up her stretchy black shirt.

The boy said, *Oh shit*, into his fist. Miles was paralyzed, abandoned by Chris, who had obligingly followed his sister's orders. Kimber's shirt covered her face like a mask. "See? Are you looking?" she asked. She wore no bra. Miles saw the chalky hollows of her armpits and the little glands of her breasts, dark-nippled, darker than he would've thought, like polka dots or painted quarters stuck bizarrely in the middle. It wasn't much different from Chris's chest. A noise downstairs, and the shirt came down. The boy was beside himself with laughter, hardly breathing. Kimber's face returned flushed and satisfied. "That's how you test if you're gay or not." Then Chris was there, saying, "She's crazy," pulling Miles toward the door, toward safety.

They never mentioned the event again, but it had happened, the word had been said, and even though the consequences, then, were nil, Miles felt a sinking surety: that this was only the beginning of something—only the first of other (many?) subsequent finger pointings, which he must learn how to answer. The worry must have troubled Chris, too, because the next week he turned cold. In class they sat in their regular seats, but if Miles asked to borrow a pencil or sheet of paper, Chris capitulated in silence, without looking up. At recess he went off alone, busying himself with homework in the library, while Miles was left to occupy their usual place, the alcove between the water fountain and the lunch room, where he drew poorly, distracted, everything bad without the incentive of Chris's praise. Such sudden abandonment shocked him. Maybe he'd imagined it all. Or maybe Chris had decided, finally, that Miles was the mistake he sometimes felt he was. His loneliness, by the time the bell rang Tuesday, was difficult to bear. On the way out of home-room, his eyes followed the orderly buzz of Chris's fade, receding as he walked. To his inadmissible fright, Miles realized how true and deep his feelings ran.

But by Friday Chris was there at the front of the 1 in their regular seats, the spot beside him empty. His eyes were wide with apology, looking every-where except at Miles and then, finally, at Miles. He offered his headphones. *Six full years of my life on your trail.* The foam circles still held the warmth of Chris's ears.

San Francisco was drizzling; water threaded the bus windows, creeping across the glass before flying off to nowhere. Nothing had been forgotten. Everything was real.

BY THE END of that year, their friendship was too firmly established to fall victim to the usual fracturing caused by summer break. Without the built-in socializing school provided, the boys had no choice but to call each other and make plans, intentionally, daily. They'd be in high school next year, Miles at Cathedral Prep but Chris at George Washington with Kimber. Everything would change in August, Miles knew without fully accepting, but consider-ing the future meant examining whatever it was that they were doing now: a thought that caused the guilt to start its cycling, further entrenching itself each time it looped, each time they did it again, the way a song stuck in your head grew increasingly unbearable.

They did their best to live discreetly in the present. Met up at the park to kick hacky sack, Miles slow and Chris fast, then walked to Clement and bought Pocky and dried mango. It felt good to Miles to wear his real clothes, but even better to see Chris in his: basketball shorts with a stripe down the side, plaid boxers ruffling out the top when he leaned to pick up the sack. Chris's mother had consented to the ear piercing, and now a gold stud glit-tered in his left lobe on rare afternoons when the sky was blue.

Mostly the sky was a static gray-white, weather that pressed people together, cordoning them off from other, more variable realities. Their arrangement depended on such unspoken consistencies: the weather, but also Chris's house, his room. Superstitiously, Miles believed that any change in the environment might upset the delicate workings of their routine, and since the beginning, Miles had made it clear that they couldn't go to his house: his mom would come out of her office and insist they eat carrots and talk to her; some cleaning woman might be buffing the hardwood floors; one of Caleb's friends would want them to do something humiliating for a video project—excuses Chris accepted without challenge. But that June, as their venturing began to feel unstoppable, a new desire edged open in Miles. To show Chris *more of himself,* despite the risks. To show Chris his room.

"You wanna come over to my house today? No one's here."

Through the receiver, Miles heard a Blow Pop clack. "Sure." Chris's lips would be a muddled, alien azure, his teeth blue-white in relief.

By noon most days, Miles's father was safely at the med center, his mother in Berkeley, and his brother already off on his skateboard, his breakfast remains strewed across the counter. Miles toasted Bagel Bites while Chris sat on the white sectional, looking small and lost inside its plushness, peering at the magazines arranged in a perfect fan across the coffee table—*Harper's, GQ,* the *New Yorker*—as if deciding how to pick one up. They'd make their way outside to the trampoline, then down the dirt path that led to a small, railingless deck and the sliding glass doors of Miles's basement room. Even with the doors closed, you could smell the eucalyptus trees, medicinal and dusty, staggering the ravine all the way to the Presidio. It was Chris's habit to go directly to the wall above Miles's desk and study, in reserved silence, the finished drawings tacked there. *You took down the tree frogs?* he'd eventually say, or *This isn't the same as the other one—you did two Princess Leias?*—the same way he made acute reports on Miles's person: *You have six freckles here that kind of make a hat shape or an Oklahoma shape.* Or, *When you hum that part you actually sound just like Robert Smith.* The observations both flattered Miles and frightened him: What else did Chris notice that he didn't say out loud? There was a kind of powerlessness in being seen, Miles was beginning to understand, that was both awesome and uncomfortable.

They watched movies on Miles's combo TV/VCR (*E.T.*, *Leprechaun*, *Laby-rinth*, and *Kindergarten Cop*—rejects from the larger family library), or they took books onto the deck, paperback hand-me-downs from Caleb—*Hatchet* and *Lord of the Flies*, which Miles read with enjoyment if also a kind of anthropological detachment, fixated on decoding his brother's random underlines, possible clues as to how Caleb had evolved from a conscientious kid reader into the person he was now, slamming the kitchen cupboards, slapping his feet against the hardwood, blasting rap in the garage, and speaking in an ever-evolving language of irony, innuendo, and reference Miles only sort of understood. Caleb had just graduated (*barely*, their father liked to qualify, though it was understood that this wasn't because Caleb wasn't smart or capable or talented, his mother emphasized—it was because he was stubborn and had cut a lot of classes and *has to do everything his own way*), and now that there weren't teachers or grades to make him feel, in his own words, *creatively restricted*, he'd committed himself to painting with a renewed vigor: *I'm going to get a gallery by the time I'm twenty-five*, he'd announced one night at dinner, shaking soy sauce onto his rice, talking more to the rice than to anyone at the table. *For real. I'm going to be a famous artist.* Forking apart his salmon, Miles cringed to hear this version of his own dream revealed so casually—a wish laid out like a prediction. Mom asked Caleb to define fame, in 1996, in terms of art. Dad laughed. *A month after almost flunking high school seems like the perfectly cinematic time to decide this. It'll play great in your biopic.* Already, though, Caleb had converted the garage into a regular studio, which the rest of the family was forbidden from entering. *Phone*, Miles would call at the threshold, holding Aurora, Sierra, Lauren on the cordless, and when the door opened, he glimpsed large, leaning canvases and plywood sheets splattered red and black and gold, floating cartoon heads, spiraling abstractions, spray-paint and collaged newspaper making crown shapes, car shapes, gun shapes. The skunk of pot covered by incense only added to his sense that this was a world intimidatingly mature—sophisticated beyond his reach. "Thanks," Caleb would say, grabbing the receiver, rubbing his eye, and the door would close again.

By July, Miles and Chris were doing the same things they'd done before, except face-to-face now, in brave confrontation of each other. Now they removed shirts and scooted their shorts down automatically, above the covers even. And they kissed like movie lovers; Chris's tongue was thick and loamy, but Miles joined his mouth insatiably, until his lips swelled and he grew queasy with saliva. They found they could touch each other until a rhythm fell into place, so pleasant that any self-consciousness could be set aside, dealt with later. Miles's veins filled with warm, new liquid, a second blood. In those moments, he was not himself—he was some perfect version of something bodiless, a soul shot out the window and singing. Afterward, he felt light and small. He looked into Chris's eyes and tried to feel unafraid. "You can only actually see a person's eyes one eye at a time," Chris said. His voice was just above a whisper. He blinked fast. "So the idea of staring into someone's *eyes* is actually not possible."

Miles moved his vision from Chris's right eye to the left, then back to the right, back to the left, trying to see them both at once. Chris was right. Even squinting, the two remained distinctly separate, egglike and biological, refusing to merge.

In the same impossible way that Miles wished Caleb would invite him places, he wished, too, that he could discuss with someone the secret of Chris. He toyed with the idea of creating a Chris stand-in, recasting Chris as female, some ambiguous girl stranger (why was it Kimber who came to mind?)—but he knew it wouldn't pass. Even if he wasn't caught immediately (what did he know about girls, anyway? Inside their pants, inside their heads?), Caleb's possible validation, his excited prodding for details, his welcoming of Miles into the teenage fold wouldn't mean anything legitimately satisfying: privately, it would only reaffirm the fact of the lie. The plan depressed him, but he returned to it still. At night sometimes, before he fell asleep, he brainstormed the made-up girl's name (*not* Kimber), and hair color (red), and a number of plausible stories to explain where she might have come from.

THERE WAS an afternoon in mid-July when the sun hung hot, illuminative and falsely happy, and a rare, exotic humidity hovered over the peninsula. Their mother had closed all the blinds and turned the air on early that morning, so it might've been the white-noise hush, pushing out from the vent above Miles's bed, that masked the sound of the garage opening. No music upstairs, no door sounds or footfalls. Later, Miles would reflect with suspicion on his brother's uncharacteristic quiet—Caleb must have had an inkling, the ambush must've been planned—but eventually he'd come to find this line of thinking delusional: in its implication that Caleb paid enough attention to Miles to wonder what he did when Caleb wasn't around.

Chris's mouth was rimed with the aftermath of too many chips, but his cheeks smelled like flowers and his chest like soap. The boom box was turned down low, and the Cure went *Woooo!* Their shirts were off but nothing else; now Chris scooted down, lowering Miles's shorts, finding him with his lips, when a sound made them both freeze. Something tapped the glass. A eucalyptus pod, Miles thought, flung by the wind. But then the tap happened again, louder, suggesting human intent. Suggesting a hand or an arm.

Awkwardly, Miles rose onto his elbows, yanking his shorts up at the same time. Behind the glass, Caleb had his skateboard raised. It was the skateboard that had made the tap, a signal meant to rouse, but when Miles looked up, Caleb's eyes retracted—pulled back inside himself, afraid. Faced with the decision of what to do next, Caleb seemed to choose at random. He pulled the board back and swung it hard into the glass. The shatter was instant, shocking. Miles had no thought as to where or who he was. In the long, paralyzed seconds that followed, he knew he would trade everything, Chris included, to have the moment back—to have not done, not been seen.

A BASEBALL, Miles told their father that night. A baseball, thrown carelessly, missed. A heavy baseball. A very hard throw.

They were grilling steaks and zucchini on the main deck, three tiers of redwood octagons that clashed with the rest of the house and stretched out in planes above the backyard. "Who plays baseball around here?" Their father wore a paper chef's hat. Caleb sat on the railing with his feet hooked through, leaning backward.

"Miles's friend Chris," Caleb said.

At the big tile table, Miles picked at the surface with a razor blade that just happened to be lying there. He couldn't look at anyone.

"Chris was over here?" Dad held the spatula. His glasses caught the setting sun. "I thought you only liked to go to Chris's."

"He has better CDs than I do," Miles said to the razor blade.

"He's been over, like, every day," Caleb said.

"And you were playing *baseball*?"

"We just got too . . . rough. I'm sorry, Dad," Miles said.

"They just got too rough," Caleb said. "He's sorry, Dad."

THREE DAYS LATER, their mother called a family meeting. In the "library," a room no one ever used, his parents waited in wicker chairs. A bottle of pink wine was open on an end table, and Mom and Dad each held a glass—white wine was for celebrations, red for crises, but pink could go either way. Mom was flushed in the cheeks, even under her makeup, nervous, smiling at Miles, looking at their father, looking at Caleb. Miles sat in an armchair with a pillow on his lap. He knew he should prepare for an interrogation, but he couldn't get his thoughts to push beyond this one thought: that he should think of something to say.

Caleb refused to sit at all. He leaned against a bookshelf with his arms folded and his bare foot balancing on the stand of a decorative birdcage. "If you're getting a divorce can you just spit it out?"—and it occurred to Miles that maybe this wasn't about him at all.

Their mother uncrossed and recrossed her legs, in drawstring linen pants, and then announced that she'd received a job offer. Their father cut in: she'd gone for an interview and a talk, remember, back in January, but hadn't gotten it. Miles tried to think back—his mother traveled often lately; she had a book out, and other universities paid her to come and talk about it—but he didn't know which interview his father meant. Well, she was saying now, they'd offered the position to another candidate, this sociolinguist from U Mass, who'd accepted it and was all ready to start. But then last week—the linguist actually *died*, as sad as that was—and now they were offering the job to her. She arranged her face in a funny smile she showed often, the one that communicated, *Isn't life strange?*

Caleb let out a crazy expulsion—a sort of strangled laugh, which their parents ignored. "It was a brain aneurysm, actually, while he was driving," their father said. "Totally tragic thing. A wife and three—"

"Jesus *Christ*, Dad!" Caleb blurted. "*Where?*"

"Career-defining," Mom said. "Your mother negotiated."

"We're talking insane to not take," their father said. "Sabbatical every other year, no committee requirements to start—give 'em the details, Lena."

"*Where*, Mom? Siberia? *Texas?*"

She sighed, "Cay. Boys. Now, don't overreact. Just give yourselves a moment to process. The job is in Ann Arbor. Michigan. It's . . . there are certainly worse places." She took an easy sip of wine.

Caleb doubled over, slapped his thighs, and howled. A pandemonium broke out. The birdcage tipped in slow motion toward the coffee table, and in Mom's attempt to catch it, her wine sloshed onto the rug. Miles wasn't sure if the panic in his chest was his own or only secondhand, environmental. Since the broken window, he'd told Chris he was sick—not to call, he'd call him later, *later*—herding him into a far corner of his mind. Downstairs, Miles had cloistered himself in tedious devotion to a re-creation of the *Ocean Rain* cover: a gift, he told himself, for Chris, once enough time had passed that the thought of him didn't bring that queasiness, a nausea that led right back to what had happened. And yet now Chris rose up like a pure, inevitable emotion, filling the space behind his sternum. *Michigan?*

In the middle of the room, Caleb was on a rampage. He flung his arms out imploringly, then clenched, his voice rising and cracking, citing all the reasons why they couldn't, all the injustice of it. He called their father money hungry, fascist, a *dictator*, and their mother—he looked her straight in the face, where he knew it would cut, and sputtered, *A selfish workaholic. Everything's about you!* She turned her face away to hide the tears that, Miles saw, had begun to leak.

"I'm staying here," Caleb announced.

"That's fine. If you want to stay and find an apartment, a job—"

"What about my account?"

Their mother sighed. "Cay, we've been through this."

Their father said, "No college, no account."

"But why can't I stay *here*? My *studio* is here, my room is here, my *stuff* is all—"

"We're renting out the house," their father said.

"As if you need the money!"

"It's not about the money."

"Rent it to me! I'll—Joey could move in—"

Their mother began, "Honey, it's not that we don't *trust* you, it's just . . ."

Their father scooted to the edge of the couch. "Look." He found his doctor voice, which made everything sound reasonable and obvious. "As a legal adult—as an artist without income or a college plan or a savings account—I'd say you're actually in a pretty fortuitous place in your life. That your fascist parents are still willing to bring you along for the ride. To house you and feed you and support you and love you. Don't you think?" He took a deep breath and looked to Miles. "Don't you think?"

2.

CALEB'S FIRST MICHIGAN WINTER (AND FUCK HIM IF IT wouldn't also be his last) came waffling in the second week of November. The storm blew relentlessly all afternoon and into the evening, rain then hail pummeling the Main Street awnings, and gusts whipping the last gray-brown leaves from the haggard trees until, sometime between his walk home from his shift at Gary's Grille and Seafoodery and his driver's test the next morning, everything froze to a mean slick, the sidewalks and roads alike, ready for slapstick or disaster.

"Just pretend the van is a Zamboni," his father said. "You'll do fine." Brian looked extragynecological standing there in the kitchen, jabbing a teaspoon into the flesh of a halved grapefruit. Beneath his white button-up Caleb could just read the shape of his undershirt. A new pager hung from his belt in a new pager case.

Sometimes Caleb hated his father with a fervor akin to mania. His skin would go tight and his vision would sharpen almost psychedelically, just looking at, say, the shirt under the shirt. The feeling overtook him from an illogical nowhere, the way acid hit you all at once or the impulse to fight flashed on like a floodlight. The same animosity boiled when he'd had to practice driving: the way his dad winced every time Caleb braked, how he braced himself against the dash and said, *School zone, twenty-five,* whenever a backpacked college kid approached a crosswalk. The whole fucking town was a school zone. He'd crank up "Sabotage" until his father's voice became a wave of sound lost to the bass—that teacher's voice in *Charlie Brown.* It was hard to concentrate on driving and on fiercely hating his father at the same time. If he failed the test today, it would be Brian's fault.

"What the fuck is a Zamboni?" he asked now, aware of the wretched arrangement of his face. He knew what it was, but he wasn't about to participate in Dad's missionary enthusiasm for middle-American quaintness—hockey and its paraphernalia. Brian raised his hands in a steering motion, made an inaccurate sputter with his lips. Caleb took his cereal bowl and his mug of sugared coffee back to his now room, which still smelled of the rental's previous inhabitants, their cleaning products and shoes.

In San Francisco, driving didn't matter. No one drove. You skated or walked or hopped Muni, then slapped stickers on your way out the back door—and there was nowhere in the city, from Land's End to Hunter's Point, you couldn't get to. But here in the Mid-shithole-west, it occurred to Caleb very quickly that wheels were the only way to mobility, that mobility was his only chance at freedom, and that freedom would be necessary to save him from actually *dying of boredom*, an expression he'd never before considered might hold truth. If he got a job by November and a license by Christmas—if he showed some *initiative*, his father had bargained (and his mother had nodded in arms-folded agreement; even on her high-and-mighty new-professor-in-town trip, she still kowtowed to Brian's rule)—they'd give him the family minivan *free of charge*, deciding to upgrade anyway. The Odyssey wasn't old but was marred already by a squealing timing belt, a peeling Clinton-Gore bumper sticker, and, inside, the olfactory reminder of Miles's carsickness last summer in Yosemite. *Free of charge*—his father had actually said those words! His father who was married to his mother whose maiden name was also the name of a building at Stanford, a street in Walnut Creek, a foundation that gave loans to farmers in Africa! *Actually*, Lena explained, that was the whole reason they'd lugged the Honda across the country in the first place. For Caleb. Anticipating just this sort of need. Her timid smile showed how much this motherly foresight pleased her.

Wow, Mom, free of charge! No way! Are you sure? I just couldn't! As if it were the offer of a fucking lifetime. But Caleb, having no other offers, took it.

"Points off for merging too soon on Packard. But you pass anyway; congratulations," the DMV guy said, with no authentic congratulations in his voice. He was like that actor in the Visine commercials.

"Cool," Caleb said. "Thanks." He'd need to get some Visine, stat, for the glove compartment. The cops here seemed extra wack, ruddy and dog-jawed, with forehead rolls—the type who'd pull you over for forgetting to signal, then make you get out of the car, sniff around, shine their flashlights in your eyes and count the busted capillaries.

When the van was his officially, he made his father sign the pink slip over and relinquish both sets of keys. The last thing he wanted was Mom and Dad snooping around in *his* van, rifling through the center console. A deal was a deal, he told them. He looked older in his ID than he did in real life: unsmiling, chin up, his Adam's apple protrusive, assertive, a vague indicator of the girth of his dick. As if Michigan were a kind of personal boot camp, he'd recently buzzed his head, but in the picture he looked marine-ish in an accidentally nonironic way.

In the driveway, if his father happened to park the Lexus too close to the van, Caleb took to saying, *Whoa, whoa, whoa, back off my Odyssey!*

HE LOST his bussing job at Gary's when the manager, Joel, caught him ripping whippets in the walk-in the weekend after Thanksgiving, just before the dinner rush. On and off since Caleb had started, the servers' whipped cream had dripped from the nozzle instead of dispensing with the customary inflation, and now, having cornered the culprit, Joel beamed with righteousness. Double-pumpkin cheesecakes had been ruined by the dozen. Not only was it *drug use on the job*, it was also, in a roundabout way, *theft*.

Joel was only a handful of years older than Caleb, but everything about him reeked of eagerness for adulthood: his prematurely receding hairline, his belted khakis and hands-on-hips stance. Caleb started to laugh and couldn't stop. Between gasps, he looked Joel in the eyes and said, *In a roundabout way, fuck off.* Had he actually said this, or had he only thought it? He had—the words still hung in the air, as did Joel's measured response, requesting he return his apron and his bow tie to the linen bin, *otherwise there'd be grounds to withhold his last—.* On his way out of the dining room, Caleb flung the apron behind him, hoping it landed on a guest, then grabbed the tub of mints off the host stand just as Lisa, the kind-of-hot hostess, shouted *Hey!* This he tucked under his arm before pushing through the glass door, buzzing with adrenaline, out into the cold night.

Who the fuck cared. The van was his, the bargain with his parents made.

He wouldn't have any money—or would have to sneak it from wallets and purses, Miles's cigar box (the allowance he'd gotten during high school had ended abruptly last summer, after the disaster of Caleb's final report card, coinciding with their decision to keep from him indefinitely—or until he broke down and went to college—the ripe fund set aside for him at birth)— but it'd be Christmas soon, checks from Grandma and Papa would arrive, cash from Uncle Gene and Aunt Deb, Mom and Dad and Nana. The thought of his name in slanted cursive comforted him—made him feel that, despite Joel and the hellhole that was this place, all was actually fine in the world; all would always be fine. Relief was a thick envelope marked *Caleb*, warm and waiting as a bed, a stash eternally replenishing.

That night he drove aimlessly through the sleeping town, past the campus with its thick-limbed trees, its wannabe-ancient libraries separated by quads, past the sports bars bumping bad Top 40, and out through the Norman Rockwell neighborhoods, each with its own variety of farmy, Republican architecture. He drove until well past the time he usually arrived home, and when he unlocked the front door, the only light inside came from a Tiffany lamp his mother kept on, on top of a long credenza that held the liquor. He sipped from Kahlua, then whiskey, then gin, felt woozy, ate cold sesame beef from a carton in the fridge. Again he replayed the scene with Joel: how good it had felt to walk out, what Lisa must've thought, hearing the story afterward. How freeing to know he'd never again have to haul a leaking bag of garbage into the dumpster out back, a heavy-ass bus tub of alfredo-streaked plates, his triceps quivering while Frank Sinatra crooned. He thought of the Christmas checks again and tried very hard to feel happy, but he was too drunk and nauseous now, and, with no one to share his news with, lonely. He went upstairs to pass out.

That Friday and Saturday, and all the following Wednesdays and Fridays and Saturdays and every other Thursday, Caleb continued to put on the black slacks and the bow tie, hollering on his way out, *See ya later, family, your golden boy's off to earn a good old-fashioned living!* On the days he didn't work (or didn't pretend to go to work), he'd been charged with the task of retrieving his brother from school in the afternoons, where Miles stood in the loading zone beside the Pioneer High marquee, separate from the loose arrangements of other kids, his shoulders slumped, his jeans bunchy, scratching his arm. How confused and forlorn he looked, in the seconds that Caleb saw Miles before Miles saw the van, waiting there like someone's lost dog, staring weirdly into the distance the way only blind people were supposed to.

"Wudup wudup wudup!" Caleb called. He liked to make the pickup a little party—blast *The Predator* or *Bleach* and backtrack so they could peel around past the buses and the car line, give the other kids something to see, a contrail of weed smoke to whiff, a larger framework in which to understand his brother. He worried about Miles (did they pick on him? How could they *not* pick on him?)—not consistently, but acutely when he did.

"Yo yo, what's up, bro? How you doin'?" Caleb asked, stubbing out a joint. He raised his hand to lay a good smack.

It took Miles a minute to offer his palm, as soft and padded as a paw. It took Miles a minute to do most things. "Hi," he said.

Sometimes, a voice inside Caleb whispered *crack baby*. He didn't *want* to hear this—the words just pushed in, and Caleb had to push them out again. "You rule this place yet or what?"

Miles coughed and cranked the window down, letting in the cold. "Obviously," he said flatly. Sarcasm was new for Miles—a quiet acerbity he seemed to be cultivating, experimenting with, since Michigan. Caleb wondered vaguely how much the change in his brother had to do with moving generally, or how much it had to do with moving away from Chris.

Even still, there was something punishing in Miles's tone, his avoidance, and Caleb had found himself working hard to regain his former footing. In his Grey Poupon voice, he asked, "May I offer young Miles a mint?" He lifted the tub from the floor of the backseat. *Gary's* appeared in cursive on each silver wrapper, as if they were the marked property of some guy named Gary, some narcissistic freak who only ate mints custom printed with his name. Caleb joked about this as he drove, until the joke ended and finally Miles asked, around the candy in his mouth, how come Caleb had the whole box.

He got what he'd been wanting then. To tell the story so patiently hoarded. What he'd said to Joel and how he'd been lying to Mom and Dad for a week now—aware of something braggy in his voice but unable to curtail it. He could still count on Miles's loyalty, he wagered, when it came to Caleb versus their parents. For years in San Francisco, Miles had put up with Caleb's use of his basement room for easy sneaking in and out, at all hours of the night, without question or threat, without demanding some reparation or asking to come along like another little brother might have. Even the time Caleb got caught shoplifting from Tower, Miles across the store innocently flipping through Misc. 80s—even when Caleb was given an involved talking-to and Miles had waited outside, pacing the same stretch of Market Street alone (later he confessed how scared he'd been, his eyes big and close to crying), Miles hadn't leaked a word. Discretion, minding his own business, secret keeping: these were his brother's best qualities. Caleb suspected it came from the gay thing.

"Dad'll find out eventually," Miles said now. They were stopped at a red light. The sky began to sleet, turning the windshield blotchy. "He'll just make you get another job."

"I'm highly unfit for employment," Caleb said. In front of them, a Ford waved a POW-MIA flag. Caleb had always thought the logo looked like a punk record more than some army thing. "Fuck the military. Fuck pigs."

"They'll take the van back," Miles said.

"They can't. That's Indian giving."

Miles turned to the window and muttered, "Native American."

Caleb didn't like this. When the left-turn arrow went green, he took the corner so fast the tires squealed. "Damn. Ninth grade in butt-fuck Michigan and look who's the fucking PC police." He gave Miles's arm a gentle shove. "You're not gonna snitch me out, right?"

Miles let the shove move him without reaction. In the side mirror, Caleb could see his face, hurt and pouty, still just a little kid's. His bottom lip stuck out even more than it did naturally.

"Right?" Caleb asked again louder, flipping off Nas.

Miles gave a nod of acquiescence, almost imperceptible, and Caleb hated himself. A nasty taste came into his mouth. Why did he do it? Always pushing when Miles was, already, so susceptible to being pushed? Why had he broken the window, before he'd even formed the thought, *Now I'll break this window*? That had freaked him out, that nanosecond of no control. How weird and dumb and betrayed he'd felt, looking in, seeing his brother's body there under Chris's. It was like looking into a stranger's room. As if Miles were someone else, or had *always been* someone else. Someone Caleb had never met.

The fact that he and Miles had not mentioned the event only made it more dreamlike, and yet the silence, which took up dangerous space in Caleb's chest, felt as real as anything. Miles used to listen to Caleb with an intensity close to awe, like a robot programmed to memorize his every word. It made Caleb feel important, to be listened to like that. It made him feel more like the person he was supposed to be, instead of whoever the hell he was. He hadn't so much as opened his tackle box of paints since they'd moved to Michigan. The tubes of oils must be petrifying, shriveling up in the dark like a nest of dead worms. By a line he couldn't quite draw, Miles's avoidance and the unused paints seemed connected.

They endured the rest of the ride in silence except for the squeak of the windshield wipers and a clicking that had started in the engine. Caleb steered with his seat reclined and his left arm rigid, gangsta-style, trying to feel gangsta, but anxious the wrench light might flash on any second.

WHERE is an eighteen-year-old to go, in a maroon bow tie on a frigid December Friday, in a world where he knows no one and no one knows him?

In the bathroom of a Liberty Street pizza spot, Caleb changed into his regular clothes. White tee, black hoodie, gray beanie, Dickies. He drove aimlessly, in a state of semiconsciousness, down the undergrad drag, scanning for girls, girls like ones he'd known in SF, anything other than shapeless layers and straight beige hair, cankles in jeans and queen-sized thighs. Up and down frat row, he cruised past mansions with yards stretched across with volleyball nets, red cups scattered everywhere, posses of jocks congregating in driveways—dudes he wouldn't mind seeing some ugly humiliation befall. He drove out through the suburbs and into Ypsilanti, past the dick-shaped water tower and across the railroad tracks, something stale about it here, something off and old, then looped back, having achieved nothing. His weed was almost gone, but even if he'd had the money, he didn't know where to buy it. In San Francisco, dealers approached any kid with a skateboard ten times a day: outside Amoeba or on Hippie Hill, lurking around Civic Center BART or walking up Van Ness. When Caleb took his board out here, he only attracted narcs. On the art museum steps, campus security told him to beat it. At the post office, big, commanding signs shouted prohibitions, and it wasn't long before two sweaty cops appeared and Caleb bounced, clacking off down the sidewalk before they were out of the car. He tried to skate outside Nickels Arcade, but there were too many gawkers, maize-and-blue dorks shouting out tricks they wouldn't even have recognized (*ollie, man! Can't you ollie?*) as if Caleb took requests. As if he were a fucking classic-rock cover band. And downtown posed the problem of his mother, too, the high potential that she might stroll right past with her arms full of books Caleb didn't believe any person could actually understand, let alone enjoy. All his life he'd harbored the belief that his mother's academic career was mostly a lie; an expertly acted charade she'd somehow gotten away with (it wasn't that his mother was a genius, but that other people were so stupid as to *think* she was), in the same way he believed his father was a closeted deviant who derived intense pleasure from examining vaginas (he probably took deep, full-nostril whiffs when he was down there and mentally recorded the visual minutiae). The common deception of their lives must've brought them together to begin with. Other showy decisions, like the adoption of Miles, were calculated to further illustrate this put-on perfection (as if being successful and educated and rich wasn't enough, they had to be selfless and kind spirited and Democrats, too—they had to be saviors). They already had Caleb—why'd they have to adopt a kid at all, let alone a Black one? It wasn't a racist question, because Caleb wasn't racist (a truth so obvious it didn't even need thinking). It was a question of why they'd *gone out of their way?* A question of *what were they trying to prove?* A question of why did his parents try so hard to appear one way (open-minded, generous, *hip*) when they were so obviously (boring, fake, *cowardly*) another?

On Friday nights, if he wove up and down the Kerrytown blocks patiently enough, desperately enough, inevitably he'd find a house party. Striding up the walk with hands shoved deep in his pockets, he vibrated with the feeling of intrusion, loitering in some bright kitchen, pouring generous cupfuls of someone else's vodka. There was always a porch or a dark, cold yard, rising voices and laughter, a circle of boys around a tree stump playing some game straight out of *Deliverance* (you threw a hammer into the air and hoped it would land on a nail). Shivering in his sweatshirt and thermal, Caleb found a wall to lean against and tried to look simultaneously comfortable and mysterious. When corn-fed girls looked his way, his heart made a racket, but he spurred himself toward them (*Don't be a pussy*), shaking a cigarette from the pack of Marlboro Reds he didn't smoke regularly but carried in the van, solely for use in situations like these. He had his own light, but he'd ask some girl for one anyway. Their northern, motherly accents flattened their Es but turned him on nevertheless. *D'ya know if there's any Redpop inside? I need a mixer.* He waited for their questions.

At first Caleb's lies came randomly and intuitively, but eventually he landed on a story he took to repeating: he was twenty-two, from New York, a graduate student in fine arts or film—knew someone who lived here, one of the *other* roommates. The girls squinted at him, gave him looks impossible to decipher. He liked lying—the challenge of inventing answers on the spot—felt a pleasant power in sparking and perpetuating another person's interest, all through the acumen of his own imagination, while leaving his real story intact, untouched. Once, three guys, overhearing his age, asked him to get more beer. The party was dry, girls were leaving. All three wore sweaters his father would've worn. The sweater-preps gave him thirty bucks, and Caleb got in the van, drove off, did not, of course, return.

But also on these nights—the times that no one showed any interest in him, and he slunk out the front door again, invisible, to wait out the hours parked and idling—Caleb missed his friends almost more than he could bear. It became a habit, to calculate the time change and imagine what Ryan and Joey and Jamal were doing. Were they sitting around at Joey's, watching *Half Baked* or *Friday* while Joey's mom blended margaritas in her short shorts? Were they busing to SOMA to bomb alleys and construction zones, or already skulking in the dark, talking more than tagging, scoping better, higher-visibility, riskier spots for next time? (The next-time spots were never realized, but because the boys' shortcomings were all the same, they'd never call each other out on failing to try what they claimed to be capable of.) Or they might be at the beach with Kelly and Sierra and Aurora, or Sierra and Mackenzie and Lauren, smoking and brown-bagging it around a bonfire, Ryan packing the pipe, Jamal and Joey freestyling, Brad trying to get the girls to kiss or take their shirts off or give him a blow job, but in a funny way, a way that made the girls laugh.

He missed the dudes cloudily and all the time, but he missed the girls with a sharp physicality—a knifelike yearning he could feel, when he thought of his various female interests, in the muscles of his thighs. Lately it was Lauren, who had recently dyed her hair cotton-candy pink and whose tits had gotten bigger. She looked like Chloë Sevigny, and everyone had been drooly for her last summer. *Bros before hoes* was a saying that sometimes circulated, in their crew, when the girl talk got too deep, too real, too awkwardly overlapping (it was weird, how quickly agreement could turn to competition), but Caleb was hardly ashamed to admit he'd hoed-before-broed plenty of times. He knew to stop with the girl's jeans for a minute to look into her eyes and stroke her face (girls practically squirted when you touched their faces, pushing their cheeks up into your hand like kittens wanting more) and reassure her, *Dude, it's okay, you guys are broken up—he's moving on, too*. He'd suffered only minor consequences, only lost friends who were too easily butt-hurt anyway. Really he suspected he was secretly revered for his rule-breaking. Pussy was king; they all knew it, even if they didn't admit it.

The night Caleb left with the thirty bucks, he drove to the nature preserve on the outskirts of town where they'd come in September as a family. His dad had freaked over some woodpecker—a bird he claimed to have been waiting to see for decades—but all Caleb had seen was a red flash in the treetops. Now he parked at the far end of the lot, clicked off the headlights, and whacked off in the dry heat to a fantasy of him and Lauren and Aurora that, despite its use, had not yet grown tired. For one elated instant, everything was miraculous—his whole life seemed to gel and lift. But the aftermath, like always, plunged him, left him haunted by a lucid regret confusingly detached from sex at all. He cleaned off the steering wheel with a wad of tissues and lit the very last of his very last roach.

Through the woods he could see the river, moving in black segments, the lit squares of windows suspended on the other side. A crust of snow made the ground reflective, patchy in places like a skin condition. He'd always suspected homesickness was an exaggeration, but suddenly there wasn't enough room in his heart for the intensity with which he wanted everything to just *go back*. Fuck his dad for not letting him live in the house; the house hadn't even *rented* yet, was just sitting there, emptily, the beds all still made. Fuck them for *not trusting him*; he was their fucking son! And yet the thought vexed him—that he'd messed up somehow, made a wrong decision. Why hadn't he just stayed anyway? Figured it out himself? Crashed in Ryan's dorm room at State, sucked it up and found a job, looked for a real apartment, in the Tenderloin, maybe, with Joey? The logic of it bristled; *No one made you come*, reminded the voice of his father. He was right. But the reality of *fending for himself*, in all its abstract implications, loomed intimidatingly large. It wasn't just that he feared the challenge of it. He feared his own absolute failure. A phone call across the country to Mom, asking for rent money—or worse, for a one-way ticket to Michigan—was as unimaginable as the picture he kept returning to: himself alone in the Lake Street house at night, in his bed in his room among all the other rooms, dark and empty, empty of family, a desolation in his heart that outweighed even the shittiness of the present.

Yesterday, out of nowhere, Miles asked why he'd stopped painting. Driving home after the usual pickup, Caleb was caught off guard by the question—surprised, he realized, because he hadn't expected anyone to notice. "Mom's wondering, too. I think she's scared to ask you, though. Like she doesn't want to pressure you." They'd been talking about him, then. His weaknesses and fears. What else had they said?

He lied without intending to: he *was* working on something, something big, still in the planning stages, sketching it out before he stretched the canvas—and Miles had seemed relieved.

That night, Caleb had even tried—opened his black book to a blank page, but the doodles that came out were lifeless and forced—dead-cat cartoons and the San Francisco Muni logo—every line the Sharpie traced smacking him generically, as if he were copying someone else's work, but couldn't, for the life of him, remember whose.

ON A remarkably bleak day in early December, the sky pressing down like an enormous gray palm, Caleb headed east on 94, then kept driving. However bland, the territory beyond the Ypsi exits vibrated with unexplored newness—fields and marshy no-man's-lands, the occasional flag-lined car dealership, McDonald's and Wendy's, then the airport and a giant tire decorating the freeway like a Claes Oldenburg. Signs announced Romulus, Inkster, Dearborn—and, eventually, Detroit, its population sign tagged to illegibility.

Up on the freeway escarpment came the first signs of city: concrete retaining walls and the cinder-blocked backs of auto shops, billboards asking INJURED IN AN ACCIDENT? and houses, grouped in twos and threes, in differing states of decline. Caleb couldn't rightfully explain how he'd already gone a month with a license but was only just now visiting Detroit. His parents had come not long after the move, to a Tigers game with one of his mother's colleagues, but their reports were that the city seemed "depressing" (Mom) and "grungy" (Dad), in keeping with descriptions Caleb had overheard around Ann Arbor: warnings of car theft and corpses; *lock your doors*–type jokes; *abandoned, a wasteland, scary.*

With no sense of the city's organization, he exited the freeway and turned left onto a wide boulevard. He drove slowly, dodging potholes, sponging up everything: storefronts papered with faded newsprint, the hand-painted signage of stand-alone muffler shops, a car wash, a Baptist church, and a liquor store with a shaggy array of figures out front. Everything, even the snow, appeared coated in the finest monochrome grime. He passed a bar that shared a parking lot with an AA clubhouse, and then the dazzlingly pillared and neon façade of an out-of-place strip club. It was unlike anything, he thought again and again; it was movie stuff, apocalypse stuff, exotic in its ugliness, beautifully unapologetic, America mugged and beat-up and left for dead, the inside-out opposite of California and the disfigured twin of what he'd only

ever known cities to be. For every open-appearing business there were three
or four closed ones, plywooded over or left to fend for their vulnerable selves,
doors torn off the hinges and their insides spilling onto the sidewalk, plaster
in chunks and furniture bearing springs, or the last unscrappable remains of
carpet, cabinetry, toilet tanks cracked off their bowls. The marquee of a movie
theater that might have once been grand read FOR SALE, the E tipped on its
prongs like it had fallen over drunk. Chain-link fences spanned certain lots,
then ended abruptly in impotent metal curls that seemed to say, *Fine then, do
what you will*. Plastic bags, paper bags, Styrofoam cups, disengaged car seats,
malt-liquor bottles, shredded bedsheets, chicken bones, hospital gowns, dia-
pers, syringes, dented traffic cones, bibles and *TV Guide*s, burger wrappers,
Kool cartons, condoms, glue traps, two-liters, crib mattresses, hairnets, dog
shit, Little Trees, wire hangers, and shoes separated from their mates strewed
the long gravel stretches of nothing, where even the sidewalk gave up. The
occasional pedestrian shuffled, stooped against the wind. A swaddled person
in a wheelchair rolled into traffic without a glance, his leg like a ramrod in
a perpendicular cast, propelling himself toward a gas station. What few cars
graced the road (the Motor City?) stood out with the quality of stragglers
when everyone else has raced off to something better. These Pontiacs and
Chevys, Fords and Cadillacs sagged their trunks and straddled two lanes at
once, drifting boatlike and without signaling, or peeling through red lights
as if they were only decorative.

Set back from the street by a flat, brown field, a twenty-story tower loomed
ghostly over the avenue. Overgrown train tracks looped off toward a tangle
of trees. It took his brain a moment to register why the building seemed
so utterly *empty*, emptier, somehow, than the other emptinesses he'd passed.
And then it clicked: without glass, the windows were just holes, dark tunnels between swaths of sky; the eye traveled through their gridded placement
unmediated, cleanly, the way Detroit birds must fly, making shortcuts across
town.

Downtown, a roundabout curved past stately buildings of another era,
then ended at a giant bronze fist. Caleb parked and got out. He was glad he
had his beanie on; the river was right there, and the wind came mean and

bright, whistling through a weird, buggish sculpture, UFO-like, in the center of the paved promenade. He made his way across the park and down to the water, where birds picked at trash and, farther down, men cast fishing poles, looking out at the tidy, slapping waves. It confused him, that a river could have waves, that the Midwest could have seagulls. Across the way, rusted smokestacks, the marshy nothingness that must be Canada, looked close enough to swim to, but if you squinted your eyes and fogged your memory, you could will yourself to think this was really a strip of ocean, the channel of the Golden Gate that separated San Francisco from Marin. A familiar soundtrack came in to match: the crack of a skateboard, wheels tracking pavement. Fifty feet down the sidewalk, a loner approached, then passed behind him, blowing on his hands. He was tall—Caleb was tall, but this dude was a head taller, gigantic for a white dude, goofy-looking in a baggy red baseball cap. A green-and-white jacket puffed around his torso, came up short at the waist and wrists. The letters C and T filled the back, CLASS OF '79, though no way was he that old—he looked Caleb's age. Climbing back to street level, he saw the dude again, mid-rise over a knocked-over trash can. He cleared it and landed it—impressive—before the wind ripped his hat off. *Jew fro*, Caleb thought—a sandy frizz. When he cruised back, dipping to grab the hat, he caught Caleb's eye on the rise. Something was off there. One eye pinned, but the other floated, unmoored, toward the water.

With each subsequent visit, Caleb circled closer to what he began to think of as the city's invisible core; its elusive, atmospheric *realness*. He found it in a neighborhood art piece that left him breathless—a block of vacant houses like giant assemblages, teddy bears nailed to the siding and upside-down boots rotting on fence posts, wonky plywood paintings of cars and clocks and faces decorating the winter yards. He found it in the labyrinthine bookstore on Lafayette—a warehouse, really, whose lone, vampiric employee gave him a tour of all four stories, pulling on the overhead lights one floor at a time (*Not worth it to light the whole place in winter, let alone heat it*). And that realness existed, too, in the many looks cast in his direction: idling car to car at a stop, or when he lowered his Olympus, or any time he emerged from the van to pump gas—looks that communicated *You're not from around here* in a way that made him feel bold—an adventurer more than an interloper—even as they gripped his insides. When the stranger's gaze moved from his California plates to his white-feeling face (had he ever quite *felt* the color of his face before? He hadn't; his skin went rubbery and false, mass-produced), lingering there long enough that something like insecurity (was *this* insecurity?) or an understanding of *out-of-placeness*, also new to Caleb, surged through him—he had to tear his eyes away. Once, in a Marathon station waiting to pay, a man eyed him long over the rims of his sunglasses, then returned to his scratcher with a dime. It was possible that Caleb had been staring at him just as intensely, actually—might've even initiated the staring, because of the man's unlikely outfit: in addition to the out-of-season wraparounds, he wore a leather beret, a brown sport coat, purple sweatpants, and several pairs of socks crammed inside shower sandals (snow and then rain had made a muddy slosh of the city, and the socks, which were wet, must have felt miserable). He mumbled, *Fuckin' crackers should contain themselves to they own zones, man, steada comin' down here, jonesin . . .*

He addressed this comment generally, to his hand on the dime and the attendant behind the glass, but Caleb's face burned. An urge rose in him to say, *Hey man, my little brother's Black.*

"Hey man, my little brother's Black." He was shocked to hear the words. How naked and silly they sounded; he wished he could suck them back in. But the man had heard him and looked up again, scooting his glasses further down his nose. "What in the *hell* makes you think I'm talkin' to you?"

Caleb opened his mouth. His chest felt tight. He hated to know his cheeks must be red. "I didn't—"

"That's right you dint." The man spoke straight into Caleb's eyes. A tease in his voice. "Boy, you look scared. You scared a *me*, an old man like this? Think I'm gonna rob you?"

He reached into his pocket and Caleb took a step back, glancing involuntarily at the door. But the man had only retrieved a bill. Andrew Jackson's gaunt face unfolded in Caleb's direction. "Why would I rob you, man? Got plenty of money. You want it? You can have it. Here."

When he took two more steps forward, the bill outstretched and waving,

Caleb turned and walked out fast, his blood fierce in his head. Behind him came laughter; the bell against the glass. Fuck the gas—he hopped in the van and peeled out of the lot. His heart raced. This particular incident didn't morph into the kind of story he imagined retelling. But it did, somehow, enter his private ledger of all that made Detroit electric. The thrum that had started in his spine, that very first trip, was only intensifying—a certain energy he'd forgotten he could feel. The specific and curious excitement that accompanied the will to explore.

After that he avoided eye contact. Kept his hood up and his face down. Was discreet with the camera, tucking it in his front pocket if he happened to park and walk around, doing his best to blend in. And yet it bothered him, the notion that, despite his interest, still he was a tourist here; a forever outsider until he was an insider. Without a reason or purpose, he knew, without friends or connections or specific involvements, he held no claim on this strange new place—a reality that seemed supremely unfair. But an auspicious stretch of forty-five-degree days thawed and dried the city, and at last Caleb worked up the courage to bring along his board. With its many stair banks and hefty, gleaming handrails, its expansive central plaza and blocky arrangements of concrete, its placement along the water and its general lack of people, Hart Plaza almost seemed intentionally designed to be skated—except that no one here seemed to skate. That first day, only a few loiterers appeared. The wind whapped Caleb's pant legs as he mostly puttered, feeling awkward and exposed, testing his footing and watching for slicks, but little by little he regained his old posture, and with it some confidence. He practiced sloppy grinds along a curved bench that rimmed the amphitheater, then cruised the circle around the UFO. A woman with a cart tossed breadcrumbs to anxious pigeons. At Caleb's approach, the birds hopped and fluttered. The wind, the water, the snap-fast elation of easily landing a kickflip—for a moment the world was good again; he could've been right back home, skating the Embarcadero.

He began leaving home earlier and earlier—said he'd been put on the swing shift between lunch and dinner—which allowed him to catch more daylight. To be freed from the casing of the van, to move, and sweat, and feel the weather on his face was a relief that welled, in its highest moments, toward joy. Reckless with happiness, he slid an eight-foot rail, crashed, and shoulder-rolled, but even the way his bones could accordion with the fall and then resurrect, his whole intact self springing up, was smally miraculous. Little by little, people appeared: kids padded and winterized, women powerwalking in custodial uniforms, old men swaggering, young men in ties, smoking quickly, then returning to the huge cylindrical buildings that reminded him of *Blade Runner*. Occasionally, other skaters arrived or were there already. In pairs or threes, they'd glance in Caleb's direction, their flannels whipping, and raise a modest hand, but otherwise kept to themselves. Maybe his solitariness carried a strong, repellent reek that Caleb himself couldn't smell (as the stinking person never could). Every trick became, subconsciously, an attempt to catch their attention.

It didn't take long to understand that the mostly white skaters, in backpacks and headphones, drove their shiny Pontiacs in from the suburbs, or, if they were younger, rode down on the Woodward bus. From his explorations, he knew that Woodward stretched north beyond the city limits, into 'burb upon 'burb that gained incrementally in bad-taste fanciness every block after Eight Mile. But it was his random countermates at the Lafayette Coney Island who, along with explaining lots of other local phenomena (like what exactly a coney dog was and why it was called that), offered fragmented social-studies lessons. *After them riots in '67 or so, a lot of us started to kinda realize, Hey, now, is this the place I'm gonna raise my family? And the city's been all downhill since then. Just overrun, I'm tellin' you. I come down for work, have a snack and a smoke, and boy, I can't tell you how happy I am to get right the fuck out again.* When these mechanics and salesmen, bankers and insurance brokers asked Caleb, through mouthfuls of chili, what the hell *he* was doing here, he offered variations on the lie he told at the college parties. He was on a cross-country drive from San Francisco to New York. He was in town from LA working on a film-school project. On the floor beneath his feet, he jittered his deck back and forth. San Francisco's hippie weirdness, New York's music and drugs, LA's health food and Hollywood—whatever associations the coasts must have conjured were enough to silence his companions. They nodded, tight-lipped, as if his answers were unquestionably respectable and disagreeable at the same time.

One day, the dude who took the stool next to Caleb had a skateboard, too—and the same fidgety habit of playing with it underfoot while he waited, to the irritation of the cooks. It was the tall kid; Caleb recognized him immediately. He'd seen him several times, since that first day, but never waved: shyness met the frustrating truth that here was a better skater. A better skater, in *Michigan*. He had that rubbery, effortless, bored stance reserved for the naturally gifted. Like Caleb, he seemed to come and go alone.

Now the dude gave him a quick chin thrust, tossing his hat on the counter. "What's up."

"What's up," Caleb said back.

He held up three fingers to the guy on the grill, then turned to Caleb. "I'm Tez."

"Cool," Caleb said. "What's up."

Tez laughed. "Man, now you say your name. That's how it works."

Caleb let out a *psh*, grabbed his nose, turned his head away. "Shit. I'm Caleb."

"Nice to meet you, Caleb," Tez said formally, and stuck out a hand to shake.

Caleb laughed reluctantly, turned, but did not extend his hand. Instead he saluted, as he sometimes did to his parents. "Nice to meet you, Tez."

Three things struck Caleb simultaneously. One, that this was the first time someone had spoken to him in Detroit without scanning and squinting. Two, that something in Tez's lack of irony and seemingly genuine niceness (something innocent?) reminded him immediately of Miles. And three, that Tez—as he'd suspected—had a lazy eye. His right iris veered toward the grill, revealing the slick, cue-ball side, while his left eye, big and brown and equine soft, looked straight at Caleb. Caleb chose to focus on his nose, where a territory of pimples looked painful around the nostrils. "I've seen you out here a bunch now," Tez said. "Where'd you come from?"

Caleb read *I've seen you* as a regular compliment: *I've seen you because I was watching; I was watching because you're good.* But he resisted adding that he'd seen Tez as well. Nervousness made his forearms prickle. Something in Tez's stare (maybe because it was only half a stare?) locked him into truth telling. He was from California, he said, but living in Ann Arbor. Temporarily. It fucking blew there. His mom was a professor.

Tez's good eye shifted off him, down at the counter—and Caleb saw himself as Tez must've: bragging, spoiled, lame. "My mom can be a fucking bitch," he added.

A smile came across Tez's lips. "I'm from New York, man. Queens. Just *living in* Detroit. Temporarily. Since I was ten. But Ann Arbor's over there. So what the fuck are you doin' *here?*"

The cook came over with two plates; Tez's three dogs and Caleb's one, and now Caleb wished he'd ordered at least two (he was up forty bucks this week, thanks to two twenties left out on his laundry pile with a note from Mom: *Proud of you, XO*, but frugality had started to become his default). Chili spilled around the papery buns. "Just tryin' to, like, see shit . . . Skate. Whatever. Before winter at least."

"Man, you gotta embrace winter here. Figure out activities. Otherwise, shit'll drag you down fast. Gotta make a game of it. Like, how can I survive today? How can I survive tomorrow?" Tez bit, slurped up the chili, licked his fingers. A stain of silver, Caleb saw, etched the nail of his index finger. Paint speckled the ball of his wrist. Rusto.

Tez must've seen Caleb seeing the paint, because he raised his right hand then and made a spraying motion, went *sh-sh-sh* through a mouthful. He swallowed and asked, "You partake?"

Caleb laughed hard enough that he inhaled a chunk of beef, coughed, had to blow it out grossly through his nose. This sent Tez into hysterics. He reared back on his stool and cackled.

A man in an apron came up from the basement stairs, as if summoned by the laughter, and looked right at Tez. "You, sir—Funny Eye."

He was as pasty and slick-skinned as any of the aproned men. His mustache hung like a whale's baleen above his bottom lip. Recovering, Tez frowned. "Man, Serge, you don't think people've been callin' me by my disability all my life? How 'bout bein' nice to your paying customers for once?"

The man stabbed his pointer finger at Tez. "I'll be nice to my customers when they don't vandalize the shit out of my bathrooms. There's a fresh coat of beautiful, high-gloss mint down there as of this morning, and if I see so much as a star, a heart, a goddamned *dot* on that door—let alone your *word*, or whatever the fuck—I'm never serving your ass again, you got it? *Karma*?"

Tez put his hands up. "Hey, we're cool; it's all good. I'll leave my art outta your bathroom, you leave your spit outta my food." Then he turned to Caleb and said, loudly enough that Serge could hear, "Hey man, you know, there's another spot next door that's actually better—"

Serge hollered, "All right, all right, all right; Jesus fucking hell, fuckin' jokester over here—you wanna go be a patriot next door, see how they—"

Tez took a crumpled five from his pocket and left it on the counter, then threw down another two dollars. He nudged Caleb; told him to tip well. "All right, Sergey," he yelled, "see you tomorrow."

Serge came over to take the cash, clear the plates. "All right, Cock-eyed, see you real soon."

Outside it was dark already. The streetlights on Fort Street were far apart, cloudy orange, underserving. Cars passed bumping bass. A distant siren moaned.

Tez's hand was out, ready to smack and say goodbye, when Caleb, in a rush, asked, "Hey, you know where I can get weed around here?"

Two men, construction workers, came up behind them, then passed. A look came over Tez, a hurtful suspicion that made Caleb regret that he'd asked. "You a cop? You seem young for a cop."

Caleb could see his breath when he blew on his hands. "Shit man, do I look like a fucking cop?"

Tez laughed. "You sorta do! Got that hairstyle—"

"I don't look like a fucking cop!"

"You kinda look like a movie cop. Like in a Cali movie. Patrolling the beach or some shit."

Smiling (though somewhat absently, hesitantly, and certainly not with the same grateful relief Caleb recognized unfolding in his own heart), Tez looked past Caleb's shoulder and down the street as if weighing something, debating something. Again, the prickly feeling in Caleb's arms. Again, an odd reminder of Miles. "I could get you some shit," he said finally. "Tomorrow?"

Caleb was amazed. "Seriously?" It was the sort of Midwestern hospitality Brian was always talking about, but which Caleb had called bullshit on. "Dude, I have money."

"No big deal," Tez said. "Sharing is caring."

3.

FOR CHRISTMAS, MOM GOT THE FAMILY FLANNEL-LINED PAR-
kas in the same cut that accentuated the shoulders and cinched girlishly at
the waist by an inside drawstring (blue for Miles, forest-green for Caleb, beige
for Dad, and rose for herself, her own already hanging in the coat closet). Sitting around the tinseled tree, they all ran their fingers instinctively over their
initials, embroidered above the left breast. Miles's spelled MAL, which he'd
recently learned meant *bad*: *malicious, malevolent, maladjusted*. At Mom's
urging, they donned the jackets over their pajamas and scooted together for
the point-and-shoot (*Get in there, get closer!*) like three members of the same
losing team—even Caleb, though later he told Miles he planned to pitch his
into the next burning building he happened to pass in Detroit.

Miles stood in the basement, having just delivered Caleb a plate of house-
shaped crackers smeared with nutted cheese, while Caleb pulled long on a
bottle of Labatt. He muted the skate video he was watching but didn't take
his eyes off the screen.

"Just roll down the window and *whap*—toss it in. Somethin's always on
fire in Detroit. You know what Devil's Night is? Night before Halloween?
People torch whole blocks. Whole neighborhoods. Not just kids pranking—
it's like, *everyone* does it. Grannies chuck Molotovs, douse that shit in lighter
fluid, crack houses or squats or whatever. And the city just looks the other
way—they're like, *Sure, Grandma, clean that shit up so we don't have to*. Tez
says if you call nine one one in Detroit, you get a recording. A fucking *answering machine* saying to call back tomorrow, or in ten years."

Detroit and Tez, Tez and Detroit—Caleb's new city and friend were
always in tandem on the tip of Caleb's tongue, waiting for any excuse to come
forth. But to Miles, Tez was just a low voice on the telephone, asking for his
brother, a replacement Joey or Brad, and Detroit was more of an impression

he'd gathered—exotically neglected, vaguely violent—than an actual, proximate place.

"You could give the jacket to a homeless person," Miles said now, thinking not of fire but of somewhere cold, inhospitable. "Like, someone less fortunate."

"You know any homeless people, Miles?" Caleb asked, biting into a house.

"Not any with your same initials," Miles said, and Caleb smirked.

Upstairs their neighbors, the Freedmans, had just arrived. Stale adult laughter filtered downstairs along with the *Charlie Brown Christmas* CD. The warming Tofurkey gave off a salty, processed smell. He joined his brother on the couch, focusing on the TV with Caleb's same intensity, though the jerky camera hurt his head, the fish-eye lens was dizzying, and the falls made him cringe reflexively. Upstairs the song switched at just the instant that the video panned the San Francisco skyline, and Miles's bare foot grazed a hardness matted in the carpet—a delicate crust. He recoiled, away from all that was no more. Chris was imprinted on the nerves of his very feet, and while he'd had no choice but to forget (a matter of survival, he'd concluded by October, so as not to drown in his own self-pity) he didn't want the memories to evaporate completely, as he feared they were beginning to. The past was only months behind him, but it had started to feel like someone else's. His own betrayal stung. "I miss San Francisco," he said to Caleb's video. "I miss . . . living in a city." That wasn't it, but it was something.

Caleb snorted and threw the beer back again. "Fuckin' duh, man. Tell me about it."

"What's Detroit like, actually? Is it like San Francisco at all?"

Caleb furrowed his brow thoughtfully and nodded. "Yeah, actually. It's a lot like San Francisco. It's like if all the rich and/or white people in San Francisco caught the same disease and died all at once and all the poor and/or Black people *survived* the disease but became fuckin' zombies instead and so the government, like, jackhammered across Daly City until the whole peninsula broke off like a snapped square of Ghirardelli and the little chocolate island floated all the way up to Alaska where a fucking blizzard was going crazy and the zombies had to hole up wherever they could for shelter and get groceries at liquor stores and, oh yeah, also the whole island is infested

with bedbugs and roaches and everyone's high on heroin or crack just to cope
and there's no movie theaters or nice restaurants or like any cultural shit
except baseball and football—somehow baseball and football still exist on
the island—and about once every night at, like, two a.m., when someone's
burning a pile of garbage to keep their hands warm, the fire gets out of control
and the whole city goes up in flames. Then another blizzard whips in and puts
everything out, and shit's as quiet and still as a graveyard."

Miles scratched his arm. He didn't like it when Caleb said *Black people*; the phrase made him squirm, the way it drew, implicitly, a line between
them, or a circle around him. No matter how much Caleb signaled that he
meant *other* people, Miles felt the pull of identification—and Caleb's implicit
reprimand—both for being Black and, simultaneously, for forgetting his
Blackness. One vulnerability tapped another. In his brother's voice, *Black
people* could've been *gay people*—might as well have been.

Two girls he sat with in art, Keera and Tiara, Miles said to Caleb now, had
gone to the Motown Museum with Keera's parents for her fifteenth birthday
and told him about it. They said it was cool, cardboard cutouts and record-
ings of all the singers Dad liked. Keera got a mouse pad that looked like a
Supremes 45. Then they'd gone for thick-crust pizza. Miles didn't go on to say
that as the three of them sat concentrating on the still life Mrs. Westmore had
arranged at the front of the room, shading the cluster of wax grapes, Keera
hummed under her breath, *Baby love, I need you love, I need you, oh how I need
your love*, occasionally tapping her shoe against Miles's ankle. Or that it was
understood among the three of them that Keera liked Miles, but that Miles,
for some reason the girls treated as an amusing mystery, only liked Keera as
a friend.

"These girls I know say Detroit has good pizza," he said.

"Fuck!" Caleb yelled at the screen. Brandishing the remote, he leapt off
the couch, crouched on the carpet, rewound, then played the video forward
one frame at a time. "Fuck, that's fucking sweet." As if Miles had already left
the room.

There was no rewriting what had happened in July, just as there was no
undoing what Miles had felt, the second their eyes met and the board struck

the glass, in seeing himself as Caleb saw him, a person split in half, one part of him known and the other strange—capable, suddenly, of being hated. His goodbye to Chris had been similarly brief and painful; a last-minute meet-up on Clement Street during which Chris had given him *The Best of New Order* and Miles had handed over the finished *Ocean Rain* drawing—not his best work, because he'd rushed to finish it in a state of anxiety, dreading precisely this moment of exchange. They discussed a few details of the LeBlancs' move, the vague possibility that the new job wouldn't stick, and then silence fell, Chris waiting for Miles to initiate some sort of affection, maybe, and Miles waiting for Chris to do the same (a long hug, a tearful promise, even), until, because they were in public—because it was only a street corner and Miles had to get back soon to finish packing and people seemed to be everywhere, suddenly, a bus emptying and plastic bags swinging—they said goodbye without touching, words only, raised hands, incapable eyes. First Chris turned, and then Miles, unable to watch Chris walk away, turned, too, and it was over.

He grabbed Caleb's beer from where it was balanced on the couch arm. The most he'd ever drunk was a sip at dinner (he always asked first), just to remind himself of how gross it was, of how mysterious and far-off adulthood still seemed. But now he chugged the bitter water, willing it over his taste buds, until the bottle was empty and his stomach puffed with carbonation.

Caleb turned around, the paused skater behind him all knees and arms. "What the fuck!" he hissed. "Are you kidding me?"

Miles ripped a large, odorous burp. He thought he might puke, except the chin-down, gape-mouthed look on Caleb's face was so perfect that Miles grinned instead. "Got any more?"

Caleb rolled onto his back and tweaked with giggles, kicking his feet in the air, then leapt up and disappeared into the laundry room. The spare refrigerator opened and closed. "What the *fuck*, little bro," Caleb said, returning with an armful of bottles. "You're like a party animal now or what?"

"How much do you have to drink to be drunk?" Miles asked. He was feeling something, a muzzying of his depth perception, already.

"I guess we're gonna see."

Caleb unmuted the video and a thrashing guitar blared, warring with its own feedback. Then he fished a lighter from his pocket and used the end to crack the caps off six more beers. "We'll race. Loser has to compliment some part of Mrs. Freedman's body. I'm already one ahead of you, anyway," he said. They sat knee to knee on the carpet. "In five, four, three—"

On *one* they clinked bottles, and Miles chugged as viciously as he could. Caleb paused between beers long enough to say, "Damn, little bro's growing up," then coughed his way into the next. Mom and Dad upstairs, the reality of being caught, of being grounded, of ruining Christmas—none of it mattered. However fleetingly, however ridiculously, the boys were linked. On the second beer, Caleb couldn't stop laughing as he gulped, while Miles was deadly serious—fixed to the single purpose of swallowing, of winning, of impressing his brother. What would it be like to be better than Caleb at something? By the third beer, Caleb was slowing, belching between every swallow while Miles guzzled on steadily. When the last bottle was empty, he felt so triumphant he could've flung it across the basement, right at the framed Georgia O'Keeffe flower (Georgia O'*Queef,* Miles would never be able to unhear Caleb say), but instead he rested it on the carpet, raised his fist in the air (a fist that was not quite attached to his body anymore, but seemed to simultaneously lag behind and float above him), and whooped, Arsenio-style, on beat with the music. Across from him, Caleb, grinning, did the same. *Whoop, whoop, whoop, whoop, whoop!*

At dinner, his cheeks were on fire. His head felt ornamental on his neck, swiveling, like the conical bauble that topped the tree. He was careful not to say anything out loud—thinking that speaking could pose a dire problem, in addition to the smell of his breath—and set to carefully, slowly, tearing off and placing in his mouth bird-food bits of a roll. But then he heard his brother tell Mrs. Freedman, bending toward her as she held the spinach salad aloft, that she had nice veins in her wrist. No lead-up, no segue, his voice slurring and smiling, a vampire on Christmas. *I like the color, like a blue-purple kinda thing.* A disturbed hush, and he started to giggle. Miles ran from the table to be sick.

ON NEW YEAR'S DAY, a post-Christmas miracle: Miles lay on his bed, using a 6H pencil to detail the final embellishments on a *National Geographic* cowboy's leather boots, when Caleb appeared in the doorway. He whapped the sketchbook shut.

"Hey. Put your crayons away. And dress warm. We're going out."

In the dining room, Caleb did the talking. It was his belated gift to Miles, he told their mother, to take him to a double feature at the State, then out for burgers. Or whatever Miles wanted. He spoke with his arm over Miles's shoulder.

The stunt at Christmas dinner had blown over easily enough. So he'd had one too many beers on an empty stomach, Miles had heard Caleb whine to their parents from down the hall. It was a holiday! It wasn't like he'd planned to operate heavy machinery! He'd been working his ass off at Gary's like a good boy, he reminded Mom. He'd be nineteen in three months. Miles claimed an upset stomach—a bug *had* been going around, Dad said—and stayed in his room sipping 7 Up all the next day.

Among Xeroxes and highlighters, Mom smiled up at them from the table. She wore the rectangular glasses that made the bottom halves of her eyes bulge. "My boys," she said. "My two sweet boys. Wait, wait." She went to her purse on the counter and retrieved her wallet. "For gas," she said, tucking a folded bill into Caleb's hand, then offered her cheek up, as she almost never did, beckoning Caleb, then Miles, to kiss it.

"It's 'cause we're wearing the fucking jackets," Caleb said, when they were safely in the van. He ripped his off and threw it in the backseat, among empty soda bottles and chip bags, work gloves and jeans, mineral spirits and rags, a deodorant stick missing its top, and a milk crate covered with a packing blanket.

Snow fell gently as they entered Detroit. Toppling, drifting, the slow-motion flakes reminded Miles of old-fashioned eras, *The Nutcracker* at the San Francisco Ballet—representations of winter more than the thing itself. "Wow," he whispered. Even Caleb, in his own version of reverence, turned the music down low, rapped under his breath, then lost the words and beat-boxed along. On one street, the stoplights were entirely dark, swaying in their vertical triplicates. Scrawny trees along the median appeared empty at first, then disclosed crows. Out in front of them, the pavement absorbed the faint, sifted-looking flakes.

Miles counted one, two, three empty houses in various states of decay, then a snow-flecked lot lined by trees and a maybe-functioning church on the corner. With little variation, this pattern repeated. Signs of life were scarce and strange. Three cars idled in an unpaved lot. A limping man jaywalked in a three-piece suit with a PVC cane. In a fenced yard, a dog barked to kill, its ears flat as hair against its skull. An asymmetrical hovel flashed its colors: draping blue tarps and red milk crates, a leather bench seat that must've once lived in a pickup truck. Two bundled men sat before a measly fire. One had something in his hand Miles couldn't make out—but then the van passed through a wall of steam, rising pillowy from a grate, and the picture was lost.

Caleb blared the horn twice in front of a crooked brick Victorian—so crooked a ball dropped on the floor would roll naturally from one room to another. A knee-high iron fence, pitched at cemetery angles, boxed in a yard crowded with dented fenders sprouting rusted rebar, sheet metal and ducting and upturned girders, deconstructed bicycles and chains and pulleys and various machine parts welded and assembled in precarious structures undecidedly architectural or vaguely human—what Miles would learn were the sculptures of Tez's grandfather, collecting scallops of snow. Behind the front window, the lights of a tabletop tree glowed in neon spots.

A lanky figure emerged, nearly as tall as the doorframe, with a backpack worn low and a red hat losing its shape. His jacket was the kind Miles associated with football players and his parents' generation. Tez leapt off the stairs, then jogged easily down the walk. At Miles, Caleb jerked his head toward the backseat. "You mind riding bitch?"

He sighed, but climbed into the back without argument, making room behind Caleb's seat. When the passenger door opened, Tez had to bend his body in half to fit. The door slammed, and this new, large presence filled the interior, the smell of coffee and fabric softener, something just eaten on his breath. "Yo yo," he said to Caleb, removing his hat. The two bumped fists. Then he swung around, offering the same fist to Miles. "What's up, fella?"

Miles's fist felt pudgy knocking the bony rock of Tez's. "Hey," Miles said. Aware that he still wore his own hat, with its itchy earflaps and spangled point (his parents had brought it back last year from Machu Picchu) Miles felt suddenly, terribly uncool. He ripped it off and ran his hand across his hair. "What's up."

Tez looked from Miles to Caleb and back to Miles, his lips stretching in a quizzical smile. He scratched his chin. "Y'all got different daddies or different mommies?" Only one of Tez's brown eyes focused on Miles. The other lolled off toward two o'clock, as if pulled by some peripheral distraction out the window. The lazy eye, the pale cheeks, the caterpillar eyebrows, and the nickel-flat nail of his thumb—the skinny largeness of his body in the passenger seat, knees up against the glove box: Tez emitted the radiant glow of a trustable giant, someone entirely himself. Miles's skin clicked on without warning. "I'm adopted," he said.

As if Miles had spoken too much already, Caleb cranked the volume and peeled back out onto Second Street, in the direction of taller buildings.

"You wanna skate first or get right to it?" Caleb asked Tez. Miles had to strain to hear them above the speakers and the heater.

"You wanna *skate*? In this shit?" A group of boys on the corner looked at the van, following them with their eyes as they passed.

"Man, you gotta embrace winter, right? Too early to get to it."

"Get to what?" Miles asked. His voice remained in the backseat, just in front of him.

"Might be slick to skate," Tez said. "Wet."

"Miles, can you handle slippery?" Caleb yelled.

"*What*?" Miles shouted, though he had heard.

Caleb pounded the steering wheel with the palm of his hand. "What's black-and-white and slippery all over? Give up? Give up? Miles's next girlfriend." He laughed in his practiced way, a Muppety *ba-ha-ha* followed by three fast head bangs, as if exercising his neck.

Defeated, Miles sank back, but Tez turned. "Man, don't let this asshole push you around. Seriously? Just tell him to shut the fuck up." In the rearview, Caleb was shaking his head, smiling, blowing out air. *Pssshhh.* "He's all nasty jokes. That shit's illiterate. I can tell just by lookin' at you you're smarter than that."

From the vents in the dash or from inside his own chest, a heat came over

Miles. He didn't care about Caleb's jokes—was used to finding himself their frequent butt, if there was someone around to impress. But he wasn't used to caring what that someone thought. "Shut the fuck up," Miles mumbled to the headrest. And then he raised his voice. "How much did Mom give you again?" He raised his hands in scare quotes—"For 'gas'? Was it fifty or a hundred?"

Tez howled. "Ooh shit, little bro's got you *outed*." He grabbed Caleb by the shoulder and shook. "How's it feel, man? Getting shit on?"

Caleb shrugged the hand away. "All right, fuck off," he said, but almost shyly. His smile emerged like a new defense, Miles saw, uncharacteristic—something else for the benefit of Tez. "So, Mom's got our field trip today. No big deal. Joke's on her."

Downtown, Miles found a bench out of the mean tunnels the wind bored but still with a view of the plaza. He sat on his gloved hands because his butt was already numbing, then half stood, occasionally, to tug his jeans down where they constricted his layered thighs. Caleb and Tez traced balletic arcs out before him, caught speed, kicked tidy flips, landed, turned, repeated. The day's earlier snow had already melted and seeped, leaving dark splotches on the pavers. Where Caleb contrived his usual stance—a look of spaced-out indifference on his face, his arms lifting just enough to accommodate the physics of a jump—Tez was scrappier, wilder. His jeans sagged on his skinny hips, the tail of his too-long belt flopping. He pumped his leg in the direction of a tower of concrete blocks, his arms splaying out, noodly, before he pulled his knees to his chin, rose to grind the corner, then fell hard on his side, contracting to absorb the tumble. Miles gasped and stood. But in the pause of debate before he called out, Tez was on his feet again, hopping in the cold, his grin cutting a wedge in the air.

It was cold enough that Miles was glad he was wearing the jacket, even if it was hideously dorky, and cold enough that he reasoned Caleb and Tez wouldn't be out skating if it were just the two of them—if some part of Caleb wasn't always seeking opportunities to *display himself*, even in Michigan, even just to Miles. All around him echoed the hollow crack, the hush of wheels, the nails-on-a-chalkboard squeal of trucks grinding, sounds Miles associated so distinctly with his brother (his easy athleticism, his aloof cool) that they sank him as quickly as they excited him—reminded him again of his own slumping posture, unwieldy legs, resonant awkwardness. There'd been one skating attempt in Miles's young life, in the Baker Beach parking lot two years ago, having succumbed to pressure not only from Caleb but from the friends who rallied around him. While Miles tried to balance on the rolling board, the boys shouted their impossible directives—verbs that didn't register and adjectives entirely wishful, as if physical coordination were only a matter of learning a new, more specific vocabulary. He'd felt like an elephant on a tricycle, a bear on water skis, his full-body embarrassment amplifying with each failure. By the time the lesson was over, Miles had bruised his hip, torn a hole in his jeans, skinned both elbows, and assaulted a beachgoer with a flyaway board—not to mention endured Caleb's loud, public suggestions that he might wanna cut out the Hot Pockets, or practice walking a straight line along a curb or balancing a book on his head, the way girls did who wanted to be models, before he tried again. He never, of course, tried again.

The session didn't last more than twenty minutes until a speed walker through the plaza cupped his hands to holler, *You want the cops on you?* before hurrying to make the light by the big suspended fist. *Go fuck your mother*, Caleb yelled, but enough traffic passed to block the retort, and they were all sufficiently freezing anyway. Caleb glided up to Miles, then stopped just in time, toeing board into hand and slapping Miles on the back. *Let's go.* The two friends in front, Miles trailed five feet behind as they jaywalked up a side street past a stone church, a brick newspaper building, antique skyscrapers plaqued with names and dates, sandwich advertisements and Red Wings posters, FOR LEASE and CLOSED signs propped behind glass. Tez motioned right, and on the corner, where a bar door opened to music and laughter, Miles caught a brief, decrepit whiff of wet carpet before it closed again. In a circular park, at the base of a large, lighted evergreen, a sleeping-bagged body rested, or maybe was dead, against a vinyl fence printed with bank advertisements. Overhead, an empty train crawled by, slow as a toy.

Their destination was a former department store—an imposing brick fortress that took up the whole block, its upper stories stacked like a Lego construction. From far away it didn't seem particularly sad, but as they neared,

Miles saw that every other window was edged by dark, jagged glass; that the ground level was cased in green plywood tagged and scribbled on, phone numbers and phrases, the crude outlines of penises and boobs. Through a gap in the boards, Miles peered: the glass of the ground-floor windows had that paraffin sheen of the long abandoned. A banner on the second story announced demolition. "They're not serious," Tez said. "Can't be. Can't blow up a landmark. You know who used to work here? Diana Ross. Swear to god. In the cafeteria, spoonin' creamed corn."

Caleb said their dad creamed himself for Diana Ross; would cream corn on himself if he heard that.

They moved along the southern edge, then around the back by the loading docks, where Tez gripped the fence and gave it a rattle, as if testing its integrity, and Miles's heart beat faster. The weight pulling down their bags, the subtle clanking as they moved, the paint dapples on the skin of Tez's right wrist, and, now that Miles thought of it, the fumy odor in the van, detectable even above the weed—Caleb and his friends had referenced tagging plenty, in San Francisco, but it was impossible to know where their real involvement figured, where embellishment ended and truth began, nor had Miles ever imagined he'd find himself along, someday, for the ride. All at once he was scared. Not of getting in trouble (trouble was abstract, unfamiliar), but of finding himself *unable* to rise to whatever unknown challenges came. If they asked him to hop the fence, for starters, or if they didn't ask him at all but proceeded to scale it, easy as squirrels, then disappeared inside the building without so much as looking back, while he remained, stranded, on the other side.

They didn't hop the fence; they crawled under it, at a part where it splayed up and the concrete underneath was busted. Tez pushed his bag through, then wiggled under headfirst, while Caleb easily followed. At Miles's turn the two wrenched the fencing up as high as they could from the inside, and Miles, too, bellied under, made it. By the time he was on his feet Tez was already up on a dumpster, testing a foothold along a drainage pipe, hoisting himself into a busted second-story window. Caleb and Miles waited with their backs against brick, hidden between dumpsters. The sun—or a faded relative of the sun—had showed up, Miles noticed, for this last hour of the day.

"You cool?" Caleb asked, breathing hard. "Shit's like *The Crow* out here, right?" Miles could hear something unfamiliar—an anxious beating in his brother's voice.

"I never saw that," he said. Remembering briefly that Chris had loved it. His own voice was strange, too—low, just skimming the surface of fear. A smear of mud appeared down the front of his new jacket.

A minute later, a metal side door opened at the top of a loading dock, and Tez appeared, the red of his hat like a beacon.

When they pulled the door shut behind them, the darkness was as thick and consuming as time in a dream. Then Caleb laughed, and Tez switched on a flashlight, and the space—a storeroom of endless shelves, some spectacularly overturned, arranged itself. Armless mannequins lay in a heap of compromised positions they had to step over.

The storeroom led to a short staircase and then a huge, columned lobby, spacious room after room that stretched away into darkness. In front of them, escalators rose with their guts all exposed, stripped of their steps, and a bank of elevators waited, doorless. A still-intact chandelier hung, caked in dust so thick no glitter or shine remained.

They climbed a once-grand staircase where light came in dull, matted. Paint hung in strips from the walls, made blistery bulges along the ceiling. Signs of visitors—splayed magazines and dirty bedding, spent syringes and Brillo pads, strange semblances of furniture and garbage bags—appeared randomly in corners. "Squatters," Tez said. "If we run into anybody, let me talk." When, on the fourth floor, they came across a lone teddy bear propped to sitting in a folding chair (a sentinel, a bouncer?), Miles resisted the impulse to grab Caleb's hand. If it were just the two of them, he might have—though if it were just the two of them, they wouldn't be here in the first place. If Miles was Caleb's shadow, Caleb was now Tez's—like those cutouts you did in construction paper, folded figures all linked at the edges.

Donkeys, lions, smiling elephants paraded across the wall in a fading procession. Their feet disappeared in water damage. "Kid zone up here," Tez said, leading them past the paintings. Into the building's darker depths.

Miles touched something in his pocket—the wrapper of a Gary's mint. "What are we doing?" he found the courage to ask.

Caleb swung his messenger bag around and unclasped it. Tez did the same with his backpack. Between them, they had three cans of black spray paint, two white, one red. "Art projects," Tez said, pulling from his pocket a Ziploc of plastic bits—caps, Miles saw—and tossing this down.

"You know what lookouts do?" Caleb asked. "It's pretty much all in the name."

Tez picked up a can of black and shook it so it rattled. To Caleb he said, "He doesn't have to, whatever. It's chill here." Then to Miles, he said, "Amateur hour." The eye—the bad one—had a way of sweeping across its intended subject before it veered away again. "I wouldn't take you anywhere that wasn't chill. Not yet at least." He smiled.

Tez and Caleb posted up away from the windows, at a wall already tagged but noncommittally—by kids, it looked like, just fooling around. Miles peered down the stairs they'd just climbed—the lobby floor was vertiginously far—but when he heard nothing but the paint cans' hiss and was satisfied no one was around, he wandered into other rooms, wondering how long graffiti took—wondering how much the smell would stick to his clothes, the way it stuck to the upholstery of the Odyssey. Miniature pants and dresses must have hung here; the familiar sound of hangers on a rack; Diana Ross in the bathroom, hustling into a hairnet. How could a store in America careen from that down into this? A wall of windows showed the flat gray tops of downtown's roofs, the green patina of an ornate nearby tower, the sky going orange like an illusion of warmth. Only once he heard something—but when he turned, expecting one of the zombies from Caleb's story—it was only a rat, skittering along the far perimeter. He hurried back in the boys' direction, trying not to think of what might be behind him.

Caleb's piece—*MUNI*—struck Miles at once as bad: balloon-animal shapes that grew in size so that the I was twice as fat as the stems of the M before he went back over them, sketching crudely with the spray to fatten them up. On the adjacent wall, Tez was finishing something twice as large, rounded white letters that marshmallowed into each other, outlined in red, dropping a black shadow. It took Miles a minute to read Tez's word, but then it popped into place—*KARMA*. He'd U-turned the cross of the final A into an arrow that stretched up and over, pointing to a tagged *Muni 1* in the upper left corner, the words *Little Bro* floating beneath; was adding, in fluid motions now, action marks that made the text vibrate. Miles's heart thumped. That was *him*. For better or worse, he'd made an impression—*Little Bro*—was not, at least, invisible. When Tez turned in the darkening room (could he feel Miles watching? Could he feel the mesmerism that had glazed, already, Miles's heart?), his face was beatific. Miles wasn't sure which he wanted more: Tez, or the feeling on Tez's face.

And then it was over. Photos snapped, down the stairs, back onto the loading dock and into the cold dusk, the wide, unpeopled sidewalk. In the van, Caleb turned up the heater and rubbed his hands together. A police cruiser pulled up beside them, the faces inside swiveling to look, then drove on again. Tez turned to Miles. "Bigger fish to fry than kids at summer camp."

Caleb let out a blustery howl and turned up the music, rapping along. *As red as my eyes get I still rock the fly shit.* "Let's light it!" He swung open the glove compartment and pulled out a baggie, a lighter, a packet of papers with the bearded guy on the front and the old-fashioned letters that appropriately zigged and zagged. Letters, Miles thought, in momentary wonderment. He'd never seriously considered *letters* before. The crazy variety of styles in which something so everyday could exist.

"Paging Miles," Caleb said, licking the paper. To Tez he said, "He's fried already."

Caleb sucked, Tez sucked, and then the joint was there in front of him, an offering from Tez, its burning end facing away. It was delicate and light in his fingers; with his lips, he sought some trace of Tez's mouth but tasted only paper. *This is weed*, he thought. *So I'm smoking weed.*

"Remember what the prez taught us," Caleb coached, "you have to *inhale*, or it doesn't count."

Miles sucked, held it, and then breathed in a second time—a seeming redundancy until his throat singed and he thought he might choke. A cough exploded and the car filled with smoke. In the front seat, hands were clapping.

A moment later or in the same moment, they were driving toward food. Tez was calling them "the Doobie Brothers," which made Caleb giggle harder each time he said it. At a red light Tez turned to Miles, his bad eye shadowed, his good one glistening. "You okay back there?"

Miles could almost feel his brain cells flaring and then dying, the gauzy trails of their last gasps. His tongue was like a sock. His nose seemed coated in paint. He was happier than he'd ever been. "I think I got the munchies," he said. Knowing it would make them laugh.

They ordered al pastor tacos and Cokes from an outdoor stand in the potholed parking lot of a carniceria. Despite the cold the cooks wore T-shirts, flipping the scrambled, sizzling meat with big, gleaming spatulas. The cilantro was slimy and the limes yellow-skinned, but even so the food was delicious, greasy and sweet and reminiscent of home. Miles licked his fingers. In the warmth of the van, they ate like inhaling.

A curvy girl in a short jacket, with hoops in her ears so large they rested askew on her shoulders, walked out of the market and over to the stand. She stood there studying the menu taped up on a series of paper plates, idly playing with her braid.

"I'd hit that," Caleb said over his food. "Haven't seen Mexican pussy in hella long."

Humiliation blushed Miles's cheeks, but he didn't cough or move or say anything. He thought of Kimber's chest—his failure to care. When Miles looked at the girl with the braid, he saw only a girl with a braid.

In the passenger seat, Tez looked up, then back at his plate. He, too, seemed to will the comment to pass over, unheard.

Maybe because he was annoyed with them, or in an effort to catch her eye, or because he really did need to pee, Caleb flung open the door and hopped out, dropped his plate in the trash bucket not three feet from the girl (who hardly glanced), then strode to the back of the lot, faced the fence, assumed a stance. Emptied of his presence, the distance between Miles in the backseat and Tez in the front seemed suddenly small. Caleb had set the song about graffiti on repeat, but now Tez pressed Stop. Miles waited for him to say something—aware that he was waiting—and then, incredibly, he did.

"So, you know who your mom is?" he asked. He turned the radio on and moved down the dial.

Miles swallowed. "No."

"Me neither, really," Tez said. Talk, guitars, pop snippets jingled and faded between static. "Mine died when I was ten. We used to live in Queens."

Could Tez hear him breathing, or was the sound of Miles's breath only audible in the immediate vicinity of his own ears? "How'd she die?"

Tez stopped on a station where a low horn moaned, then rose, like a voice. "Cancer. Moved here to live with my grandpa. He makes all those crazy sculptures."

An instant passed in which Miles could think of no worthy reply—considered, *What about your dad?*—but Tez went on, "You think you'll find her ever? Or, like, hypothetical, if she came looking for you, you'd give her the time of day? Walk in a park with her or some shit, like on TV?"

Miles considered this. Many times, he'd imagined a woman like the mom from *The Cosby Show* apprehending him in the grocery store (*Miles? It's me, your mother. Don't you remember?*). But his imagination failed him beyond that; the fantasy always ended with his reaction—pride at having been reclaimed, or instant, biological love, or the shame of not recognizing her face—and melded, then, into a story his real mother told him each year on his birthday, of a kind of hallucination. Those first weeks after they'd brought him home, mother and baby would doze together in the afternoons, fed and warm in the big bedroom, until she'd wake with a start: an unmistakable weight in her womb and the visceral surety that Miles was inside her, stirring, before reality settled again and she saw him, in the bassinet actually, already born.

"I already have a mom," Miles said. And then, because something about Tez made him want to be honest, even if it meant risking silliness, he added, "She loves me a lot." He knew it, of course, with the force of something he never actually thought about.

The door swung open, and Caleb threw himself back in the driver's seat. "Fuckin *jazz*? Dude, my *grandpa* likes this shit."

"Mine, too," Tez said. Then he turned to Miles. "Don't forget it, now."

That eye. That one eye, and Miles thought of something Chris had said.

"Don't forget what?" Caleb asked.

Tez put his seat belt back on. The horns harmonized, then separated. "Just going over lookout protocol."

"Oh yeah?"

"For next time. Right, Miles?"

Miles sought the rearview mirror for Tez again but saw only the frizz of his hair. His head was bent, reigniting the joint. "Yeah," he said coolly. "Next time."

MILES was lookout in an abandoned plant in a Polish part of town. He was lookout from the glassless windows of a school whose halls drifted surreally with piles of books, and from the doorway of a closed and chained liquor store, and from the forested roof of a picked-clean warehouse where, Tez said, last winter a body had been found, hanging in the elevator shaft, suspended in a column of ice like a bug trapped in amber. He was lookout along frozen train tracks, on a wooded freeway embankment, at the icicled mouth of a cavernous, unused underpass where he'd given the signal to bail, but the stirring in the snowy brush turned out to be only a possum, red-eyed as a rodent ghost.

Caleb tried to roast him for that, but Tez came to his defense: *Who knows, man, that possum coulda been packin' some fuckin' prison shank, got territorial.* Even as Miles got over it, he couldn't help reliving the fear that burst up his spine in those long, quiet minutes standing guard at invisible thresholds (because what if someone *did* appear? Other taggers, bored gangsters, drooling warlocks wielding weapons—what good would it do to hoot the ridiculous faux owl call Caleb had taught him, into the dark bowels of the building?). And yet at the same time, the notion of real danger in Tez's vicinity seemed almost impossible. Circled by a halo of immunity, a kind of force field of safety cast by five letters, *KARMA* was a talisman violence wouldn't dare approach. As if Tez, superheroically, were the *real* lookout, his untethered eye capable of X-ray vision, of predicting the future. The power was tested Miles's fourth night out, when the silhouettes of two men appeared around back of the ruinous shell of a St. Aubin Street factory before the boys had even pulled out their paint. Miles was scanning the perimeter in the opposite direction—the men came around the other side (cops, he thought at first, but no—they weren't uniformed, wore winter coats, and dragged their steps; junkies, maybe) and one hollered, his voice mean, *Hey—hey now*, as he reached inside his coat. Tez led the escape—nowhere to go but down the snowy hillside, sliding into the wet gulch fifty feet below. *Too much work for them to follow*, Tez panted when they were all together, crouching in the sog behind a wall of brush. Miles's pulse rang in his ears, having sensed, for the first time, the threat of a weapon—even just its possibility—at his back. Up above, the figures moved back toward the structure. Miles's palms were shredded and bleeding. Caleb had torn his Dickies and lost his beanie. *They're not interested. We're fine.* Tez—Tez was unmarred.

Later, they swung by a liquor store Tez said would sell to toddlers, and, because the relief of their escape had brought a certain levity to the night, Tez and Miles even agreed, at Caleb's urging, to stop at an all-ages show Caleb had been hoarding a flyer for. Bursts of sound, equipment frying out, screeched from a skinny Victorian. Out on the street, Tez raised his chin in small hellos to several kids but didn't join their groups—seemed content to stand with Miles alone. *Let me see*, he asked, and poured water from a plastic bottle over the scrapes on Miles's palms, then took them in his own hands, turning them, inspecting them—*You'll be okay. Use some peroxide when you get home.* Down the sidewalk, Caleb was talking to two girls, throwing his arm back over his head in a kind of armpit-baring flex, scratching at his neck. *I ever tell you about my encounter with Chainsaw Dude?* Tez asked, popping open his can. *Over in North End—we were in this cut, trees all around, just doin' our thing, when we heard it—I almost shit my pants—bbbbbzzzz, buzzzzz, and this dude yells out, 'Hey, fellas, it's cool—just cuttin' me some firewood for winter!' At three o'clock in the fuckin' morning! Old Man Dee-troit Winter stockin' up, no big deal.* But Miles could hardly concentrate. Tez had touched his hands like that, so gently. He was wondering what Tez's arms would feel like, encircling him, pulling him close, their hearts meeting chest to chest. Out the backseat window an hour later, the night moved by cold and black and as unpunctuated as reverie.

When school started back up, days inevitably passed in which Miles couldn't accompany Caleb, and he fell into mean sulks that rivaled those first weeks after the move. Then Friday rolled around again and Caleb whispered, *Tonight, okay?* As soon as Tez appeared again—long-striding it down the walk or waiting on the corner outside Can-Do, the hardware store where he worked, that smiling, two-eyed look on his face that matched so perfectly the image of Miles's daydreams—his despair dried up, seemed ridiculous in hindsight. By way of excuses, he invented and exaggerated friends he'd only partially made, left Mom and Dad first names without lasts on countertop Post-its, feigned forgetfulness over phone numbers and addresses, fabricated sleepovers and school projects and whole drama-club productions, entire set crews, in order to explain away the secondhand spray of paint on his shoes and cuffs. (*But how do I lie?* he asked Caleb. *Dude, don't be a pussy. Just own it. Dive into it. Lying is a part of life. You better learn how; you're in high school now—it's practically expected.*) Once, the three of them spent a valuable midnight hour searching for a pay phone in Russell Woods, one that wouldn't pick up the howling of sirens, just so Miles could call home with a generic update: *I think we need just another two hours probably. I'll call the restaurant and have Caleb pick me up after work!* If the bottom fell out of a story at any time, he'd need to have a second story ready, Caleb advised: a girl he liked, a party he was at, something normal freshmen did—*What you have to remember is that never in a billion fucking years would they guess what you're* actually *doing, right?*

What *was* he actually doing? To Caleb, he was simply fulfilling his little-brother role. But what Caleb failed to notice was all the noticing Miles was doing in the process, all the looking and listening and learning as they drove around the city—all the mental practicing, and the buoyant realizing: *I could do it, too.* In the car, on foot, Tez read them the landscape like translating hieroglyphs—marks, scratches, nonsense, waiting for an expert to interpret. *WAXMAN, 2TIME, RANK, MEEK*: moniker, crew, real name, story. Waxman, known for his calligraphic flourishes, was a freak enigma, a train-hopping transplant from Philly via Houston via Saint Louis, where he'd brought along the SLT crew, all of them living out in a crusty, ramshackle

compound in a Jeff Chalmers field. Nomor was a revered veteran (Caleb
cruised them past a vintage *NOMOR '93* on the wall around a scrap yard)
whose wide-legged characters reminded Tez of his childhood, holding his
breath on the IRT platform as a rainbow car rolled into view. *2TIME, ORF,
MADNIS*, up sporadically and in pairs, were old news—they'd all stopped
writing a year before, mostly gone over, now, by *CLONE* and *BLUZE*, macho
white boys from the 'burbs who beefed with MC crew—*MEEK* and *CARL*—
young Black dudes, Detroit natives, known for scrappy hangovers and impossible freeway stunts, *the real deal*. Shit had peaked a month ago when Clone
and Bluze teamed up with two Swedish train writers to burn, notoriously,
the People Mover, until Meek and Carl and a handful of young apprentices
one-upped them, bombed half the length of the Chicago-bound Amtrak during its three-minute station stop, topping every one of Carl's Cs suggestively
with Viking horns. Meek was locked up now for shattering Clone's ribs in
a parking lot on Joy Road, but Carl's girl was involved somehow, too, and a
long-circulating rumor that Bluze slipped roofies at parties.

"But what about . . . like, how does beef . . ." Miles didn't know how to
phrase it. What he wanted to ask was, how does *paint* become competitive?
Where lay the boundary between *field trips* and this more dangerous world?
"I mean, what kind of trouble—"

Caleb blurted, "It's *crime*, Miles—I mean, seriously? What did you think
we were doing, just fucking *pretending* to commit—"

But Tez cut in. "At the end of the day, beef isn't about spray paint." It
grew out of everything behind and around the paint, he explained, the egos
at the center of it, some of which were rotten. "It's just like in life. You have
your good people and your bad people. Or your trustworthy people and your
shady ones. I guess the hard part is figuring out who's who."

One tag, *KURU*—clean, legible, mirroring itself at the fold between the
syllables—seemed to be everywhere. Like a symbol, like a brand, they encoun-
tered it large and small, *KURU*s scribbled and perfected, glass-etched and
sticker-stuck, so often that it didn't always consciously register but staked its
claim just the same. A handful of times, they passed *KURU*s and *KARMA*s

together, in shared colors or at uniform heights, floating atop clouds, their styles similarly simple, equally legible. But beyond saying the strange moniker out loud (after Caleb had stumbled: *Ku-tu? Ku-ku?*) Tez volunteered none of the commentary, none of the context, that had become so usual.

"So, what's up with him?" Caleb finally pressed, turning down the radio. They passed under a viaduct scrolled *KURU KARMA KURU*, so close together they formed a pattern. "You guys used to write together, obviously."

"Sorta," Tez said. "Sometimes."

"Dude's hella up."

"I guess."

"Wow. Karma doesn't want to talk about it."

Tez turned the radio up again, but Caleb flipped it off. "What the fuck is *kuru*, anyway?"

Tez exhaled. From the backseat, Miles could see the flare and release of his left nostril. "You know what kuru is?" Miles had been quiet, but now Tez turned toward him. "It's a disease cannibals get from eating brains. For real. From people eating people. Makes you go crazy." He turned to Caleb again. "Then you die a lonely motherfucker 'cause you ate all your friends." He turned the radio back on but kept the volume low. "We used to be crew."

In other places, Miles began to notice, *KARMA*s had been covered by *KURU*s, the second laid flatly over the first in colors that obliterated—white over black, black over red, red over yellow. Accompanying these were the letters *CT*, slanted or stamped like a copyright: *City of Terror*, Tez explained, or *Carnage Time*. "Whatever you want. Fill in the blank."

"Cock tease," Caleb said. "Clown toy."

"Like the CT on your jacket?" Miles ventured.

Tez placed his right hand on his heart, as if to make sure the felt letters were still there. "Cass Tech, man. This was my dad's. It's—I know it's weird, but that shit's pure coincidence. I mean, the jacket and the crew. Kuru loved that. Thought it was fate or something, bringing us together."

On one occasion, Caleb's headlights grazed a pink, straight-lettered *KARMA* on a Bagley roll-up gate—*Whoa, slow down, slow down*, Tez urged—crossed out with a single line of black, and, in prosaic all-caps arcing above, the words *CWEER TRAITOR*. Another CT.

The van still slowing, Tez swung open the door and hopped out, against Caleb's objections, hauling his backpack with him. They were right in the exposed middle of downtown, close enough to a club that the crunch of bass, hollow and industrial, pulsed up from underground. Through the window, Miles watched Tez shake two cans at once, reach his right arm up to full extension, and begin the fast, elliptical motion that marked Karma's tag—an ovular scribble cut through with the peaking M. A car sped past, churning through the muck. Another car, and then a bus. One tag, two tags, three—while Caleb chanted *Come on, come on, come on*, checking the rearview. Another car, a purple cab, and then a box truck passed: emblazoned on its hatch with the sixth *KURU* they'd seen that night. Miles had been counting.

"How have we not run into him?" Caleb asked, annoyed, when Tez was done and they'd peeled off. "If he's so up."

They pulled into a parking lot to smoke. "Truthfully," Tez said, thumbing open an Altoids case, "it's only a matter of time."

His real name, Tez told them, was, disarmingly, *Drew*. His family owned two commercial blocks in Grosse Pointe, a dairy in St. Claire Shores, apartment buildings in Warren and Roseville. "That I know of," Tez said.

Caleb laughed. "Some rich little shit? What could he do? Dude's not gonna fuck with three of us."

Long seconds passed. Tez pinched at the weed, then crumbled it into the trough the paper made. He licked and rolled, meeting Miles's eyes in the rearview. "If we ever do run into him—you both gotta swear—you'll let me handle it, right? I know the dude. Know how he works. Unfortunately."

A calendar week later (had Caleb's question somehow summoned him?) Kuru did appear, though not in the way Miles had worried he might. They'd taken to frequenting a certain Midtown coney precisely because it was a spot, Tez admitted, where Kuru didn't go. And yet there he was, beneath the fluorescence on the other side of the counter, sharing a booth with two dudes Caleb and Tez's age.

The waitress, Yolanda, told Tez, "Your friend's here," pouring water from a plastic pitcher. She and Tez had gone to high school together. "What's his name? Mean-lookin'? Shit-eatin' grin?"

"How do you know we're friends?" Tez said. His voice came out carefully, quietly.

Yolanda rolled her eyes. "Come on, Tez. Two white boys who dress the same? In this city? Anyway, you were together at that Halloween thing."

Through the panes of the pie case, Kuru slouched, big and Bic-headed, his arm stretched out over the seatback, taking up the whole booth. He laughed heartily at something his tablemate must have said. A blond tuft of beard shook as if pasted on. He scratched at it. There were tattoos everywhere.

Miles felt his pulse in his neck. It wasn't that Drew was so terrifying to behold—it was the disturbance of watching Tez rip his hat off and sink his posture, his face drained, suddenly, of color.

Caleb giggled idiotically, edging forward to see. "So that's him, huh?"

"Y'all know, or you need a minute?" Yolanda asked Tez. She clicked her pen. Her hair was cropped at the ears and clipped back in a way that accentuated her cheekbones. A faint line showed along her temple where makeup met real skin.

"Onion rings, extra crispy," Caleb said, straining to see Drew. "And coffee. Extra hot."

"Don't," Tez mumbled. He didn't put his hand up to block them—that would've been too obvious—but Miles felt him erecting a mental shield, a boundary of magical separation that prevented evil from penetrating good. So far, it was working. Drew laughed, the beard bobbed, and his vision didn't wander past the bounds of the pie case. "Nobody even look."

Caleb frowned. "Well somebody's shakin' in his fuckin' boots, huh? What if we need to piss?"

In a small voice, Miles admitted, "I kind of need to pee," then hated himself.

"Man, just trust me, okay?" Tez said to Caleb. "Best thing we can do is eat our grub, get outta here, no eye contact, no problems."

Caleb leaned forward. "He's not gonna try shit with three of—"

Yolanda clicked her pen. "Y'all, I got tables."

"'Cause if he wants to start something, man, you know I'm ready; I don't care who the fuck he is; we *got you*, right, Miles?"

It was enough to make Tez's lip twitch up. A small grunt sounded in his throat, something approaching a laugh. "Waffle for me," he said to Yolanda. "Sorry."

Miles said, "Same."

He *did* have to pee—and now that he'd said it out loud, the pressure in his bladder doubled so that he squirmed uncomfortably, youngly, in his seat. Caleb was lying to Tez about his exploits in San Francisco—some tall tale that involved hopping the fence into the Muni yard, *bombing the fuck out of three buses back to back*—when Tez turned to Miles and kicked his duck boot. "Man, *go*. Don't give yourself a fuckin' infection. Just don't look at him."

Blushing but released, Miles made his way to the restroom, his eyes trained carefully on the scuffed floor, the wooden restroom door. But drying his hands on his jeans, opening the door, and dodging a waitress with a wide tray, his mind was blurry with the usual mixed wonderment and insecurity and euphoria that came over him any time he was in close proximity to Tez (that kick beneath the table—that flirting, physical kick!) and he glanced in the forbidden direction at just the moment that the big, bald man looked up. Miles's heart stopped. Despite the surrounding clatter of forks against plastic, of ketchup leaving glass, of talk and mastication, the room went silent between their eyes. His pupils, Miles saw, were pinpricks.

Miles pulled his gaze away and hurried forward. But Kuru reached a jacketed arm out to block him. "Hey bud, slow down, slow down, huh?"

His forehead bulged, hippoish and stupid, and his face was blotched with rashy islands. Tattooed around his neck were two skeleton hands, inked in a permanent choke. Above the burnt-potato smell, Miles thought he caught a whiff of Gillette—fumes coming off Kuru's gleaming, globular head, freshly shaved. "Don't be scared, man. We have friends in common." When he smiled, the skin on his face looked too tight—as if it might burst.

Kuru withdrew his arm and offered his hand. When Miles reached his own out to shake, the grip closed and clamped. "Hey," Miles said.

"I seen you over there with Tez—we're old friends, me and Tez—how do you know him?"

He didn't turn to see Kuru's buddies, close by on his right, but he heard them, suppressing their entertainment. "I just know him," Miles stuttered. "From around."

This made Drew chuckle. "*Oooooooh*. From *around*. I like it. So, you two are what he finds, huh, left to his own devices? *From around*. Makes sense. Look, what's your name? I didn't get your name."

"Mi—Michael," Miles said. Feeling the eyes of the second audience now—the eyes behind him. Knowing Tez must be watching, too. Watching Miles fail him.

"And what do you write, *Michael*? You write *MUNI*, or is that the other toy?"

Miles wanted to swallow but had no spit. "I'm not Muni."

Drew laughed again, and his upper half shook. The tattoo—a needle poking on repeat into your neck, Miles thought, must have been unfathomably painful. *What kind of person signs up for that?* "Well you're lucky there, man, cause that shit is fuckin' wretched. So, okay, look, little Michael—I'm not trying to interrogate you, man. You just tell your bud Karma I miss him. Okay? Just that. Kuru misses him. Oh—and tell him to lose the jacket. He can't be sportin' that shit, after what we've been through. Can you remember all that?"

He was saved by Yolanda, who came up with the check. "You boys bein' nice?" Miles stepped back to let her in. His eyes were free again. Heavy-footed, he slipped away, pushed and pulled by a force outside himself.

AFTER SCHOOL the next day, Miles walked to the downtown bookstore, bought a new blank journal and three Sharpies. In the back of Café Ambrosia he nibbled a stale cookie, stared at the college kids, then slipped on his head-phones and opened the book. *So please, please, please, let me, let me, let me . . .* He wrote *SMITHS, MUTT, OGRE, PLEASE* before the word appeared to him: *CRUSH*—his crush, the truth of it. A revelation—a camouflaged confession. In the weeks since they'd met, Miles had spent countless hours (in bed, in class, on the couch, in the car) conjuring and holding the specific architecture of Tez's face, the choreography of his stride, the cadence of his voice and the tickle of New York accent, the exact memory of some phrasing and intonation, as if to let the slightest detail of Tez slip would be somehow to lose him, the *possibility* of him, entirely and forever. Each replay afforded the chance that some deeper message broadcast by Tez, overlooked before, might now be uncovered. And yet, at the completion of its cycle, this hope gave way, again and again, to a stomach-dropping guilt. The pressure of so much want, so much hope, so much *unknowing* was relentless. It amazed Miles, how quickly elation could plummet into despair. *For once in my life, let me, let me, let me . . .*

He filled seventeen pages with *CRUSH*es in every imaginable style, then walked home in the eyelash-freezing dark.

ON A STEELY Friday evening, the sun already down, Caleb and Miles were just past Ann Arbor's outskirts when Caleb cut the stereo volume. It was the part on *Enter* that Miles always braced himself for, where the Wu threatened to shove burning hangers up each other's butts, to hang each other from skyscrapers by their dicks. "Look, I want to tell you something," Caleb said.

Miles's long johns were giving him a wedgie, but he didn't dare rise up to pick it now. That morning, their parents had driven north for the weekend, to snowshoe and scout vacation homes on the lake, entrusting Caleb as *babysitter*—though really, their mother had whispered into Miles's ear, it was more like the other way around. *Just don't let him do anything you wouldn't do, okay?*

Caleb drove with both hands firmly at ten and two, his eyes fixed to the freeway with uncharacteristic alertness. "What I want to say is, I don't care if you're gay. That's what I wanted to tell you. I mean, I don't want to *hear* about it, what it's like . . . *smoking pole* or whatever—I just—I'm saying this as your brother because I don't know who else will. It's going to make shit harder for you. Way harder. That, plus being mixed. I'm seeing the way you look at

Tez and I'm tellin' you, man, be cool. I don't wanna see you get your ass beat because you're, like, drooling over some dude who doesn't appreciate—"

"I'm not gay!" Miles exploded. His voice was strangled and dry. *Just own it. Dive into it. Lying is a part of life.* He hated Caleb, for making him have to say it.

Caleb sighed, glancing in his direction. When he turned the music back up, they were rapping, at least.

Miles was crawling into the backseat before the van had properly stopped. Loping out of the hardware store, Tez spun his hat on his index finger, though it was ten degrees out and only getting colder. He whistled.

"Damn, what's with this crew?" he asked, yanking on the seat belt. "You guys have a fight?" He turned from Caleb to Miles. "Some Ann Arbor shit? Who got the last chocolate-chip cookie?"

Later, the night was dark enough, the van smoky enough, and Caleb and Tez lost enough in shouting along with Method Man that Miles was able to slip two cans of paint out of the backseat milk crate and up under his jacket.

"Post up here," Caleb ordered him, indicating the nook of an alley between two empty apartment buildings. Tez leapt and clung to the lowest rung of a fire escape, pulled himself up, and was on the roof in seconds, Caleb following a story below. Soon Miles heard the rattle of their cans and Caleb's laughter. Edging to the sidewalk, he wandered left, where streetlights cast their occasional, eerie pools. Six lanes of empty boulevard. No movement except the wind, which lifted and hovered a shower cap, then floated it like a jellyfish toward the big black gash of night. He shook his first can up under his shirt to muffle, as best he could, the sound, then walked back into the alley.

The challenge was in controlling the flow of paint from vessel to nozzle, from cap to wall. It was about gauging the liquid density, then committing to the gesture from beginning to end. When he hesitated, when he paused and doubted, it all fell apart—the letter dribbled and sagged and the word buckled in on itself, afraid. But when he was confident—when he imagined the line in the split second before he actualized it, repeating nothing to himself but *crush, crush, crush*, it was hardly different from practicing in the black book. The stream of color became an extension of his arm and his arm an extension of his heart, crushing love into every curving S.

By the time Tez and Caleb were back on the ground, Miles had reached the end of the sixty-foot wall, crouching and rising and reaching with his eyes closed, spraying or pretending to spray, hardly caring that he'd run out of paint several tags back.

4.

IT STRUCK HIM AS DEEPLY UNJUST. THE REWARDS MILES WAS magically, overnight, reaping.

For Caleb's whole teenage career, and even before that, he'd devoted himself to the sole occupation of *figuring it out*—*it* being *life*, and *life* being *coolness*. Where to go, what to say, how to say it, how to listen or not listen, what to wear, what to smoke, what kind of girls, what to care about versus what to laugh at, what to call *jock* or *poser* on, and how to firewall yourself, in all circumstances, against criticism from anyone uncool, less than cool. Painting, skating, hip-hop—and now Detroit, graffiti, a bud like Tez: Caleb's reality had pulled a fast one-eighty this last month, from the desolation of jerking it in the forest that frozen night to the present pitch rising in his heart as he scaled a ladder beneath Tez, the city as quiet and dark as a child's play fort. He was happy—there was no other word for it—he was smack in the middle of his own active happiness. Adrenaline made a box around his concentration, so that all he saw was the color saturating its mark, and then, stepping back, the frame widening to accommodate the whole view, his own *MUNI*, upright and proud, visible and recognizable, *his*. Even if a throw-up wasn't good (they often weren't, but they were getting better—even Tez said so), there it was, permanent or at least suggesting permanence. Something he'd long been practicing was, finally, culminating. On a day in the future, he'd return to the 415 with a hard wisdom in his voice, a mystery about him like Tez's, hinting at things he'd done (survived?) in real life that his friends had only seen in music videos.

But what about Miles? What was graffiti, what was Detroit, for *him*? It couldn't be a culmination because no work had gone in before—nothing had ever *accumulated*. He'd taken none of the risks Caleb had—all those bad grades, punishments, fights with Mom and Dad, lies that made his heart pound—following, instead, the rules, telling the truth, earning Bs, clicking through the Oregon Trail on the living room desktop. The worst things Miles had done were in his own imagination—whatever nastiness he dreamed of with Chris, now Tez—images that left a sulfuric taste in Caleb's mouth.

What Caleb wanted to say to Miles was: *Get your own life.* Get your own friends, interests, paint—*Pay your own way*—because vying for what Caleb had (rightfully) earned (all by *himself*) made his fur bristle and his back arch, his hands grip tight around what he had (that elusive spraying joy, and the sweetness of Tez's companionship). And he wanted to tell Miles to toughen the fuck up already. Wipe that sorry-for-yourself, broken-winged-baby-bird look off your pudgy face. Especially when you look at Tez. When all he's doing is buying a fucking pack of gum at the gas station. Staring at him in a way that begs *Love me! Love me!*

That one tag (that stupid fucking tag!), and Tez's focus shifted away from Caleb, squarely onto Miles. *CRUSH*, of all the words, queerest of the queer, and their lookout was promoted to crew. *All crewed up now*, Tez had taken to declaring, apropos of nothing, even though Caleb wondered aloud (chill—careful not to reveal even the edges of his envy) who would look out now? No big deal, Tez said, so long as everybody checked their shit, watched their backs, stayed alert. *In crew, everyone is equal.* Accordingly, when it came to deciding on a name, Caleb lost, two against one. Tez and Miles wanted TLC—Three Lost Children, The Loser Club—a name Caleb thought was stupid, played-out, too referential. *As in the girl group? As in tender loving care? I don't get it.* And Tez sang, *Don't go chasin' waterfalls, please stick to the rivers and the lakes that you're used to . . .*

The nights Miles didn't come along (school nights, nights he couldn't escape Mom and Dad's awareness), Tez would climb in the van, look to the empty backseat, and ask, disappointed, *Where's little Crush?*—liking the feeling of a protégé, Caleb thought, liking the novelty of a preternaturally good fifteen-year-old tagalong. *Tagalong*: its double meaning matching Caleb's double irritation that not only had Miles stolen the spotlight, he *was* better—much better (impressive, verging on miraculous)—than Caleb, better, maybe (and the reality enraged him) than whatever Caleb had the potential to become. And yet without Miles around it was, in some ways, worse: Tez was free to talk, ask, gush unchecked (*So you don't think he ever handled paint before? Had somebody showing him shit? Those little feet he's adding on the R and the H, you know what I'm talking about? That shit's dope, reminds me of Mono kinda, straight off the Seven, nuts to think of what he'll be doin' in six months, in six years . . .*), inevitably rehashing the last successful outing: a crazy, balls-out three-color blockbuster on a Conant roof Miles had pulled off in half the time it had taken Caleb to create something half as skilled (*How? How the fuck?* he thought). In the long silences that gapped Tez's praise, as if the two had nothing else to talk about, Caleb knew acutely the pain of being second.

Their spots—limited, at first, to those Tez deemed chill—were changing, too. As Caleb got better and Miles was promoted, Tez, along with taking them higher (they were edging across second-story ledges now and, last week, had pulled hangovers on a Lodge overpass), was also circling them back over ground they'd hit just days before. *KURU*s covered their *KARMA, MUNI, CRUSH*es one for one—*KURU*s that must be gone over again in turn (*KARMA, MUNI, CRUSH*), only to await another eventual erasure. Tag over tag, throw-up over throw-up, piece over piece. Caleb's chest clenched when they returned one night to an upper story of the train station to find his and Tez's spaghetti-lettered *MUNI-KAR* burner eradicated by the ten-foot-high, black-rollered exclamation *KURURULES*. He stood there in the fog of his own breath and just looked—Tez shivering beside him and the lights on the Ambassador Bridge twinkling like a lost cause beyond the missing windows, while Miles walked straight up to it, shaking his can of white, and set about the arduous, multicoat task of vandalizing the vandalism.

In the last few weeks, it seemed to be the start of an endless game, one neither side could win. A stupid game that Caleb had no real investment in. Who the fuck was this Kuru dude anyway, and why was he so bent on beef? *What went down?* Caleb wanted to know. But Tez withdrew, reticent when questioned, protective and afraid—another mood Caleb recognized in Miles. *He'll get tired of it eventually*, was all Tez would say. *Dude's a coward on the inside. Us going over him is just our way of saying we won't be stopped.*

Us. Our. There had been no discussion, no consensus that the crew forming around Tez would make this war its mission. While Tez and Miles went over and went over, Caleb looked for a fresh wall or pillar or side of the box truck to do his own thing, his own way, on his own terms.

And yet another, concurrent phenomenon was helping enormously to soften his irritation. For the first time in months, Caleb was getting laid. Beyond the power he felt in marking territory, the delicious adrenaline high or the rush of pride that came with flipping through fresh prints (those flicks of you crouching by your finished piece making, now, a document of it, a record), Kelsey proved that writing graffiti carried ample fringe benefits. On a night when "little Crush" couldn't get out of algebra tutoring and Caleb didn't have the energy to suffer Tez's questions, Caleb rolled up on an Ann Arbor party that seemed, for once, worth crashing. In a crappy apartment by the Residential College, film majors and philosophy minors and dropouts and townies drank wine out of coffee mugs, smoked inside, formed a line down the hall for a bong called the Event Horizon. Under colored lights in the living room, girls ground in hot, skanky clumps to the Fugees. They looked just as down as SF girls, in their spaghetti straps and jeans tight at the ass but flaring at the socks. A blue gem shone inside the knot of the center girl's belly button. Plastic barrettes—yellow bears—were clipped close to her center part. An hour later, Caleb and Kelsey stood on the back porch waiting for the motion-activated light to go off. *Have you ever been arrested? But what's the highest thing you've ever climbed?* Her mouth was weedy and warm, slick with winter mucus. She gave him head right there in fourteen degrees, amid the garbage-can effluvium—looked up once with a wild and desperate want in her eyes, then dove back into the task. Caleb couldn't believe his good luck.

The first time they met up, he bought her hippie hash at the Fleetwood, then yanked down her tights in the backseat of the van. She lingered in his memory for days. The second time, he went straight to her dorm room after a night out with Tez. She picked up his paint-stained hands, inspected and sucked on the blue digits before he pushed them inside her two at a time. They did other things, too—wholesome things, like ate pizza and listened to music and saw a campus play that one of her friends was in (Caleb couldn't have synopsized the plot if his life depended on it), but these activities passed like school used to between weekend parties, like palate cleansers between courses.

The most he really knew was that Kelsey was a dance major from Dayton, with tits as perfect as halved oranges. She kept herself tidy and shaved and smelling of fruity soap. One night, she whispered into his neck, *You're the hottest guy I've ever seen.*

He whispered back, *Thanks.*

On Friday, Tez called. *Where you been, man?* because Caleb had bailed on last weekend's excursion, and then again on Wednesday, claiming a cold. For days, Miles had been slamming doors and abruptly leaving rooms, switching MTV to VH1 without asking. Now, Caleb coughed meekly into the receiver. "Yeah, still feelin' pretty shitty."

"You better chug some fuckin' Robitussin, 'cause I got a spot for us tomorrow." A billboard along 75 was blank as a canvas between ads, set back enough from the service drive that the deep shadows cast by the crossbars would, if they were quick about it, cover them. Tez wanted to debut their first real crew piece. "Put TLC on the city map. Tough Loving Care or Tender Lost Children. What do you think?" He'd racked the paint, he said, already.

Caleb felt himself frown. His mother walked into the kitchen carrying a stack of mail and a single mitten. She smiled at him and he turned away, careful, always, to hide his left hand. "So that's—that's decided then?"

"You were outbid, brother. Two to one, remember?"

Tez Loves Crush, Caleb thought. *Two Lonely Cocks.*

"You're down, right?" Tez asked. His voice sounded oceans, freeways away.

"I'm down, I'm down," he said. Tomorrow was Valentine's Day. He and Kelsey were supposed to see the new Adam Sandler movie, and afterward, he had a resolute plan to drive out to the bird sanctuary, share a bottle of Jameson, and coax her into anal. "I might bring a friend," he said now, unable to surrender the idea. "But yeah, no worries, they're cool." Careful to avoid *she*. He'd never done anal before.

When he hung up the phone, his mother's smile was still there, tight-lipped and ugly across her face. She looked up from the mail she'd been sorting. "Who was that?"

"Just Tez. From work. He wants to see this movie tomorrow. But, like, I have a date planned, so—"

She scrunched her nose, looked back at the mail. "Kelsey, right? You should bring her over for dinner some night. We'd love to meet her."

Caleb's hands were sweating in his hoodie pocket. "She's not, like, my *girlfriend.*"

His mother frowned, looking up again. "She's—you've been sleeping in her dorm room, right? If I'm to believe your phone calls . . ."

He sighed heavily. Lena should be happy he called home at all. That he should *be* so courteous. He was legally an adult. "Look, it's not like it was when you were my age, you know, going to the sock hop and then getting married or whatever—"

His mother's eyes went hard and her chin jutted forward—an indication that she might, at any moment, bring up the topic of sex in her most antiseptic, I-read-a-parenting-book way. But her jaw remained closed, and she retracted. To the mail, she said only, "I hope I raised a son who respects women."

IT WAS SNOWING and it was going to snow.

Some line from an English-class poem he'd accidentally memorized, but it was unshakably right.

It was snowing, it had been snowing, it would continue to snow all night. Winter (he was beginning to understand what people meant when they groaned about its duration) had a way of compressing time, of packing a whole season into one monotonous span of waning daylight, dry skin, simulated warmth. Traffic crawled on 94, and his eyes itched and blurred. In the slow lane, he followed the taillights of a pickup truck's dangling steel nuts, as hard and frustrated as his own. Already he was thinking he'd made the wrong decision. Could've been sitting in the dark eating Junior Mints, Kelsey's hand down his pants. Instead, she smacked her gum in the passenger seat and sang along to the mix CD she'd made him—some whining Lisa Loeb bullshit he hoped desperately would be over by the time they picked up Tez. Caleb couldn't tell if all girls were this annoying when you weren't pressed up against them, or if this was only particular to the girls he'd been with. No sooner did physical space develop (it had been, what, an hour since they'd made out in her room, and then he'd driven irritably across town to pick up Miles?) than he felt the need to shut her up again, to pull Kelsey back into the silent occupation of bodies only.

She asked Miles questions that had never once crossed Caleb's mind. Every few seconds she'd swivel around abruptly, as if something urgent had just occurred to her, and ask, "What's your favorite food?" or "So where do you think you'll apply to college?" or "So you write graffiti too, huh? What's your word?" and Miles, clearly perplexed as to what Kelsey was doing here, would lift his headphones, ask her to repeat herself, then look to Caleb for guidance.

So the fuck what. Let him wonder why he'd brought her along. Say, *This is what it looks like—to be not even a sliver gay. You keep girls around to watch. A girl watching makes a straight dude feel alive.* Deep in the fibers of his dick, Caleb intuited that without a girl watching, nothing he did quite mattered— was quite real. Make Miles jealous, make him see what he was missing. And make Tez—because where, in the schema of Miles's gluey-eyed crush, *did* Tez stand?—make Tez see clearly the brothers' difference: wake him up to something, observe closely his reaction.

And yet when they picked up Tez, his Timberlands kicking fresh powder down the dark walk, the mood in the car suggested a division. Tez, who'd never ridden in the backseat, now sat next to Miles, and Kelsey, after a timid *Hey*, placed her hand on the back of Caleb's neck. She stroked the shaved hairs there as he drove—a gesture he would've welcomed any other time, but which now felt wifely, ridiculously *laying claim*. He shivered and inched forward.

He could barely hear them behind him. Miles was passing his headphones to Tez, saying something about the tape (all these corny-ass bands from England—Caleb didn't get it) while Tez nodded seriously, sagely, his bad eye bulgy as ever. The stoplights on Brush Street were dark for blocks. Caleb blew the intersections one after another, nearly swiping a hunched body pedaling hard on a mountain bike. It snowed and it was going to snow. "Baby," Kelsey said and was going to say. Making a comment he didn't hear.

In the middle of an empty lot, the billboard stood high and unlit, an air of lonely resignation in its blankness. Slabs of demoed concrete and frozen, churned-up earth made a mound above the embankment, which would obscure them from the freeway, but not the overpass or the frontage road.

"This is the spot," Tez said. "Pretty visible—we gotta be in and out. Or, up and down. Like, twenty minutes tops." Fucking duh, Caleb thought—noticing, for the very first time, that Tez had an annoying habit of stating the obvious. Of liking playing teacher.

Caleb pulled the van into a cut behind a roofless wooden structure whose former life could only be guessed at. He kept the engine running and got out, opened Kelsey's door as she watched Tez in the backseat, divvying up the paint. Under glittery makeup, her eyes were wet with excitement.

"Look, so just get in the driver's seat and stay there," Caleb told her. But he was watching Tez and Miles pack up, distracted. The lid tops were white, silver, a faggy pink. *Pink!* "If you see anything weird," he said, "any cars up the service drive that look like cops or whatever . . . just back out and swing over by the field. We'll see you and come down."

She nodded, climbing out, then nuzzled her head up under his chin. "Be careful, baby."

"She knows to lock the doors?" Tez said as they crossed the field. "Makes me nervous, honestly, having a chick out here."

"Whatever," Caleb said. "No one's out tonight. It's snowing."

"*Psh.* People are out. We might not *see* 'em, doesn't mean they're not out."

"Yeah," Miles piped up. "Like that dude on the bike you almost ran over."

"Look, she practically begged to come. It's like, what the fuck was I supposed to tell her? I'm so fucking sick of jerking it in the shower."

Tez's voice was almost a mumble. "Not the wisest move."

"Fuck, man, let's just figure out this piece." Caleb could feel the blood moving in his neck. It was the only warmth in his whole body. "What's the fucking plan? I don't even know what we're—"

"Crush's leadin' this one," Tez said.

"The Lost Children," Miles said. He had his backpack around on his fat front and was removing cans of white. "All caps, narrow blocks with the shadow dropping up. I'll outline, silver. Tez'll shadow pink. Caleb, you can fill. The bars make a grid already."

Miles piled four cans of white into Caleb's arms. "*What?*" he hissed. *Caleb, you can fill. You* can. What a privilege! "What the fuck is that? Sounds like some kids' movie. I don't even get a say in—"

Tez clamped his hand around Caleb's neck. "Dude, it's *one* fuckin' piece! Plenty more—time for plenty."

They walked the rest of the way in silence, but inside Caleb's head a racket of half-formed arguments raged. He let Tez and Miles go first. Who the fuck cared; he didn't give a shit about *THE LOST CHILDREN*—planned on half-assing his end anyway. If Kelsey hadn't been there he might've just refused—*Fuck it, do it yourselves, bitches*—but how would he explain it, and where would he stand, then, in the crew? The bars of the ladder were slick and freezing even through his gloves, and the ledge was narrow, flimsy-feeling beneath his weight, the ground below dizzyingly far. By the time he found himself hugging the insufficient surface of the board, his anger was gone, replaced with the more immediate fear of falling, of snapping his back on the frozen ground. Filing behind Miles, swiping white paint in the thoughtless, back-and-forth motion, sweat soaking his forehead and beanie, he was, actually, grateful he'd been assigned the easiest of the three tasks. It saved him from failure (already he was lagging, working at half the speed of Tez), and he found himself realizing, his heart racing with the knowledge, that they must've had their own conversation, behind his back (had Tez called Miles, or had Miles called Tez?): *Let's give Caleb the fill-in. You know, something he won't fuck up.*

He was only at the L on *CHILDREN* when Miles returned behind him, going over the outlines, and Tez, finished with the shadow, craned and reached, detailing now—silver and pink!—like they were decorating a fucking wedding cake. Like the magazine-cover cupcakes Miles and their mom baked and frosted and sprinkled together, both of them aproned, for family birthdays. Miles scooted around him and climbed the right-side ladder to crisp up a T. His foot was at Caleb's eye level. A whir in Caleb's heart and he wanted to yank the ankle out, watch his brother fly.

A voice called up, "Write my name!"

A girl's voice—contained between her hands. Down below, Caleb saw Kelsey's upturned face, smiling and boring in the falling snow. "What?" he yelled back. His heart, throbbing with anger, swelled and then closed like a fist.

"It's Valentine's Day! Write my name!"

Tez came up on Caleb's left, highlighting the tops of the I, the L. "Sick of jerking off, right?"

Caleb's can spattered and ran out—he was halfway down the N. "Fuck!" He dropped it, heard its distant whap as it hit the ground. His heart didn't stop. "Give me a fucking can!"

"Baby!" The voice yelled.

Tez handed him his own, though the color was wrong. Below them, Miles was already halfway down the ladder.

Above the N Caleb scrawled K-E-L-S-Y.

"You spelled it wrong!"

Tez turned to him. "Come on, man, let's wrap it up."

The angry throb hadn't stopped. The pulse in his ears seemed to palpitate. He heard the load of Miles's body land, and a moment later, Tez's lithe hop behind him. The billboard seemed to float, to rise. "Who the fuck is watching the van!?" He was up there, all alone, struggling to finish.

"Don't cuss at me!"

"Dude, just shut the fuck up!"

At last the N was filled (spottily, grainy, half pink instead of white, but fuck it, it was done), and Caleb inched his way back across the sticky, fuming surface as carefully as he could.

A moment later, he was on the ground. Kelsey pushed his shoulders hard, and he stumbled back. "What the—" They fought like that, their voices fierce in the cold, until Caleb had no choice but to conjure an apology, just to make it stop. Tez and Miles were already a heads-bent pair moving across the snowy lot (was that a laugh? His brother's rare, salty snicker?). When they stopped, Miles pulled a camera from his bag (when had he gotten a camera? It was an Olympus, just like Caleb's) and lifted it to his eye. The flash went off like a shooting star, just before it crashed to earth.

NOW IT WAS two against two. In the booth at the coney, Caleb and Kelsey raised their hands to vote—they wanted to hit another spot; it was early still, there was plenty of paint—while Tez and Miles sat motionless on the other side, ready to puss out, go to bed, get back to their wet dreams of each other.

"Man, I'm fuckin' tired," Tez said.

"Me, too," Miles muttered, his lip turning down.

"You can sleep when you're dead," Caleb said.

They'd rock-paper-scissor, he suggested, he and Tez, to break the tie. Rock met rock. Then rock met rock again. But the third time, Tez went paper, while Caleb, anticipating the move, went scissors. Kelsey slipped her hand in the pocket of his Dickies and squeezed. Miles tipped over the saltshaker he'd been staring at glumly. Tez might be a better graffiti writer, but Caleb was smarter—of *course* he was smarter—and he had more luck.

Across the plates of fries and pancakes, they smacked hands on it—*Fair and square,* Tez said, good-natured, manning up, looking Caleb in the eye, at least with the eye that could; the other lazed in the vicinity of Miles's saltshaker. (*Poor Tez,* most of Caleb thought, whenever he was reminded of the imperfection. But the eye generated a tiny, electric buzz, too—another reminder of his own superiority, and the almost-imperceptible suspicion that maybe Tez somehow deserved it.)

Tez hadn't wanted to come to the diner, either—still spooked by the encounter with Kuru. *I dunno, if he sees the van—maybe we don't push our luck.* But Caleb had been driving. And Miles had been deep in his headphones, muttering lyrics as if no one could hear, cleaning his and Tez's caps with Mom's nail polish remover. Then it had been two against one. *Oh, come on man, you're gonna let that chode dictate where you go? Seriously?* and hung a left onto John R.

It felt good to be regaining some of his lost ground. "I got this, fellas." Throwing down a twenty, swallowing the last of the coffee, Kelsey's warm hand. The fight had been nothing. Back in the driver's seat, he took a swig from the Jameson he'd brought along, then passed the bottle to her. Miles's eyes were freaky in the rearview mirror—gold, gleaming, and giving him a look.

Backing out of the parking lot, navigating the hardened ruts, Caleb had to stop to let an incoming van squeeze around. Through the windshield, above the glare of the headlights, Drew's unmistakable face furrowed with concentration. The pubey beard, the neck as thick as a head. When it was clear he wouldn't scrape anything, Drew glanced up—a cursory look—but long enough for their eyes to connect. Caleb peeled out into the alley, Kelsey squealing, and back onto the safety of Woodward.

It was so fast. His heart raced, but his voice was steady as he swung onto MLK. *No way did he see you*, Caleb said to the rearview. *You're all the way in the back. No way would he put two and two together with the van. I don't think he recognized me.* He wiped his palms, which had sprung sweat, on his pant legs.

Miles swallowed.

He looked scary, Kelsey was saying.

How long do you think it takes to recognize someone? Tez asked.

It was snowing again, and it was going to snow.

5.

THREE DAYS BEFORE, ANXIOUS TO PLAN THE BILLBOARD debut but unable to track down Caleb, Tez had faked a name—*Jonah, from school*—and asked their mother for Miles. He'd waited with the receiver in the crook of his neck, Can-Do's ancient heater emitting its metallic smell, but at least the store was warm. Mr. Clive had slipped on ice that afternoon, wrenched his back, and left Tez with the after-hours inventory. He hadn't earned back his key privilege yet, but Mr. Clive had called it an emergency; Tez's old set still lived under the tray in the register.

He stretched the phone cord down a dusty aisle and began with the insecticides. Sprays and foggers, gels and powders. Counted and guessed. Recorded it on the clipboard. At the rate he was going he'd be there till sunrise.

"Hello?" Miles's voice came on the line, small and close.

Through their initial talk, there was a breathlessness on Miles's end—an almost palpable anxiety that made Tez's heart flare, nervous in return. "What're you doin', anyway? You outside?"

"Yeah," Miles said. "Just walking around the backyard. Our mom's a total eavesdropper."

"Where's Muni? He won't call me back." Because it seemed weird, not to mention him. There was something narrowly transgressive, just this side of secret, about a phone call between only them. Leaving Caleb out made Tez cautious—Caleb was a baby like that. Also, he had the wheels.

"Who cares," Miles said. "Probably with his girlfriend." Tez could almost see him, circumnavigating the landscaping of a nice, cozy house. Bushes all neat and snow-draped. His short, shuffling strides, retracing his boot tracks. "Are you ever gonna tell us what's up with you and Kuru?"

So this was all it took. The safe detachment the phone afforded, and Miles mustered the guts to ask. "We used to be crew but now we beef. That's all."

"Yeah, but why? What happened?" he panted. "He told me to tell you he *misses* you."

At night the hanging lights turned everything otherwise normal in the store a decrepit greenish. "We had a falling out," Tez said. The roll-up gates were down, the back door was locked; he'd checked it twice.

"Like, if we're crew now, your beef is . . ."

"It's your beef, too," Tez finished. "Fair enough. Shit."

"Did he, like, teach you how to paint?"

"Sort of. Not really. He thinks he did."

What Tez meant was *only indirectly*. It hurt to think about Drew, and then before Drew, the deeper past; made his brain ache, deep in its crannies (or was it his heart?) to go back there. But Miles was waiting on the phone, expecting an explanation, asking something of Tez that Tez supposed he owed.

After his mother died, he told Miles (where else could he begin?), he spent those first months in Detroit learning to whittle wood. Mute on a stool, he carved fish, apples, duck heads while Grandpa grunted to AM radio and the backyard workshop filled with the smell of the space heater incinerating dust. Time passed in an ellipse that did not feel like passing at all—it was more like *cycling*, bending around and around, every hour and day, this rupture at the core of his life, so brightly burning that to look at it directly might destroy him. No more mother, no more father, no more home: new home, new city, new people, not yet real, but the gentle scrape and release of wood leaving wood, the delicate and raw shape evolving beneath the knife, provided him, at least, with proof that he was still alive. And so Tez learned the palliative capacity of busying the hands. Of making something, however unimportant, where nothing had existed before.

There was no precise moment he could pinpoint, when the attraction first bit. Graffiti he associated with New York and thus his life before, but so, too, did it come to mean the Cass Corridor and the present, a bridge connecting the old, warm feeling of hot air blowing through subway tunnels with *now*, windows down and Monk on the radio, driving to the scrap yard with Grandpa. Tags big and small, indecipherable or clear, cryptic or obvious scrawled on mailboxes, concrete, brick—were as much a part of the landscape as clouds, houses, trees. His cousin Max sent a *Style Wars* tape for his fifteenth birthday. "I was your age, I guess," he told Miles, when noticing slipped into reading, words became sounds, and the volume flipped on, the city suddenly babbling, *I am here! I exist!* and a cacophony of names. And then at some point, two or three years ago (maybe it happened in a dream? Maybe it happened during a memory? Maybe it happened in a lazy gap between two otherwise conscious thoughts?), the desire rose up in him to do it, too. *I want that.* Reading, studying, doing: one activity gave birth to the next, he explained. "As you know."

As his literacy improved, his powers of deductive graffiti reasoning, he soon understood that the writers he most admired—Madnis and 2Time, Jasp and Kuru—were all of the same crew. *Cannibal Time. Crew of Thieves. Crazy Thugs.* Footnoting the corner or emerging from a speech bubble, the code, CT 313, signed off the pieces he craned, again and again, to see out the smeared bus window. Clean, animated, understated—they struck him with their symmetry and simplicity, their legibility and quirk. And Kuru was the best of the best. A K kicked out at a jaunty angle. Mickey Mouse hands, bubbly gloves, topped the final U, reaching in an illustrated climb. Tez used Grandpa's Instamatic to capture all the *KURU*s he could, then pored over the glossy photos as the bus jolted and rushed.

The dude was up all over town. He was all-city, he was king, a royalty Tez recognized even before he knew the vocabulary. Whole bombed stretches of Vernor, of Van Dyke, of the blocks around the Fisher Building, glowing tall and alone at night like a candle about to go out. Every Gratiot muffler shop, dead or alive, bore some trace of Kuru, from downtown to Seven Mile. Dude was up on the Boulevard underpasses and the *Welcome to Hamtramck* wall, the pedestrian bridge in Eastern Market and the north-facing side of the Russian "bathhouse" that was actually, everyone knew, a sex club. A two-story *KURU* dripped crazily down the bricks of a Rivard Street storage facility, its spewiness achieved, Tez later learned, by a paint-filled fire extinguisher. White tags, mistakable for some official city marking, *KURU*ed every black-barked trunk in a random Antietam locust grove.

He'd had the job at Can-Do for more than a year at that point, and the extreme good fortune of it was almost too perfect to be true: the Krylon in the cage to which Tez had a key; the dented shipments of primer deemed unsellable; the *oops* paint, bad-idea mixes of Spring Bridesmaid and Goat's Jaunt; even the greasy streakers they used for pricing. Mr. Clive was an old friend of his grandfather's who'd put increasing trust in Tez; when the moment came to steal, Tez could only bring himself to sneak from dusty back stock he was certain would go unnoticed. After that it was a matter of a single unoccupied evening, and courage. A walk with a backpack into the wilds of North Corktown. A blank wall—his very first—the cinder-block exterior of a once–liquor store, hidden by thick spring growth, like an outpost in the deep of a mythic jungle. The spray he'd swiped was an ugly, generic green, but color didn't matter. What mattered was doing it. What mattered was clarifying, *I am here. I exist.* Over the layers of language, the symbols and scribbles—*Fuck off Carlo* and *Sheri L gave me the clap*—Tez shook the first can. That first unsharp line, in the itchy choke of weeds, and Tez thrilled with the realization that he *could*. His K mimicked Kuru's as best he could, but where the king's swung out and up at the leg, Tez's K tucked under shyly, a nervous foot midstep.

KARMA had been teasing him for weeks. The idea of it—an invisible force of balance and justice, a world-leveling physics, had come like an epiphany— and now, the letters having finally actualized in the bad tag before him (bad, but not hopeless; bad, but *improvable*), the word thunked into place like a deadbolt in its lock. *What goes around comes around.* It wasn't real, of course; how the fuck could it be, given poverty and cancer, war and slavery, prison and the Brewster towers, the rottweiler that had cleared a Trumbull fence and sunk its teeth into the skinny backs of Tez's eleven-year-old thighs one day on his way home from school—his wood-whittling period. *Why do bad things happen to good people?* How could karma be real, given his mom and dad and Detroit itself? Karma was as wishful a thought as god, he understood—and yet another part of him held out modest hope. A timid faith in the universe's order. "Maybe it's all bullshit," he confessed to Miles. But the idea that it wasn't made him feel less alone.

All his life, he'd seen a change come over people when they looked at him long enough to notice his eye. They'd go quiet while their brains fumbled. And when their voices returned they were gentle with embarrassment. He was used to pity—to the distance it imposed.

By spring of last year, school felt done and gone; junior year had not been good to him. For this long, Tez had managed to survive the halls and his classmates, teachers and the neighborhood; rather than marking him easy prey, his bad eye, combined with his height, bought him a kind of social amnesty, provided an easy answer to every unasked question. He always said *Wudup* when *wudup*ped himself, slapped hands, kept his mouth shut. But then he'd started skating (the board another gift from Max, when he'd visited the previous summer, stayed over three nights, and demonstrated the basics), and a forming neighborhood clique made it their extracurricular to tease him, threaten him, start shit when they weren't dealing. These were two kids he'd known since he'd moved in with Grandpa—Devon and his sidekick, Charles, newly muscular and menacing—plus others new to the block, a stepbrother, a foster kid. *Special needs, Albino retard, Beanpole bitch, go back to Connecticut,* they yelled from the corner. His impulse to ignore them might have made it worse. In a drag-ass Chevy Cavalier, they shadowed him from the door of his house to the door of school and back, parked, posted up across the street, grew bored, grew interested again, broke appendages off Grandpa's sculptures and flung them, ringing, into the gutter. He was white, too tall, wasn't native, talked and looked funny; he lived in the weird house with the weird old man and bought his weed as he always had (insulting to them), from Rodney, out the back door of the liquor store on Forest. But Tez knew their hate came from a deeper restlessness, a more profound fury that had nothing to do with him (they, too, knew the burning core). *Who the fuck you think you are? We own this block, man—you come to us or get the fuck out.* It got worse as the weather got better. They frisbeed hubcaps, tomahawked bottles. On a Sunday, Devon rang the doorbell, asked Grandpa if Tez could come out to play while the others waited on the sidewalk. Tez hid in the bathroom with the door cracked, his heart pounding, not knowing what he'd do if Devon pushed the old man down. He didn't. It had been a kind of dare. But the next day they ambushed him around a corner, and Devon grabbed his board—Max's board, that gift from his own mother's brother's son, swung it at his head and then against the fender of a parked Oldsmobile Cutlass. Miss Joyce, three houses down, came onto the porch to yell. Tez wrestled back the board and ran, dropped it, rolled. Miraculously, the deck hadn't splintered. A nod, it seemed, from heaven. *Go ahead, then. Ride away.*

Sometimes Tez read the books for English, the chapters for history: *The Outsiders* and *The Metamorphosis, Brown v. Board of Education*. But when teachers—especially the white ones—pulled him aside to push SATs and GPAs, acronyms that always ended with *college* (a word jam-packed to bursting with everything they deemed important and he deemed impossible), Tez shamed and went cold. *You're a smart guy, Tez—you have potential.* But they were talking to some other Tez, a Tez he had fooled them into thinking existed. Terrified this double would subsume him, he forgot pencils for tests, rolled his eyes, skipped class, shoved Devon back—hard, into a brick wall, gashed where his skull met his neck and blood began to drip—*Fuck, fuck, fuck*, he'd sat next to Devon all through fifth grade; now *he* was on the wrong side of karma, scrambling inside himself. The crew had it out for him doubly then, triply. He rode the bus in zippers up and down the city. Got off, skated, walked; snuck into his own house through the back door, walked out at night through the front. Snapped photos on the Instamatic. Skated one parking garage, tagged another. Switched out the factory caps for oven-cleaner nozzles, perfected a thinner line. Loitered at Zoot's, practiced in his black book. Went to work, measured wood, counted change. Feigned movement when Grandpa hollered in the mornings to *get yourself going*—waited at his window for the old man's hunched shoulders, bow legs, saggy drawers to cross the yard toward the workshop, so Tez could return to the warm slot of bed, again, till noon. The evenings were sunlit and long that April. He never went back to school.

Alone at the wall, he did not think of the rottweiler or Devon. He didn't think of his father on a rec yard at Coxsackie, no longer waiting for visitors, his own family's abandonment a fact that must've long ceased to surprise him. He didn't think of the portrait he'd once found hidden in the workshop, tacked to the wall behind a calendar, his father's cheeks gleaming as apples and a smile that matched Tez's tooth for tooth (could your smile retain its original character even after you'd killed someone?). He didn't think of the mother who'd married his father very young, remembered in flashes of flower prints and hairspray but not whole conversations or events, because most of his life had been the suffering end of hers, in the dim fourth-floor walkup, her friends from the salon stopping in to comb her hair and then, when she had no more hair, to paint her fingernails. He didn't think of the stupefying fact that your body could fuck you over like that—let these pathogenic nodes take root in your innermost parts—until you couldn't walk without leaning on something. He didn't think of the days after the ambulance, across the hall in Nina's apartment, telenovelas on loud and holding in the fear when it was explained that she would not be coming back. And he didn't think of the press he felt, a constant pressure in his own chest, to somehow *understand* how he'd come to arrive in *this* life, instead of some other life. These torments were outside the ring of his concentration; no space for them here, no air. In the moment of painting, he was free.

"But you didn't really ask me about how I started to write. You asked me about Kuru. So."

Tez was fearless that spring; he had paint on his side, agility and energy, two decades of stored inertia, and a willingness to fail so pure that it inoculated him against failure. It didn't take long for confirmation to arrive: that the codes he was tapping out were likewise being received. Just as Tez had stalked Kuru, now it was Kuru stalking Karma. Tez only learned this later, during one of those early conversations, akin to how new lovers luxuriate in confessing their first impressions—their tentative premonitions of love. *I thought you were fuckin' with me, like, on purpose. You ripped me off, 'specially in that bomb out on Fort. I was pissed, man, some young-ass fool I never heard of, coppin' my style like it was nothing. But I was impressed, too. Like, who taught this fool his shit? Who does he roll with? Overnight, I'm seein' KARMAs five, ten times a day. I'm seein' KARMA on the inside of my eyes at night. I'm thinkin', man, this dude is either gonna be my worst enemy or my bestest friend.*

Two hooded figures tromped toward Tez through waist-high grass one afternoon in the Mt. Elliott train yard. He was spraying a field of asterisks around a black-and-yellow fill-in as tall as he was (it was his first freight: you had to practice some funny kind of art-class perspective technique, to compensate for the raised ribbing of the surface) when he stepped back and saw them. They were somewhere between boys and men: straight posture, hard jaws, hands in kangaroo pockets. Concrete faces. The sun pressed hot on the back of his neck.

They stopped twenty feet away. Waiting, it seemed, for Tez to finish. They weren't railroad guys, not in hoodies, and they couldn't be cops—or could they? If they were cops it was too late now. Tez finished three more stars, his pulse moving in his wrist, and then he turned.

One of them pulled down his hood. *You got a crew?* Twin barbells studded the outside edges of his eyebrows. He was dark in the eyes and hair, gelled and shaved. Only older than Tez by a handful of years. Except for the piercings, Tez saw a nice young bank teller from Dearborn.

Who's asking? Tez called.

The other one was taller, broader, with a square, fair head and a smutty, accidental-looking mustache. He twisted a finger into his ear. *Jasp*, he called. *Jasp and Madnis are asking.*

The bank teller hollered, *You ready to go, or you need a flick first?*

Tez lifted his backpack and picked up his board. *Where?*

He went with them voluntarily. Out of curiosity as much as fear, and because it seemed somehow meant to be: a good time to test the light of karma. Up close, Jasp's fingertips were coated red, the nails bitten down, a *Mom* tattoo across his wrist. Acne scars pocked his cheeks; the sag of his pants matched Madnis's. So this was what graffiti writers looked like. Jasp who would soon become Jasper, Madnis who'd soon be Arman.

In the backseat of a rusty Safari, Tez allowed the CT ambassadors to blindfold him. Jasp's breath was mossy and too near, leaning in to tie the knot: *Pretend it's Pin the Tail on the Donkey.* Inside the adrenaline pound, Tez actually smiled. It was a short drive. They didn't take the freeway, just the neighborhood streets. Tez knew Detroit like a house felt through at night: the Hamtramck one-ways and North End service drives were familiar enough that the mask served no purpose. In the dark, he followed an inner map, and when they opened the door, he asked, *Puritan and Hamilton? About?* Sheepishly, hiding pride; the same voice he used to ask Grandpa if he'd noticed the dishes he'd washed, the laundry folded. *See, Gramps, I'm paying my rent.*

Jasper, leading him across gravel, laughed. *Wow. A psychic, too.*

A metal door scraped, and Tez stepped forward. The smell of weed was overwhelming: sticky and vegetal, so potent he could taste it. Their hands steered him by the shoulder, down a passage, a turn, and then, the acoustics changing, into a room. When the blindfold came off, he blinked against the brightness. He stood in the central nave of a vaulted church, heavenly light streaming in through a series of tall, skinny windows. The décor was 1970s; burnt greens and October oranges, carpet stained from innumerable treads.

In a pew across the aisle, a man sat with his head tilted, staring quizzically at Tez. He stood. Who else could it be? The aura behind the paint took on, now, a face, walking toward him. The dude was fatter, and older, than Tez had expected. A tattoo, a bony optical illusion impossible to ignore, encircled his neck. And his cheeks had the same beery ruddiness as the guys outside the Old Miami. *Andrew Wallace Kirkpatrick Junior,* he said, stepping forward. *Or just Drew. Nice to meet you.*

When he reached out a hand, Tez had no choice but to shake it. *Kirkpatrick like the milk?* He meant it as a joke. The name recalled a bright red logo and the script of *Grosse Pointe Farms* on delivery trucks around the city. The rubbery orange cheese he and Grandpa grilled on bread.

Drew smiled. *Whole milk, two percent, heavy cream, ice cream . . . nasty, runny yogurt . . .*

Tez pictured the school in Grosse Pointe, brick buildings and shaded lawns, and the sailboats on Lake Saint Clair. He looked down at Drew's feet, half expecting boat shoes. But Drew's Vans were worse off than his own; a socked toe showed through a hole. *Shit,* he muttered.

And you're . . .

Karma, Tez said.

That's it?

For now.

Good boy, Tez. He grinned, showing straight, yellowy teeth. A deep bay of scalp receded up his forehead before strawberry wisps began. *What's that short for, anyway?*

Tez turned around, as if Jasper or Madnis might be there with his wallet in hand, his school ID out, but they were only lounging a few pews behind, ready, he guessed, to grab him if he tried to bolt. He looked at Drew's round, fleshy face. *Taylor,* he said.

Drew laughed. *What's wrong with Taylor, Taylor? Tez is kinda a wigger name, if you ask me.*

Heat filled Tez's face. *Yeah? No one fuckin' asked you.* The pew creaked— Jasp and Madnis had stood. *You don't know me.*

Drew raised his palms. *Whoa, whoa, calm down, man. You're right. Don't know the first thing about you. Except that you got good style.*

His tone was hard to read; if it was sarcasm it was subtle enough to be almost undetectable, but if he were serious . . . what could Drew want with him? Be cool, be cool. *Oh yeah?* And a tiny fear snagged: he'd borrowed Kuru's K. He'd ripped the dude's trademark right out from under him. *Where've you seen my style?* Deny, then get the fuck out.

The grin again. *All over, man. I get around. Just like you do.*

On the ivory wall behind Drew, Tez's eyes landed on a bleached T where a crucifix must've once hung. *What am I doin' here?* he asked.

Drew asked, *What* are *you doing here?*

He was conscious of holding his chin an inch higher than usual, and of walking in a way he never walked, following Drew down the aisle with his arms behind him, right hand gripping left wrist. And he was conscious, in the time it took Drew to roll a blunt on the waist-high altar table, that this was the first time anyone had matched Tez to Karma, Karma to Tez. He had the keen sense, all at once, that he was more alive, now, than he'd been an hour ago. Where he'd shaken Drew's hand, a tingling remained, warm and animate.

Jasper and Arman brushed off the seats of office chairs on castors, arranged in a semicircle around orange five-gallon buckets filled to various capacities with fresh green bud, a makeshift clubhouse of sacrilege. Marijuana trim messed the floor, dry and feral as a forest carpet. *We don't deal—just our personal stash,*

Drew offered, as if he could read Tez's mind, wondering if he'd stumbled, inadvertently, onto his own supplier's supplier. Scattered around the scene were Olde English and Stroh's empties, a stack of greasy Little Caesar's boxes, *Rolling Stone* and the *Free Press*, *Playboy* and harder stuff. On an overturned bucket lay a glassine baggie Tez knew to be cocaine—crystalline as snow, not like the yellowy rocks, earwax crystals, passed hand to hand outside the Milner Arms. He thought of his father as he always did, wanting to and not wanting to (the same way Grandpa, sometimes, spoke of him, caught between sorrow and resentment, after too much whiskey), because it was coke that got his dad locked up—insane, that such a passive, powdery, nothing-looking thing could cause a person to shoot; could get you put away forever. Tez looked elsewhere.

A stand covered in a doily still held little churchy things: a brass bell and a red votive candle beside an ashtray overflowing. Drew brought the blunt over and sat down, blowing smoke. He passed to Jasper, then looked at Tez. *You were born like that, huh? Wall-eyed?*

Tez met his gaze with the only eye that could. He held the stare. *Been told I was.*

Jasper coughed. Drew's smile stretched. *Mommy's pussy so ugly you had to look away?*

Tez leaned forward. *Was just trying to get a better look at the nurse. Got stuck like this.* He picked at the yellow that had dripped down his thumb.

Drew laughed low in his throat, swiveling in the chair. *Can't you get some kinda surgery or something?*

When at last the blunt came to him, Tez took his time, let the sweetness line his mouth, the dizziness knock and calm him. *Fuck this guy.* He blew out. Forced himself to look at Drew through the wafting smoke. *What about you, man?* He motioned at Drew's neck. *I don't believe you don't look in the mirror every day and regret that shit. I mean, you're, what . . . thirty? What the fuck's that gonna be like when you're sixty?*

Jasper and Arman were absolutely silent. Drew ran his fingers gingerly over his neck, the blue-green ink, scrunching his brow. *Shit*, he drawled. *The ladies, though—when I'm hittin' it, I'm tellin you, their hands go right here. Like magnets.* He faked at choking himself, rolled his eyes back into his head, and stuck out his tongue, laughing. *As your elder, let me tell you—chicks love your flaws. Arman's mole on his ass. Jasper's shit-wipe mustache. Your eye. My theory is, the uglier you are, the hotter they feel.* His laugh became a cough as he sucked on the blunt again. *Use that to your advantage.* He passed to Tez.

On the tour of the church, Jasper and Arman dropped away—it must've been prearranged like this, to leave the two alone, once the ice was broken and it was clear Tez wasn't a threat. *Bought this place outright for thirty grand,* Drew told Tez, *cash. Some family money came my way and everyone was like,* Invest, fool, invest. *Coulda just got a house out here but I thought,* Fuck it, why not go big? *Saw it listed and it just . . . called to me. The Church of Holy Names. How could I pass on that?* High, and hypnotized by Drew's meandering voice, Tez began to make sense of where they were: A graffiti boardinghouse that grew its own weed. An orphanage for misfit vandals. A three-storied, roof-collapsing Church of Holy Coincidence. *So up on floor three you got myself—master suite, high priest's quarters, the Vatican. Ground floor is Orf and Rob; you'll meet them later. Then down here's Jasp and Arman.*

The basement was lit up fluorescent, a drop-ceilinged room where youth groups and prayer circles must've once met. Now the walls were covered with tags. A series of doors led to the converted bedrooms and the grow room, a Do NOT ENTER sign hanging crooked. In one corner of the space, beer cans covered the counters of a kitchen, and just beyond this, a sort of den—randomly placed sectionals, a La-Z-Boy, a television and VCR on a milk crate. Black books were open on the couches; USPS stickers in stacks and piles; markers, streakers, caps everywhere. Bikes leaned against a shelf crowded with tools, loose tubes hanging from their handlebars. A washing machine and a dryer were stacked off-kilter beside a toy basketball hoop, a gory, severed Halloween head stuffed in its net, too large to pass.

Santa's workshop, he said. *Community center for fuck-ups. Where we just were? Upstairs? That's more like the formal dining room.*

A dog toddled out from behind one of the couches, a velvety gray pit with eyes the same color as her coat. Her chain rattled expensively. Drew knelt and closed his eyes. *Roxy, baby, meet Karma.* The dog licked his face clean.

It smelled like Tez's sock drawer; he had the bad habit of bunching his dirties in with his cleans, and his weed permeated everything. When Grandpa found him out last year, he took to carrying his stash in the side pocket of his cargo pants. Cops in Detroit, if he was ever stopped, took one look at the eye and let him off with a nod.

In the kitchen, Drew opened a cupboard crammed with ramen packets and belly-up roaches to retrieve a Crown Royal bottle, still in its cheap purple pouch. He poured two shots and handed one to Tez. Markered across the freezer door, a tag read *RIP SCABS*. They raised their glasses and drank. The booze was smooth on the tongue but fiery in Tez's throat. His high muddled and spread.

Drew poured a second shot and raised it in the direction of the freezer. *My mentor*, Kuru said. *To Scabby.* And shot again.

Tez only knew Scabs from an old lavender roller piece, faded and kinged on a wall off Livernois, and from a tribute on the back of a charred house visible from I-96. Twelve years before, Drew explained, it was Scabs who'd initiated Kuru—*way back when I was a widdle baby just about your age.* He had seen something in young Kuru and taken him under his wing. *It's like anything. Like baseball, like being a concert piano player—a fucking pee-an-ist—someone's gotta show you how to go from talent to mastery.* But Scabs's name, at first novel, became, eventually, literal, with dope. Rehab, relapse, homelessness, overdose. *The thing with junkies is, eventually they die. Remember that. Dude died with his scabby face in his own puke. He taught me everything I know. Even what not to do.*

When Tez nodded, the booze seemed to slosh inside him. He sensed a vague proposition rolled inside the story. *Took me under his wing.* Was this Drew's way of telling Tez he'd been chosen? He experienced a feeling almost entirely new. He was flattered, and inside the flattery, proud.

The hot, cricket-studded evenings of the coming summer—working, Grandpa's, watching his back in the neighborhood, sneaking out alone at night—the approaching season seemed incredibly long. And after summer? The life in front of him? Longer, lonelier, hardly imaginable.

So, rule number one, in memory of Scabs, we don't fuck with smack in this crew. Anything else, fine. Got it? He poured Tez a second shot, himself a third.

Across the main room, Drew led him to a storage closet where metal shop shelves lined the walls, crammed with Rust-Oleum and bucket paint, turpentine and WD-40, bags of caps, coffee cans of markers, stacks of stickers.

How much paint you got?

On me?

Yeah, right now.

Tez swung his backpack around and removed a single can, left over from the freight. When Drew motioned for him to add this to the shelf, Tez complied.

Sharing is caring, Drew said. *It's like a fucking preschool here. Everyone on crew brings in a dozen cans a week. It's like dues. Like taxes. Where do you rack?*

Tez thought of Mr. Clive. Most Sundays, the old man came over for canned soup and store-bought rolls, played cards with his grandfather or toured the workshop—come Pistons season he'd be there Thursdays, too. Mr. Clive, fedora resting in his lap, telling in-my-day stories, Black Bottom and playing the numbers. The gentle hand he set on Tez's shoulder. The keys to Can-Do's gate, front door, and back door, safe on the ring in Tez's front pocket. He told Drew, *I take the bus out to an Ace usually. The one in Clinton.*

Drew grinned and smacked his back. *When you're here you can go with the other guys. Make a day of it. An outing. You bring in extra, great. Keep your room clean, bring in beer now and then—pills are always welcome—you're going above and beyond. I see it all, just remember that. I see everything, I remember everything. You do good, good shit will come back to you. That's karma, right?*

It was the moment, Tez tried to explain to Miles, that he agreed with Drew, *That's karma.* It was the moment he set that can on the shelf, signing on the figurative dotted line. Or the moment guilt flashed hot in his chest when he thought of what his grandfather would think, if he knew what he was planning . . . to throw some clothes in a bag and skate off tomorrow and move directly into the spare basement room, where Ideot, the boy who'd lived there before, had tagged *Mad run the mad house* like a manifesto or a warning, dripping purple on the wall over the mattress.

Kuru's hand was on the back of Tez's neck.

When does the cleaning lady come?

A guttural laugh rose up—*Gwa-ha-ha!*—and the hot hand squeezed.

SO THAT was the beginning, and five months later would come the end, but in the middle, Tez tried to explain, there was joy in belonging to a group, in having found yourself worthy, in committing to a shared endeavor. The dictates of their mission, at least at first, eclipsed all else.

Their mission was to cover the city. To comb it with paint. To canvas it, literally, with their holy names, in color, between sundown and sunup. Jasp and Madnis, 2Time and Orf, Kuru and Karma moved in pairs and pairs of pairs, tracing ever-widening circles out from the church. For farther-reaching treks (in Brightmoor, in Regent Park), Jasp or Dylan drove the crew in Jasper's Safari or Dylan's Ford Tempo, or Drew, on occasion, drove his factory-new Astro, white as a commode (obsessively Drew licked a finger to remove a smudge, checked the tire pressure once a week, and, when a nick appeared on the passenger-side door, interrogated them: *Who the fuck rode shotgun last?*). Closer to home, they biked. Pedaled standing up, navigating potholes on the blocks without streetlights, the backpack of cans tugging on Tez's shoulders. If the ride was long enough, sometimes he entered a state of blankness— forgot where he was going, what he was doing, who he was . . . until Drew cruised up beside him, whacked him on the back, and sped past—*Look alive, Karma*, the deep laugh roiling in his wake.

His boogers came out black. His hands were always paint-stained (there was no point in scrubbing and scrubbing with Palmolive when you'd be back out in another twelve hours). The manic addiction to reaching at least a baseline euphoria, night after night, was consuming work—took a lot of not-thinking and just-doing, the goal, above all, to score—to maintain, for as long as possible, the high. Kuru and Karma were sometimes brotherly, sometimes best-friendly, sometimes master and pupil. Kuru might pull the can away to alter Karma's outline, correct a highlight. And Tez painted aware of Drew's evaluating stare, always awaiting the sweet nectar of praise—*Fuck yeah. Shit's ill. Just don't ever bomb harder than me, right? Wait till I retire*—all the sweeter for its rarity. Toward other graffiti, even within CT, Kuru was harsh—*Wack spot. Obvious spot. Too sharp. Pretentious. Artsy-fartsy-faggy.* During an evening trim session at the altar, drinking coffee and smoking cigarettes, preparing for their night, Drew might lay into Rob and Dylan, who, at twenty and twenty-one, occupied the bottom rungs of the CT hierarchy. *Let's not repeat last night's disaster, all right you two? Howdy and Doody? That shit was too time-consuming. Way, way out of reach. Keep it simple, all right?* And the boys would nod, shamed, these smart-enough best friends, mutually lost, who struck Tez as having wandered from the suburbs into a kind of strange vacation—*Kuru-World: An Adventure!*—though who was Tez to judge? After big nights out, while the others slept, Rob and Tez skated in Palmer Park, fucking around in the parking lot to quell the adrenaline, druggy and wild, still surging through their veins. It was Rob who offered those first hints. *He's got two sides, you know. Ever wonder why you've never seen an* IDEOT *tag? Dude didn't leave for no reason.* Implications Tez chose not to hear.

There were tricks for getting onto roofs, using car hoods and dumpster edges, drainage pipes and fire escapes. You handled squatters one way, dope fiends another, lurking drunks another—tossed five bucks to a guy and suddenly he wasn't so threatening, had reason to lurk his way to the liquor store instead. You waved at passing cops from your bicycle—*Hey there, officers, just a couple of paper boys out at midnight!*—and if they somehow managed to care enough to make it onto a roof behind you, to draw their Maglites and get all fucking Terminator—you dropped your can, put your hands up, let Kuru do the talking. *Officers. Good evening. May I reach for my wallet, please? Procure identification?*

Drew's uncle was a retired decorated detective. In the seventies and eighties, he'd taken two bullets to the shoulder, locked up pedophiles, murderers, notorious dealers, and the assassin of a city councilman. One name dropped, one glance at Drew's license, and the cops backed away. *You boys be careful up here, now. Lotta bad people on the streets, right?*

He quit his job at Can-Do through a note in the mail slot along with the keys. *Dear Mr. Clive, I want to thank you for everything you have done for me up until now.* Pushed the guilt down, blotted and blacked it out by climbing higher, going harder. Knowing Mr. Clive would show his grandfather, that they'd sit around the kitchen table asking the same things over and over— Where had he gone, and how would they find him? Should they call the police? (*Had* they called the police?) Heavy sighs over coffee that tasted of the sponge before climbing into the Buick to drive loops around the city, looking, looking, the way Tez looked, too, any time a bulky silver car passed, his heart hammering to wonder. The old man didn't deserve it—the way he'd stood bare chested in the hallway the morning Tez left, hair sticking up crazily from a bad night of sleep, his glasses not on yet, the fragility of age apparent in his skinny arms, his feeble bottom lip as Tez unlatched the screen. He made up a room to rent, a room from a friend, never mind that he *had* no friends. *Who? Where?* Folded in his back pocket was a snapshot of his parents feeding each other wedding cake, pupils red in the flash, a crease between them. All Grandpa had asked was when he'd be coming back—*But when are you coming back?* The voice trembling with restraint—as if to say *No! You'll end up like your father!* would've broken him beyond repair.

I have this fucked-up eye, he could've told him. *Something incredible is happening. I'll return triumphant.* Instead Gramps hobbled out onto the porch calling *Taylor, Taylor, Taylor*, and still Taylor had left. Knowing that whatever the old man imagined must be a hundred times worse, more dangerous and criminal than Drew and the church, a few aerosol cans.

In the middle, he told Miles, he racked in long johns under a shop suit he still had from Can-Do, stuffed the cylinders down his legs three in one, three in the other, two in the waistband, and walked straight out the front, sure to make eye contact with any orange-vested employee—let them see his deformity and wince. Or he went out through the lumberyard with the loot in a five-gallon bucket, a prop receipt visible in his hand and a satisfied-customer look on his face. Once, Rob and Dylan, in college sweatshirts, each holding a ficus, engaged the door clerk in a very serious conversation about soil nutrients while Jasper wheeled a fully loaded cart straight out of the garden department—Tez angling a sheet of plywood to block another clerk's view—and they were stocked for the next two weeks. Other times they just packed and ran, past sensors and alarms, banking on the probability that minimum-wage earners lacked incentive to chase and tackle a seven-foot-tall, lazy-eyed teen. Stealing didn't fit into Tez's karmic code, but without Can-Do he didn't have a dime. *Fuck it, it's corporate bullshit anyway. Fuck with the system however you can*, Dylan said, ripping off the sweatshirt, edging the van back onto Gratiot.

The Fourth of July came. Drew took Tez (only Tez—and the favoritism was lost on no one) to a party at the house of the decorated cop uncle, a flabby-necked man with a don't-fuck-with-me voice and a wife with the largest breasts Tez had ever seen. Their mansion was all stone and cream, boxed in by trees sculpted like ice-cream cones, in the neighborhood where Henry Ford once lived. Silent Black caterers carried trays of pigs in a blanket. A DJ in a tent played classic rock and Motown. *I'm a joker . . . signed, sealed, delivered . . . born in the USA!* Drew led him upstairs to a study attached to the master bedroom. Leaded windows followed the curve of a circular wall. Leather-bound books filled shelves that might've been doors to secret passageways. The sofas were leather, too, and the desk was the size of Tez's bed. It was the richest-feeling room he'd ever been in.

Drew poured them two glasses of a chestnut-colored liquor out of a big crystal decanter, then excused himself to piss. Through the window, Tez could see the bald scalps, the dyed and shiny up-dos, the forks and champagne flutes catching light. The distance of Drew's planet from his own was momentarily bewildering, uncrossable. When Drew returned from the bathroom, he carried four white, round pills. *Uncle had knee surgery last year. These'll make you feel amazing.*

Tez said, *I already feel amazing.*

Drew set a pill in Tez's palm. *You know what's crazy? Your daddy in prison? It's like, my fuckin' uncle down there coulda had some part in your daddy going to prison. Now how fucked is that?*

He sipped the booze but it tasted like smoke. Drew's playing confused him. *No, he couldn't have. My dad got busted in Queens. Not shithole Detroit.*

Drew shot his drink, throwing a pill back with it, then poured another. *Shithole Detroit my ass, man. I fuckin' love my city. This place is good to me.*

Good to you, Tez thought. Good to Andrew Kirkpatrick from Grosse Pointe Farms. *Well. Not as good to a lot of people. I mean, whatever man, I don't claim Detroit; I was ten when I moved here. That means, like, more than half my life—*

I know, I know, bud; you lived in New fucking York. Back in the day. When you were just an itty-bitty fool.

Tez smiled and held it. If he knew anything, he knew to never let on what hurt. Between his shoes the rug was red, antique. Goofily, he rapped, *Fool— defined in Webster's . . .*

The look that crossed Drew's face was perplexed, irritated. *What?*

Tez furrowed his brow and almost laughed. *Tribe? Q-Tip?* Drew's face remained blank. *It's nothing,* he said, but a funny awareness rode in on the next sip of scotch. Drew didn't listen to music. There were no boom boxes, no speakers, not even a kitchen radio at the church. How had this escaped his notice before now? The Astro was outfitted with a stock cassette player, but Drew never inserted a tape. These past two months—beyond a blare from a passing car, movies watched on the couch, and the recurring soundtrack of his memory, Tez had hardly heard a song, a melody, a note. Grandpa liked to say, *Never trust a person who doesn't like jazz,* as he lowered the needle on *A Love Supreme.*

The pills were still waiting in his palm, and now Tez swallowed one. He drank until the glass was empty. *Let's go back down.*

For the next three hours, they danced in the tent with the relatives. The pills brought a brimming warmth, a bootlegged sense of belonging that pushed out anything else—*Bring me a higher love! Bring me a higher love!* Drew moved off-rhythm, raising his knees clumsily, grinned at Tez like a coconspirator. Tez held Drew's mother's bouncing hand until it went sweaty. Fireworks burst in the distance like sparkling, dripping geraniums, and he had this small epiphany, that happiness required not thinking: there would always be a problem, curling up life's edges, but acknowledgment was his choice, his power. By the end of the night, his face ached from smiling.

"You could say I doubled down," he told Miles. Moved deeper into this new, unexamined life. In Ideot's former bedroom, he slept all day and was out all night. Drew shaved his head to lessen the impact of his balding, then promptly met a girl. In her struggling black Camaro, Carmel came over in the late afternoon, walked Roxy, disappeared upstairs inside Drew's room. Other girls—girls carrying their platforms by the straps, girls clogging the toilets with their tampons, their faces sick-looking in the mornings—had to follow the rules or they were out. They weren't allowed to drive there, for example (*Pick their skinny asses up, I don't want their Geo Metros drawing attention to my home*). And they couldn't spend more than two nights in a row. Drew lectured the crew during sticker production: *I see their stuff around—their fuckin' scrunchies and bras—it means they're comin' back. Pare these relations down to their essentials. Fuck them and get them out.*

One night in late July, Jasper and his date entered the pitch dark of the basement through the side hallway. The light above the oven came on, casting a square into the main room. Tez heard the refrigerator open and close, the crack of two beers, footsteps and murmurs, the fleshy suction of kissing. Surrounded by the room's deep stillness, Jasper had no reason to assume the basement wasn't empty—Drew and Tez upstairs or out, instead of stretched out long on the couches, luxuriating in the deep sedation of acepromazine, pilfered last week from Royal Oak Veterinary during Roxy's teeth cleaning. They listened to Jasper regale the girl with shit talk: critique Kuru's style as *going downhill*, reveal Drew's real name, speculate on his net worth, psychoanalyze his character (narcissistic, egomaniacal, his graffiti an elaborate defense mechanism against the embarrassment of being so rich). *It's like he's trying to be a mafia boss. He's got this new partner, this confused kid who doesn't know any better, thinks he's special, and Drew's basically, like, waiting for him to kneel down and offer to suck his dick, is my opinion.* The only reason he'd recruited Karma so hard in the first place was because Karma posed a threat. *He's already better than Drew. It's keep-your-friends-close-and-your-enemies-closer shit.*

It was almost work, to tense up on doggy Valium—and yet every nerve in Tez's body went rigid. He was sure Jasper would hear his pounding heart around the kitchen corner and turn. When Drew clicked on the floor lamp, Tez kept his eyes shut.

Drew's voice labored just above a whisper. *I'd suggest you get the fuck out of my house before this shit wears off.*

After Jasper moved out, the crew was tasked with eradicating every visible trace of him. CT, now a ragtag task force, buffed and beautified every *JASP*-touched surface they could find. *Don't even go over him—just erase him. Like he never even existed.* Guilty by association, Arman left two days later, and then, in quick succession, Rob and Dylan left, too. Their excuses were flimsy: Rob claimed he'd gotten a girl pregnant in Ferndale—had to go deal. Dylan's father was "sick." *Anyway*—Dylan swallowed—even if he hadn't been, *I think it's time to move on.*

Drew was speeding in the slow lane, southbound on 75, when Rob and Dylan broke the news. Incredible timing, Tez thought, as Drew's laugh began, a rumble rising with the speedometer. In the passenger seat Tez gripped the armrest—they were accelerating toward the back of a sixteen-wheeler—before Drew swerved onto the shoulder, then through gravel that met the frontage road. *Ahhh, cause it's such a fucking terrible thing, living with your friends, doing whatever you want, smoking endless weed, never having to pay . . . You're right, boys. Back to Ferndale. Back to Mommy and Daddy. But look, when you get the itch—and you know you will, you know you will—when you get the itch to come down to the city and fuck shit up again, remember whose territory you're in. Remember what you gave up.*

The morning Rob and Dylan left, Drew and Tez sat on the wide cement steps at the church's entrance. They watched the pair haul armfuls of stuff out to Dylan's car. Didn't offer to help, didn't say a word. It was a thick-aired day in August, the sky on the verge of a storm. Drew smoked a cigarette, Tez a joint, and every few drags, they swapped.

The unease—the moral cramp—that had gripped Tez's stomach the night they overheard Jasper had been there for a week now. He hadn't shit in days. Heavy with fear, constipated with a special kind of ineffectualness, every second he sat beside Drew and smoked began to seem like another second of doing the wrong thing. Like in doing nothing, he was precisely *not doing something*. Now, he couldn't forge the connection, between what he was doing or not doing and *karma*, that abstraction, no longer belief but only pure word, two syllables of sound and five flashy letters. A *symbol*—except Tez, for the life of him, couldn't remember what it stood for.

KARMA and *KURU*, Kuru and Karma. That's what karma meant now. Drew's leg in shorts was there beside him like a hairy, blown-up bone. Remove this leg, this person, the word, and Tez was no one again. Partnerless and nothing. *When you get the itch—and you know you will—remember what you gave up*. The ground shifted beneath his feet, slipped and receded.

When the last bag was tossed in, Rob climbed into the passenger seat without a glance. But Dylan, slamming the trunk, turned and gazed up at the church, shoved his hands in his pockets, and sighed. From this vantage he looked small and young. A lightning bolt struck the White House on his black T-shirt. At the edge of the parking lot, ooze-green trees of heaven bowed and rustled in the wind.

Man, I know you like to scare people, he said, his eyes on the ribbed gray sky. *But whatever you think you're all about—you're really just a bully. Just a scared-ass bully. You're not fooling anyone. Except maybe Karma here.*

Then he got in the car, reversed, and drove off.

Drew studied the cigarette. Tez could hear the panic of crickets, thunder rumbling its warning. *See those bushes over there?* Drew motioned with his chin toward yellow grass, tall along the steps. *I'm gonna flick this cigarette. If a flame lights, it's a sign: No more Dylan. Gone. They won't even know where to find his body.*

Tez listened backward, as if he were already off in some alternate future, remembering this.

Drew looked at the glowing tip, then tossed it. It disappeared between the stalks, where Tez's eyes were glued, expecting the first thin line of smoke. And if there *was* a fire—Dylan aside—if there was a fire, then what? The church, the two of them running, Carmel and Roxy and everything inside . . .

There was no smoke, no flame. Drew dropped his head down between his knees and laughter pealed. When he flung himself back up, his face filled with rushing blood, and in the pre-storm light his eyes were spookily blue.

Man, I've been throwing my butts over there since I got the place. Never once, nothing. Two fuckin' years. You think I'd kill Dylan? Think I got secret guns and shit? Ah, Karma, think better of your best friend, huh? We got better things to do. You and me.

A sprinkle began. Dark dots appeared on the broken concrete. Back inside, the church was warm, cavernous as ever, echoing.

Your best friend, your partner, your number one. Summer faded, the sun arced lower, the light got sadder, fall arrived. They painted together, shared the serotonin surge, returned the next day to take pictures and admire. But something seemed to be sliding. Sometimes, when Tez stepped back to admire five stories of stairwell throw-ups, or the new decorations along an off-ramp embankment, he had the strange sense that he hadn't painted it at all—had hardly even been there. They woke at five o'clock in the evening, observed the last blazing hours of daylight from the balcony outside Drew's bedroom window. Drank Folgers and ate pork rinds, shared another blunt. Tez had moved upstairs by then, to the only other room on Drew's floor. Drew suggested it as a safety precaution—in the giant church, if there were ever a break-in . . . but his voice had trailed, and the rationale was never clarified. At dusk, he skated alone through the neighborhood, letting his wheels shuffle and gather up leaves. Hands deep in his pockets, he stared into empty windows, past doorframes turned to charcoal, saw the rotting carcass of a cat where one overgrown yard met another. What did a dead cat mean? Its fragile, pointed skull was just beginning to peek through the tight, icky mulch of its previous self.

Where'd you go, bud? Got scared maybe you were leavin' me.

What Tez didn't tell Miles was that, in an overlookable corner of himself, he had dared, then, to hope that Drew wanted him near for all the same reasons Tez wanted to be near. He'd felt so proud, the first chilly night in September, to trot downstairs wearing his dad's jacket—knowing the *CT* would blow Drew away but not knowing Drew would turn him, spin him around like a beautiful thing, admiring, saying *Whoa, whoa, whoa, you do us right, Karma.* That *us.* He didn't tell Miles how he'd tortured himself wondering what exactly it was that caused his cells to light up, his guts to pull toward Drew—his blood to yearn traitorously in his neck. He didn't tell Miles about the sheer exhaustion of that period—not from graffiti, but from fear, the constant niggling dread that Drew might find him out—would know, somehow, Tez's feelings more than Tez knew them himself—and did not feel them back. And he didn't tell Miles that he dreamed of Kuru, lips finding lips in rooms so dark they couldn't see their hands. Dreams that brought immense relief, then disturbed him in the daylight, visions returning, demanding he digest them.

On Wednesdays and Fridays, Carmel brought over tamales, Schlitz, pizza, and cocaine, which she cut into manageable lines with her Wayne State ID. The girl in the picture had baby-chubby cheeks and wore a black ribbon choker. Carmel still wore the choker, but her cheeks had thinned and her eyes were deeper set now, her collarbone desperate-looking beneath her halter. Through the wall, she and Drew made noises like rearranging furniture; pianos dropping, bones breaking, grunts and screams. On Halloween, Tez followed them to a party in the same labyrinthine warehouse CT had bombed just days before the big exodus. Women as tall as Tez wore electrical tape across their nipples. A hairy man was naked but for Pampers and feathery black wings. Carmel wore a Cleopatra wig and mesh: *I wanna dance*, she said. Drew slapped her ass like *Go ahead*, and she disappeared into the fold, of glitter and ghouls and aviator goggles.

Yours hittin' you? Drew asked. They sat on the tailgate of a truck strapped with nitrous tanks, where a stringy-haired dude rapidly inflated balloons, then handed them over the side. Tez turned to Drew and nodded. The tab he'd swallowed on the way over was changing the color of his blood now, turning his muscles to jelly. Out across the parking lot, dust puffed and hovered in the floodlights. From this distance, the music was a sonic fog in the open concrete bunker where their corner piece, KARMRU 313, still ran, obscured by speaker stands and draping black fabric. Someone was stroking his arm, and he didn't want them to stop. A weight settled on his shoulder: Drew's head, heavy and close. The ear as delicate and new-looking as a baby's.

Where's Carmel? You think she's okay? Tez heard himself say. His voice was gelatinous, outside time.

I'm not thinking about her right now. Drew's hand slid into Tez's. He turned it over by the wrist, then pressed it open from palm to fingers. *It's okay, man, it's just the drugs.*

Every nerve in Tez's body was alive, awake.

I'm glad I found you, Drew said then. *I can't imagine shit without you.*

Every nerve was alive and then it wasn't. Something moved—the tab closed again. For a hard second, Tez feared Drew was baiting him toward a trap. He waited. Sirens rang in the distance; the smell of smoke tinged the air. The hand in his hand continued to press, massaging his palm as if rubbing away a pain. Then the nerves flared again, and pleasure was back, and Tez said, *I can't imagine shit without you either.*

Tez said to Miles, "But he did shit like that, man. Set traps. I mean, I meant what I said back to him but it—you know, only about half of me trusted him at that point. Maybe less than half."

Three nights later, biking the perimeter of Belle Isle, Halloween was a washy dream. Drew's voice was aloof now. Teasing and distant. *Why don't you get a girl?* he called to Tez. Currents of cold, moving air separated them. *You got urges like the rest of us humans, right? Or are you human, Tez?*

They'd just finished the windows of a waterfront warehouse and were debating whether or not to attempt the roof of the boathouse. To the east, the water was zebra-striped with moonlight.

I don't know, don't think about it a lot, Tez said. The organ in his chest contracted.

What, you don't jerk off? Drew asked.

Tez was quiet; caught.

You're tellin' me you don't jerk off? That's like sayin' you don't shit. Don't breathe.

Sometimes, he said.

Sometimes—I seen you jerk off, man. Saw you doin' it last night. Carmel got out of the shower, came in my room, you closed your door to do your business. Right? Am I right? All it takes is one look at my girl in a towel? Drew made a scowling, comic sound. *Come on, man, I won't get mad.*

It wasn't possible. Was it? That Drew had seen him? Could see through walls, or could predict the exact time his stoppered-up desire would demand release? And if he could do all that, what was to prevent him from reading Tez's mind?

Naw, man. I don't look at Carmel like that.

Drew chuckled, moving his head in deep circle-eights. He let the bike veer lazily on the blue pavement. *Oh-oh-ho. Excuse me, Mister fucking Picky. My girl isn't good enough for you? What, you need younger pussy? Hotter?* A car bumping bass came up behind them, and in the sweep of passing headlights Tez saw Drew's familiar grin. The nakedness of his face, wanting a fight. *Come on. Let's do the boathouse. We got the whole night ahead of us.* And he swerved left, down the path that cut through the woods around the pond, deeper into the dark center of the island.

I think I'm done for the night, Tez called up ahead. The back of Drew's neck, the pale skin of birch trunks, the toe-shaped moon in the sky were all the same glowing blue-gray white.

Drew slowed; circled back and stopped. *You scared?*

Tez saw the pair of them inching across the slippery terra-cotta tiles. Relying only on the tread of their sneakers and their forward-leaning weight for balance. It would take just one slip, one push, one accidental jolt on Drew's part for Tez to go down. In a flash he saw himself on the concrete dock, his head cracked and leaking like an Eastern Market gourd. *I'm not scared. I'm just done for the night.*

Okay, Drew said. *Okay. If my partner's done, then I'm done, too. Carmel's comin' over, anyway. Maybe she'll stop by your room. A sympathy fuck. Man, Carmel—she'll fuck you so hard your eye might pop back into place. If my girl climbs in with you, Tez, just know that I okayed it. Preapproved. Like a gift from me to you.*

Man, I don't want to—

You know the saying, 'Don't look a gift horse in the mouth'?

It was an adage his grandfather used. If he brought Tez home new gray tube socks instead of white ones, or skimped on the sides with the fried-chicken order, or pinched seventy-five cents out of his pocket when Tez had asked for a dollar: *It's all I got. Don't look a gift horse in the mouth.*

He turned his bike around to finish the island circle, his breath short, his palms grimy on the handlebars as the tears welled and ran uncontrollably, hot down his cheeks. How good it felt, to cry unseen, unheard, Drew somewhere behind him, though he didn't turn to look. He rode back over the bridge, down Jefferson to St. Aubin to Mack, his nostrils stinging, fending off a wordless panic as he crossed the Cass intersection, knowing he was only four blocks away from home—wanting to be only there—and the craziness of knowing it was impossible. He seemed to slow down even as he pedaled faster and faster, as if he could simply outride Drew, shake loose the choice he'd made. As if one left turn onto Second was all it'd take, to run up the porch steps, fling open the door, and cross the threshold—and everything behind him would magically disappear. A phantom evaporating as easily as he'd manifested.

"He was all bluff," Tez told Miles. "All bullshit. Of course, I locked my door that night, and yeah, no, Carmel didn't come in my room. But it was the beginning of the end. You can't live like that, thinkin' eyes are on you all the time. Can't be close to someone you don't really trust."

The end came two weeks later, when, cruising in the Astro, debating what to hit, their headlights rolled across Jasper's decrepit Safari, half-hidden in a weedy cut off Rosa Parks, given away by the faded *NIN* decal on the back bumper. An abandoned school, set back from the road, appeared as empty as ever, but when Drew cut the engine and rolled down the windows, they could hear the softest echo of hiss.

Holy fucking shit. Couldn't stay away, could he. Drew flung his arm around backward, rummaging for something in the crates behind him. When he returned, he didn't hold the paint cans Tez imagined but a wadded black sweatshirt. *Come on; we gotta be fast.* His eyes were buggy, giggling in his skull. On the drive, he'd uncapped an orange pill bottle and taken two of something—uppers, Tez saw now. Tez himself had passed.

The sweatshirt contained exactly what Tez feared it might. The gun was matte black and petite and looked fake to him, as Tez thought all real guns looked. Identical black toys had come into his world more than once. He'd seen a gun floppy, unserious, in a suited man's hand outside the Blackstone apartments, pointing at someone in a parked car—a huge, brassy wig in the way. He'd seen one on a summer night, tucked in the back waistband of jeans as Tez watched from the dark of the stairs, hardly breathing, while a thief detangled the wires of Grandpa's receiver, ripped the cords out of the turntable, and carried the pair back out through the open window, as easily as he'd come in. And at the Sphinx gas station he'd seen one, while lost in innocent perusal of the Better Mades, watched it emerge from a plastic bag and focus on the cashier. The register opened with a ding, and money was set in a modest heap on the bulletproof lazy Susan. Tez heard the clerk's muffled voice, giving the Susan a spin: *Fine by me. Not my money.* And he knew, of course, their sound—the unspectacular *pawp-pawp-pawp*, like firecrackers but rhythmic—the same sound he heard now, as Drew blew out one, then two, then three, then all four of Jasper's tires. Tez stood with one hand still on the Astro, unable to move. From this distance he could wonder if it were really happening. It was nearly freezing, the night air dry and mean and still, and yet Tez could feel the damp across his forehead, to see Drew's eyes so big with glee.

Help me! he hissed.

The van was sinking to its defeated rubber knees. The gun in Drew's hand turned him into someone Tez had never met before—the person he'd been becoming, it was clear now, all the time he'd known him. The evolution was, just like that, complete.

Get a fucking rock!

Tez just stood there, paralyzed with not-knowing.

Come the fuck on!

The gun was pointed, now, in Tez's direction.

At last Drew shoved the weapon down his pants, hurried into the brush, then hurled a jagged hunk of concrete like a basketball in an overhead pass. The crash through the windshield tore the air. In the direction of the school, there wasn't a sound.

Tez's heartbeat filled his ears. *You forget everything?* Drew revved the engine, spinning trenches in the mud. *You forget who the fuck I am, who we are, what I'd do for you?*

His words came out brittle and hard to say. Spit flew. Tez took it. *Fucking pussy. Fucking faggot. Unbelievable.* Haunted houses and nighttime lights, black spots blotted past the windows.

Just fucking standing there.

He spouted about empire. A rolling, tripping monologue, tearing through red lights, fishtailing around corners, checking his rearview, and swiping his tongue across his yellow teeth. About going down with sinking ships. About Rome, burning.

Should we light the church up tonight? Finally? Been wanting to—I tell you, been contemplating it, while you and Carmel are sleeping.

"He stopped at a liquor store—this one over on Holbrook, and while he was inside, I fucking ran. That's all. I had my board with me, don't know why, but I'd brought it out that night—anyway, I had my backpack and my board and I fucking ran. I thought for sure he'd get in the van, chase me, put a bullet in my head. I really did. I hid in some bushes in someone's yard, like a fox in a hole, for what felt like hours. It was so cold. Then I skated home. No van. Thought my feet would fall off by the time I got to the porch. Broke into my own house; Grandpa almost clocked me with the skillet. Thought I was a robber. I'm gonna tell you something that I've never told anybody, Crush. I mean, I've never told anybody *any* of this, but I'm gonna tell you one thing more: I slept in my grandpa's bed that night. Curled up next to him like a little baby. He didn't know what to think."

What he didn't tell Miles was how his heart, that night, shattered like Jasper's windshield. How he burned, in that foxhole, with humiliation and fear and love and grief so mixed and terrible that he wondered what sickness of the brain, what dementia of the heart, he'd been born with, to have fallen for someone so monstrous. What he didn't tell Miles was how, before Drew went into the liquor store, he'd put the gun to Tez's temple and, unzipping his jeans with his free hand, ordered, *Blow me*, right there or he'd kill him—and when Tez, hyperventilating against the tickling press of the barrel, could hardly speak or see, began to bend down, Drew pushed him back by the shoulder so hard—*Get the fuck off me, queer!*—that Tez's head whapped back against the passenger-side glass. *I'm getting booze*, Drew had said. *And when*

I come back, shit, man, straighten yourself out. He laughed then. *Have some fucking dignity.*

But what he did allow was this: when Miles's exhale hit the receiver, followed by the simplest declaration, *I like you*, stripped and quivering in the open utterance—Tez responded in kind.

"Shit, Crush." He pictured Miles's face, the way his chin and eyes pulled down. How good to hear sincerity, and to give sincerity back. "I like you, too."

6.

MILES SUCKS ON A PEPPERMINT UNTIL IT IS A GLASSINE
wafer between his teeth. Beside him in the backseat, he's aware of Tez's worry,
over that fast vision in the parking lot. Every ten seconds Tez's jacket chafes
the seat belt as he turns to peer behind them, or at any pair of headlights that
sidle up. Checking for the van, Miles knows. Checking for Drew.

Sh, sh, sh. It's okay. He didn't see you, Miles wants to be able to say. He wants
to say, *Remember the phone? Remember what we confessed?* Despite the smallest
itch of doubt (but had Tez really meant it?) Miles is lifted now by a powerful
sense of rightness and righteousness, euphoria that reduces everything else
to minutiae, even the threat of Drew. Tez had said it back. Love had been
returned. Now possibilities are taking shape that Miles had hardly allowed
himself to imagine. *I like you, too.* Futures.

The van bounces over train tracks that split the road like stitches. Half
of every block is another field of snow, walled off from the street by dirty,
waist-high banks. A bus zooms around them, lit up and entirely empty,
appearing hell-bound. Flakes fall in spinning columns before the headlights.
They're heading farther east than Miles has ever been, moving deeper and
deeper into the socket of the night. The van swerves around a pothole, then
slides, Caleb tapping the brakes, before they're on their way again.

Déjà vu comes over Miles. "I feel like I've been here before." Intending the
comment for Tez.

"You haven't," Caleb answers. "It's just that most of Detroit looks the same."

That isn't it, Miles thinks, annoyed. It's the confluence of the phone call
and the nearness of Tez's body and the haunted landscape outside and the
home he is making in *I like you, too.* The same safety Miles used to feel with
Chris—*You're coming over, right?* The wonder of a gift reciprocated. Tez's voice
had been so clear, so just-for-him, telling the story only for Miles, trusting him
with a chunk of his life. *I never told anyone any of this.*

They enter a neighborhood where the houses loom bigger, three stories, and the yards make wider, tree-thick borders, but all is still dark. At the end of this block is a squat stand-alone brick building with a sign jutting out over what must've once been sidewalk. The wooden cutout of a shoe hangs creaking in the moonlight. Above the front door, faded white letters spell REPAIR, but the windows are glassless, soggy cardboard behind the bars, and the front door is roped in heavy, rusted chains. Miles reads a few looping, eye-level tags as *HOPE, HOPE, HOPE*, but Tez corrects him: *NOPE, NOPE, NOPE*. For the first time in an hour, Tez laughs.

Despite the fight he put up at the diner, or maybe because of it, Caleb announces that he and Kelsey will be up in a minute. So casually, putting the van in park.

"Seriously?" Tez says. "Dude. Shit was your idea."

Caleb glances in the mirror. "What? The partners can't handle it alone for a minute?"

Miles scoffs, shaking his head. "But you're the one who—"

Kelsey turns to Miles and smiles like she's trying to sell something. Caleb turns around, too, his eyes pleading. He says it to both of them but looks at Miles. "Guys. Please. It's *Valentine's Day.*"

Tez is shaking his head, climbing out, muttering, "What the fuck ever . . ."

Yeah, what the fuck ever, Miles thinks. It's just him and Tez now anyway, Karma and Crush, the way it's supposed to be. He shrugs on his backpack and scoots out, too, slamming the back door hard. Without Caleb around, Miles thinks, maybe he and Tez will kiss.

Around the side of the defunct shop, they climb a dumpster easily enough, leverage a close-growing tree to get onto the roof, Tez going first, then offering his hand out to Miles.

They'll paint the shoe, they decide: a *KARMA* on one side, a *CRUSH* on the other. At the ledge, Tez kicks snow away to clear space on the shingles, pulls out his first can, then drops to his stomach. His throw-up is fast, silver with black highlights. Out on the street, the landscape is dark, pitted and peaked with black roofs, the occasional light that seems just for show. There's no sound except the van's steady engine down below, the muffled suggestion of music coming from inside. The sign is blanched and old enough that, wiggling forward, Miles can see the wood grain, swirling around knots and eyes. He reverses Karma's colors—goes black with silver pops, dragging up his C, scrunching his H, to match the rise of the boot, the point of the toe. Back on the ground, they are pleased. It's too dark for pictures, they agree. They'll come back tomorrow or Sunday or next weekend. They have, it seems then, the rest of their lives.

"Come on, let's let them do whatever they're doing," Tez says. "Take a walk. There's some crazy houses over here."

Down the side street, the snow makes a perfect shallow carpet of the sidewalk. There's a lovely satisfaction in messing it up; in feeling your own clean footprints form. Miles sees what Tez means—the block has the feeling of wartime abandonment, of a memory forgotten. House after house is charred, collapsed, or missing its front steps, appearing to levitate over the reflective ground. Plywood patches the luckier ones, spared, where signs read THIS HOUSE IS BEING WATCHED above illustrated, feminine eyes. Tez laughs at this—"By who?"—until a car passes and both boys turn fast. But it's unfamiliar and on its way elsewhere, a one-headlighted sedan casting a waxy glow.

Halfway down the block, they come to a once-grand three-story, a corner turret and no front door—just an X made of two-by-fours. Miles's heart thumps fast as Tez steps forward. "I've been in this one. Never met any trouble." Miles hasn't had the thought that they'd actually go inside, but it's too late, Tez is tall enough to scissor his legs right over the boards—"I think there's a piano in here"—while Miles waits, afraid, on the porch.

"Hello?" Tez calls in at the threshold. "Squatters? Ghosts? We come in peace."

They listen for a response, their breath making clouds, Tez wagging a flashlight around the foyer. "Come on, I think it's cool." Miles climbs over in two cumbersome moves. Inside, snow has drifted, shored itself against the foot of the stairs in slopes of natural collection. Tez shines the light behind him, into the dark rooms of the wider house.

The part of Miles that is scared is only the outer layer—the part that still takes in information and processes its meaning. But the inner part—the inner part still thrums with *I like you, too*, safe against Tez, so tall and so sure. "Abandoned-house patrol," Tez calls, and Miles is comforted by the sound of his voice. "Neighborhood watch."

He can hardly see Tez in the darkness, except for the breath that the flashlight catches. Miles takes off one glove and grips the edge of Tez's jacket. If Tez notices, he doesn't say so. Miles's heart is audible in his ears. Knowing that they'll find a room. That at last they'll press close, touch their freezing noses together, seal their mouths. For an instant it is such a certainty that Miles sinks to remember his own cowardice. But he doesn't let go of the jacket.

Around the staircase is a dining room or den, its floor punctured and splintered, and then a kitchen without counters or cabinets, just a ceiling bubbled with paint. Across from the kitchen, a larger room reveals the lid-less body of a piano, still there but stripped of keys and legs, like an elephant shot down. Tez's light shows a square plaster scar where a mantel must've been, and walls ripped of molding, and arched, once-beautiful windows now glassless like all the others, letting in the night air. They toe at an avalanche of yellowing portraits, broken-framed snapshots, scattered and mud-printed across the floor. A black-and-white wedding on courthouse steps. Dresses and suits, caps and gowns. A girl with a cheese-wedge haircut sits at the piano in a pinafore, her legs dangling off the bench, her hands gentle on the ivories, staring right at them. The eyes, which have been colored in green—the only color in the picture—give her an eerie livingness.

"You think she sees us?" Tez asks.

They are right up against each other, arm to arm, when Miles hears the noise. At first, he thinks it's outside—off in the twiggy winter trees. But no, the noise is inside, and close. The beam of a flashlight shines in from the door-way, except Tez is right there beside him. A moment of sickening topsy-turvy in which Miles allows himself to hope—*Caleb?*—but two knit masks float in the dark across the room.

His fear is a ball set loose in a box. Who and what—a frenzied mental ricochet. The beam of light points and Miles raises his arms like a shield; when it lowers, he glimpses, in the other mask's hand, the black edges of a dinky tool, pointing. How Tez had described it, like a toy. The gun can't be real, but the way it's being held is real. Raised and dead straight, two hands on it now, trained at his chest, ready to go off at any time.

The voice beside the gun says, *Bags off*; orders them to drop the flashlight. "Do what they say," Tez whispers. The words undo themselves the instant Miles hears them. Tez clicks off their light. Sets it down with hands up.

"Hats off. Jackets off." It's a calm voice. Unhurried, unconcerned. Spit-lipped. "Shirts off. Socks." The one holding the light bends to unzip their packs. *They only want our paint*, Miles lets himself think. The notion is so comforting as to feel almost plausible. The masked man is removing the paint, setting it out, then propping the flashlight on the dead piano, so that it makes a blinding spotlight—pinning them, trembling, to the dark.

"Now shoes. Pants. All of it." As if the gun itself has a voice. Strip down, unwrap, one excruciating skin at a time. Working at his fly, Miles's hands are barely capable. It is cold, it is freezing, but every molecule of his being is too clenched to feel. A can, shaking, a spritz, tested. "Down on your knees." The gun and the light are trained on him and on Tez, on *them*, like a single, impossible demand. The floor is freezing; his palms press the grit; the scattered pictures are everywhere. *Do what they say.*

In a week, in a month, running over and over and over that night, Miles will wonder, *How long had they been following us? How long had they been waiting?* He'll wonder, *When did I let go of his jacket?*

7.

CALEB ISN'T ENTIRELY SURE WHAT'S JUST HAPPENED—IT was *that* kind of coming, that stars-bursting-behind-your-eyes and world-going-black feeling—but he is all too sure of what's happening now: Kelsey is crying and saying, *Don't touch me, don't touch me!* She is, actually, choking on the words, every time his hand moves in her direction, and edging herself closer to the window, as if Caleb's hand were on fire or venomous. But he has to touch her. He has to set his hand gently on her T-shirted shoulder, inside the too-hot, too-dry air of the van, stinking now, a sick stink, the way China Beach at low tide would sometimes reek of rot. He has to be *allowed* to touch her, in order to know that everything is fine. He needs Kelsey to tell him it's fine. And yet she's wailing *Don't touch me* and grabbing at the door handle, which Caleb holds pressed down to lock on his side. *Let me out. Let me out. I don't care, I'll walk.*

Look, let's calm down, he's telling her. He sounds like his fucking father, but he's scrambling, desperate. His heart is a roller coaster careening on the downhill drop. He's lost control of its beat. *I'm gonna take a walk and let you calm down, okay? I gotta find these guys. Look. Kelsey. Seriously. It's okay. It just happens sometimes, okay? You can trust me. It's—sometimes sex—like, it's not always great, but it's fine, right? It's not your fault. I still love you? What I'm trying to say—*

She has her hands covering her shaking face in a way that must make it hard to hear. Like a kid trying to turn invisible. The last thing Caleb hears, before he closes the door, is the deep, concentrated attempt at inhalation, then exhalation.

He came in about thirty seconds flat. Maybe it had hurt (he guessed it probably felt like taking a giant dump, but in reverse), but thirty seconds couldn't have hurt bad enough to warrant this scene, and he was sure there must've been some twisty pleasure at the center of it. The way she'd bitten his hand, hard.

The way she'd gripped the door. Her freak-out was born of embarrassment more than anything, Caleb thought: the grimy slick she'd left on him, what he was surprised to see was blood, and wiped away as discreetly as he could, with napkins from the console.

Caleb smells his hands now—not great—and shoves them back into his jacket where the car keys, at least, reassure him. He follows the footprints in the snow—Tez's bigger ones beside Miles's smaller ones—anxious to find the lovebirds as quickly as possible, to get back to the van, to get Kelsey home, to get her acting normal again before she starts thinking . . . or worse, *saying* . . . what Caleb fears she might be thinking (might be thinking and might be thinking she might *say*). That she didn't want to. That he went so fast . . . that she thought he was doing one thing but then he baited-and-switched her and did something else . . . that his hand was over her mouth so that she couldn't say no. Fuck. His heart is flipping now, freaking—dancing unnaturally in his chest. Just find the dudes, get on home. Let Kelsey calm down. The footsteps lead to a house with an X boarding the door. There are no cars parked on the street, but here, with one wheel up on the mounded sidewalk, is the white van that Caleb knows to be Kuru's.

Time slows. Time slows, and sort of drags, dulling his senses like he's suddenly watching the world through water, trapped in an impossible dream. His legs carry him between a tangle of hedges and the side of the house. The sound of boots stepping, inside. Above his head, a beam of light shows through the arch of a busted window. Like a child, scared and yet determined—driven not by rational thinking now but by a blind, animal will to do one thing and then another, Caleb steps on a water spigot, hoists himself up, balances his forearms on the stone ledge, just high enough to see inside.

He smells the paint before he hears it, hears the hiss before he registers its aim: ten feet into the room shiver two bodies on all fours, one heaving silhouette blocking, at this angle, the other. Their nakedness is immensely unreal. The body closest to Caleb hangs its head, chin collapsed, eyes shut tight and bearing the stream, a *hush, hush, hush* back and forth across its pale shoulders. Beyond, the smaller body, mounded, is rising and falling, rising and falling, as with the labor of impossible waiting. A gasping—Miles's—and a whimper—Tez's—except these bodies and their sounds don't, somehow, match those names, those persons, who must still be safely back, as they were an hour ago, in a different stratum of existence: what will become *before*.

Another person—not the bodies on the floor or the crouching, shadowed painter, but a dark pillar in the doorway, a ski mask making a worm of his face, points at this version of Miles what it occurs to Caleb is a gun.

What if they see me, what if they see me, what if they see me? Fear has never felt quite like this—a surge he must act inside. The painter rattles the can. Logic clicks off by degrees. He has caused this, somehow, by doing that to Kelsey. By bringing Miles, by lying to his mother, by doing that to Kelsey. The gun looks almost bored in its long-resolved pointing. *You invited this*, the voice in the room declares. Caleb's foot on the spigot is aching. His hands are like rocks on the window ledge. When he looks down, surveying the ground for flatness, the decision, already, has been made. Fear is a gravitational force. He lets go.

Don't slip, don't slip, don't slip. Tearing through brush, leaping off the curb, sprinting down the center of the street, looking back once, expecting to be chased, but all is absolutely still. If Kelsey is gone, he'll leave her. He'll whip right onto Kercheval, he'll scream at a gas station attendant, *Call nine one one*—he can see the gas station in his mind, back on MLK—clings to the image for his life.

He'll never admit, not even to himself, how soon he began to revise the story of that night. How quickly feeling guilt became the impulse to cover up guilt. That even as he ran, in those first minutes of psychedelic panic, a lie was seeding itself, one he wouldn't manifest verbally for years. The locked-in fact of *having witnessed* was only a step away from the blurrier almost-fact, of having been, himself, a victim. One word, substituted for another, was a trapdoor, an alibi, a strangely fortuitous *opportunity*. A loophole inside the reality of who he might otherwise be.

8.

PAINT ISN'T A TASTE NOW, IT ONLY JUST *IS*. IT IS THEM AND IT is poison. They can't breathe, because paint can't breathe. The air, the ground, is like glass to move across. Infinitesimally broken. How can they speak, with silver lungs? They can't. Their tongues wag, to keep the poison away, except that it is everywhere already. A relief to vomit. To expel and to trail it, metallic drool, burning with the heat of insides that still work. Is it possible to amputate skin? They run—or drag their legs across the ground—like twin nightmares escaping the block. The sky (or do they imagine it?) is lightening. How impossible. A sunrise inside death.

A sunrise, and a garbage truck, here inside death.

The driver coughs, pulls up the mucus, hocks it clean into his hanky, wads this back into his fist. The fresh pink dawn of another February day. Down a ways, in the middle of the street, silver people wave silver arms. He slows. Their armpits are normal but the rest of them—no, they're gleaming, naked, even shoeless, befouled, the one of them puking. Shit. Climbed up out of the river like winter swamp things. Some beyond-him party, drugs and face paint. He hopes. He hopes that's it. Can't let 'em ride up front, no way. He pumps the brakes, careful on the ice, looks down into the shiny-flecked hair of the tall one—real tall—wet-looking, white under the silver. Other one's young, pudgy, like he was at that age. Even their shriveled dicks shine silver. What does frostbite look like? Can't get paint on these seats— city-owned—let alone the puke. They're shaking bad. Eyes so swollen no way they can see.

He cranks down the window. The tall one starts to blubber, but he cuts in—it's brutal with the window down. "Hop on back. Hang on tight." Rolls it up fast and blows into his hands. A shiver from nape to tailbone. February is a nightmare. The irony is, garbage everywhere, but no garbage to pick up.

Should he take them to the precinct or the hospital? Precinct is closer. Yeah, the precinct, to cover his own ass.

He's thinking, at least it ain't me. He's thinking, this is why I don't have kids. He's thinking, the things you see out here. He hopes to god they're with it enough to hold on.

III.

I LOVE NEW YORK

2016

"May this never happen to you," Mother is saying,
when everything has happened to Mother.

CHRISTINE SCHUTT,
"Daywork"

1. Friday

ON THE FLIGHT FROM SACRAMENTO TO LAGUARDIA, BONNIE O'Connell considered for a moment what it would smell like, taste like, feel like to have a drink for the first time in seven years. Brought on by the cart clattering down the aisle, it was a thought exercise not new to her and not particularly alarming, being no different from the harmless way she sometimes imagined (didn't everyone?) sprinting into oncoming traffic, opening the plane's exit hatch, or chugging down Clorox, if she happened to be bleaching Greg's whites. Her brain had been like that forever: a bully daring her to self-destruct, whom she'd learned to laugh at and ignore.

And yet. A superstition had long persisted in Bonnie, that eventually some Terrible Thing would befall her, bad enough to drive her to drink again, as if booze were, once and for all, her inarguable fate, her one true birthright. She'd gotten used to fearing bankruptcy, cancer, her uterus prolapsing, or Judy cutting off ties completely, but this news about her ex-husband tested her wildest predictions—took a form she could never have expected, dragging her cruelly back in time. She sensed her predicament had something in common with those stories you heard of perfectly healthy wives living with smokers for forty years, then dying of emphysema while their husbands lived on and on. If she wanted to relapse, Rick was her ready excuse.

Ridiculous thought! The drink cart arrived. Jeff, her dead brother, voiced reason in the cotton-ball clouds out the window. *Just cool it, Bonnie. People get emotional on airplanes, and you don't fly so often, right?* Ice fell into plastic. Single-shot spirits were snapped and poured, unleashed to the world. Was she thirsty for it? Did she remember? Of course she did: the burn and warming, the dark and quiet hideout bourbon could make in an otherwise unbearable string of days. Rick's face came to her like her brother's evil opposite. It was the same expression he'd worn in the internet picture, mid-yell at a girl on the court. *That's it,* he chided her. *Blame it again on someone else. Rick ruins your life once and for all.* Since she'd stopped answering his calls, he busted in this other way, mixed up in his aura. Who he'd been twenty years ago collapsing into who she now understood him to be. Haunting, scowling, Rick might cuss, then bust up laughing like it was all a dirty joke. *How 'bout we go down to TJ for the weekend and throw back some cervezas, forget this shit ever happened?* The past tense of it made her brain hurt. Rick was supposed to be someone she never thought about anymore, like her father.

The flight attendant's young face was close enough that Bonnie could see her mascara clumping in real time. To order a gin would be like singing along to an old favorite on the radio.

"A ginger ale, please."

The painted eyes smiled. Bonnie outsmiled her back.

At Bonnie's age, any woman with from-the-box blond striping through her silver had only two options: to be hippie-cheery or hippie-witchy, something happily haggard or just haggard-haggard. As a rule Bonnie pursued the former, even when smiling was a lie (being of the mind that faking it could lead, eventually, to the real thing; being of the mind that prayer was still powerful, even if you knew that heaven was a crock of shit). "Thank you so, so much," she told the flight attendant, tilting her head, accepting the cup.

The bubbles stung her nose, the area above her lip she'd waxed earlier that morning, readying herself for Judy. Bonnie hadn't seen her daughter in two and a half years—not since Judy had come to visit friends in San Francisco and driven a rental up to Auburn. They'd caught up generically over Southwest chicken salads at Taco Tree, and Judy had insisted on staying in a motel instead of in her mother's small but cozy trailer. Now, the long-awaited reality of Judy came nearer and nearer each second, the four-day weekend Bonnie had so been looking forward to, even in her anxiety over what she must tell, a notion that riddled and scattered her brain. She hadn't thought out what exactly she'd say, instead relying on crossed fingers that an opportunity would just *fall into place.* She'd know the time when it was right. On a bench some evening, they'd gaze out at the city. Bonnie's voice would be measured and wise, revealing the girl's story as tactfully as possible. In the best-case scenario, Judy would interrupt—*Mom, please. I don't want to know.* But in the worst—the more probable case—she'd want everything: the gory details, the names and dates, and then, of course, the more brutal line of questioning: *You didn't sense something? Or see signs? How could you have been* married *to this person and not* . . . her tone mounting. But she would not ask, *How could you have chosen him over me?* She might *think* it, but she wouldn't voice it. Even Judy had her limits.

Her baby, her once-suckling best friend, her toddling, hungry towhead, had grown into a shrewd, attractive girl-woman—*Jude*, now, curious but critical, opinionated and resolute. (There was some link, Bonnie knew, between Judy's need to *analyze* everything and the hard-to-see-the-point-of stories she wrote—obscure little episodes that often left Bonnie flipping backward, wondering if she'd missed a page.) And she twitched to remember how easily Judy could flip-flop: could demand everything of you one minute, then close up, pensive, the next. Could look right over your shoulder as if anything in the world was more worthy of attention than whatever brainless topic Bonnie had raised. It was amazing and awful to have birthed a creature like that. How on earth had *she* made *Judy*? And how was it possible to so love and fear someone simultaneously?

She was annoyed to realize her eyes were wet; not *crying* but *tearing*. *Hush now*, Jeff's voice cooed. She dabbed at her face with the Delta napkin. In the imagined scene with Judy, she made a promise to herself: no matter how scary, you must ask the inevitable. Use open-ended, not closed-ended questions. *Did he ever try anything with you?* not *But he never tried anything with you, right?* Bonnie was working, with the help of a library book, on bettering her communication skills.

She could imagine asking *Did he ever*, but she could not will herself around the bend to Judy's answer.

An infant who'd been quiet all this time began to howl behind her. On the small screen above her tray table, the airplane icon fidgeted and froze somewhere over the middle of the country, one of those states Bonnie would be hard-pressed to identify.

*

THEY WERE ONLY TWENTY-SEVEN HOURS INTO THE WEEK, AND already the rope had rubbed a business-card-sized rawness where Jude's top met her jeans. The smallest gestures, the simple movements—climbing into the cab at Caleb's exact pace, leaning forward to mute the news on the back of the passenger seat while he reached behind him to unpocket his phone— now had to be thought through, verbalized, executed with careful coordination. The day had sucked. She hadn't stopped itching or sweating. As if the chewable heat of New York in July wasn't oppressive enough, Jude found herself ungraceful and irritated in her bondage, reduced to the worst version of herself, whining *Ow!* and *What the fuck?* more often than was necessary as they brushed their teeth, navigated the stairwell, did something as easy as ordering coffee. (People would glance, double-take, snap a picture with their phones, then drop their heads back down, perhaps to google *New York couple tied together* before looking up to stare again, as if staring itself wasn't a thing that could be seen.) But Caleb seemed not to mind the chafing and slowness, remained patient through the obviousness of Jude's frustration, was maybe even *enjoying* himself. The weed must've helped—all day he'd nursed the pen, his eyes so placidly flat they brought new literalism to *stoned*. And all day he'd pulled her drowsily against his lean torso, whispering into her neck, *Baby, I just want to be closer to you*, relentlessly sarcastic. That evening they'd napped in the air-conditioning's blast, ordered in sushi, then showered, a thoroughly involved experience for Caleb while Jude waited on her end of the rope, shivering in the periphery of the nozzle stream. He scrubbed his scalp luxuriously, lathered his forehead and pits, screwed up his face with the effort of self-care. He was so handsome it shocked her sometimes, her proximity to its potency but also her distance from it: she felt so *ordinary* next to him, in the disenchanted shell of her body. It was a feeling, she knew, best kept to herself.

The cabdriver, who'd made no comment regarding their predicament, turned to ask which it was—Central and Troutman or Central and Myrtle?

They'd given conflicting directions: Jude the former, Caleb the latter, and now Caleb repeated the cross streets in the backseat. He turned to Jude in the dark and moved his fingertips down her arm, as if her skin was suddenly fascinating. "I thought if we got out early we could walk a few blocks first. Fuck against a wall or something."

His molly had blossomed already, Jude saw; her own was still wrapped in a tissue, nestled in the cup of her bra. She nudged his knee and snorted. She was beginning to know how he worked: he wanted a cinematic entrance, the illusion they'd trudged halfway across Brooklyn like this, or at least ridden the subway to Jefferson. As if anyone's first question, seeing them tied together at the waist, would be whether they'd cabbed or trained. Caleb lifted the arm he'd been touching and ran his tongue along its inner length.

She turned on like a lamp. All at once she was giddy, pushing him back against the seat to lick the side of his face until he cried out, and the cabdriver glanced worriedly in the mirror. They giggled. He fished down her shirt, found the Kleenex-wrapped pill, slipped it in her mouth, and then kissed her again as she swallowed. Mouth to mouth, Jude's mind drifted toward another pleasure: at the end of the piece, the photos would hang in a grid on the gallery wall, and aloof opening-goers, Jude's well-dressed peers, would whisper, *He did it with his girlfriend*. The pride she'd thrill with.

The car let them off in front of the twenty-four-hour pizza/falafel place where, later, a mob would gather when the bars closed. Jude bought three bottles of water, then drank half of one as they walked, their paces matched, the rope slack between them, Caleb squeezing and releasing, squeezing and releasing, her hip.

The club wasn't really a club—it was a white-washed cinder-block yoga cooperative profiled on Japanese blogs and appearing in bespoke city guides, slim as chapbooks. Its founders—three reinvented heshers—took pains to sync the event calendar with the phases of the moon. Jude had been there a half dozen times, but never with Caleb. In the backyard, a geodesic tree fort remained half-built above spindly tomato plants and an herb garden everyone stepped on. The single bathroom accumulated a line so long and impatient it became its own sort of party-alongside-the-party. From the street, bass thumped like a big baby's heartbeat. The sound intensified and gained depth when someone opened the door, then flattened again when the door closed.

Two girls leaned against a chain-link fence, smoking, one tall and one short, both with flat white bellies bared above their shorts. They ashed their cigarettes and stared. "Whoa," the tall one said. "What's *up?*"

"Hey," Jude said.

"Is this, like, a secret kink party?" the other asked. "We didn't get the message."

The tall girl said to Caleb, "Wait, are you that artist guy? What's your name? I totally recognize you. You know my friend Suzie, right?"

"I don't know if I know Suzie," Caleb said. He bent his head to remove an Olympus point-and-shoot he wore by the lanyard, his name scratched into the plastic front with a glass etcher. He asked neither of the girls in particular, "Would you mind?"

Suzie's friend stepped forward to take the camera and turned it over, inspecting it for a dumbfounded minute, then shrieked, "Oh my god, it's a *real* camera!"

In *Art/Life: One Year Performance 1983–1984 (Rope Piece)*, the original rope connecting Tehching Hsieh and Linda Montano was eight feet long, not the three feet of Caleb and Jude's, and they'd endured their linkage for 365 days instead of just seven. Caleb called their piece—*his* piece—*One Week Rope, July 2016 (Relationship)*, and added the documentary element of photographs: a picture taken once every four hours would capture their plight on film (film was more authentic than JPEGs, which could be edited and deleted, retaken). Last night, spooned together in the center of the mattress, the alarm on Caleb's phone chimed Jude awake. The camera was there like an eye in her face—a flash, and she'd winced.

The original statement signed by Hsieh and Montano read: *We will stay together for one year and never be alone. We will be in the same room at the same time, when we are inside. We will be tied together at waist with an eight-foot rope. We will never touch each other during the year.* In his art studio the evening before, Jude had watched Caleb scrawl his own manifesto in all-caps Sharpie on a square of paper, then tuck this between two sheets of vellum in the top drawer of a flat file. Luke, Caleb's assistant, had already left for the day but had arranged the supplies: a Home Depot bag, tape measure, and industrial-looking scissors, plus a bottle of champagne and two plastic cups. A sticky note suggested, *Have fun!*

Jude sat on the worktable while Caleb uncoiled the rope, the kind used for horses or nooses, and fitted it around her waist. Except for a noxious, chemical smell that signified, to Jude, "art," there was little evidence of making in the space. A number of older paintings rested in crates against the wall, and desks edging the room held two large Macs, a 3-D printer, piles of media: magazines and a New Museum catalogue where Caleb's work made an appearance. On his phone, a supposed sailor demonstrated knot tying on YouTube. Caleb belted the other end around himself, measured the distance between them, and tied the same knot again. When he lifted the slack and let it fall, she thought of those blankets you put on dogs, to comfort them during storms.

WE WILL STAY TOGETHER FOR ONE WEEK AND NEVER BE ALONE.

WE WILL BE IN THE SAME ROOM AT THE SAME TIME, WHEN WE ARE INSIDE.

WE WILL BE TIED TOGETHER WITH A THREE-FOOT ROPE.

WE WILL TOUCH EACH OTHER OFTEN.

When he kissed her, he caressed her throat like something at last cherished. Sex on the table was brutal against her tailbone, but then the scales tipped, and pleasure overwhelmed her. Just once she turned her head—Manhattan's floating, sunset skyline, moated by dark water—and her breath caught.

It was only midnight but the party was full and hot, smelling already of sweat, palo santo, manufactured fog. She found herself dancing before she decided to dance. Sound—bass and its tinny top layer—came in through Jude's very pores. Within minutes she was all hips and liquid pulse, gravitating toward the crowd's center, though Caleb, on his end of the tether, stayed still, imperceptibly moving his chin, gazing down at his phone. Jude closed her eyes, slipped her hand up his back, danced into him. *Let's find Alec*, he yelled in her ear. *I think he has blow.*

Arm fragments swam, heads swerved, pupils dilated in the gauzy pink womb. Faces floated past that she knew and didn't know. When the haze subsided, Caleb's friends appeared—Alec and Bryce, Jahari and his girlfriend, Zoë, and a DJ whose name Jude forgot, gyrating in a huddle among banana leaves lit purple. Long, sensuous hugs were given, cheeks kissed, beers passed out. Zoë said something Jude couldn't make out, then lifted Jude's hand, kissed it, and receded into the swell. The rope made only a minimal stir; no follow-up questions met Caleb's explanation (*Just this piece I'm redoing*). It was too loud to talk. They drank and danced. Even Caleb was bobbing now, to a deep, persuasive beat. One track blurred into the next and suddenly everyone—every*thing*—in the room synchronized (a feeling she knew from rolling at other parties, in other emailed locations), intoxicated by music that was better, somehow, than music could be. Her brain sparkled like the glitter around Bryce's eyes. A stranger passed out Dixie cups of mushroom tea. Caleb's face turned away, bent over Alec's outstretched hand, wrenched up with the force of the snort. Had anyone stopped dancing? Whole hours folded and released like Chinatown souvenirs.

Something tugged, yanking Jude from her thrall. "Hey, I gotta take a leak."

In the backyard, where it was cooler but still loud, she waited patiently while Caleb pissed in the mud. A pretty girl, buns like pastries atop her head, met Jude's eyes and distinctly frowned. Her mood plummeted then, dropped off into lucidity, and everything was horribly normal. "Should you be peeing out here?" He either hadn't heard or pretended not to hear—he was turned away from her, shaking off. A snap crisis, an epiphany flipped wrong side out. Who *was* this person, and why was she *tied* to him? Her saliva was too thick to swallow; even her mouth felt claustrophobic. Her life from a month ago rushed up: her Bed-Stuy apartment, her own room with her own books, Jen's jarred kombucha creatures crowding the kitchen cabinets like a store of alien embryos—a setting she suddenly yearned for.

Caleb turned and held her, bringing his pricy odor of bergamot and oud. His lips pressed her hair. "Wait it out. It'll come back."

It *did* come back, once they were back inside and Jude had chugged more

water, and that freak desolation passed as easily as it had arrived. Among the
friends they danced, kissing, receptors of sheer pleasure, bodies syncopating
outside with inside, riding out the lows because the peaks—all of the gratitude and love you'd ever felt for anything welling up through time and space,
culminating in the perfect repository of whoever was beside you—were pure
euphoria. Unquestionably, it would all be worth however they'd feel tomorrow.

THEY'D MET in real life (as never seemed to happen anymore), two and a half
months ago. One empty weekday, a stranger sat down at the bar near the end
of Jude's lunch shift, arresting her with his tallness, his blue eyes, the perfectly
casual way his clothes fit. In its repurposed dining car, the restaurant evoked
a pearl-and-glass past that had probably never been, Toulouse-Lautrecian, and
at its best when it was raining. That day, it happened to be raining.

He listened to her required oration of the entire menu, then ordered
the half chicken and a beer brewed by monks. They chatted about the new
Whitney, the catastrophe of the waterfront, a "there goes the neighborhood"
conversation while he sipped and she adjusted tips. The cuffs of his thermal
(he wore a T-shirt over it, recalling the boys of Jude's youth) were flecked
with gesso. Like other gorgeous men, he was comfortable taking up space:
his jacket, phone, knit hat, a long black vape pen, and a Bukowski paperback
(Bukowski! Could she forgive herself?) were piled on the zinc beside him, his
elbows rested wide, and he made no attempt to rein in his gaze, roving from
her face to her collarbone to the long mirror behind the aperitif bottles, glowing like jewels in the natural light. Each time his sangfroid eyes met Jude's,
they seemed to touch her incidentally, as if he were running his hand over
everything and just happened to land on her. She found herself begging, *Look
at me.*

When his food came, he told a story set in some corny seafood restaurant
where he'd worked when he was eighteen and been fired for doing whippets,
an anecdote that made her feel both exposed and commiserated with, even
as it flustered her (for there was no casual way to say, *But this isn't my real
job! I work at a magazine, a very cool one!*). Instead, she asked, "Have you
read Orwell's *Down and Out in Paris and London*?" and then hated herself

for beginning a sentence *Have you read* (a friend's voice came back: *Whenever anyone asks 'Have you read,' what they really mean is 'I have read.' They mean, Me, me, me*) but forged on, to save him from having to answer. "I only read it recently, for this review I was working on—"

"You're a writer?" he asked, tearing off a wing.

How could she qualify: *I'm trying*? "I work at a magazine." She felt herself flush.

He bit into the meat, talking as he chewed. "I love magazines." He smiled, swallowing. "Do I know it?"

She set to polishing a row of already polished wine glasses. "*Hierarchy*?" No matter that she was only asked to write when a contributor bailed or a hole needed filling. No matter that she wasn't on the masthead but managed subscriptions for contract pay that covered less than half of her rent each month.

"Totally. My friend Manuel used to do stuff there."

He wrote a column for the blog; Jude had met him exactly once. "Manuel! Manuel's great."

"Anyway, you were saying? About some book?"

"Oh, it's just—it's all about Orwell working in Paris as a plongeur—or, like, a dishwasher—"

"Man, I was in Paris last winter and it—*French*! It's like everyone's about to spit a huge fucking loogie. I didn't even try—"

Jude laughed. "Just traveling? Or—"

"This residency thing."

"Cool." She could feel her skin warming, her scalp tingling. "An artist residency?"

"Yeah," he said, sucking on a bone. The track switched on the management-selected mix. "Through this museum."

She'd die before she'd ask what museum, but she felt herself running out of questions. "It's—what's winter like there?"

"Cold. I mean, I used to live in Detroit, so—" He shrugged.

A life stretched out behind him, replete with mysterious previous chapters. "Oh, cool," she said. Detroit—she thought of bankruptcy and techno, photos of hulking, empty structures and nature-reclaiming rooftops. Some friends of hers had just moved there, she told him—Julian did sound performance, and his husband, Jeremy, made furniture. "Anyway, I think they really like it; they're renovating this house . . ."

Did he roll his eyes, or was that only the way eyeballs migrated, sometimes, when swigging back a beer? "Read the hype in the *Times*?" he said, setting the bottle down. "Found a foreclosure at auction that a poor Black family owned for generations? Julian and Jeremy. Entrepreneurs, too, right? Trying to open a ceramics-slash–vintage clothing shop in a *safe* neighborhood." His hands made air quotes around *safe*, and then he laughed. He laughed at her.

She gathered herself inside herself, as she'd learned to do in this life, so effectively and without thinking that the immense effort of it went consciously unnoticed. She smiled. "Oh, no, different Julian and Jeremy. Their shop sells air plant arrangements and essential-oil perfumes."

"With names like Mist and Rust," Caleb said.

"Macramé everywhere."

"Tarot readings on Wednesday nights."

"Deep listening sessions on Thursdays."

"Drone, mostly."

"Yeah, it's more of a *space* than a shop."

The rain intensified, percussing on the metal roof.

Ten minutes later he was gone—braved the downpour while she was in the kitchen helping Jorge unclog the food trap, Jude a lowly plongeur again. He'd tipped exactly fifteen percent, she was flummoxed to see, and there was no phone number or *Nice to meet you* scrawled boyishly on the credit-card receipt. But she had his full name and searched him anyway, over her shift amaro and warm Castelvetranos, sitting on the same stool he'd occupied. She clicked the links and zoomed in on the photos, anticipating disappointment. But what Jude learned that evening was that Caleb was Someone—a nineties graffiti writer ("under-recognized") turned very recognized artist—celebrityesque, even, living loosely in the neighborhood of fame, if fame meant usernames on nostalgia blogs arguing over the origins of your "handstyle" (though, mysteriously, the internet lacked photos of his tag). If famous meant an image search yielded more pictures of your face than of your actual art (in more

than one of these, he stood in a suit before branded red-carpet backdrops Jude
only knew from tabloids—Tribeca Film Fest, a NYFA gala—beside one, then
another beautiful woman). Famous if fame meant fifty thousand followers
while Caleb, in turn, followed only nine accounts. Always-in-the-right-place-
at-the-right-time famous, she supposed; never-early/rarely-smiling famous, as
if smiling was reserved for his private, not his public life (she'd made him
smile, at lunch, more than once). By the time he graduated from Parsons he'd
already sold out a solo show (who *did* that?) at a now-extinct Stanton Street
gallery Jude remembered from her first years in the city, before he moved up
to Chelsea, with cameos in Brussels, Sydney, Dubai. His CV showed how
one domino hit another—Spring Break, the Armory, Art Basel (Miami),
Art Basel (Basel)—an enviable momentum, successes stacked year by year.
And she understood why. He was good, actually. It wasn't her usual thing
(masculine? maximal?), but she liked his work, at least in the postage-stamp-
sized images she was zooming in on now, paintings (oils, early stuff) recalling
Basquiat's messiness and Bruegel's panoramas, if you replaced the hunting
grounds and codpieces with blighted houses, flaming cop cars, amputees in
wheelchairs and, floating overhead, a chubby-cheeked boy draped in lilies,
sprouting wings. No profile or review seemed complete without referencing
a tantalizing biographical detail: in his fringier youth, Caleb and his brother
(*adopted*, it was also occasionally clarified) had suffered a bizarre assault—
attacked with their own spray paint almost two decades before, effectively
ending Caleb's graffiti career and, after a drawn-out illness, his little brother's
life. A Miles LeBlanc memorial page showed a trapped-in-cyberspace thumbnail of an awkward boy, *so young*, standing on a distinctly Californian deck, a
resigned half smile it was impossible not to see as somehow prophetic, knowing the brevity of his life to come. He died in 2002, but the posts on the page
were from later—2006 and after, mostly from old classmates and addressed
to Miles directly (*I sat by you in science. You were always such a kind and funny
person*), emphatic as yearbook inscriptions, differing only in their tense. How
awful, Jude thought, from deep inside the wormhole of her phone, and for
Caleb, too—to have lost a brother. She could see past the Bukowski now,
the bad tip, the eye-roll; he was shifting, in her understanding, to someone

pained, even tortured, wizened by tragedy; a reluctant survivor. She swiped back to a painting from 2007. The boy peered out from a smoldering oil sky, smeary and atmospheric, like a spirit in a Chagall.

Was it possible to fall in love with someone via their hodgepodge, achronological, pixelated digital biography? In an interview from 2014, Caleb explained how *uninterested* he was in traveling down a well-worn art-world path in which the limelight led to fadeout, fatigue, a deterioration of the work's essential quality. *I refuse to be pigeonholed. When you're making paintings, selling out shows, you have all these collectors on you suddenly, treating you like a fucking painting machine, like you're IKEA or some shit. Then there's all these copycat dick riders basically ripping off your style, then DMing you, asking if they can do a studio visit. The art world can be toxic. Cannibalistic. You have to stay one step ahead at all times.* (Jude had a general understanding of what he meant. Just after college, her first year in New York, she'd found Craigslist work as an assistant for one such toxic dealer until, at a West Village happy hour, he put his hand on her leg midsentence, while discussing exactly the kind of copycat dick rider Caleb was describing, and propositioned her outright.) The more recent work attested to this view; his paintings became sculpture, which merged organically into installation, which led, naturally, to photo, video, performance, and the murky, unclassifiable genres that mixed them. Caleb's Wikipedia entry (which was brief and needed sweeping up) dubbed him a "multimedia street artist." Most recently, he'd been making *Edits*—his chosen term—remakes, reenactments, or referential riffs imbued with art-historical allusions. He'd rewritten a dozen Yoko Ono event scores to include drug use, vandalism, and satiric references to Beatles trivia. Last year, he'd painted the Futurist manifesto in red enamel on the hood of a Chevy Cavalier, then set fire to the car in an empty field somewhere. The footage—the burning metal husk interspersed with the slow-motion demolition of an old Detroit department store—was scored by a warped recording of David Bowie's "Panic in Detroit." Bowie's voice wailed and wobbled. It occurred to Jude that Caleb looked a little like Bowie himself, in his wide-set eyes and sulky mouth, *Hunky Dory*–era but without the lipstick or long hair.

Sofia, who edited *Hierarchy*'s portfolio spreads, knew everyone in the art world. *Caleb LeBlanc?* Jude texted, and the paint palette emoji. *Just met him. Wtf. Single?* Immediately came Sofia's emphatic *YES!*—and a string of tiny flames.

A week later, a boon in Jude's inbox: he had a piece in a group show opening that Friday, at a gallery on Broome she just happened to get emails from (she didn't go in for signs, and yet here one was). In the days leading up, she rearranged her work schedule, stressed over her outfit, decided not to go (the likelihood was too high that she'd leave the event defeated, without even having talked to him), then finally, the evening of, reversed course at the last minute. Sofia couldn't go but she persuaded Jen—bribed her with free beer and a promise to clean, that weekend, the bathroom.

The outfit she regretted immediately: a voluminous velveteen coat (too hot) over a pale, low-necked bodysuit (naked as an undergarment), had seemed appropriately laissez-faire at home but now struck her as both frumpy and slutty. Jen had approved of the rest of her—bright lipstick, hair parted and pulled back, no jewelry—but now, looking around the room, Jude felt her motives must've showed; she was too obvious and too distinctly poor. For years she had avoided big openings, *Manhattan* openings, afraid of running into the dealer—dog hair and a petite Scandinavian on his arm, holding her hostage with small talk. But now she felt lame, to recognize only three or four faces in the bright rooms, and even then, whether from real life or the internet she couldn't be sure. She scanned for Caleb—*You'll know him when you see him*, she told Jen, *he's stupidly hot*—but there were so many sculptures in the way, more like social obstructions than works of art, and he was nowhere. Eventually they found his installation, the centerpiece of the second story. A small drywall room was accessible to the viewer only by a tiny window in the green, industrial door. Inside was a kind of outsider reconstruction of Duchamp's *Étant donnés*, in which the lantern above the recumbent nude (was she papier-mâché?) was, instead, a jankily suspended desktop computer displaying a video feed. When Jude approached the door, the screen showed a girl, fourteen or fifteen, buzzing her shoulder-length hair. Close-up and blue in the camera's lens, she mowed from forehead to crown as clumps fell surreally away. *This is for you, Mom*, she said to the camera. *This is for you.*

"Oh my god," Jude said. She pulled back and turned to the space where Jen had been. But standing there was Caleb. "Is it a live stream or—" shocked, struggling to calibrate the real him against the imagined him.

He asked, "Can I see?"

"Of course!" she blundered. "It's your thing."

He stepped forward and took her place. Was Jude supposed to walk away now? "Oh man," he said, as if knowing she would stay. "It's live, yeah. All anonymous."

"Is she crying yet?" From inside, Jude thought she heard the beginnings of a sob.

"No, she's laughing. She's losing it." Caleb was smiling. "Good for her. She's going for it. Doing her eyebrows now."

When the channel switched, he turned to her again and swigged his Tecate. "You want a beer?" She saw the recognition puzzle across his face— saw his brain working to match her with someone he knew, a friend's friend or an art-world person, and for one hot-cheeked instant she was terrified she'd have to say, *I was your waitress in Williamsburg.* But he broke the moment himself. "It's Jude, right?"—as if already aware of the power her name, in his mouth, could wield.

On their first date they ate hand-pulled noodles off Styrofoam plates, watched tai chi in the park, downed several Negronis at a bar on Canal, ran through a midnight tropical storm, then locked themselves in Caleb's apartment for the next forty-eight hours.

That was in early May. Saffron pollen dusted windshields and sidewalks. Rosé was chalked back on the city's menus. Dopamine surged and squirrels freaked, and Sundays were for squandering again, everyone woozy with life force, sex urge. For days, weeks, Jude and Caleb didn't sleep. They stretched themselves long into the night, accidentally and on purpose, incapable of not touching, talking and talking as if sleep were just a pesky hurdle to bigger urgencies: marveling at the contours of each other's bodies, for example, or learning what songs the other had loved as a teenager. Jude broke glasses at work, stopped responding to friends, ate almost nothing, neglected her writing and felt fine neglecting it (an old teacher's voice echoed: *Most of the time, art surpasses life. But sometimes—very rarely—life surpasses art. When that happens, take it*). Condoms became a ridiculous notion—a thing for other, less besotted people. At the magazine, she sat at the plywood desk, in the dusty ground-level Dumbo office, and composed ebullient emails: *We apologize profusely for the delay in processing your subscription! Please accept a complimentary* Hierarchy *tote, which will arrive with your *ON TIME* spring print issue, "Error & Errata," in 5–7 business days!* He slipped a key to his apartment into Jude's jacket pocket, so that she didn't discover it until she was halfway home, one delirious morning on the G.

Stories were told, histories sketched, past romances tallied and delineated. Jude had to pry a little to get Caleb to open up (what was her name, how had they met, how long had it lasted, and why did it end?), but when he did, she detected a trend. There'd been one long-term relationship in his twenties (Hannah, cute but dumb; they'd run into her once on the train), then a series of yearish-long *things* (*We had a thing*, as Caleb put it) pressed back-to-back-to-back, as far as Jude could calculate. *And why did it end with Mira? What happened with Bianca?* she nudged, prepared for betrayals, overlaps, cheating—but the answers only oscillated between stock and deflective: *It ran its course, We didn't see eye to eye, Because she wasn't you.*

She could entertain the notion that, sure, maybe in the past Caleb had been a *serial monogamist* (who hadn't?), but the idea that Jude might be part of a larger pattern was incomprehensible, given the private specificity—the rarity, she felt—of their connection. Again and again, he held her face in his hands and said, *What did I do to deserve you?* with a candor that startled her. *I feel like I've known you forever* and *I've never felt this way about anyone* and soon, most significantly, *I love you.* The phrase was new enough between them that it still carried its original meaning, confessional in quality, ripe with all the excitement of vulnerability and a fearless acknowledgment of magic. Any previous utterance of those three words shrank in Jude's perception to an embarrassing miscalculation. In hindsight she'd been so naïve(!), to have said it to a balding cellist who wept when he played and, before him, to a wannabe cowboy poet who actually wore the boots and, last year, to an espresso-machine repair guy with an honest-to-god phobia of buttons—someone she'd kept on the back burner until the unbearableness of February had driven them finally to *try it*. Simon, Aaron, Reid—the "loves" of Jude's past became so paltry once described to Caleb, in translations that laid ballsy waste to the reality of their once-powerful positions in her life (so many dinners! So many estimated cross-borough travel times, Sunday plans, birthday gifts; arguments, weekends upstate, tears, texts, movies, breakups, back-togethers, museums; so many exhausting conversations with friends over drinks, deciphering the subtext of such-and-such action, such-and-such word choice or phrasing, as if these dudes were high experimental modernists and Jude and her friends had nothing better to do than treat their under-the-breath murmurs like the masterworks of Stein or Pound). Now the exes took on the cumulative purpose of *practice*—of having existed merely to ready her for Caleb. *I can't think about you with other dudes*, Caleb said. *I'm sorry, but it's disgusting to me*. It was disgusting to Jude, too, now! In her heart they became a sort of human staircase, meant only to lead her to him.

One of those nights, upon learning Jude lacked a father (she didn't know, she told him, much more than a first name), Caleb observed, *It's amazing you don't have daddy issues*, to which Jude took no offense. Where daddy issues lacked, she said, she had enough mommy troubles to last a lifetime. Bonnie was a topic she'd learned to make anecdotal (to friends she described the relationship as *a long work in progress*), but now she tried hard to tell a kind of truth, trusting that Caleb, estranged as he was from his own parents, would get it. Her mother had had an unlucky life, Jude explained, complicated by alcoholism, abuse, a dead brother, and a string of bad men—all the psychic instability that combo brought. When Jude was fourteen, in the fall of her freshman year, Bonnie had steered her Dodge Colt off the 405, underestimating the curve of the ramp, on her way from Jude's school to their then house, where they lived with Rick, Jude's pervy, pedophiliac stepfather (*That's a whole other darkness . . .*). The car had rolled three times before ramming into a retaining wall, inflating an airbag like a punch to the face, shattering her mother's nose. The windshield was a web of glass, and the entire passenger side—where Jude would've ridden, had she not left campus on foot that day, right at dismissal, with her friend Melissa—came out crunched as a beer can in a backyard crusher.

The accident earned Bonnie a DUI and thirty days in a treatment facility, mandated by the state. Legally, Jude became the temporary ward of her stepfather—a decision so infuriatingly stupid that she refused, to the outrage of Rick and with the blessing of Melissa's mother, to abide by it. The Geisens were profoundly kind. Half of Jude's clothes were already at Melissa's, folded in stacks on the baby-blue chair. The pullout section of Melissa's daybed stayed permanently pulled out, two inches lower than Melissa's own bed. Monday through Friday, Kathy packed fruit leather and egg-salad sandwiches, cut along the diagonal, and Melissa's father, Cody, enforced a rational set of rules around curfews and Parental Advisory stickers, which Jude dutifully followed. She smiled and laughed and responded when called upon, helped clear the table and made her own bed, playing a Geisen girl, in survival mode for four disorienting years. Even when Bonnie got out of rehab, ten pounds heavier, stripped of her pride but healthier in the eyes, Jude stayed with her new family, a choice meant not to punish her mother (though that would become Bonnie's long-suffering understanding) as much as to avoid her stepfather. The truer narrative—the one adult Jude wished her mother would recognize—was that Bonnie, having failed to protect Jude, had left her no other choice.

She kept straight As in high school and won an award for zero absences in all four years. She edited the school literary magazine under the guidance of her English teacher, Miss Hicks, read the Beats and their girlfriends, and didn't lose her virginity until she was twenty, in her sophomore year at UC Santa Barbara. The guy was no one, a friend's friend. By the time they slept together she'd already been accepted as a transfer student at Sarah Lawrence, on loans and a partial scholarship; sex for the first time was akin to laundry done frantically before a big trip. *New York!* she expressed to Caleb—goodbye Santa Anas, hang-looses thrown from Jeeps, pajamaed classmates who never did the reading. Hello whole Russian novels assigned over the weekend, feminist professors who went by first names, train rides to record stores in the city. Civilization.

Now Bonnie lived in a depressing town in the Sierra foothills, where she'd been sober for seven years. (*Supposedly* seven years—though Jude found the town, with its unshaded parking lots and pine-forest margins, its sidewalk-less central highway and roving tweakers, to be exactly the sort of California wasteland that would drive one to drink. That is, it reminded her of the Valley.) Now, things between them were generally level. They spoke on the phone once every month or two (Bonnie called much more) about weather, health, money, scarcity. Their geographical distance, the end of Bonnie and Rick when Jude was in college, Bonnie's submission to "getting help," Bonnie frequent vocalizing that she wanted to "be closer" (*How?* Jude always wondered) made the phone calls possible, if not exactly emotionally satisfying.

For years, Jude had waited for her mother to work the steps—to call her one Sunday, or sit her down on the built-in trailer couch during one of Jude's visits, and initiate a formal amends. She had envisioned herself listening, nodding and nodding, taking in Bonnie's tearful apology, letting it run through her veins and heal her. By the end, both of them would embrace, transformed. (As if one apology could do that.) When it did finally come, not long after her twenty-fifth birthday, it was quick and surreal—scripted and sad. Jude couldn't help feeling she was simply one other person on a list of coworkers, old friends, ex-lovers that her mother had to get through. And at the *What can I do to make it better* part, Jude, too, had failed—choked out *I don't know*, because she didn't, and *It's okay*, although it wasn't. On her end, she was tired of doing "work." How many hours had she invested, already, in sliding-scale therapy, Al-Anon, journaling, endless thinking walks? The city commanded, *Look forward*; it had no time for the past. Her peers all seemed so free, unworried; without guilt, they glided around her, drinking beer on gentrified stoops, browsing the new releases at the bookstore, crowding the A train, Rockaway-bound. She wanted their *ease*, and with it a head so clear that she could, seriously, write. She was plagued, she told Caleb, by the persistent fear that *time was running out*—as if everything she desired might slip out of reach if she didn't claim it by some nebulous, approaching midnight. The last time Jude had asked her mother about meetings, Bonnie answered, *Oh sure, as often as I can*, with an airiness that signified well-intentioned lying. *I mean, I skip a week here and there, but mostly* . . . As if Bonnie, by contrast, had all the sweet time in the world.

Two birthdays ago, Bonnie had given Jude a star—or rather, bought a mail-order certificate that said a star at such-and-such coordinates, pulsing in the night sky, was now named "Judy"—never mind that what Jude really needed was a better winter coat and help with her student loans.

"I wonder how many other stars are named Judy," Caleb whispered, three weeks after their first date, picking a pubic hair off his tongue.

"What a scam," Jude said. "That should tell you everything you need to know."

"I want to meet her."

A siren passed outside, pinking the walls. "Do you mean that? Because she's coming here. In July. I can't believe—in a moment of weakness I agreed to it. Four days."

"Great; she can stay with us."

"With *us*?"

"Why not?"

"We don't live together!"

"We should, though, shouldn't we?"

"You're crazy."

"Come on, isn't she broke? She lives in a trailer."

An old defensiveness rose in her. Maybe she'd said too much. "She's not *that* broke. She bought me a star."

When Caleb talked about himself, growing up in San Francisco and then, briefly, in Michigan, Jude began to piece together the extent of his wealth. She gleaned that he was private-school rich, family-summer-house rich, owned-his-Greenpoint-apartment rich, generations-deep rich; and yet she didn't, to her own surprise, find herself cutting him down, writing her own silent counternarrative of resentment and contempt as he spoke—her general response when she learned someone "came from money" (as if it were a ripe, green seed). On the contrary, the shaded embarrassment that came into Caleb's voice when he answered Jude's questions—her beloved's insecurity—made him all the more attractive, stretched out, fawnlike, on a cool bed. He feared being judged for his privilege, she intuited, the perception that his life had been a cakewalk, his success something he'd bought instead of earned. Her hand found his chest and stroked.

"I mean, there's a lot that people don't know about me. I'm not some fucking *trustafarian* . . . I haven't even spoken to my parents in like ten years."

He'd hinted at the silence before, but not precisely at its shape or reasons. "Not at all?" Jude asked. Her first night in the apartment, in a small frame on the bookshelf, she'd seen a photograph, the distinct gloss and color saturation that signaled midnineties film development. It was a Halloween picture. The little brother held a bandana on a stick, the father wore a blue police hat, and the woman who must've been their mother was dressed as a clown, in a polka-dot jumper hooped out at the sides and a green, flipping-up wig. Only Caleb was without costume, all teenage posture. The photographer must have snapped at just the right moment—someone had said something funny—because everyone smiled naturally, even Caleb, looking at his mother. They didn't *seem* like a troubled family. But the next time she was over, the picture was gone. Removed.

Irritation came into his voice. "I just couldn't deal anymore, you know, with feeling like . . . not only did they not support me making art, but"—he cleared his throat—"I really think they blame me for what happened with my brother."

Guilt pricked her. She arranged her face into something puzzled and concerned, to veil what she already knew from the internet. "What . . . what happened with your brother?"

Caleb rolled onto his back, looked up at the ceiling, and exhaled. They'd been graffiti partners, he said, in Detroit, when the family moved to Michigan. Developed a style together, went out together. Miles had been good. Everything came so naturally to him—he was only fifteen, but you wouldn't know it, the way he bombed, fearless and exact. Anyway, they met this kid—this local tagger, sort of a loner, sort of *lost*, a displaced white boy in

Detroit—who they let write with them. Took this kid out, showed him stuff. Had no idea the kid was trouble—had beef with an older crew, dangerous, territorial dudes of a whole different ilk. One night, the kid took them to an area where they'd never been, a neighborhood that was supposed to be safe, low-stakes. He had this girl with him, and he might've been showing off . . . neither Caleb nor Miles had wanted to go. But they did, in the dead of winter, fucking around in a big, abandoned house . . . and when the kid went out to the car, disappeared with the girl, two dudes showed up. Jumped Caleb and Miles. Forced them, at gunpoint, to strip. *Painted us like furniture*, Caleb's voice shook, *head to toe*. Jude clenched to listen. Her breath was a pain in her chest, imagining. "Silver—silver paint is really toxic, whatever is in it to make it metallic . . . and Miles got it worse than me. They got my back, my legs and feet, but Miles got it across the chest, the face, in his fucking mouth. I couldn't do anything to make it stop. I was . . . I was so scared."

Was he crying? He wasn't, but his eyes were glossy in the dimness, and a mask of pain armored his face. She ached to see him like this. "I'm so sorry."

Two months after the attack, Miles had his first seizure. Chronic bronchitis became asthma, debilitating stomach pain revealed bleeding intestines, and his kidneys, the doctor said, suffered from exhaustion. The decline was gradual at first, then all at once—the same way decay overtook Detroit houses, whose roofs sank and doors blew off in big storms. The roof sank, the doors blew off Miles. He was in and out of the hospital; their father took a leave of absence; Miles grew depressed, nearly silent, locked himself inside himself. Diagnosis after diagnosis made the psychic burden as hard to endure as the physical symptoms. Then, one afternoon in the Ann Arbor dining room (*I was in New York by then—I had to live my life, you know?*), drawing at the table while his urine collected in a bag, Miles seized so violently he stopped breathing altogether. He had been, Caleb said, alone.

Now he cried. Oozed like a puddle, his grief deep and hungry, an insatiable frustration. Jude brought his head to her chest and felt the tears collect at her sternum. She struggled to know what to say. "You did everything you could," she tried.

He sucked in snot. "*I know. I know.*"

Certain phrasings, she couldn't help but notice, matched those he'd used in interviews. It was only natural. She, too, resorted to scripts often enough (*You did everything you could*—how cliché!) and, even in therapy, sometimes caught herself *reciting* instead of really *reflecting*. Because the past, arranged as syntax, was easier to stomach. A perfectly human defense against reliving anything too vividly.

SHE MUST'VE blacked out. One second they were in Bushwick waiting for a car, and the next they were back on Nassau, passing McGolrick in slow motion, new blisters on her heels rubbing against her sneakers. The water was long gone. Her throat ached; she had the feeling she'd talked the whole night, though she couldn't recall anything she'd said. Was Caleb there? Yes, he was right where she'd last seen him, on the other end of the rope. "Advil," she said, but couldn't hear herself above the *untz-untz*ing of her inner ear.

The sun was just rising, the first birds trilling in the plane trees, practicing their car alarms and smartphone rings. Caleb practically carried her; her body felt as shapeless and used as an old pillow. Nearing the apartment, Jude noted curiously how much the homeless woman on their stoop looked, from this distance, like her mother.

2. Saturday

IN THE NEW YORK OF BONNIE'S IMAGINATION (A POTPOURRI of scenes from Eddie Murphy movies, the Macy's Thanksgiving Day Parade, *Sesame Street* flashbacks, and what little Judy had told her) the streets were abundant with taxis, hot dog stands umbrellaed every corner, and the boroughs' residents—shopkeeps with brooms, stock-market guys swinging briefcases, kids jumping double Dutch—were affable, accented, gruff. All of these presumptions had been shattered in the hell that was the previous night, but now, under bright, midmorning sun, Bonnie was determined to start fresh, to give the place a second chance. She patted her pocket again (the spare keys were there) and stepped out into the happy weekend thoroughfare. Joggers trotted around her with the same purposeful stride they affected in California. Two women with glossy black hair brushed by, pushing strollers, arguing in a language like English pulled apart and reconstituted. Across the way, the park, which had so disconcerted her in the dark (like a forest in a folktale, the place had lurked with ill will), looked, in the daytime, exactly how New York should look. She welled with a certain brand of excitement, connected, as it was, to the pride of survival: after everything, she had arrived! Enormous, shade-offering trees wore their dappled barks like animal hides. Benches lined the diagonal walks where people read newspapers, sipped coffee, let their dogs sniff around and poop (she bent to pet this one, dodged that one's excrement). Then she moved on, toward a busier intersection of awnings and storefronts. It was hotter than she remembered heat could be.

It was the heat that had woken her that morning. Beyond depleted (by her flight, the time change, and then the distress of her sojourn on the stoop), she'd slept deeply and totally on Judy's new boyfriend's couch, despite the stiff cushions and the pokey wooden arms, the sun lighting up the curtains to blot and brighten her dreams. When she opened her eyes, she was sweating.

The excruciation of the night before rushed back at once, making her jumpy and alert, anxious to get outside and dispel the memory. Misery, pure misery, was the only way to describe it: pacing, pulling her bag, staring at her phone, waiting, calling, walking the block, circling the park, asking a number of passing strangers, a corner-store clerk, *Do you know Judy? Judy who's supposed to live here?*, a coil of worry tightening in her chest as the minutes, then hours, crawled in painstaking increments. She'd been so consumed by her own helplessness, by her lack of ideas when it came to knowing what to do, where to go, how to solve anything, that at last she'd simply sat, paralyzed. Her battery down to three percent, she saw herself the mother of a three-year-old again: one minute Judy was right there at her knee and the next she was gone, Bonnie was drunk, Rick was a rapist—store security and intercom announcements—a panic that grew more and more tangible the longer Judy did not manifest. Then the tables turned, and a bizarre blankness of feeling came up in Bonnie upon the discovery that she had, at last, been totally and completely abandoned. That was right before she dozed. Right before Judy rescued her.

After an argument (or a series of looping accusations and explanations—they were both too wrecked to make much of a claim), they agreed it was only a misunderstanding, and both of them were to blame. Judy was right; Bonnie should have texted—sent a message, as people did in this millennium, to say she was boarding her flight, she'd land at such-and-such hour. But Bonnie was right, too; possibly even more right. Judy should've gotten the date correct—written it somewhere in ink. July *ninth*, not July *nineteenth*—call her old-fashioned, but wasn't *the date* the most important detail of any visit? Judy should've read the flight email Bonnie had forwarded (she'd *insisted* Bonnie forward it, even walked her through the steps—so why had Judy not *read* it?). And had she not seen Bonnie's calls and texts that night? She'd left six voice mails, to her humiliation now. On the last two she'd downright whimpered. She'd thought maybe Judy was dead.

"We were at a party," Judy had said. "I'm sorry."

But the explanation seemed measly, and the words failed to do their job.

Bonnie (she was ashamed to see it now) had sulked. "Well, sorry doesn't undo—"

"Mom, please! Let's not, okay? My head is—I'm sorry, really, I really am. It was an honest mistake, I just—"

Why had Bonnie pressed? "I guess some *enthusiasm* would be nice, I came all the way out here—"

Judy's tongue looked awkward in her mouth, a thing she seemed to struggle to speak around. She said slowly, to Bonnie's shoes, "Look, I'm sorry, okay. I just confused the dates. There's been a lot going on. I took the whole week off work for this."

It took Bonnie a moment to realize she didn't mean the visit. Judy picked up the slack of rope (a party costume?) tying her to this new person—this *Caleb*—and let it fall. The two were living together, Bonnie learned, though she hadn't heard so much as his name before now, and when Judy had said, last month, that she was *moving into a new apartment*, she'd failed to elaborate, *with my new boyfriend*. He stood there in tall, mute witness to the scene, as if the fact that Judy had a mother was as much of a surprise to him as the fact that Judy had a live-in boyfriend was to her. That, or Caleb was studying her: had heard things about Bonnie already.

It had not been the welcome Bonnie had hoped for, but that was hours ago! Before they'd all gotten some rest, and now, in the new, bright question of the unknown city, she willed positivity. At the intersection she turned left, past a redbrick school and a stretch of sidewalk produce. From behind, she passed a woman whose varicose veins ran rootlike beneath her shorts. Veins like that made Bonnie feel lucky, feel not as old as she knew she was, even while she felt sorry, too. When the woman caught up with her at the crosswalk, Bonnie noted the sack she carried: white paper logoed with a bagel. Bonnie inquired, and the woman stopped there on the corner to give scrupulous directions. "That's just so kind of you, thank you, *thank you*," Bonnie beamed, lifted by the generosity of this stranger—by the ease of her own returned kindness—and when the woman went on, and Bonnie doubled back toward the bagel place, she felt something sharp and splintery, some pain of *missing* people—though who, exactly, she couldn't say, and there were people, people, right now, everywhere.

The bagel man hollered, "And what can I get for you, pretty lady?" He was stout and bald, with copious ear hair. His accent elated her—she hollered back, "Gimme the most New Yorky thing you have! For three!"

"New Yorky for three, comin' up!" He was a man who'd heard everything before. When he finished her order, he called the next woman *pretty lady*, too.

She thought she remembered how to get back. If she could find the park, she could find the apartment. She had her smartphone, all charged up, and knew how to use its mapping tool (her coworkers, the teenaged boys who helped with donation drop-offs, had showed her a dozen times), but she was allergic to the idea of it—she didn't like to have to pull a thing out of her pocket and go *online* all the time, just to know where she was and what the weather was like. There was satisfaction in finding one's bearings alone; it forced your eyes open wider, your senses to sharpen. Or you could ask people—make a new friend while you were at it. Sweat made the butt of her capri pants stick already, but little could dampen her mood. She stopped a couple Judy and Caleb's age—"Is this the right way to the park?" Hmm, they weren't sure which park she meant. Perhaps there were many parks nearby, park upon neighborhood park, patterning out endlessly, a green, gridded paradise.

She got lost, circled, wandered, and eventually reached the line of trees from the opposite corner from where she'd begun. Finally, she found the number. The key fit the lock—miracle!—and the second door past the vestibule was open already. The entryway was dark and cool, and the banister that ran along the dingy staircase tilted at such an angle that Bonnie feared any weight applied might push it right off—an accident that, if it happened to anyone, would happen to her! What did it cost to rent an apartment in a building like this, a small but nice apartment in a shabby-but-not-bad building? Judy hated to talk about money. Bonnie knew New York was expensive, but she didn't have a clue what the numbers actually looked like. At Five Pines, her lot rent was up to $285 a month plus $220 for the trailer itself.

She'd bought her plane ticket with savings from the modest account she'd opened after her mother passed away. The money was not for dipping into, but she had made this small exception.

BY THE third floor, Bonnie was out of breath. Safe inside the apartment again, she removed her clogs, two sweaty leather foot pockets—sniffed the insides, and they weren't terrible, but she regretted already having packed just this one pair of shoes. Behind the closed bathroom door, she could hear Judy's whine, and then Caleb's voice, calm and low, before the toilet flushed. Bonnie filled a Mason jar from the kitchen sink and drank. When they entered the room they were still, to her disturbance, in their little waist shackle. They'd been too tired, then, to remove the costume? Or perhaps they'd lost a bet, and these were the terms? Before Judy was born, Bonnie had once woken up in a dry bathtub, in the seedy part of Hollywood, wearing a stranger's sequined dress. Last night, Judy had said, *We'll explain tomorrow.*

"Good morning!" Bonnie piped. "It's hot, huh?" She stood in the room's center, but now she shifted, unsure of where to be.

Judy went straight for the faucet. "Morning," she tried, faking cheeriness.

"Morning," Caleb said, picking up the teakettle, reaching in over Judy.

Judy gulped thirstily. "Did you sleep okay? Mom, look, I'm sorry again about last—"

"Oh"—she scowled—"Don't even give it—I haven't even given it another thought." She motioned at the rope. "I see you two are really *joined at the hip.* The honeymoon phase, huh?"

Caleb smiled, spotting the paper sack on the counter. "You found the bagel place."

"I did! A sweet woman helped me." She touched her hair, which had frizzed wildly to twice its usual size. "The people here are just—*friendlier,* you know, than they seem in the movies." She'd need to wear it up, she reasoned, but hated to reveal her temples, where only wisps were left. "I—this *city*; I'm just *thrilled* to finally be here."

Caleb adjusted the stove's flame. "You've never been?"

His eyes, catching hers, were something to reckon with. Blue, and what

Bonnie supposed you'd call *piercing*. "No," Bonnie said. Though surely he knew that already; surely Judy had mentioned the importance of this visit, being the first, ever, that Bonnie herself had made to Judy (that Judy had *let* Bonnie make) and not the other way around.

Her first real impression of him, as he turned to grind the coffee, was that this man, whoever he was, had the power to destroy her daughter. Or at least the daughter Bonnie once knew, an insecure adolescent with a life not yet staked out as her own. His neck was long, his head shaved into an off-kilter widow's peak; an old rag resembling a T-shirt and a pair of droopy boxer shorts were all that covered his fit frame. Spider webs and chains and cartoons and jagged lines decorated his skin at random, but two tattoos in particular struck her strangely: the word *WHY* above his left knee and *NOT* above his right. It took Bonnie a minute to read them, because they were upside down—a question clearly put by Caleb to Caleb, and not to any admirer of his legs. An actor, that's who he looked like: some heartthrob cast to play a bum or delinquent but whose striking good looks made his story come off as fake.

Judy could've been his sister. There was something strangely alike about their faces, a shared intensity in their brows and a length and grace to their fingers. Judy's hands must've come from Tom: Bonnie's own were stubby and utilitarian, too wide in the knuckles for rings to ever fit properly. Though Judy, slouching in silk shorts and a tank top, wasn't looking her best this morning, truth be told. Her eyes were puffy and bloodshot—gave Bonnie a headache just to look at. Was it only the aftermath of last night, or was there something else? She held the rope in one hand, enduring Caleb's circular pouring. "Is everything all right?" Bonnie finally asked.

Judy looked down, blinking. "Everything is fine."

So that was it. She'd been crying. Caleb smiled again. "She can't handle the whole bowel movement thing." He watched the coffee as it dripped, into a beautiful glass carafe. "We're forty hours in, and so far it's two points for Caleb, zero for Jude. I'm telling her"—he looked at Judy then, playfully— "I'm telling you, it's going to be a long, uncomfortable—"

"I know, I know," Judy moaned.

"It's healthy!" Caleb exclaimed. "It's normal!"

"I'm not saying it's not *normal*, I just—"

Caleb looked to Bonnie. "Was she like this as a kid? Anal retentive? It seems so Freudian . . . repression or whatever—"

"I'm not *repressed*," Judy said, "I just don't want to *shit* in front of my *boyfriend*. Is that so—"

Bonnie was struggling to catch up. "But—you're—you're doing your *business* together?" She looked at the rope. Had they not even *tried* to get it off? "Look, I don't think you even need scissors, we can probably—"

But as she stepped forward, Caleb reared back, and Judy cried, "No, *no!*"

Not the result of a dare or bet, it was intentional, actually, Bonnie learned. Caleb was an artist, and this was a *piece*, Judy clarified as they settled around the kitchen table. Bonnie did her best to listen, sipping her coffee, nodding and smiling, but only bits and scraps computed. *It's part of this series where, by reenacting seminal . . .* Caleb started, and Judy added . . . *Really create a chiasma between the art-historical and the contemporary* (more to Caleb than to Bonnie) *through these autobiographical adjustments . . .* and Caleb again, *Plus, I like the risk . . . appropriation and everything . . .* and Judy again, *And the photographic record means it's more than just somatic, like there's a degree of post-internet nostalgia . . .*

The *performance* part Bonnie got right away, but the rest . . . When a pause arrived, she started, "It's . . . it sounds so interesting. I don't *totally* see why . . . but that's . . ." What she wanted to ask was how *this* was art. And did Caleb have a real job? He must; the apartment had big windows and a view of the park, and the furniture, the table they sat at, was expensive-seeming, made of smooth, dark wood, with leather upholstering the chairs. He picked up a long black tube and sucked. The smallest puff of mist escaped his mouth: marijuana, and Bonnie filled up with want. "And so you . . . you'll take some pictures while you're . . . tied together, and they'll be on display . . ."

He nodded and sucked again. "The show's in November. You should come out for it."

Judy looked at him over her coffee cup and, for the first time all morning, smiled genuinely. How lovely to see Judy smile! She seemed, to Bonnie, happy.

Bonnie passed out the bagels in their cute paper jackets. "How much longer will you wear it, then?" Thinking that it only took a minute to snap a few pictures.

"Through Wednesday," Caleb said casually, unwrapping his.

She nearly gasped. "*Wednesday?*" Her flight home was Tuesday, early in the morning. She appealed to Judy. "But—but—my god, you're going to go to the *bathroom* together till—how humiliating!" Judy had said of the visit, *Four days is plenty of time*, and Tuesday had been the cheapest return.

Judy nodded, chewing. "Insane, right? At least I'm not on my period."

And Caleb said to Bonnie, "You can help, actually. With the photos. It'll be good to have a third person around for that."

I thought maybe we could go to a museum today, Judy was saying now, and Caleb was agreeing, *Sure. We might as well do the touristy stuff*, but Bonnie couldn't speak. A third person, a tourist. The fleshy, flayed smell of the lox, the teeming city she'd hardly yet glimpsed, the nearness to Judy at last real— everything was zapped, suddenly, of any magical effect. How would she discuss the thing she had come to discuss? She'd have no time alone with her daughter. And Bonnie had come all this way.

The bagel was thick, exploding with filling—there would be no graceful way to eat it, but fuck it, fuck everything. "*Mmm, mmm, mmm!*" she sang as she chewed. "This is perfect. A feast!"

Maybe their enthusiasm would fizzle by tomorrow. Maybe they weren't as serious about the rope as they seemed. The way they rose and moved across the kitchen, now, to refill the water pitcher, navigating each step, looked so tiresome! (And was that a scrape, already, on Judy's side?) A week of this! Even back at the table they moved in sync, attending to each other's timing. Judy ate the capers and cucumbers, one at a time, but left the rest. They wiped their fingers on a shared napkin and sipped their coffee simultaneously.

"I hope it's okay for you, Judy; I didn't know if you were doing no wheat or whatever." The last time Bonnie had seen her, Judy refused pasta, and French bread, and even oatmeal. Something about her skin and inflammation, though Bonnie assumed it was a weight-loss thing. Now she was looking thinner than two years ago, especially in the face and arms.

"Wheat is fine," Judy said, and sipped her coffee.

Bonnie's weight used to drop, too, every time she met a new man; maybe the tendency was genetic. "Well, I think you've got a great figure, with or without wheat. For what it's worth."

"Thank you?" Judy said.

A string of salmon had wedged itself between Bonnie's molars, and now she picked at it. "Are you getting enough to eat, though, Judy Patooty? In general, I mean?"

Judy swallowed and looked skeptical. "Why is it that within minutes of seeing each other we're always talking about bodies? Of all the things in the world we could—"

"Oh!" Bonnie said. "Let's stop it now! I'm sorry!" As much to herself as to Judy, to this petty, blaming spirit that always came over their togetherness, seeping like a draft and turning things cold. "You're *gorgeous*, Judith Petunia O'Connell, inside and out. You're absolutely beautiful and perfect just the way you are, and you will be until you're old like me."

Caleb looked from Judy to Bonnie, entertained. "You know your voices sound the same? If we were on the phone I wouldn't know who I was talking to."

"That used to happen with Rick, actually—Rick is Judy's ex-stepfather . . ." In the time it took the memory to become speech, Bonnie had forgotten— she'd actually *forgotten*—about Rick all over again. In the onrush of truth the anecdote shrank stupidly. Her voice lost its oomph. "He used to call the house and think that Judy was me."

A timer went off on Caleb's phone—it was noon already, apparently, and some bustle ensued, to retrieve the camera from the bedroom, to check the position of the sunlight, to arrange themselves seriously, *artistically*. Bonnie did as she was told: framed the couple horizontally, counted to three, took only one photo. Afterward she carried the plates to the sink, forging (gracefully, she thought) on. But when she turned to grab the coffee things, the couple had entered the private dimension of their love. Their foreheads were pressed together as if communing telepathically, and Caleb had one hand up under Judy's shirt, presumably on her ribs, a vision that left Bonnie feeling stranded.

In such intimate proximity to affection, she had the impulse to blurt, "Oh, I'm seeing a man, too!" But on the airplane she'd told herself, had a long Bonnie-to-Bonnie talk: *No blurting; read the room; be deliberate; wait for conversational connections.* Yet the thought of keeping Gregory unmentioned shamed her with its suggestion—it was not a real relationship, they were not real lovers, not like these two, and Greg, try as Bonnie might, was not capable of ousting Rick from her heart. Having recently lost his wife, Greg was only interested in *companionship*; he'd made that clear from the start (companionship being a euphemism for celibacy, Bonnie read, either *I'm paralyzed by grief* or *I can't get it up*, which both amounted to the same rejection: her body would continue to gather dust). They spent Wednesday evenings and Sunday afternoons watching television, sipping club soda; held hands on walks around the duck pond, where kids lured crawfish with baloney scraps on coat hangers and Bonnie cracked abortion jokes. His heart medication made drinking impossible—a relief, Bonnie had thought at first, though old habits died hard, and sometimes she found herself fantasizing the two of them sipping whiskey in a High Street bar, dancing back to front to the Stones, looking sexy in the beer light and manifesting a realer version of the relationship— one that never, of course, would be. As it was, the dry rub of his thumb on her hand, the framed photos of his wife, the furred dimples around his lips, where no razor could ever quite reach and which should've stayed hidden by a beard, were enough to make Bonnie want, simultaneously, to kill herself and to hang onto him for dear life. *Leave me alone* and *don't ever leave me*—a pairing so familiar it ached. Greg would stand over the electric range shaking the pan intently, listening for the last kernels to pop, while Bonnie waited politely on the island stool. Then the loneliness would creep. What was there to talk about? In no small way, her life was nearly over. A truth that shocked her almost as much as the fact that she could go whole days without remembering it.

She insisted on cleaning up while Caleb and Judy got ready. From the living room, Caleb called, "Do you like jazz?" Bonnie could hear the gentle thwap of LPs as he flipped. *Albums*, they used to call them, when there was only one thing an album could be.

"I certainly don't *not* like jazz," Bonnie sang over the faucet. "I'd say half the men I ever dated were jazz lovers."

"Mom only listens to Neil Young," she heard Judy say.

"And Cat Stevens!" Bonnie chirped, piqued. "And Graham Nash, and Van, and Joni, of course."

"And Joni, of course," Judy mimicked. But sweetly.

"So your favorite movie's *The Last Waltz*," Caleb called.

Bonnie gasped and shouted so she was sure he could hear. "*The Last Waltz*! I *love* *The Last Waltz*! I can't even remember the last time I—that booger of cocaine in Neil's nose!"

Judy muttered something she couldn't hear, but Bonnie felt she'd broken through somehow—judged Caleb, maybe, prematurely. She yelled over the faucet, "He gets me, Judy! Your new man! I don't know why you wanted to keep him a secret when we obviously . . ." A movement caught her eye between the dish drainer and the tiled backsplash. A cockroach had appeared, feeling its way forward antennae first. She was talking, still, she could hear the sound of her voice, but her tone became less sure. "We're going to be good friends, I think," she finished.

No one said anything in response. They couldn't hear her, maybe, over the running water. She turned it off and dried her hands and listened to the crinkle of a record leaving its sleeve, the static pop of the speakers turned on. The roach scooted across the counter and disappeared into a crevice. It wasn't Neil, or Van, and certainly not jazz, as if Caleb's question had been merely rhetorical, or they were playing some kind of joke on her. The sound warbled strangely: spaceship-reminiscent, carwash-sounding music, if it could even be called music, with an alarm-clock ping going off in the background, beep-beeping in no discernable rhythm, then an icky swell of broken melody . . . what sounded to Bonnie like a chimp practicing kazoo, and made her feel as if she didn't understand—had never understood—the first thing about anything.

*

IT WAS AFTER TWO O'CLOCK BY THE TIME THEY LEFT THE HOUSE.
The sun was a laser beam tracking them all the way to the L. Bonnie lagged
three paces behind, hiding herself under rhinestone-edged sunglasses, but
when they descended underground and a station loiterer gawked at the rope,
she perked to new life: *What's the matter, you've never seen live art before?*

On the platform, Bonnie gravitated toward the subway map, to study it
beside a man with Dungeons and Dragons facial hair and a bulky laptop bag.
Jude heard her ask if he knew what went on at Jamaica station (*That sounds like
an interesting stop*), and what about Roosevelt Island? Did people live there?
"Maybe we should take your mom to the Transit Museum instead," Caleb
whispered. Jude sighed. Talking to strangers was Bonnie's way of clarifying
that her reticence was intentional and Jude-specific; that she was pleased as
could be by New York, with or without her daughter. When the L whooshed
in, Bonnie waved to him—a girlish goodbye—though they were all getting
onto the same car.

She let three people fill the space between herself and Caleb and Jude, and
made an effort not to look in their direction. If Jude knew her mother, she
knew that she must have been shocked by the existence of Caleb. Confused
and probably hurt as to why the fact of him hadn't been revealed earlier, let
alone that she'd moved in with him. And yet the idea that Jude's withholding
needed explaining at all was a problem in and of itself. The frustration that
surrounded any discussion of her love life with her mother was an old, stale
feeling. Bonnie prided herself on being such a veteran of love (or: alcohol-
induced promiscuity, dependency and codependency, the traditional performance of gender roles, the normalization of misogyny and victimhood) that
she doled out bad advice as if it were sacred, sagely. Worse, Bonnie couldn't
recognize her own bad listening. She read Jude's updates—a new boyfriend, or
a good series of dates, or a breakup, or a betrayal—as an automatic invitation
to file through her own psychic archives for the memory that best matched
Jude's situation, then cut right in. *Well, it sounds to me like he's the love-her-
and-leave-her type. I remember when this person Donny I was just obsessed*

with—we were Donny and Bonnie for a hot minute—caught wind of my old friend Tina's boob job—you remember Tina, right? From Scorekeepers? Though Jude didn't remember Tina and had never heard of Donny—probably she'd been three years old, crying in a makeshift playpen at an unlicensed daycare while Bonnie and Donny and Tina took shots naked in a hot tub—and the winding, long-winded comparisons left Jude morose on her end of the line, not understanding how she hadn't learned, yet, to just keep her mouth shut. All she wanted was some acknowledgment, from her mother, that her various predicaments were real; *That sounds hard* and then the pertinent follow-up questions. Reassurance that her feelings weren't delusional, and to share, she supposed, something of her present with her mother, so that they could, ideally, move forward, out from the mess of their past.

Louanne, her therapist, had given her an opener: *I'd like to tell you about something, Mom, but I want you to just listen and not feel the need to respond. What I'm going to tell you isn't about you, it's only about me.* She had tried it once, about six months ago, after learning that Simon (the cellist) was engaged to a girl she knew. She hadn't even known they were dating, and the betrayal she felt, the jealousy and regret and pettiness, were so disproportionate that winter afternoon that the only person she could imagine confiding in was her mother, who was, despite it all, still her mother. She recited the opener and then told the news, but Bonnie stayed absolutely quiet. *Mom?* she asked. Bonnie said nothing. Not even a huff, a breathy, *Well what am I supposed to say, then? What do you want me to say? You should never have broken up with the guy, if you're jealous, it sounds like.* The control it must've taken to not speak . . . it was far outside her mother's range. So the cut had gone deep. Jude said, *Mom, come on, okay, you can say something. Say whatever you want. Mom? Mom?* The silence endured like a painful metaphor—a flashback to other absences. Finally, Jude had pressed the red circle. *Call ended.* For all their fights, all their spans of not speaking, she'd never resorted to hanging up. The image of Bonnie so silenced, all alone in the world's smallest kitchen, had been more than Jude could bear.

The L wasn't bad, but the F was packed and reeking. Squeezing off at Fifty-seventh, they tugged an old man with them—their rope caught on his cane—and the detangling was almost violent. The museum, too, was swarming; by the time they got their tickets, Jude felt too zombified to wait in another line for the special exhibit. Instead, they moved through the permanent collection, where Bonnie proceeded ten steps before them, her hands tucked reverently behind her. She moved up close to certain canvases, seemingly at random, as if examining them for authenticity. A guard approached her before a Matisse and made the *move back* gesture, pointed to the taped white line. Embarrassed, Bonnie scuttled on.

Struggling to keep up, hardly glancing at the paintings, Jude lost sight of her behind a man ferrying a child on his shoulders. "That should be illegal," Caleb said as they passed. "Also kids in general. Why are kids allowed in museums? Don't they have their own museums?" Caleb and Jude agreed that children were mostly a masochistic time-suck for people too boring to find more creative ways to spend their lives, but still she resented his need to remind her of it—her thirty-two-year-old, thumb-twiddling uterus. As if she'd signed a contract he kept folded in his pocket.

Three galleries later, Jude spotted Bonnie stalled before a painting she'd never seen before. "Is it Hopper?" she asked Caleb, but he was looking intently at a Rauschenberg assemblage and just shrugged. It had to be—the yellow had the same buttery glow she knew from *Nighthawks*. The painting showed a second-story corner apartment, viewed from the vantage of the dark street below, three lit windows revealing a woman inside (was she wrapped in a towel?), bent and mostly obscured, banally midaction, presumably rummaging in a drawer. Bare walls and a radiator somehow made her more solitary. Jude knew Hopper was all about loneliness. It was the figures on the canvas who were to be pitied, she'd always thought, but suddenly she saw it in reverse. The *viewer* was the lonely one, invisible in a passing voyeur's shoes, outside looking in. Bonnie tucked her hair behind her ears, as if aware of being watched, but did not move away. She looked small, Jude saw; unlovely and too real before the painting. Jude would make an effort, this time. Be good. Be nice. Be generous.

She needed to sit down, she told Caleb. The Advil wasn't working, her head wasn't quite attached to her body, and coating her mouth was a hard-boiled chalkiness no amount of water seemed to satisfy. When Jude told Bonnie they were heading for the courtyard, her mother hollered, "I'll meet you there in a bit," though the gallery was hushed. "I'd like to get the full experience."

They rode the escalator down, side by side, while the people moving up looked at them, bored, as if they were just another piece of art, which, Jude guessed, they were.

"I just want to sleep for a hundred years," she said. "I'm never doing drugs again."

"You say that every time," Caleb said.

"*Every time?*" She balked. Stepping outside was like passing into another reality, landing on a planet with six suns. "You've known me for two months."

Caleb appeared hurt. "I've *known* you for two months? Not, we've been *in love* for two months? Not, you've been my girlfriend for two months?"

There was no line at the café. They ordered a big, sweaty bottle of Perrier, then found a table in the shade of a birch grove, close to the water, obsidian-black. "I'm sorry," Jude apologized. "I'm just tired, and being around my mother is so . . . emotional, I get . . ."

"I like her," Caleb said. "She's kooky." He was enjoying this, his tone said, this *mother-meeting*.

"She's mentally ill, actually," Jude corrected, annoyed. Was she, though? She had casually diagnosed Bonnie years ago: delusional and prone to mania.

"Oh, come on. She's just . . . like . . . of a different generation. She's kind of a hippie?"

Jude rested the cool bottle on her forehead and closed her eyes. "Just because you like Neil Young doesn't make you a hippie. Hippies don't micro-wave their dinners. They don't shop at big-box stores. She *wishes* she were a hippie, is the problem, this whole held-over sixties infatuation . . . But she doesn't, like, follow politics; she doesn't really read, I'd be shocked if she had a library card . . ." Jude made herself stop. For each grievance rattled off, another appeared on the list. She knew this was unfair. "I mean, she can only *afford* those stores . . ." she revised. "And she's not a Republican, at least . . . But our voices are not alike. I can't believe you said that."

Caleb took the bottle and drank. "They *are*, though. And you walk the same."

Jude moaned. Her mother's clogs caused her to clomp. Her hips swung with a life of their own. And she swore by a pair of special sneakers shaped to tone your ass. Those shoes, thankfully, hadn't made it on this trip. "You can't even *see* my walk when we're in this three-legged race together." She lay her head down on the table. "I'm sure I walk like you now."

"Dude, you're like a teenager again. You've totally—what's the word . . ."

"Regressed," Jude said miserably. She hated it when Caleb called her *dude*. "I was hoping you wouldn't notice."

He laid his hot hand on her thigh. "Should we go into the bathroom?" he whispered.

She snorted. "At MoMA? You're joking."

But as his hand crept up, it didn't seem so insane. They hadn't had sex since Thursday, and with Bonnie around, wouldn't, probably, until Tuesday—a lifetime.

Except here was Bonnie now, clutching a branded bag from the gift shop, which she refused to show the contents of. "No, no, no. There might be a surprise in there." An announcement was made—the museum would close in fifteen minutes—and soon men in lanyards came to usher them out. They decided on dim sum downtown (*It's all Greek to me*, Bonnie consented), and all at once she was enthusiastic again, begging Caleb to let her hail the cab herself (it was cute, Jude supposed, how she'd elected him the authority). *Be my guest*, he said, as she rushed eagerly into the bike lane. But she was watching for smears of yellow instead of heeding the lights, and for one terrifying instant, Jude foresaw a tsunami of Sixth Avenue traffic rushing grilles-first into her mother. Instead, a taxi braked and pulled up adeptly, and the three were in and off. Out the window, Bonnie looked up and up and up.

EACH TIME a cart passed, they took another dish, and soon their table was crowded with bamboo baskets. When Jude lifted a lid to reveal steaming, translucent dumplings, Bonnie exclaimed, "Oh, they're just like hot little breasts!"

Jude had made it a rule not to drink in front of her mother, but, desperate for something cold and restorative, she didn't protest when Caleb ordered beer for both of them. A waiter brought over mugs so frosty Jude's fingers stuck. "Hair of the dog," Bonnie said, nodding her approval, and tucked a pink napkin into her T-shirt.

A thought occurred to Jude reflexively. "You know, Mom, I could look up a meeting for you if you want. Maybe for Monday?"

Bonnie's attention was on gripping, then lifting, a pancake with chopsticks. Her eyebrows rose. "Here? In New York City?" She gave up, set down the utensils, and picked up the food with her hand.

"Yeah. Here. I'm sure there's one in our neighborhood, if—"

"There's one on Twelfth Street every morning at ten," Caleb said. He raised his beer and looked at Bonnie. "My friend goes. Or at least she used to."

Jude bristled at this unexpected *she*. Caleb, as far as Jude was learning, didn't have female friends; any woman he mentioned so lightly had surely been a past *thing*. She couldn't help herself. "Who?"

He burped into his napkin, and when he lowered it he was smiling. "Jude, come on, it's anonymous, remember?" and Bonnie chortled.

Caleb suggested Bonnie try what he said were sauce-covered vegetables, some sort of Chinese root, and when she bit what was really a fried chicken foot, her expression changed, became bewildered and excited. She whapped him on the arm. "Naughty boy! Playing tricks on a sweet old lady!"—delighted to be let in on a joke, even if it was on her.

"Now this is *fun* food. Not like Chinese when I was a kid." She clicked her chopsticks, surveying the spread. "My father would get so mad about Mom's cooking he'd get right up from the table and say, *We can't eat this crap. C'mon, we're going down to Ming's*. He'd order all this duck and noodles and everything, but Jeff would look at me like *Don't eat any of it*. You know, to side with our mother. And Dad didn't like that, you better believe. We had a clean-plate rule in our family, and he'd start in on us, adding more and more to our plates, *What, you don't like monkey brains? You don't like snake meat?*"

Jude glanced around the dining room, half expecting stares. But the tables were far apart, and the place crowded and noisy enough that no one could hear them. Bonnie was smiling so widely that Jude could see hatch lines of real lip her lipstick hadn't covered.

"Mom, that painting you were looking at—" Jude tried, but Bonnie wasn't having it; a door to the past had opened. She put a hand on Caleb's arm and leaned toward him, her sudden confidant. "I lived in Southern California for forty-one years, from the day I was born until they closed down Sunset—oh, more than ten years ago now—and I had to move."

"Sunset is the name of the dialysis center," Jude clarified. "Where Mom used to work."

Bonnie continued, "They closed the one in Burbank. I could've tried to stay in the business, but I had this opportunity up by Sacramento. I work in retail now—well, Judy's probably told you—at a secondhand store. It's *amazing* the things people throw away. Perfectly good cookware, shoes never worn, appliances and furniture—"

"Bathrobes, underwear . . ." Caleb added.

"Yes! You name it, it'll show up brand-new. When I moved up north I had nothing. Nada. Now my whole trailer is decked out. Employee discount's forty percent off, but the boys in the back—hell, at the end of every day, they let us go through the overflow before it gets shipped to the warehouse. No one really keeps track of the overflow."

The last time Jude had been in her mother's trailer, wooden novelty signs— cow-shaped cutouts hanging by dusty twine—made proclamations like *Put one foot in front of the udder!* Afghans crocheted by other people's grandmothers made triangles on the couch and recliner. An apple-and-cinnamon candle burned with the Goodwill price tag still on. But Bonnie's version of the "moving up north" story omitted the real reason she left Van Nuys. She came home one day to find Rick in bed with someone new—or *not* new, Jude would later (to her disturbance but not surprise) learn, one half of a neighborhood couple *he was always wanting to swing with. Darby!* Jude was almost done with college by then, halfway across the country, already spending her Christmases on campus and summer breaks subletting windowless bedrooms in Brooklyn. And it was true that the dialysis center closed, but Bonnie had lost her job well before that, for mixing gin with her Diet Coke and her gin-and-Diet with Xanax. Another DUI cost her another car, a night in jail, and finally she was evicted from a Reseda halfway house she called a *subsidized living situation* for stealing a pair of diamond earrings from another resident. That was a favorite war story of Bonnie's: as she liked to tell it, she'd denied the theft to the resident director (*In my blackout I didn't remember!*) even as the earrings glinted in her lobes. The diamonds turned out to be glass.

Caleb nodded at Bonnie but said nothing. He chewed on a spare rib, and a long pause followed, like the pauses they'd experienced on the train and in the museum, in which their three-person arrangement failed to click organically into place. Jude felt the pressure of the MC; a host sleeping on the job. Why wasn't Caleb *helping*? He paid more attention to his beer and his phone, which he flipped over and checked whether or not the device pulsed, than to Bonnie. Not happily, Jude zoomed in on these bad manners, and a behavior she was beginning to fear was a trait: this impolite unawareness that he should ask her mother a question, or, ideally, a string of them.

Even with her, her brain churned, he sometimes failed in this way. When she happened to mention her writing (her *real writing*—which, she'd revealed to him as they'd gotten to know each other, meant fiction, not the bits she sometimes composed for *Hierarchy*), a glazed look came over him; his eyes would float to the door of the bar or restaurant and, having offered a generic platitude to whatever her current creative problem was (*I'm sure it's great; maybe just take a break?*), he'd move on to another topic. She'd clung to his early shows of interest: their very first week together he'd asked, *So, when can I read one of your stories?*—even though, after she gave him a journal, the book stayed buried in a stack on Caleb's coffee table, never to be mentioned again. It was a story she was, actually, proud of—it had won, subsequently, a modest year-end prize, a five-hundred-dollar check she put into her savings.

Maybe he just hasn't gotten around to it? Sofia tried to help. *Or maybe he's intimidated. He's probably scared? Most people don't read, we have to remember. And he's so hot!* As if there were a corollary.

Regardless, she couldn't help imagining her writing as Caleb must have—unserious, a *hobby*—even while her heart knew otherwise: that the weird act of hunting and arranging words was, actually, the only way she'd found to transform herself into someone other—*better*—than who she actually was (did hobbies do that?), even if the fruits of her labor were underripe, uneven, unoriginal. In fits and starts, in coffee shops and on the bus, she scribbled down insights and structures and observations that always seemed *brilliant!* in the moment but soon embarrassed and disappointed, once they shrank from imagination into language—always less capacious, duller, on the page. When she worked up the courage to submit for publication, the best-case scenario was her work *in print!*—full of typos, in an ugly-covered journal no one read, but still! The worst—the more usual outcome—was a form rejection email, which immediately made her cry, every time, regardless. Her colleagues at the magazine encouraged her in their ways: *You're not too old! You should apply to MFAs!*, said Jesse and Sofia and Yajira, who'd known Jude since her days as an intern, while the other camp, TJ and Chaim and Kai, advised, *The workshop route is so . . . homogenizing. Just stay put here, work your way up, wait till one of the editors gets pregnant . . .* stranding her in a purgatory of indecision. Every month or so, she'd click to the websites of Brown, Iowa, Austin, peruse the bios of faculty (half of their books were on her shelf), revisit the application requirements, wonder, *But who will write my recs?*, then open dozens of her own disorderly Word files, one after another, scrutinizing her sentences through the put-on jadedness of an admissions panel until she determined everything she'd ever written was total shit. At the end of such a crisis, it always seemed to be three o'clock. There was work to go to, *paid work*, and earning money was, at least, a utilitarian distraction—until the existential itch came back, and the cycle repeated, as it had for the last few years.

When Jude had first mentioned grad school, casually, not really thinking, days after she moved in, Caleb frowned and said, "The cornfields? There's no way in fuck I'm moving to Iowa," then laughed. She was taken aback. She had not said *we*. But this revelation, that he saw their futures entwined, softened the force of the statement as much as it mixed her up, and a part of her agreed: How could she ever leave New York?

The table chewed quietly on. Jude cleared her throat. "Mom, Caleb's from California," she tried. "San Francisco, actually."

A dumpling split on Bonnie's bite and pork spilled to her plate. She covered her mouth and hummed, *"If you're going to San-Fran-cisco . . ."* then swallowed quickly. "I just adore Frisco. We used to—before Judy was born, I went out with someone who knew folks in Sausalito, and we drove up once—it must've been seventy-eight or seventy-nine—to stay on a houseboat. Anyway, we got caught up in North Beach—you know the strip club where those people died having sex on that piano? Well, these were peak cocaine days. Blew through all our vacation money in about two hours! We never made it to Sausalito. What is that story, Judy, about the couple that died on the piano? The one Carol Doda used to dance on?"

Jude hadn't the slightest clue, but Caleb was consulting his phone. "The Condor," he reported.

"Yes! The Condor! That's it!"

Jude fixed her stare until Bonnie caught her eyes. *Compose yourself. Dear God*, and Bonnie's smile deteriorated. She sipped her water demurely, poked at the food on her plate, and when her voice came out again, it was smaller. "Now, do your parents still live there?" she asked Caleb.

Caleb held his beer midraise, his mouth ajar. "They do, yeah," he said, and drank. "Out by the Presidio."

Jude stiffened. His parents still lived in Michigan, as far as she knew. As far as she knew Caleb knew.

"Oh, the Presidio. Now where's that?"

Maybe he thought it'd be the fastest way to dispense with the subject. To say yes and move on. Or was it possible they'd moved back there? That Caleb got updates from another relative? "It's, like, northwest. By the Golden Gate Bridge."

Now—*now*, of all the times—Bonnie seemed interested. "And do they—what do your parents do? Are you close with them?"

Jude rested her hand on his leg. He downed the rest of his beer. She was ready to rush in and help, whenever he needed her.

"My dad's a cop, actually. He's retired now, but he was with the SFPD for a long time. And my mom's a clown. If you can believe it. She still works. Mostly, like, private events. We're pretty close, yeah."

"A cop and a clown!" Bonnie exclaimed. "What a match!"

Caleb continued, smiling, "I couldn't deal when I was younger. I'd lie and say my dad was a doctor and my mom was a professor. But then, like, in elementary school, my mom would show up at birthday parties, and kids would recognize her. And in high school, my dad would bust my friends for tagging, smoking weed in the park."

Jude was frozen. What was he *talking* about? Was this a thing, a story he told, that she hadn't been let in on?

"Does she wear wigs and all that? Your mother? How wonderful!"

Caleb signaled for another beer. "Oh yeah, wigs, hats, fuckin' face paint, all that shit. Rides a unicycle."

Bonnie shrieked.

"You'd like them, Bonnie. I visit every few months. Maybe we could all meet up out there." He looked to Jude, smiling. "At Christmas or something."

She met his eyes, stunned, pulling her hand away. He grinned back at her, a *What?* in his expression like it was some sort of game, until his new beer arrived, and he drank long. Why on earth tell Bonnie that? She didn't even *know him* yet—if it was a joke, it was callous and random—what was the point? Now Bonnie was going on about Christmas, how she and Jude hadn't had one together in years and years, how fun San Francisco would be then, the hills and the lights and the after-Christmas sales. The cop and the clown—something there rang familiar. The Halloween picture came back all at once, those four smiling people, but the image hardly answered Jude's questions.

Perhaps some psychic residue had seeped from her brain into the outside world, because, with exquisite timing, the alarm sounded—eight o'clock.

Caleb waved to a waiter carrying a tower of plates, so that, to Jude's mortification, he had to set down the whole heavy stack to tend to them.

Caleb yanked on the rope without looking at her, a signal to stand. She could murder him. "I'm not a pony," she said flatly, scooting back her chair. He looked at her—surprised, then smiling again. Was he *drunk*?

"Bonnie, we want you in this one," he said, off-kilter for a moment.

Instinctually, Jude took a step back. The rope, which had frayed and darkened and loosened a little in the last two days, stretched behind her mother in the middle, Bonnie's arms around both of them, her head awkwardly at crotch level, the refuse-strewn table in the foreground.

ON EAST BROADWAY, Bonnie stopped at a bodega window and pointed to a faded advertisement for a Statue of Liberty tour. "Oh, Judy, can we? Tomorrow? To see Lady Liberty?" Already Jude knew tomorrow was out, but, thinking of Caleb's cruelty, she told her mother yes.

*

THEY WENT TO THE TROUBLE, AS THEY HADN'T THE NIGHT BEFORE, of pulling out the sofa and of making it up with sheets and pillows as a proper bed. But Bonnie was still so hot in the room, even with only her nightdress on and the windows open and the box fan going (the air conditioner was in Caleb and Judy's room, their door already firmly shut), that she only lay there, sweating and breathing, staring at the silhouettes the trees made against the streetlight. It was Saturday night, and on their walk home the neighborhood buzzed with activity still, but Judy had gone sulky; she was exhausted, she said, but Bonnie knew she must be anxious, already, for time away from her. Most things Bonnie said and did were wrong, apparently, or to some degree embarrassing to Judy, try as her daughter might to hide her exasperation. But Bonnie could only be herself. Judy's annoyance was her own problem. It was her habit, anyway, to make mountainous disturbances out of molehill irritations. Bonnie herself was quite the opposite.

She turned on a lamp and looked around at the room. By the window, a large tropical plant was perched on a cinder-block stand, too fecund, everywhere at once, its roots draping over the pot's edges. There were a console full of records and the record player, various framed prints and photographs haphazard on the wall, and long, built-in shelves holding art books, cookbooks, novels; variously sized spines with titles evocative but intimidating: *Meditations in an Emergency* and *Diving into the Wreck* and *Regarding the Pain of Others*. She had brought neither her menopause book nor her better-communication book (for fear that Judy would discover them somehow; judge her), but now she wouldn't mind something to help her relax. She rose and went to the coffee table, which they'd shoved up against the radiator to make room for her bed, and sorted through a stack of magazines and paperbacks, where she hoped to find something more her speed. A cover caught her eye, a title and number, a species of book Bonnie recognized as the kind put out by colleges, where Judy's stories were sometimes published. Judy used to send these to Bonnie, in padded envelopes, and to Bonnie's delight, there would be Judy's name, in the table of contents and then above paragraphs of text Bonnie mostly understood but didn't exactly enjoy. (Girl characters floating unhappily through their twenties, Judy thinly disguised . . . what Bonnie wouldn't give to float unhappily through Judy's twenties!) Such a package hadn't come for Bonnie in a year, maybe two. She'd thought—thought without asking—that it meant Judy had, probably, outgrown the pastime.

But now, opening the journal, her expectation was confirmed: halfway down the table of contents appeared *Judith P. O'Connell*, pretty in print, all those regal, vertical letters holding her name up like columns. The issue was from last winter. So she *was* still writing, just no longer passing the stories on to Bonnie. In the past, she'd never known what to say—*I liked it! I liked how you could see it all, like in a movie*—shallow truths that seemed to let Judy down. Upon second inspection, the book Bonnie flipped through wasn't from a college. It was sturdier and nicer-looking than those other ones, its pages smooth and heavy, and a lot of white space had been left in the margins. Was this the magazine Judy referenced sometimes, the one she was an intern at? She hardly ever mentioned it, but no, no, that magazine had a different name, something beginning with an H Bonnie could never remember. On the final pages, a description of each contributor appeared—but Judy's was only one sentence. *Judith P. O'Connell is a writer living in New York.* It read like a mention of someone Bonnie didn't know. A person distant, anonymous, without history or family.

Pride bled into despair, and she was, she realized, suddenly so tired. She closed the book, slipped it in the side pocket of her day bag, and switched off the lamp. Murmurs came from the bedroom—tense, maybe—but she could make out no words; the effort of straining to listen put her, instantly, to sleep.

3. Sunday

FOR THREE LONG SECONDS, BONNIE DIDN'T KNOW WHERE she was. Then her eyes found the window and her suitcase heaped on the floor. She felt as if she'd just swum up through a hole in the cosmos and was late for something important.

The door must've woken her. "I feel like I died and have been born again," she said to Judy and Caleb, who came in through it now, balancing a carton with three paper cups.

"Good," Judy said. "We didn't want to wake you with the grinder. It's almost noon, Mom."

"Is it?" Bonnie said. Her father would've yelled, *Half the day is shot!*

"It's only nine on the West Coast," Caleb said.

But Judy scrunched her brow; the lines across her forehead were settling, as Bonnie's had at her age, into unfortunate permanence. She was pretty today, though, the rope making a kind of meant-to-be-there belt around her olive dress, and she'd penciled a line of black on just the bottom of her eyelids, the way they'd done it in the seventies. "You're feeling okay?"

"Oh, I'm great, I'm perfect!" Bonnie said, rising. Her knees took a minute to work. She should be doing something, to compensate for sleeping so long. She picked up the thin blanket and billowed it, folding it in half.

"You don't have to do that," Caleb said.

But Bonnie folded anyway. "Oh, I'm just—you two are all dressed, I have to catch up. Do we know what time the boats leave? Or where to buy tickets?"

She meant for Lady Liberty, but Judy's expression made it obvious that the visit wasn't on their agenda. They'd had a thing come up, Judy explained. A magazine had scheduled an interview with Caleb, in SoHo that afternoon. It was *sort of a big deal*, she added, in place of an apology.

"You really don't have to do that," Caleb said. Meaning the bedding again, but Bonnie was on to the sheet. "Because you're staying again tonight, right?"

As if Judy hadn't discussed it with him at all. As if Bonnie's whole visit were a sort of spontaneous accident, a layover on her way somewhere more important. But Bonnie had nowhere more important to be. She crumpled the sheet and tossed it down. Anger shook into her voice. "Yes, I was planning to stay for another night. And tomorrow night, if that's okay with you. I don't have money for a hotel, truth be told, and I haven't seen Judy here in about two years. I'm not sure if she's told you that. My flight is early Tuesday, and then you'll be rid of me."

Her own tone humiliated her, with its senior-sounding hurt. She didn't dare look at Judy, who let out a long moan. Instead, her eyes moved to the plant by the window, its leaves unfurling like giant, eight-fingered hands, reaching for whatever they could get.

It was just one afternoon, Judy was saying. Bonnie should *do her own thing* for a minute, do whatever she wanted, it was her first time in New York! And then they'd meet up for dinner. By the end of the speech, she was pleading. "My treat," she said. It was a phrase Bonnie herself used.

Caleb tried to interject—*I didn't mean*—but Bonnie cut him off. "Judy's right. It's only an afternoon. I'm a big girl." She didn't like that she was still in her nightgown, heather-gray and flimsy, her bare legs showing, three days unshaved. When she looked at Judy at last, her daughter's face was anxious, sorry, ready to placate. Bonnie felt inexplicably old, a nuisance. "You'll have to remind me how to work the subway."

AND SO Bonnie set out in the relentless heat, the paper that held Judy's hand-drawn map wilting in her hand. Her senses were braced, on high alert. She walked through drafts of trash and perfume, a stench that might've been a rotting corpse, until it was subsumed by pizza exhaust. Jackhammers pounded, box trucks rattled down a violent central boulevard while the subway rushed beneath her like a dirty underground river. She thought she'd never *been* somewhere so alive . . . but the train was here, and she clutched her bag close, the way the robotic voice instructed. On the map, Judy had drawn in N/S/E/W and written the number of the pier she needed, the names of the cruise company and the restaurant they'd meet at later, again in Chinatown but this one not Chinese (*Grain bowls*, Judy had said, whatever the hell those were). Bonnie had hoped for alfredo sauce and garlic bread and drippy candles shoved in wine bottles, but they hadn't asked her; it had all been decided already.

Never mind that eight o'clock was seven hours away. That, for seven hours, Bonnie would be alone, her trip exactly half over, taking in not her daughter's company but a monument she couldn't now remember why she'd so wanted to see. Sometimes a truth overtook her meanly: the fact of all the time she'd already lost with Judy. The lost time was impossible to reclaim, but so was it impossible to prevent such loss from happening again, over and over, from continuing to happen.

By two o'clock she sat shoulder to shoulder with strangers in a scooped plastic seat that burned her thighs. When the boat's horn belched, she felt it in her feet. Only a layer of SPF 30 and her sunglasses protected her from the glaring day (why had she not packed a visor?), but she felt liberated in a new pair of red rubber sandals, sparkles on the straps, bought for cheap from a sidewalk vendor on the way. Her clogs she'd thrown impulsively in a trash can, probably to regret later (they were her most practical work shoes), but security allowed only a small bag on the boat. Anyway, Bonnie reminded herself, she deserved certain luxuries from time to time.

The ferry scooted off, a clean unmooring from the land, a rotten tooth extracted. Sea spray rose and tingled. Kids chortled, mothers chastised, the crew seemed grumpy, and a seagull messed on someone, but Bonnie was happy amid the human commotion. Floating in the distance, Lady Liberty looked as forlorn as a seasonal decoration left out after the holiday, patiently resigned to waiting. Something chimed—a phone—and didn't stop, kept on chiming, until Bonnie realized the sound came from her own purse. She so rarely received calls! "Excuse me, excuse me," she said to the bodies all around her. But when she took it out, shielding the screen to block the glare, the name jarred her, and her stomach cramped. *RICK BRINGETTO* appeared like a formal announcement, insistent, a summons. Rick across the country, demanding she pick up.

Don't you dare, Jeff warned. She stared at the name, waiting for it to disappear. In her panic she couldn't remember how to silence the ringer, and she didn't want to touch anything, for fear she'd accidentally answer and then somehow be trapped—as if Rick had the power to reach through the device and physically force her into saying something she didn't mean, some commitment she could never undo, like a pact made in dreams or nightmares.

When the ringing at last stopped, Bonnie opened her contacts and tapped around hesitantly; it was as easy as swipe-swiping, she realized, and pressing Delete. In the new millennium, you could clear someone out of your life—erase all trace of them—with such simple, delicate gestures. She deleted Rick's name, and then she deleted his call from the missed-call list. A message popped up; he'd left a voice mail. He had not left a message in months, and her curiosity flared. *Get rid of it*, Jeff told her. No good could come of it. She opened the log of voice mails and swiped this one away, too, before she could persuade herself otherwise. It was gone! Her heart buzzed, afraid, but she liked this control. It was the same power, magnified, that she'd felt dumping the clogs.

They docked, and Bonnie followed the signs for the Crown Tour Elites, navigating the throngs. Earlier, at the kiosk on the pier, it was explained through the Plexi that *crown access tours filled up months in advance* (Bonnie was a bad tourist!), but a pissed-looking woman had saved the day, stuck a computer printout brusquely in her face, while children all around her screeched and made requests—*Here, we have an extra. You don't even need to pay me for it, all the mothers chipped in.* Bonnie thanked the woman profusely, said she was beginning to think that people in New York were the nicest people, actually, she'd ever met in her life. But the woman said she was from Ohio.

Now the Ohioan was up ahead, cutting across the wide lawn at Liberty's base where clusters of people applied more sunscreen, threw back trail mix. A tour guide was spieling out names and dates, then reciting the famous poem—the one about the poor and the huddled and the tempest-tost (surely Judy, if she'd come, would have something political to impart, some opinion that had never crossed Bonnie's mind). But Bonnie picked her way around the groups' margins, lithe and free in her new sandals, then up the big stone steps and into the museum. Up another flight of stairs, past another line (*Keep it movin', keep it movin', people*), around displays, and finally, outside, she gazed up at the solid green robes, the hardened, sea-foam folds made huge above her, funny at this angle, trying to feel something, trying to match this up-close materiality with the picture in her mind. Boys—young men— posed perversely for cameras waving on sticks, sticking their tongues through V-shaped fingers and reaching up their hands, as if to lift the statue's skirt. Judy would have had something to say about that, probably, too. But it was harmless. Just people having a good time, enjoying the sights, like her.

Now Bonnie saw they weren't bluffing about the climb: the staircase to the crown was a dizzying corkscrew up, silver as a drill bit, into the statue's brain. A guard checked her ticket and unlatched the velvet rope. Bonnie hadn't had a cigarette in years, but she had a vision of smoking a delicious Camel in the high altitude of Liberty's head. In the tour brochure she'd seen a photograph of Nancy Reagan and some other people leaning right out the crown windows, waving as if it were a Greyhound bus.

She had to pause several times to catch her breath. It was hot inside, claustrophobic and un-air-conditionable, and for a frightening moment Bonnie imagined suffocating—didn't know whether it was better to keep going or to descend, defeated. But there were voices right behind her, and she pressed on. When she reached the top, it was worth it. The breeze came in through small windows—much smaller than she'd thought. There was Liberty's arm! A girthful, blue-green thing, and there, on the other side, was the city, floating murkily across the ruffled water, framed by two armored spikes. From here the cityscape was not as clear as she'd hoped—more a cluster of gray and brown buildings than a breathtaking panorama—but who cared; it was *knowing it was there* that mattered, not so much what it looked like. She wished Judy was beside her—felt very high up and extra alone, now, to think of it. The polluted geography to the east would be Brooklyn—but where was Judy amid the landmass? Where was she, and *who* was she, and was she happy, Bonnie wondered suddenly, in this huge place, which she'd discovered (how *had* she?) all by herself? *I just want you to be happy*, Bonnie was fond of repeating—but what, really, *was* happiness, to Judy? She squinted, willing the view to yield, but Judy remained a pixel in the haze—off somewhere unknown, becoming evermore not quite her daughter.

A couple was behind her now, panting and oohing. She recognized them from the ferry; the woman was hugely pregnant, past the navel-popping stage, too far along, Bonnie thought, to have risked the ascent. When they moved beside her to gaze out, she couldn't help herself. "You know, I read in the in-flight magazine that if everyone in New York came out of their apartments or offices or whatever all at the same time, there wouldn't be enough space on the street to stand? Or air to breathe? You would suffocate. I mean, can you imagine?"

The woman turned. A delicate gold cross rested on her clavicle, above an I ♥ NY tank top, warping over the big breasts and belly. "Wow," she said, but leaned closer to her husband, placing her hands, protectively, on her womb.

It isn't what you think it will be, Bonnie could've said. *Prepare yourself for that.* "Do you have a name yet?"

The woman offered a short list, Bible characters and a grandmother, but Bonnie hardly listened. A memory—a reminiscence of wailing, like labor, like *bloody murder*—butted in from nowhere (was it the children stampeding up the staircase now, announcing themselves so loudly?). In her first days out of rehab, after Judy moved in with the Geisens, Bonnie took to waiting in one of Rick's cars from the driving school, out of sight down the block like a goddamned spy, until Judy emerged from the doors of Grant High, she and Melissa striding and chatting, smiling and gossiping (it had fractured her heart to see her daughter so normal, carrying happily on!). She'd cruise up alongside them, and Judy would glance her way but act like she hadn't seen. Would continue talking, staring at the sidewalk and showing her half smile to Melissa, as if nothing at all were strange in their periphery. How insane Bonnie had felt! Screaming for her own daughter to *Get in the car!*, begging, pleading like that, maddened. Only eight feet of air separated them, but Bonnie could not close the gap. Melissa clutched Judy's arm through the intersection. *You're not even supposed to be driving*, Judy yelled at last, her voice betraying her upset. *Get in the fucking car, Judith Petunia! I'm your mother!* and Melissa sprang forward—*Leave her alone, she lives with us now!*—as if Bonnie were a kidnapper. Once, Judy spat righteously, *You're not my mother anymore!* And another time, Judy's hair was different: bangs cut across her forehead, obscuring her eyebrows, *changing her.* Past the scope of Bonnie's watch, she was slipping away. Loss had devastated Bonnie before, but loss while sober was a new kind of torture. She'd peeled off savagely that day. Considered burning down Melissa's house or slitting her own wrists. Instead, more easily, she'd bought a handle of vodka.

She nodded at the woman. "How nice. Congratulations."

On the descent, her thighs quivering, regret hit her heart like the back of a spoon: she had deleted Rick's number. She had not listened to his message, and then she had thrown it away. In his last email, he had written that he still loved her. She hadn't answered his calls, or his texts, or that email, and an hour ago she'd deleted him. How terrible, to have to say no to love, when its invitations were so rare.

IT WAS AFTER five o'clock when, recognizing the lightness in her arms, Bonnie realized she'd eaten nothing all day except a dish of Judy's yogurt. This neglectfulness disturbed her; when the ferry returned them to the terminal, she was off the boat at once, looking right and then left, driven by purpose, her sole wish in the world to find a hamburger and a glass of iced tea.

After soldiering several blocks through pedestrians, tourists semicircled around street performers, convenience stores and pharmacies and office buildings and a big bronze bull people were lined up to photograph, she found a narrow, old-timey street with a sandwich board perched halfway down the block, advertising Guinness and fried things. Shamrocks glittered in the windows. Inside, an Irish flag hung festively beside a dingy American one.

Stale beer particles hung out in air that felt recirculated, insufficient. The place was almost entirely empty. She took a seat near the middle of the bar and ordered straightaway.

"One burga for the miss," the bartender said.

"Oh god, thank you," she said, settling herself. "Are you Irish?"

"Aussie," he said, pouring her water. "That work all right for you?"

He was, she now saw, extremely handsome. His long hair was pulled back in a ponytail, and biceps round as grapefruits made the sleeves of his black polo tight. A young Val Kilmer; a heyday Mel Gibson. His *you* sounded funny. "Thank you so, so much," Bonnie said, gulping. The glass tasted like detergent. "You're saving my life, really. *Reviving* me."

"Sure you don't need something a tad stronga?" He raised his eyebrows, looking at the empty glass.

"Oh, I'd love to, but I shouldn't. Iced tea?"

He was even cuter when he smiled. Two dimples came out in star shapes at the bottoms of his cheeks (what Greg's dimples might've looked like, had Bonnie met him in his prime), and his eyes were the same blue as Bonnie's— those glass-coated, clear-flecked, hiding-between-the-lids minerals that had been the pride of her appearance, growing up. She'd always been attracted to men that matched. Judy's father. Rick. Caleb, come to think of it, was blue-eyed, too.

She spread her hands wide on the bar, her new domain, and leaned forward. "Dan, do you think we have the same color eyes?" His name was printed in white cursive above a hard, square pec. She blinked a few times, as if to make their color clearer.

He played serious and inspected her face, clinical. "It's uncanny, actually. We must be kin. Or destined for one anotha."

Bonnie drew back in mock alarm. "Oh, I know your kind," she said. "It's all about the big tip with you charming, foreign bartenders. You'll say anything to get a big tip."

Dan grinned badly. "Oh, my tips are plenty big already," he said. "Bigga than you can imagine."

She swatted the air, and Dan plopped down before her a caddy of Dijon and Worcestershire. Two men in gym clothes settled themselves at the end of the bar, and Dan, who Bonnie was now sufficiently yearning for, took a lot of time attending to his new customers. It was for the best, probably, because the burger, when it came, proved to be a massive, shifting catastrophe she couldn't properly fit her mouth around, with unexpected bacon and blue cheese Bonnie did her best to pick off. Juice ran down her chin, and she dabbed, quickly, with her shredded, bloody napkin. Now Dan turned his back and was busy unboxing a shipment, running cases of liquor two at a time up a staircase behind the bar. Hoping to distance herself from the plate, from overindulging

and coming off piggish, and because all of the other patrons were in twos and
threes, talking, Bonnie lifted her purse to retrieve one of the Statue of Liberty
brochures. But here in her bag was a book—Judy's story! She'd nearly forgotten about it. She wiped her hands again, not wanting to stain the pages.

The story was called "Freaky_Kiki," a title that unnerved and confused
Bonnie (why was it written like that?), and began with twelve-year-old Kiki
traipsing along a California highway, a small blue suitcase in her hand, sticking her thumb out at passing cars. Kiki was on her way to the desert, where
her mother lived (she'd never met her—Kiki was adopted). In the first pages,
Bonnie felt the familiar frustration of Judy's writing: the sentences were jam-
packed with minutiae (get to the point, Judy!), and Bonnie had to strain to
keep her focus attached. But when the girl arrived at the mother's, and Bonnie
saw, to her utter dismay, that the mother lived in a trailer, that the mother had
hair Judy described as *silver made all the more visible by her attempts to mask
it with cheap, smelly dyes*, and the flap of skin between her chin and neck was
something the mother said she'd *clip like a fingernail, if she had the money*,
Bonnie's concentration sharpened. The mother's name was Deb, with a Rick-
like boyfriend named Jed. Deb and Jed drank Wild Turkey on ice and offered
Kiki spoiled milk. Deb did her makeup in a hand mirror while Kiki asked
questions about her birth—why her mother had given her up and so forth,
to which Deb gave blunt, casual replies while rubbing color on her lips. It
was revealed that Kiki had met Deb and Jed on the internet somehow—and
eventually it became clear that Deb wasn't, after all, Kiki's mother, something
the reader was clued in on but poor Kiki didn't see. At one point, while Kiki
changed clothes in the bathroom, the suspect Jed walked in on her—played
it off like an accident but let his eyes linger too long. *The eyes detached from his
face and hung in the air like two floating marbles.* In another scene, Kiki offered
to perform a dance routine on the Astroturf patio. She danced without music.
The couple watched, chain-smoking and sipping. When she did the splits at
the grand finale and looked over at them for applause, she found them *hysterical with laughter; tears ran down Deb's gummy cheeks.* The story ended exactly
as Bonnie hoped it wouldn't: Deb was out walking their dachshund when
Rick—Jed—held Kiki down in the bedroom and did the unthinkable. Here

the descriptions got fuzzy, and Bonnie couldn't quite see it—or, she *could* see it, but more by the power of her own shameful imagination than because of anything clearly stated. She was aware of how rigid her body had gone, her crossed legs gripped together and her spine like a wire, hunched over the book. It was impossible not to think of Rick, again—his crime disconcertingly close. After the suggested rape, Jed went to the kitchen to crack a beer while Kiki lay on the water bed, *the waves jiggling beneath her like something alive—like yet another living thing to contend with.*

But how could the story end *there,* Bonnie's heart raged, without the mother returning, with nothing else happening, just the cold dismalness of the trailer turned crime scene? Had Judy been able to imagine such ugliness because it had happened to her? Or did the fact that Judy had written it cancel out this possibility (no one *actually* faced their worst traumas, Bonnie felt, not in memory and so certainly not in writing; Judy's fiction might be fully autobiographical until precisely the moment it couldn't be)? *She was able to write it because she didn't live it,* Bonnie told herself. And yet the newly chewed food rose in her esophagus in a gray, vengeful lump. She drank her tea until the glass was empty, then suppressed a painful burp.

"Whatcha readin'?" A voice split through.

Bonnie looked up. He was a savior. "Oh," she said, and closed the journal quickly. "Just something a friend wrote. A writer friend."

"Ah, a *writer* friend. Make sure you don't do anything to end up in his book."

He was even more handsome than she remembered. The work with the boxes had made his forehead slick, and the faintest smell, musk and deodorant, mingled with the dirty taps. She laughed loudly, raising her chin to tighten the flab at her neck. "It might be too late for that!"

"How're we doin' otherwise?" Dan asked, gesturing at her plate. "Finished?"

She feared she was losing him. Losing him to the formalities of customer service. She leaned forward and gripped him with her eyes. "You tell me."

He grinned, turned, and pulled down a tall gold bottle Bonnie knew—used to know—well. Again, his dimples revealed themselves. He held the shot glasses two in one hand, then rotated their rims one at a time in a dish of salt on the bar. For a long beat, she allowed herself to assume the glasses were for two other people. But then he clarified, "You're a tequila woman, I can tell"—*tequila* with the subtlest R tacked to the end—conscripting her. When he poured, the gold liquid turned convex at the rim, then spilled over the edge so that some of the salt saturated and dribbled.

As kids, Judy and her friend, Meghan Rorty, had been in the habit of making up their own little routines to cassette tapes, dragging the recliner and the coffee table to the living room's edges to make floor space. They somersaulted and cartwheeled, folded their arms and flapped their hands, made Egyptians of their postures, did the Roger Rabbit and the running man, moves copied from music videos. Once, having come home hammered with someone she was seeing (Trent, who wore bowling shirts embroidered with other men's names), Bonnie got it in her head that Trent just *had* to meet Judy, who they found camped out in the bedroom with a watery bowl of Top Ramen, a library book, and a grubby stuffed cat she was, at that time, particularly attached to. Bonnie asked Judy to dance, to do one of her routines for Trent— he'd come *all the way down from Sylmar* just to meet her! *It's a two-person dance*, Judy had protested. *Meghan's not here.* Trent suggested, *Call her up!* but it was well after ten o'clock. Eventually Judy conceded; Bonnie could tell she was pleased to have been asked and was only acting coy for Trent. They helped with the recliner and the coffee table. The boom box was plugged in, the Whitney Houston tape found. Judy began with her shoulders hunched and her hands covering her face, in her P.E. T-shirt and fuchsia sweats. At the song's intro, her fingers shivered away from her eyes as her head slowly rose, then she turned a cartwheel on the synthesizer burst. Beside Bonnie on the couch, Trent put two fingers in his mouth and whistled. But Judy had been right; without Meghan the choreography was crooked. The wavy hand thing didn't work; the four-armed-person move was lost; and impossible was the part where they crouched, then popped up over each other's shoulders, leapfrogging toward the audience, Meghan bending into a bridge for Judy to worm beneath. Rather than improvise, Judy stuck strictly to the plan— performed her half to a tee, freezing in certain positions to give imaginary

Meghan time to do her bit, even clapping the patty-cake sequence with no one to clap back. But as the music wore on, Bonnie saw, in her daughter's face, the cracking of resolve. The song—ironically, the song went, *Oh, I wanna dance with somebody!*

When Judy dropped into backward push-up position and did a funny, crabby thing, lifting her arms first right, then left, in time, grabbing out toward the balancing weight of a partner who wasn't present—Bonnie had finally busted up. The preciousness of Judy's sincerity! The failure of the dance! Hysterical, she fell onto Trent, who was shaking, wiping the tears from his eyes. Judy leapt to her feet. Their laughter went on. She pounded off the music, enraged, her voice twisting on *I hate you!*, and ran out, sobbing.

It was one of a thousand incidents Bonnie had always hoped Judy didn't remember, but there it was, laid out like evidence, unforgettable, permanent. The Deb character, too, was proof of something: to Judy, Bonnie was still *that* mother, singular and stationary, a constant incapable of change. *Yet another living thing to contend with.*

If Bonnie hadn't changed to Judy, then why should Bonnie change to Bonnie? Take the drink, and her world could flip, turn, change course yet again—or at least go still for a minute. She was all alone in New York City. She could have this one, and no one would ever know.

"To kin," the bartender said, raising his shot, "and destiny."

She didn't look at his face but at the two golden ounces in front of her. Like a vow, Bonnie repeated the toast.

*

SHE TENSED TO SEE HER MOTHER AT THE TOP OF THE STAIRS. Bonnie's face looked pale and searching in the low light of the basement bar, and when Jude saw her locate their pushed-together table, Jude and Caleb among their friends, Bonnie waved a moment too long. Jude's throat closed. She knew that off-kilter timing—Bonnie was drunk. This was confirmed as she began her jerky descent, tilting dangerously forward.

A disorienting déjà vu—Jude's body did a mental double-take—was she really an adult, in 2016, hosting her mother in a faraway place? Many times,

Jude had played out this scenario, or one similar. But the imaginary relapses happened at a distance, came with telephone calls late at night, suicide threats and ancient revelations—far enough in the future that Jude was married and publishing books, more safely insulated by her own encumbering life. Half-way down the stairs, Bonnie stopped to peer down again, as if she'd lost faith in where she was going. Again she spotted Jude and waved.

The frustration she'd felt at Bonnie's missing their dinner reservation, at her not answering her phone and her inability to respond to texts—all of it evaporated now. In its place, dark disquietude fell. She found a modicum of comfort in reasoning that this couldn't be the first slip in almost a decade. Probably drinking had been back for weeks or months or years now, informa-tion Bonnie had simply withheld, keeping Jude in the dark, white-knuckling it between benders. And yet the change in her mother was indisputably new: the lapse had happened on Jude's own watch. She shrank to someone very weak. This helpless person thought, *Let it not be.*

On stage, three girls in NYU T-shirts wrapped up the final bars of Cyndi Lauper. Their boyfriends catcalled and whooped, and Jude's own table clapped minimally, without setting down their drinks. Then Bonnie was there, at the head of the table, leaning awkwardly on one foot in ugly new sandals. "Hello, hello everyone, people I've never met. I'm Bonnie Bringetto. Judy's mother, from California. I'm just—I'm really *loving* New York."

She slurred in that almost imperceptible way—slurring that's aware of itself still, and so tries not to. And she'd said her married name—Rick's last name—instead of her own, her maiden. She was gone, gone. Jude did not speak or move.

Jesse, an editor at *Hierarchy*, and Erika, from the restaurant, both rose to give Bonnie their chairs, insisting they liked to stand. Her friends—bless them—she could count on to be graceful and kind, especially the indus-try ones, to whom satisfying needs was second nature. One by one, they went around and introduced themselves, half stood, shook hands, smiled, complimented. The friends were mostly Jude's but included a few of Caleb's, too; the convenient swath of overlap the couple had discovered in their social worlds and which Jude had been working hard to cultivate. (The nights when they were only among Caleb's friends, who were fancier, artier, quicker to drop names, left Jude generally insecure, easily miffed.) An hour before, Jude had mentioned to the table her mother's current visit (*I'm warning you, she has no filter. And she's very . . . glib*). Half of them had heard talk of Bonnie at other times, in other bars, Bonnie who always came out of Jude's mouth not as a sober, middle-aged minimum-wage earner but as the Bonnie of old, a Gena Rowlands character in a Cassavetes film. They would've expected this, then: Bonnie flipping, accidentally, the straw from Zach's glass as she gestured with a flying hand. Now Jude was guilt-stricken, as if her comments had been prophecy—she'd even assembled an audience to bear witness. And if Bonnie had heard Jude qualify her, an hour ago, as *estranged*, it would have crushed her beyond measure. She leaned into Caleb and whispered, "She's been drinking."

She looked to gauge his reaction. His barely listening face searched for the joke. "It'll probably chill her out, right?"

Jude's chest felt tight; she was aware of her own rapid breathing. "She's an *alcoholic*, Caleb," she hissed between inhales. Outside of sex, she almost never used his name. "She's *sober*."

"I mean, it's just—whatever—she's on vacation?" He raised his own drink, and the ice hit his teeth.

Nancy Sinatra started up. Jude hated this song—imagined ripping herself away, but could only scoot closer to the wall. His response baffled her. Did he know *nothing*?—even with an ex-girlfriend in recovery? Jude's intuition had been right; last night in bed, during their whispered fight, he'd admitted that the friend he'd brought up at dinner *was* a woman he'd been involved with (though still he wouldn't say her name). But the revelation was quickly lost in the tumult of the bigger argument. *Why would you make that up about your parents?* Jude needed to know. She'd done her best to express herself calmly, rationally. It was the first time she'd been mad at him, *really* mad, and she didn't like the feeling—as if they'd already failed at something, as if she herself had miscalculated. *She doesn't know anything about you yet, and you've*—but Caleb had evaded. Avoided the question, then flipped it. *Look, she's sleeping on my couch, isn't she . . . You're making me feel like I did something wrong . . .* Jude had taken a deep, leveling breath: *You* did *do something wrong.*

At last, she dragged out a sort of confession (but she didn't want to *drag* any-thing out of anyone, the way it brought to mind *nagged* or *hag*). He explained that he'd only told Bonnie what he assumed Bonnie wanted to hear. That Jude had found a nice, normal, well-adjusted boyfriend, with a family to match. *It's not like it hurts anyone*, he finished. But Jude asked him to clarify *it*. Making that up, he meant. He did not say *lying*. It was harmless, it was small. He begged her to let them sleep.

He'd lost his family, she'd reasoned while Caleb snored. He'd lost a brother, and then a mother and father, and Bonnie's visit might've been salt, subcon-sciously shaking into old wounds. And yet why *didn't* they talk, specifically, and what steps had Caleb taken, or not taken, to make it better? The cop and the clown in the photograph, the doctor and the professor—liberal, affluent San Franciscans—did not strike Jude as people unwilling to reconcile. She would ask him directly, she told herself, after the rope, but a small part of her—a quadrant of her heart just awakening—was less eager to hear his answer. Could he be stubborn? Unyielding? Someone who harbored grudges? Her perception turned a corner into new wilderness, even while she reminded herself that no one was perfect, no romance ideal, generosity and understanding were part of mature relationships. And they were still only at the beginning.

When the introduction line came to them, Bonnie swatted the air at Jude and said, "Well I *know* you. Twenty-six hours of labor; I better!" Then she waggled her finger at Caleb but spoke to Sofia. "But this one . . . what do we think of this one? I'm not sure yet. He's awful cute to be trustworthy, don't you think?"

Sofia smiled and nodded like a good sport, slipping Jude a sideways look. Never in Jude's life had she been so happy to be called to a karaoke stage.

They sang a staid duet of "Dirty Work," alternating verses and then com-ing together at the chorus, but with no attempts to harmonize. The KJ took a photo with his phone, presumably because of the rope—the fucking rope—which Jude had expected would, by now, have become less noticeable, bur-densome, oppressive, instead of more. Earlier, in SoHo, the interviewer had asked Jude only *Sparkling or still?*, then turned his attention fully to *the artist*. Caleb wavered self-consciously between keys: *But I stay here just the same . . .*

None of the friends left their seats (*You don't dance to "Dirty Work,"* Jesse had said, *you empathize to it*) except for Bonnie, who Jude saw now, under the red glow of an exit sign. She swayed with her head down and her hands raised, as if she were evangelizing, or on a hillside at Altamont. Her hair, which she generally wore swept back in a loose, half-up beret shape that trailed into a scrawny braid, had fallen out of its rubber band, fell limply into her face, frizzing and thinning. When the chorus returned, Jude watched Bonnie mouth the words, her eyes closed. *I'm a fool* . . .

The room clapped politely, but Bonnie shook her hands wildly and screamed, *Woooo!*

Next Kayla's new partner, a person named Xara with a shaved head and a septum piercing, sang an easy Sadé, and Peter landed "Purple Rain," and an NYU girl butchered "Juicy," and then Zach, who'd been in a successful garage-rock band, crooned a virtuosic "I'm on Fire." Bonnie was back at the table now, across from Jude and Caleb, gaping at Zach on stage with wet, starstruck eyes, no doubt tingling for him, his assured stance, his white T-shirt and dark, curly hair lending him a Bosslike appeal that only added to the performance. Jude twitched at the lyrics turning yellow across the monitor: *Like someone took a knife baby edgy and dull and cut a six-inch valley through the middle of my skull.* Across the table, Bonnie had the big song binder open on her lap and was conferring seriously with Sofia, until the waitress appeared with a loaded tray and set a drink in front of her (a tall, clear, pint glass of a drink: a double, Jude thought; she could practically smell the gin from here). Bonnie rushed to open her purse, then crammed a dollar into the poor girl's hand, clutching and shaking it gratefully, as if Bonnie were a desert sojourner who'd at last been given water.

What could Jude do? Intercept the drink, pull already-drunk Bonnie aside, scold her and forbid her, *manage her*? If she was going to drink she was going to drink, a voice in Jude, long-ago hardened, reminded her—and a familiar distress rose up, the unjust perturbation that, try as she might, Jude was *not in control of her own life.* For much of her childhood and some of her adulthood, she'd thought there was something wrong with her—a shapeless disfigurement, she told Louanne—but only more recently had she been able to admit: *since there was so much wrong with my mother.* It came as an enormous relief to find that, as a young adult, she liked alcohol just fine, but not too much.

Jude sat transfixed, immobile, Caleb's warm hand on her back. The drunk woman across from her rose, holding a slip of paper, and wobbled her way to the booth. *For better or for worse, in sickness and in health . . .* the words came in freakishly and made a mess of Jude's heart. She hadn't been to therapy in months, but now she thought she'd make an appointment, despite the cost, the second her mother was back on a plane.

Bonnie dropped the song in the jar and offered the KJ a wink—a wink that took her whole, effortful face. On stage, Zach howled the song's final yips, and everyone clapped and yelled. When he leapt off the stage, Bonnie grabbed him—tugged him to her by the arm and kissed him hugely on the mouth.

From the speakers, the KJ's voice boomed, "Bon-ee! Miss Bon-ee, it's your up! Happy birthday to you!"

She heard Paul ask, *It's her birthday?* and Jude turned, suddenly very tired, to look at her friends. "No. It's just a card she likes to play." To skip the line, to weasel a free drink. She'd used it once when a cop pulled her over for running a stop sign: *But officer, please, not on my birthday!* The cop who held, of course, her birthdated ID. "This is insane," Jude appealed, to no one in particular, to the semicircle of faces, like so many rocks on a distant shore. "How is this happening?" Caleb's hand on her back moved as if to say, *Hush.*

Up on the stage, Bonnie struggled to adjust the mic stand and hold her rapidly disappearing drink at the same time. She figured it out, sighed loudly, tapped the mic twice, then flung her head back, readying herself. "Go Bonnie! Happy birthday!" the KJ cheered. Several of Jude's friends clapped, caught between politeness and concern.

"Suite: Judy Blue Eyes" appeared on the screen unsurprisingly. Those opening guitar chords, so familiar, a soundtrack to Jude's childhood, a thing often played on her birthday, actually, her own, *real* birthday, on Bonnie's ancient turntable accompanying cake from a mix, or on the radio in the Dodge, Bonnie singing along with her whole heart, and Judy understanding that the song represented a time in her mother's life that had been greater, magically, than the sum of its humble parts. Never mind that this was the era in which Bonnie had run away from home, lived in a car for several years, developed an addiction, suffered a litany of traumas Jude hardly knew the half of—a certain something-in-the-air nostalgia (denial?) somehow prevailed. Judy Collins stared out, beautiful and sad, from the water-warped cover of one album among a stack. *Laurel Canyon was—you know, it was practically next door, even if we never went up there, but we did go down to the Whisky sometimes—a gal I worked with at my very first job had a boyfriend who'd done some studio things with the Eagles, so . . .* Whenever Judy had complained of the old-fashionedness of her name, wanting to be a Miranda or an Alicia, Bonnie would say, *But you're named after a masterpiece!* Judy's eyes weren't even blue! she'd protest. *Bonnie* had the blue eyes; Jude's were simply brown, or, as Meghan had once described them, *a color you never think about.*

Now, on the first hesitant notes of Bonnie's voice, the clenched thing inside Jude cranked tighter. *It's getting to the point where I'mmmm no fun anymore.* Quivering, earnest, quietly theatrical, but not *bad*—in fact, if Jude could be objective, her mother was almost good. Difficult-to-bear good. Heart-cracking good. Tears rushed to Jude's eyes, but she forced them to hold still. *I am sor-ry*, too low for her range. Each word lagged a semisecond behind the music.

Nothing erupted, as it could have: she didn't rush the stage, or grab the microphone away, or ferry her mother back to Brooklyn, as she might have (should have?)—which gave the song an aura of preemptive apology and also, oddly, of thanks. Now Jude was the mother allowing Bonnie, the child, to stay up past her bedtime, to join the adults at their party, to drink. Bonnie's eyes moved from the screen directly to Jude's, locking her in painful serenade. *I am yours, you are mine.* But Jude pulled her eyes away. She didn't want this. *You make it ha-ah-ah-ah-ard.* To be the burning, awkward nucleus of the night, or of, unasked for, her mother's life.

It continued, and continued, for so long—an endless song—with its various parts and breakdowns and voices, which Bonnie flipped among like a vaudeville performer, a one-woman show, rushing to keep up. It was no small miracle that Jude wasn't crying—she hadn't during the opening bars and so wouldn't, now, at the sag in the middle, the suite's empty corners. Zach joined Bonnie at the mic. Tickled and laughing, they danced through the instrumentals. The NYU girls gathered around the stage, doing sexy, snaky moves. *Chestnut-brown canary,* the KJ sang, accented and serious, from his booth. Everyone at the table was laughing uncontrollably now, snorting to keep it in—*Oh my god, Jude, your mom!*—even Caleb. Was it embarrassment she felt? No; embarrassment was easy. It was miles, oceans, years of distance. And yet here they were, in a room together. The song a mockery of all that had, supposedly, changed. Bonnie's arm encircled Zach low, clutching the denim of his skinny hip. For a flash, Jude was able to laugh, too—to zoom out and above and see the comedy of it. At the *do-do-do-do-do* breakdown, they all *do-do-do-do-do*ed together, shouting, yelling now, even, softly, her.

4. Monday

THE RENEWAL OF BONNIE'S CONTACT WITH RICK BEGAN SIX months back, with an email that opened, *Hello again.*

Hello—how impersonal and generic—and yet, *again*: as if nothing had changed and only a moment, not thirteen years, had elapsed. All the intimacy of their past had rushed back—she missed him deeply and all at once, with a force that frightened her. How atypical of Rick's voice *Hello again* sounded, and yet how strange, that a phrase could contain, still, a voice.

It didn't hit her that the email was an amends until the second read. The realization cheapened her pleasure; so it was only Rick moving through the program, doing what he was supposed to. He could've at least had the balls to *call*, she thought at first, or to drive north and say it to her face: Why the hell not? And yet the concluding paragraph pricked: *When I remember what a woman I had, how beautiful you were on our wedding day and how much love you gave me . . .* So often Bonnie's thoughts led back to how she used to be, the good parts of that past, that the sweetness overwhelmed her—to know that someone else, too, remembered.

On her own eighth step, Bonnie had skipped over Rick completely, an omission she'd kept from her sponsor, but so be it, her pride was what it was, a flower trampled on so many times she had no choice but to protect its few intact petals. Through the grapevine she'd learned that he was already remarried by then, to someone from Reno named Darcy (how preposterous, that one man could be with both a *Darby* and a *Darcy* in the same lifetime! Darby, the side piece who'd been the end of their marriage, still haunted Bonnie, the image of her unsunned legs astraddle Rick's face the day she had walked in on them, Darcy's walnut-colored hair fastened up with Bonnie's own abalone-inlaid butterfly clip, no doubt lifted from the nightstand at the suggestion of Rick, who liked Bonnie's hair to be off her neck and had the habit of handing her the clip whenever he rolled to her, hard). *Thirteen years ago!* Bonnie let two days pass before she replied with polite forgiveness, congratulating Rick on his recovery. She checked her tone for maturity and distance, for a certain degree of securely sober wisdom. But right away, he wrote again.

To emails two and three Bonnie didn't respond at all. She was mulling over what to do with his increasingly personal revelations. He explained how his marriage to Darcy, too, had recently ended; how alcohol and infidelity had again comingled to destroy something precious—though not as precious as what he and Bonnie had had. *Remember how we . . .* and his smell returned, distant but potent. A trip to Catalina when Bonnie emerged from the surf with tar on her heels, sticky patches Rick scrubbed off with baby oil, his torso jiggling as he laughed. The way he started sentences, *How 'bout if we*—plans Rick had already decided on but formed into questions for Bonnie's sake. *How 'bout if we go for steak tonight? Fuck it, put it on the driving school's plastic. How 'bout if we ask the Robinsons over for drinks? Get Judy out of the house and wear that black bra? How 'bout if we go out to Palm Springs the weekend after my tournament?* He danced as few men did: confidently, on rhythm, nearly *graceful.* It was his confidence that always got her. As if he'd been given a key to his life at birth, and all he had to do was use it. He'd scoop you right up, used to like to carry her, squealing and kicking, across parking lots and hotel lobbies and domestic thresholds. In his big arms, oh, how young and feminine and weightless she'd felt, hardly there, joyfully removed from herself.

To the fourth email, she responded. Emails soon became phone calls. Clichés like *rekindle* and *second chance* were introduced. He spoke generously of regret. It was March, a season of damp gray and ennui, of income taxes and overeating, of green-tag sales and grief breakdowns from Greg. A season in which, many times, she considered attending a meeting (she hadn't been in more than a year), if only for something to put on her calendar other than her shifts and to avoid having to lie to Judy—and yet the guilt she now associated with the long hiatus, plus the effort it would take to spur herself from this late-winter lassitude, plus the reality that she'd had flings with too many of the men from the usual Bowman group and so would need to try DeWitt Center or the church over on Nevada Street . . . she wrote down the times but didn't go. In a funny way, all Rick's talk of sobriety created the illusion that Bonnie, too, was keeping up with a decent amount of maintenance just by proxy. The familiar recovery language, the tropes and phrases long tarnished by over-use, arrived in Rick's voice loaded as revelations, with all of the rightness with which they'd first struck her, too. *Oh yes, he's changing*, she began to think. She willfully forgot how, during their marriage, any talk by Bonnie of "cleaning up her act" went entirely unsupported by Rick, who ruled again and again that drinking itself wasn't the problem, but rather Bonnie's silly routines *around* drinking (if Bonnie would eat a bigger dinner, if she'd put on a little weight, if she wasn't already run down by the stress of her job and her daughter, if she'd stick to just beer or Jim Beam straight, instead of mixing it with Sprite). And she ignored the reality that Rick had begun his assault on her program the moment she left detox: *There goes our social life. Our sex life. How 'bout a few margaritas with my baby?* He wanted to dance with her close at Padre's Tacos, to show her off at his buddies' parties, to do a few lines and stay up late. He wanted to hit the Blue Zebra after he'd finished a long week of lessons—give Bonnie a stack of bills and watch her squirm, tucking them into G-strings—*But all that'll be going down the crapper, too, won't it, now that you can't handle your beer.* For a decade, she slid back into booze, crawled out again, slid back, crawled out, up onto, again, the wagon. It was during a particularly strong dry run in 2004 that she'd discovered Darby (Rick: *Well what did you expect me to do? Sit home and watch the news every night while you're off drinking the Kool-Aid, getting saved?*) and fallen, again, off.

And yet this Rick, this new Rick, was actively apologizing for *enabling her*, for his *manipulative behavior*, admitting to living so long in denial of his own sickness that his judgments of Bonnie were, of course, defenses against his own problem. His sponsor, his new friends, were helping him understand. It flattered her and made her nervous, the foreignness of his respect. She was patient; she said the right things back, though the itchy part of her was ever waiting for more talk of *us*. When he mentioned the house—renovations to the kitchen and cookouts on the weekends—the life that had once been hers tugged. She could almost see the rotting fence boards, the thicket of jelly palms, the barbecue on its concrete square in the sea of watery grass where

Judy and Meghan used to "lay out" in their two-pieces, spraying lemon juice in their hair.

I miss you, Bonnie. I miss you as my girl. A window opened in the dark and stuffy room of Bonnie's life. The notion that her existence could again be shared, and didn't have to be, forever, something she alone was responsible for. The possibility of two sober divorcés reconnecting, after all these bitter years, like a feel-good story in a local newspaper. And things starting back up with Rick made her time with Greg simpler. Demoted to a placeholder, he became sweeter in Bonnie's eyes, more like a friend she didn't mind kissing but wanted nothing more from. The hardest thing would be Judy—breaking the news of this reconnection, *convincing* her—but there would be time, Bonnie thought. She was getting ahead of herself. She'd take it, this time, slow.

Inevitably, a visit was suggested. Rick brought it up, then changed the subject when Bonnie expressed interest, and then, when Bonnie proceeded as if no visit had been mentioned, again Rick circled back. He was semiretired now and well enough off—he'd sold the driving school, cashed in his inventory, and did contract work for traffic schools, web stuff on the side. He offered to buy her flight to Burbank—an offer she held at bay for days, knowing all along that she would, of course, take it. But *slow this time*—plus she was waiting to talk to her doctor about a hormone cream, something she'd read about, that would make sex at her age less of a catastrophe. She wanted it, with Rick again, to be special, and to be special it would have to be functional.

Then one day in May, on her fifteen-minute break, Bonnie logged into her email on the employee computer in the storeroom. Hoping for something from Rick, she saw his name, instead, in the subject line of a message from her old coworker Diane. The women had once power-walked on their lunch breaks together, complained of the same bitchy boss. Now Diane lived in Phoenix with her son and his wife and spent inordinate amounts of time online. Every few months Bonnie heard from her: chain letters, political stuff, videos Bonnie didn't watch.

There was no greeting. *You're gonna hate me for this, but I thought you should know. Don't shoot the messenger! P.S. See, this is why you should get facebook!*

Beneath the email was a blue link Bonnie clicked, bracing herself. A confusingly laid-out profile appeared, of a youngish, happy-looking blond woman shining out from a quarter-sized picture above her name, Katie Hendrickson.

It was easy to find what Diane meant for her to see, because there at the center of the screen was an old photo of Rick on a volleyball court, his hair parted in the Kenny Rogers shag Bonnie knew so well, a whistle around his neck and his face composed in the angry expression of a coach midyell: an angry, possibly drunk coach, Bonnie thought. The disinfectant they sprayed in the shoes polluted the air back here, and Bonnie's eyes watered. She was alone in the world except for that chemical sting, and the screen, and the text beneath the picture.

This is the man who raped me in 1997, when I was fifteen. He was my junior varsity volleyball coach. He had singled me out as a favorite that year, and for away games it was expected that I'd ride with him, alone in his car, while the other girls took the bus. He would put his hand on my leg like there wasn't anything strange about it, or stop and buy me a present somewhere, then kiss me really quick, before I could even process what was happening. I didn't tell anyone because I was afraid they wouldn't believe me. Also, I loved volleyball and didn't want to leave my team. My mom was a single mom and was forking over a lot of money for me to be able to play. Then, away at a tournament in San Bernardino, he came into my hotel room one night and convinced me to follow him down the hall. I don't remember where the other girls were. The rape occurred in his room, with the television on. It was Jeopardy; *I'll never forget. Afterward, when I was crying and told him I hadn't wanted to, he reminded me of all the other things we'd already done leading up to it: I let him kiss me, and I took his presents, and I had changed into my uniform in front of him, once, in his car. This was just the next step, he said. It was normal. In my panic to convince myself I actually liked him, I forced myself to sleep in his bed that night, and then, the next morning, we had sex again, but that time I initiated it. While it's perhaps pointless to compare*

two different forms of trauma, I think that second time did more damage to my
psyche, because of my own denial. I am only able to write this now after a decade
of professional help, the support of my loving husband, and Jesus's grace in my life.
I have decided not to pursue legal action against this person almost twenty years
later, knowing God will judge him accordingly.

By the time Bonnie read it twice, a deep, pulsing pain had radiated from
her forehead into her jaw, the nerves of her teeth, and the spongy makeup of
her brain. When she returned to the register, her body was not her own. The
pain was a guilt was a shame was a let-it-not-be, as severe as if Bonnie, herself,
were the survivor, both victim and criminal rolled into one. To her coworker
Natasha she called this a migraine.

She didn't leave her trailer for three days. It was like watching an endless
movie in which you hated every last character. She felt invaded, body-snatched,
after so much time spent imagining on repeat. She replied to Diane, *Go to hell*.
Then she focused her energy on this Katie person, whom she despised, too; spilling her guts so publicly, flaunting her Jesus and her God. What was the point
of it? To show no shame in describing your shame. A part of Bonnie was even
suspicious of the girl's supposed innocence. Though she had been *fifteen*, Bonnie argued with herself. Fifteen. Judy's age, around then. It was almost beside
the point that 1997 was, of course, the year they'd gotten married. The year
of her accident, and of Judy leaving. She tried to recall San Bernardino, but so
much had happened, and the tournaments were frequent and unmemorable.
For six years then, the math went, she'd been married to a rapist.

When her anger at last transferred to Rick, the disgust was total. The
picture of the act was a visceral torment she could not push out of her brain.
She sat on the couch as the hours passed, more or less immobile, while Rick
transformed into a monster, driven by an uncontrollable will to devour.
What fondness she'd recently revived went black now, the memories blotted over and any naïve hope—of *visiting him!*—sucked away, doubling her
betrayal as it went, searing her with fresh guilt. So, that had been it: Rick
knew that this was coming, or it had come already, from the girl; perhaps
he'd even tried to reach her, to apologize, and the attempt had backfired.

He'd dredged the crime up, probably, writing his inventory. And there was Bonnie, he must've figured, pathetic old Bonnie, scraped from the bottom of the barrel, the last woman on the planet who might still have him.

And what else, in those six years? During driving lessons, after practices? *Who* else? Of all the swirling questions, at the end of those three days, she decided on only one. Her fingers shook as she texted it. It burned diamond-sharp on the screen. *Did you ever touch Judy?*

His reply came hours later. *You know I wouldn't.*

She could almost laugh. *You know!* What *did* she know? *How* could she know? *I wouldn't*, not *I didn't*. She did laugh, once, crazily to herself in her kitchen, busted up until it rolled her to the linoleum and she thought, Here I go, loony at last and never coming back. But she did come back; she turned on the television and took the hottest shower her water heater could supply. She got Judy's voice mail but couldn't bring herself to leave a message. She didn't go to a meeting. She didn't speak to anyone, not even Natasha and Sal when they swung by, left Campbell's soup and a tin of butter biscuits on her trailer steps, *Get well soon!* Bonnie was a canned-food-drive charity. She broke down at their kindness. Judy did not call back—Judy was off living her life, had no idea what was happening, but still Bonnie resented not hearing from her. Unsurprising and yet terrible, the world, of butter biscuits and daughters and sick days, continued on with no discernible change. And yet everything—*everything*—had changed. Even the stand of pines out her kitchen window, overhanging the wire fence in their perennial springiness, weren't just trees now but bleak reminders of Christmas, once your only child has gone and nothing, anymore, is festive.

Rick called several times but left no messages. In place of his voice, his texts read strange and oddly grammared, as if conceived in fits:

> I am not that person, you're thinking I am.

> It's not fair not to give me that.

> We all deserve another, chance and you should
> no as well as anyone that people change.

Despite everything, even through her anger, she struggled to not respond. Pathetic old Bonnie. What kind of woman marries a rapist? What kind of woman *falls for, marries, divorces, and then falls for, again*, a *rapist*? There must be something malformed in her, to ever have been attracted to him. Or there was something in his hideousness that subconsciously compelled her; perhaps she hated herself that much.

EARLY THAT MORNING, confusion twisted in the gulf between sleep and wakefulness. She turned away from Rick, pleading in the wings of her dreams, but beyond him, reality burned even meaner. Her brain felt swollen, waterlogged, punched, as the landscape of the living room merged into focus. The night before crashed back. A damage too great to comprehend. When she sat up, she spun.

In her toiletry bag she found ibuprofen, took four, and lay back down again, waiting for the capsules to dissolve. Her mouth tasted like disease. Twenty minutes later she dressed, silently and shakily, in her last clean outfit. Nothing came from Caleb and Judy's room except the low chug of the air conditioner. She needed badly to use the bathroom but felt she might have diarrhea and worried about the sound, the smell, the toilet flush. The dawn lit the room its first sherbet colors. Bonnie slipped out into the dark, humid hall.

Vaguely she thought she might sleep in the park. But once she was on the street, the pain in her head began to dull and dissipate, and a few lone dog walkers were already out. Her phone said it was just past seven. At the corner bodega, she looked into the refrigerators of juice and water and big pickles in plastic bags, of wine and beer and malt liquor. The universe, with its insistence on choices, would crush her at last. She stared at the masculine cans and bottles and weighed, for one struggling moment, the possibility of a tallboy of Steel Reserve. *Do not*, Jeff whispered—and yet the impulse was in her mouth, her throat, nerves inaccessible to logic. She stood there for a long time without thinking, in the vortex of her own insanity, then returned abruptly to the safety of the front of the store. The clerk poured her a coffee and asked, "Regular?" She didn't know what regular meant but she nodded, and when he added cream and sugar, her eyes filled gratefully with tears. The cup was blue and white, with a Greek motif. It was the nicest paper cup Bonnie had ever seen. She managed a tip, a whole dollar, in the can by the register, knowing Judy would approve.

In the park the pigeons were spastic already, pecking at crumbs and dawdling down the walk, ladylike and nosey. She found a bench on which to sit and sip and let the tears do what they were bound to do. Her arms and legs felt battered; perceptions lagged and lurched; some degree of her was still drunk, she recognized, though she wasn't as bad off as she might've been, since she'd vomited last night in the gutter. For a peaceful moment, her regret was mostly conceptual, not weighted with real despair. But then it sank into memory: how Judy's anger had exploded, her flashing face pushing Bonnie into the cab; the fight between Judy and Caleb that came back in washy clips. How she'd sung CSN. Mortified Judy, undoubtedly. Now, on top of everything, she had this making-up to do.

It was ugly, wasn't it, to recognize fuck-ups all your life, and then one day to know for certain that you yourself are one. Early in recovery, Bonnie, following the lead and knowing she must acquaint herself with a "higher power" if she were to survive, had rigged up a faith in *connectedness* and *grace*, a riff on *Everything happens for a reason*, enough spiritual logic to get her through the bad days. *I do believe we're all woven together, like a big blanket*, she'd tried, Styrofoam cup in hand, *and there are reasons we can't always see . . .* sharing in the back room of Sherman Oaks Presbyterian in 1999, or in the basement of Our Lady of Perpetual Sorrow in 2006. If you believed in connection, you could believe that just loving someone was enough for them to feel it. That even without contact, energies communicated and comingled. *If we do our best, stay grateful, remember kindness to each other . . .* Then what? Rewards would come? Guarantees? *We all deserve another chance . . .* Maybe Bonnie was remiss, to think she might deserve anything more than what she already had.

Her napkin was soggy with coffee and snot. Self-pity was a well you could fall into, like a peasant girl in a fairy tale, never to crawl out of. She pulled out her phone and composed a text. *Judy, I am so sorry about last night, I made an ass of myself and I am eager to make it up. Do you think it could be possible to put the rope on hold? So we can get some one-on-one? There's something I want to talk to you about. Love, Mom.* The message sat there on her screen. She read it twice and then erased it, deciding she'd lost the right, even, to ask this much. Bonnie rose and left the park, heading once more for the subway, fairly confident she could find her way by heart.

*

JUDE WOKE BUT HER DREAM STILL LINGERED, AURAL, ATTACHED to a memory that came back with the startling intensity of the long dormant.

On a fall day when she was maybe nine, the power went off overnight, and when mother and daughter awoke, the heat of the morning sun said it was well past eight. In bed beside her, Bonnie hinged up to sitting like rising from the crypt. The way her hair bunched and matted, mammalian, was a ritual comedy for Judy. Judy thought, *I will never get old*. Bonnie, then, was just past thirty.

The old apartment—the peeling linoleum, the roach traps growing sticky in the corners, the mold and grime and gas smell around the wall heater. The hulking off-kilter hutch in the dining nook, where Bonnie kept real silver silverware and gravy boats bought at thrift stores and a lava lamp that glowed but didn't liquefy, the hutch they were lucky didn't topple during Northridge (the thing shuddered and threatened but held its ground). The old apartment she'd hated every second of but in hindsight missed senselessly—her last real home with her mother, their collaborative world, however imperfect.

The power was out, and also the water. *Mmhmm, mmhmm*, Bonnie said into the receiver, *look, I've got a daughter here, I've got a little girl who needs to get ready for school and brush her teeth and you're telling me that we can't get this thing turned on again until Monday? Monday? It's Thursday. Thurs-day!*

Some problem in the city's system, Bonnie told Judy, though at school the following week, Meghan assured her it meant Bonnie hadn't paid the bill. It had happened once at Meghan's house, too.

They'd go camping. Bonnie called in sick to work and then turned into a madwoman packing—flinging open the back closet, pulling out tents and tarps and big canvas bags that smelled peculiarly rancid, like vomit or parmesan cheese, hauling it all toward the front door, her bathrobe falling open to reveal her floppy breasts, her skinny ribs and legs. Judy slipped on a sundress, packed her book and her Etch A Sketch and a bathing suit she'd outgrown. They filled the cooler with ice, hot dogs and Kraft singles, a six-pack of Coors, and a bottle from the freezer. While Bonnie dressed and did her face, she told Judy to make as many peanut-butter sandwiches as they had bread for. Judy made five.

They'd never camped before; she was elated and scared: visions of bears mangling them in their sleep, premonitions of her mother falling into a fire. It was nothing like that. The campground was at the southern end of a long public beach on a strip of coast between Ventura and Santa Barbara. They backed the Colt into a site and unloaded everything on a picnic table. The fire ring had an old, charred-black grill, which her mother showed her how to flop over, for cooking over hot coals. Trees tilted by the wind made shade above their new home, and a layer of red-brown needles coated the ground like a prickly carpet. Beyond a low ridge of dunes, the ocean crashed and hushed. When people said they were *in heaven*, Judy knew, now, what they meant.

The camping supplies belonged to a forgotten boyfriend who'd left his tent and lantern, for reasons oblique, at their house. Soon Judy realized her mother knew what she was doing—sweeping the ground with a fallen branch, feeling for stones and tossing them aside, laying down the tarp and then the limp body of the tent, working the poles in expertly, showing Judy how with a patience and care Judy hardly recognized. At night they built a fire and listened to sounds, the washing-machine rhythm of the sea and ambiguous cries up in the hills, animal noises in the dark, on the other side of the highway. She and Jeff, Judy's uncle, had camped all up and down the state, Bonnie said, when she was just sixteen and they'd left home. (Jude didn't then know the extent of the abuse—the violent father and the stony mother—didn't know, yet, how textbook the case study of Bonnie would prove, nor how up to Jude it would feel, eventually, to break the tired, inherited cycle.) When Judy asked about Jeff, Bonnie smiled like saying, *Thank you*. Her voice went wispy as a greeting card, and she could talk for much longer than any of

Judy's questions required. He'd died of a heart attack (cocaine, she'd also learn later) when Judy was still a baby, but before that he'd been her mother's best friend. *My ally. My old reliable.* Jeff knew the names of plants and birds, Bonnie explained. Could rig up an outdoor shower with a five-gallon bucket and a hose and cut his own skimboards out of plywood—a skimboard, Bonnie explained, was just what it sounded like; a way to sort of skate, suspended, across the drifting surf.

Judy said, "Maybe that's what Jesus did—skimboarded? But no one saw the skimboard and thought he was just walking on the water." Because recently she'd argued this impossibility, with a Christian girl during tetherball.

Bonnie laughed. "Jeff would like that theory, I think." She turned their hot dogs; the skin bubbled and went glossy.

Jude knew how memory functioned: like patchwork, by doing its modest best. But while it pained her that she couldn't replay it all exactly—could never retrieve that trip just as it had been—she was grateful to have, at least, these impressions of happiness. Of the long days at the beach, testing the frigid Pacific, the way the sand sucked down beneath your feet and left perfectly curved prints, and the residual salt made your calves sting and itch. Of the safety inside the tent, beside Bonnie's steady breathing, the silk of the sleeping bag and the heat coming off her sunburn, the shadow of the trees against the pale mesh ceiling, the knowledge of the ocean, right there, insulating despite its vastness. And how the book she was reading blended with reality more fluidly than books ever did at home or school. As if she were living inside her class-issued copy of *Island of the Blue Dolphins*, as if the other families at the campground were really members of her tribe, the other children her own little brothers and sisters. She dug with them in the sand, engineered their castle's moat. And at the water spigot between sites she turned the faucet on, helped the littlest ones wash their tiny hands, like an older sister should.

Without warning, Jude began to cry. Boomeranged back to the present, the here-and-now disorganized her completely, made her feel as if no other experience had occurred between that camping trip and today—only a long, eventless sleep. She cried silently at first, not wanting to rouse Caleb, but then the outpour was too much, she had to roll onto her side to breathe, scraping, again, the raw patch on her hip, sniffing in big drafts of air. How devastated she'd been last night. And how terrible to Bonnie, practically pushing her into the cab. She had called her a drunk. She had spat the word.

Now pity overwhelmed her. Caleb rolled, his armpit damp, and clutched her. She could feel his heart thumping in her back, beating with its own private life. He waited for a long minute before he groaned, *Are you crying?* to which she cried on, quietly, afraid Bonnie would hear. There was no way to say the goo of what she felt. He tightened his grip, pressed his face into her neck. Everything, he murmured, would be all right.

They got up unsteadily, stumbling like hunchbacks into the bathroom for toilet paper. Jude blew her nose and splashed her face and, no doubt aided by last night's drinks, sat on the toilet to move her bowels. She was still sniffling; nothing mattered; the relief was immediate and immense. She felt evacuated, high. Caleb stood at the end of the rope with his back turned respectfully, but at the last minute, as Jude was wiping, he turned around and snapped her photo. She moaned, flushed, lit a match to clear the shameful smell. Then he kissed her hard on the forehead in ridiculous congratulation, laughing, which had, at least, the effect of stanching her last tears.

They found the living room still and quiet. An ice cream truck's tune came up from the street. The couch had been put back, and sat there, empty, with its forever-waiting quality of unpeopled furniture. Jude's heart dropped: Bonnie must be on a plane now, halfway back to California.

But no, there was her suitcase, her toiletry kit mended with a safety pin, her crumpled paper bag from the MoMA gift shop. Jude found her phone in the kitchen. A message from Bonnie read: *I'm going to find that 10 o'clock meeting. I love you.*

Caleb looked over her shoulder and scoffed. "Just don't respond." Reflexively she turned, put her body between him and the screen. The thought of her mother braving the city alone seemed incomparably sad now, as it hadn't yesterday. Another sob welled in her chest, then settled, unvoiced. *Be careful*, was all she managed to write.

They moved through the coffee routine, Caleb pouring with the maddening attention of a real barista while Jude's head pulsed. Nothing was said of the night before, the screaming catastrophe on the street, in front of their friends and the cabdriver and Bonnie, who'd leaned on Zach, fading in and out of consciousness. Following "Judy Blue Eyes" Caleb, wasted himself, had ordered a round of shots—*birthday* shots—and lifted: *To Bonnie!* But now Jude's anger returned with a force that flipped her stomach. She wanted suddenly to smack the kettle out of his hand. To see boiling water fly everywhere.

"We need to talk about last night," she said. Aware of the pointedness of her tone.

"I thought we talked about last night last night," he said.

She exhaled through her nose. "Are you even going to ask me how I feel? I woke up crying."

Caleb crumpled his brow, looked at her, and scoffed. "Oh shit, I'm so sorry. Stupid me." He made his voice imbecilic, mechanical. "How do you feel, Jude? Why were you crying, Jude?"

She looked at her bare feet, fuming. Tiny fragments of oats and dirt, coffee grounds and crumbs, were pressed into the gaps between the floorboards. Many people—countless couples—must have lived in this apartment before Caleb bought it. "You're being an asshole," she said.

He threw his head back and sighed loudly, put-upon. His big Adam's apple pointed up. "Jesus. It's like you want me to say something specific, and then when I can't *guess* what it is, you, like, accuse me of—"

"I don't, I just want you to *ask* me—"

"I did! I asked you what was wrong, but you can't seem to answer without—"

"Without what?" she said, her voice shaking. "Without calling you out? Don't act like you're not"—but it was too late. The tears started up again, their store immediately replenished. She turned her body and gripped the knot at her waist, working to wriggle her fingers between the fibers, impossibly tight. "I'm done. It's over. I'm taking this fucking thing off." She scrambled, mucus running to her lips now, not knowing if *done* meant only with the piece or with Caleb, too.

His hands were on hers, gently, pulling them away, "Hey, hey, hey. Calm *down.*" But Jude jerked—"Let *go!*"—and Caleb's elbow bumped the kettle; scalding water splashed down his leg. He cried out. Jude dropped the rope. "I'm sorry!"

The *ping* of his phone interrupted them. On the kitchen counter, first one, then another text.

She wet a towel under the faucet, but when she turned, he was already looking at the screen.

Throughout their bondage they'd remained tactful, looking away, feigning disinterest while one or the other texted or read emails, scrolled and commented. The privacy of individual and device was respectfully understood. But now, pissed, handing him the towel, Jude saw without meaning to: Persona *later at IFC. Always makes me think of u.* And then the second message: *Can u go?* from an unnamed New York number.

She wiped her nose with the back of her hand. Her heartbeat made it hard to breathe. "Who the fuck is that?"

Caleb turned the screen facedown, took the towel, and pressed it to his leg. "Did you just read my text?"

The fight that ensued was crazy-making. Jude let herself go wild; her voice rose up, Stravinskyesque, peaking in hysteria and then collapsing to sardonic depths, gravelly as she moved from question to accusation to self-flagellating conclusion. Caleb sighed tolerantly, a model of decorum and patience, answering as if he felt sorry for her, her suffering insanity, like a fucking doctor with a clipboard patrolling the madhouse. The messages, he explained, were from Hannah; he thought Jude understood that they were still in "polite contact." *You met her that one time on the G, remember?* As if this explained anything. She cut him off—of *course* she remembered, how would she not remember meeting his most serious ex, who, he'd gone out of his way to tell Jude afterward, *modeled* for a mutual friend's shitty lingerie brand, as if to explain her ludicrously scanty outfit, braless and perky in a silk tank top, her labia practically hanging out the leg holes of her booty shorts, the childish tattoo of a deer's face ringed with flowers that bent up over her shoulder like a relic, now, of a bad aesthetic spell in the early 2000s when forest creatures and derivative folk music had no doubt captivated this button-nosed innocent from Georgia? A lingerie model with a Southern accent! Jude shrieked. The audacity! *It was ten years ago!* Caleb countered. But how often did they text, she demanded, and why did Hannah think it was okay to send this; did she not realize that Caleb and Jude were *serious*? Had he not made that clear? She *must*, to ask the question the way she did, *Can you*, as in *Can you come out to play?*—as if Jude were a fucking *mother* Caleb might have to sneak around. Did she think they were *open*? Was he still attracted to her? Still in love with her? Had he kept the door to Hannah just-perceptibly cracked, like an escape route, like a backup? And why—*why, why, why*—was her name not attached to her number in his phone, if it were *friendly*, if it was *nothing*?

She caught her breath. The kitchen tilted. Caleb looked tired and hungover, his eyes fixed carefully on a banana blackening in the fruit bowl. Calmly now, she asked, "Are you keeping something from me?"

He pulled his eyes up with effort. "No," he said. "You know I wouldn't."

Persona, he explained, wasn't some romantic thing between them, it was only a movie he'd written a failing paper on during sophomore year, in a film class he and Hannah had taken together. This was funny, Caleb explained, because, before the paper, Caleb had given her shit about not having seen the film, not even knowing who Bergman was: she was so . . . *uncultured* like that, *just sort of uncool, and really insecure.* But then the F had come, and Hannah's B plus, meaning she had won after all. *It became this inside joke, like, about how I could be an elitist.* He smiled.

Or just a dick, Jude thought. Self-deprecation looked odd on him. She, too, had been with men who'd made her feel stupid and pedestrian, a student needing guidance in taste, and the part of her that knew itself to be a woman bristled. It sucked to think of Caleb fitting the archetype so easily. And the thing he wasn't saying, Jude thought, was that what Hannah lacked in cultural capital she made up for in malleability, in willingness, in body. He was talking still, a tone bent on conviction, but Jude was struggling to hear. It all translated to the simplicity that Caleb and Hannah's three years together, then their on-again/off-again aftermath, had likely been based on such predictable tensions, such sexy and ordinary inequities of power.

"She thinks highly of you, you know. She told me," he said seriously. "I think she wants to be your friend."

Jude balked. The line of his mouth said, *I rest my case.* "I don't need any more friends," she said venomously.

He called her catty, then, and she told him he was playing dumb. He called her dramatic, and she accused him of just *loving this*, that his ex was still after him, while all of Jude's had moved respectfully on, gotten married, committed to good jobs, and invited her to view group photo albums of their newborn babies. *What are you even talking about? You sound so jealous!* And she spat back, *I'm not jealous of your superficial friendship with your corny ex!* Eventually she came to the preposterous ultimatum that the only thing for Caleb to do was to respond to Hannah with a kind of passive-aggressive test. *Yes! Thank you for the invite, Hannah. Jude and I would love to join for the film! What time?* Jude, sniveling and shaking, typed this herself under Caleb's eye-rolling watch, then pressed Send.

A calm set in after that. Jude's breath came raggedly. She was aware, again, of the empty apartment, and how cold and sad their coffee had become. She wiped her face with a paper towel. "I don't want to fight," she sniffled finally, meaning it.

Caleb spoke to the rope. "You have to give me more credit, you know. Like, trust me. I'm fucking *tied* to you, Jude."

His phone buzzed on the table, and she jumped. Hannah agreed to the movie date, with triple exclamation marks that seemed competitive in their reach.

"What will we do with Bonnie?" she asked. Her voice was small, inside herself now.

"Do you think she's a big Bergman fan?"

"I guess we'll have to invite her."

"Maybe she won't want to come?"

Jude actually laughed then, and Caleb did, too, though less.

*

BONNIE WAS FIFTEEN MINUTES EARLY TO THE BROWNSTONE ON the shady street, but most of the seats were already taken. She hit the coffee, then found a free chair pushed up against the wall in the outer circle. A poster on the wall read, EXPECT MIRACLES. In her periphery, the men and women chatting in clusters were no different than the people she'd ridden the subway with. Most were young, Judy's age, shouldering bags printed with nonsense phrases, or closer to Bonnie's own age but with young-looking hairstyles and shoes. No one she saw shuffled; no one dragged the muddy heels of sweatpants or picked at scabs on their cheeks and arms. No one reeked of hot, leaking booze, or vomit, except perhaps Bonnie herself, though before coming here she'd taken care to buy a toothbrush-toothpaste kit at a pharmacy and wash up as best she could in a Starbucks bathroom. A wave of dizziness rose in her, then receded. She blew ripples across her coffee and tried to compose her body in a posture that laid claim to something. That belonged.

A girl plopped down next to her, laden with a yoga mat and purse, her own coffee, and a small white pastry bag. She arranged her things under the seat, then ate greedily, shedding flakes of croissant in her lap. The blue spandex of her bike shorts made shiny tubes of her thighs and emphasized her small, enviable figure. When she looked at Bonnie, Bonnie saw how pretty she was in the face, with fiery hair cropped smartly at the chin and a nose that turned up, as in an old-fashioned picture book, but with a nose ring. A pronounced dip between her mouth and nose accentuated her lips and reminded Bonnie of someone, someone she couldn't place. Bonnie smiled, and the girl smiled back, chewing. When she swallowed she said, "Sorry about my breakfast."

Bonnie waved away the apology. She liked the girl at once. Her voice did a country thing—twanged to match her nose.

The room grew quiet as the chairperson took a seat at the front; he was older but not bad-looking, with a silky ponytail and belted black jeans, like someone Bonnie would've hung out with thirty years ago, except now here they were, growing old together in a twelve-step program. She had a vision of them speaking—flirting, maybe, afterward—until he began, "Hello everyone, welcome to the Monday-morning Twelfth Street group. My name is Rick, and I'm an alcoholic . . ."

She let out something like a squeak.

"You okay?" the girl whispered.

The room was crowded and stuffy despite the air-conditioning—every seat was taken, and a dozen people stood against the wall—and as the preamble droned, Bonnie felt, for a moment, like she was back at a school assembly at Garfield Elementary, disliked by her classmates and so wanting to be naughty. "Oh, yes," she said. "I just—have you ever met a good *Rick*, honestly?"

The girl's smile showed very white teeth. "My landlord's name is Rick. Talk about a *slumlord*. Never fixes anything but always around, know what I mean? And my rent keeps going up. Rick the *prick*, if you ask me."

Bonnie gave a soundless laugh. A woman to Rick's left recited, *Our stories disclose in a general way what we used to be like, what happened, and what we are like now . . .*

When the time came, three newcomers rose to introduce themselves: Dave and Naomi and Chase, who had just moved, were visiting, were counting days. Bonnie hadn't intended to stand, but now she did, lifted by a desire to display herself to the girl. Once she began talking, she found she didn't know how to stop.

"Hello, I'm Bonnie, from California. I'm just here on vacation—I leave tomorrow morning, unfortunately. I've never been to New York before, and now that I'm here I'm thinking, holy Toledo, why didn't anyone *tell* me, I mean, my god, what a beautiful and exciting place . . . Anyway, I've been stone-cold sober for seven years, and on and off for quite a while before that . . . but I actually, I . . . I had a slip last night, a relapse-type thing, you might say— frankly, I screwed the pooch, and my daughter was there to see it. There's been a lot of negative stuff swishing around in my head lately, *resentments*, I suppose, and—"

Rick's voice cut in. "Thank you, Bonnie. We like to cap these introductions at just a hello. But I know there's a lot of recognition in this room." Faces—rows of faces—were looking up at her. She lowered herself, mortified.

The tears were back again, stinging their way up her sinuses. Bonnie blinked, whispering to the girl, "Do you know a good tall building around here I could jump off?"

The girl reached over and patted her arm, just twice, a kindness that meant everything. "Oh, there are lots," she whispered. "You'll have your pick."

She could hardly concentrate on the speaker. He wore those glasses where the lenses changed, went from clear to smoky and were now a spooky violet, and his shirt was too crispy-clean, his facial hair groomed to disconcerting points. He told a boring story of overindulging in blow, spoiling a big promotion, losing money on a stock thing Bonnie didn't follow. Rich guy, she thought, and tuned him out. She thought of Jeff, poor Jeff, his death a cataclysm as powerful as Judy's birth—the two phenomena running parallel but in opposite directions. For ten months following conception, Bonnie had been wide-awake clean—high on the sheer miracle of her daughter and needing nothing more—when she'd driven over to Jeff's one Saturday, Judy a bundle in her arms, to find him facedown on the floor by the sofa, as if he'd been struck dead while trying to outcrawl something. His head tucked under at a fetal angle, his bare feet splayed and extra white, a half-eaten pizza and a bottle of ranch, an empty fifth of scotch and a mirror on the coffee table, retaining the faintest crystalline spackle, the lonely dregs of his final night. What else could be expected, after life in that family of theirs? High-pitched voices issued from the TV, small blue men in psychedelic hats. Judy began to fuss. After that, certain cartoons would forever turn Bonnie's stomach.

They all stood—*God, grant me the serenity*—and Bonnie's new friend gripped and squeezed her hand. When they returned to their seats to gather their things, the girl looked down at her phone for a moment and made an unhappy face, then shook her head. Bonnie thought she'd just slip away, but the girl looked up smiling and asked, "Are you heading east or west?" Bonnie said she didn't know where she was heading.

"I'm Hannah, by the way. I don't think I told you that."

"I'm Bonnie," Bonnie said. "In case you happened to fall asleep during my speech."

"Honestly, Bonnie, you were better than the speaker, I thought." And she leaned forward to whisper, "He's just a rich creep. I know for a fact."

There was a juice place Hannah liked around the corner, and also a sweet park. Bonnie found the idea of pulped beets and spinach disgusting, but she was so grateful to have been asked, invited into a cordial New York fold with this lovely person that she, of course, accepted. They strolled down the dappled sidewalk in the full morning sun, which warmed Bonnie's face, her neck, her toes. She was happy to be dressed as she was, colorful in a gauzy turquoise tank and lime capris and the new red sandals. When she ordered her iced tea from the juice counter, she confided in Hannah how she yearned for a screwdriver, her old morning-after cure. Hannah nodded, smiled, moved her finger back and forth between herself and Bonnie. "There's a lot of recognition in this room."

They took their drinks to the park, where the mellifluous notes of a saxophone floated on the breeze. Hannah, Bonnie learned, was from Georgia. She'd moved to New York for college more than a decade before, done a degree in fashion she didn't know how to use, made her living teaching yoga and modeling occasionally, but really she was a musician: she wrote her own songs and sang, played guitar, piano, a modest amount of Celtic harp.

"Do you like Judy Collins?" Bonnie asked, big eyed. "Joni?" She was falling a little in love.

"Oh, god, who doesn't?" Hannah gushed. "Idols. And Sandy Denny and Vashti Bunyan."

"Oh! Bunyan!" Bonnie said. Who she didn't, actually, know.

Boys with swagger like Caleb's—younger, but the same breed—rode skateboards fast across a basketball court, their T-shirts pulling against their chests. It was thrilling to watch, even as it made Bonnie feel she'd never been physically coordinated at anything in her life.

"I'm still trying to figure out if I belong there," Hannah confided. "I don't have a sponsor or anything yet. To be honest, I don't—it's hard to tell if you're really an *alcoholic*, you know?" She said the word in a spooky voice, and Bonnie thought sadly, no, it's easy, really, to tell.

"I think sometimes," Hannah continued, "I mean, is my drinking any more of a problem than my friends'? The real problem might be a *sex* problem as much as a drinking problem. I can't seem to stop sleeping with my terrible ex. Especially when I'm wasted. But also when I'm sober. So there. There is my dilemma. Or one of them."

Bonnie chuckled at this. "Oh, honey," she said. She wanted Hannah to like her as much as she was liking Hannah. "That just sounds like a *human* problem. Is he that good-looking?"

She sighed, flung her head back, and groaned. "It's terrible. I don't even *like him*, but I'm, like, *addicted* to him. And he has a new girlfriend, now, to complicate things."

It was impossible for Bonnie not to think of how much this conversation was exactly the type she wished she and Judy could have. How desperately she wished Judy could just *talk* to her, confide in her, be a woman with her. "And is she—is she much competition?"

One of the skateboarders zoomed up a ramp, landed with a crack, then rolled on, leaning back coolly. Bonnie clapped.

"Is she much competition . . ." Hannah mused. "I'm trying to figure that out. She seems smart. She's plenty pretty."

Bonnie scoffed. "Oh honey, *you're* plenty pretty! I'm sure she's—whoever she is—I'm sure she's not prettier than you." Bonnie meant it. Hannah had perfectly clear, lineless skin, a smattering of beauty marks that made her face unique, and eyes like a petting-zoo animal, rimmed with generous lashes. A very unique tattoo, of a deer's face and a garland of flowers, wrapped up her bare arm.

She smiled at Bonnie. "Oh, you're just so sweet. Thank you so much for saying so. My mother—not that you're anything like her; you're much *hipper* than she is, but—she never says things like that. She couldn't give me a compliment if her damned life depended on it. Maybe that's why I end up craving these unavailable men. Always seeking the impossible. You know, looking for love in all the wrong places."

She hummed a bar of the song, and Bonnie smiled. "I wonder if you'd like my daughter. I think I could see you two being friends." She sort of meant it, though she wanted to mean it wholly. She had the disappointing intuition, actually, that Judy might find many things wrong with Hannah. Things Bonnie herself couldn't fathom.

Twenty minutes later, the women embraced and exchanged phone numbers. Bonnie promised to call Hannah the next time she was in New York, and Hannah promised to call Bonnie, too, if she were ever in California—both, of course, knowing they'd never see the other again but needing to acknowledge, somehow, the goodness of having met.

*

THEY ATE POACHED EGGS AND SMOKED TROUT, CHAMPAGNE AND greens, at a café where all of the staff knew Caleb, then headed south on Wythe because Jude needed to walk. The weather was confused: low gray clouds to the east but white, cauliflower ones to the west, a sky in split decision. Holding Jude's hand, Caleb vaped as they passed a new ten-story hotel and then a block-long excavation, the measured beep of a construction site behind green mesh—the rising monstrosity of the new waterfront.

"Even if you could afford it, I don't understand who'd want to live here," Jude said, of the hideous glass-and-steel tower Caleb was steering them toward.

"I know. It's disgusting," he agreed. But it was to a ground-floor window in precisely this building that he was pointing with his pen. The boutique had sprung up overnight—Jude didn't recognize it—and several couples inside browsed the minimal wares. A woman in linen lifted an asymmetrical teapot, a man appraised an ambiguous wooden brush. On a rack in the window hung brightly woven blankets, what Bonnie would call *throws*. "See? Right there," Caleb said, pointing to the textiles. It was one of his paintings—an older one, a Detroit scene, reproduced in black and brown and yellow threads. Those signature floating heads, and pink and yellow tags rendered (*re*rendered?) and repurposed and hanging, now, among other art-turned-décor, other designs and patterns, to keep the inhabitants of the upstairs condos warm. Corinne, the woman whose business it was to make the blankets—or rather, to buy

the rights to artworks, then contract a factory in Taiwan to do the manu-
facturing, then distribute them to shops such as this one at prohibitive price
points—Corinne, Jude knew, was also someone Caleb had been romantic
with, not long before Jude, though neither of them mentioned this connection now. She complimented the blanket. It was beneath her to take up the
issue—the punishing and banal issue of *other women*—twice in one day.

Instead they went directly home, latched the door chain, shed their
clothes in the living room in bold reclamation of their lovers' domain.
Jude wanted it suddenly—thought, *use the rope*—found herself, after the
weekend's doubts and the morning's fight and the frightening inklings of
but who else *is he?* needing more, needing *other*—turned herself over and
pressed her forehead to the floor. To be ground down, to be fed, to have
something unknown answered, appeased, or driven out, obliterated—once
he was inside her, even the trace scent of Bonnie's coconutty shampoo
couldn't diminish Jude's rapture. In the past, with other men—*boys*—she'd
been timid and they'd been bad. Her, relentlessly passive, and them, proce-
dural and scared, until their eyes went wide at climax, huge and freaked out
as arboreal animals caught on film at night. She'd never thought herself a
faker, but oh, how Jude had faked with the others, not just orgasms (though
she'd faked her share of those, too) but a deeper pretending, that love could
be channeled into sheer, euphoric sensation—*pleasure*—and pleasure channeled, back the other way, into bright, liquid love. With Caleb, the bound-
aries at last burst; words became mush; in the bonding of human materials,
an ineffable something was finally complete. His thighs locked around hers
and his hand gripped her neck; they were an inch away from violence, but
she shuddered ecstatically along its edge. What Jude had learned to love
about sex was simple: how deftly desire could coerce the mind in service
of the body; how, like grief and jealousy and the truest conditions, real
pleasure left no room for irony. An image invaded, ridiculous: Hannah in
the room, both specter and spectator—and Jude came in the deepest pit of
herself.

Afterward, they lay doggishly on the hardwood, listening to traffic, comfortable in their own silly secretions. They said their *I love you*s, and Jude

confessed her recurring revelation: that sex with him amazed her—because she felt she'd be depriving them of some truth if she didn't. Caleb could never quite return the sentiment, but Jude refused to feel self-conscious. Why should honesty embarrass her? "I'm sorry," Caleb replied instead, "about earlier." And she kissed his forehead, forgiving him.

They showered and then dried themselves, sensitive to the red marks on their torsos. Then they dressed carefully, one garment at a time, took the four o'clock picture, and set out for the city.

*

STANDING IN THE DARK PASSAGE, BONNIE HAD TO WAIT FOR A lighter frame to come on screen before she could identify Judy and Caleb among the watching faces. They were up near the back, Caleb's hand raised in her direction. They'd saved her a seat. She side-stepped her way down the row and settled in, patting Caleb's arm and leaning forward to wave at Judy—when she saw, one seat past her daughter, a red bob of hair, the same upturned nose, the exact profile of the girl she'd met that morning. Hannah! Was it *her*? It *was* her. Hannah was digging around in her bag and didn't notice Bonnie's arrival. The strangeness of it disoriented her—for a moment reality pulsed. Then, abruptly, Bonnie sat back. The coincidence was so uncanny it seemed somehow wrong to acknowledge it head-on, like a breach of cosmic trust.

At first Bonnie thought (although this would've been just as strange; it would've meant something entirely different) that Hannah was only sitting there by chance. But then she realized they knew each other; Hannah leaned in to Judy and whispered something in her ear, and the two girls shared a smile. So they *were* friends; and Bonnie tingled—she *did* know her daughter, after all. She felt elated by her own relevancy, as if she herself had introduced the girls. There was no such thing as coincidence, Bonnie believed. There were seemingly accidental comings-together for secret, under-the-surface reasons. There were strange signals thrown out by the universe, whose meanings weren't made clear until later, or never. A prism from the Goodwill hung in

Bonnie's kitchen window, throwing its rainbows around the trailer with a rhyme and reason only it knew.

The movie was impossible to follow, slow and boring and hopelessly foreign—an irritating detour between Bonnie's discovery and the time when she could share it. They would marvel! Especially Hannah, but *especially* Judy. And yet she made herself, studiously, catch enough of the film that she could form an opinion, knowing she might be called upon, afterward, to think something.

*

FIRST BONNIE HAD COME LATE AND NOW SHE WAS SLEEPING—JUDE could just make out her inhales, nasal and hollow. Whatever tenderness she'd felt toward Bonnie earlier evaporated, victim to the same mysterious vicissitudes that made some mornings full of potential and others leaden with apathy, some Manhattan streets magical to walk down while others were unbearable. What had she *done* with herself, all day, alone? Jude only half believed that Bonnie had gone to a meeting; the other half of her guessed she'd passed the hours in some nasty Times Square bar. And yet she hadn't seemed drunk when she came in, and Jude didn't smell that old odor of gin breath, bourbon sweat.

On the screen, the actress and the nurse tiptoed around each other with spiteful restraint, both irritants to the other's peace. It irked Jude, to think of this male director guessing at female relationships; how women in films were always either pitted against one another in envy or close to the point of merging, even if the root of that closeness was, also, envy. Jude shifted, aware of her discomfort beside Hannah. *Always makes me think of you*, this woman had typed, accessing a whole other Caleb, a Caleb of ten years ago, whom Jude had never met. They had watched this very scene, Jude guessed, on a New School library DVD from the futon Caleb no doubt once owned, the kind that loses its square, becomes a parallelogram after too much sex. By sheer force of will she kept her eyes straight ahead, though Hannah was there in her periphery, flickering, knowing things, surely, Jude didn't.

Bonnie woke up perfectly on cue at the credits, blinking like a baby. Jude motioned her forward, and she and Caleb shuffled out, navigating the crowd.

Out on the sidewalk, they joined the huddle that had gathered beneath the marquee. A summer drizzle became, with one clap of thunder, a downpour.

She'd forgotten her umbrella at home. "What should we do?" she asked Caleb, only to turn and see her mother and Hannah embracing.

A serene smile stretched across Bonnie's face. She looked at Jude and blurted, "We know each other! We met this morning! Isn't that—"

"Is it okay to tell where?" Hannah asked Bonnie. The women were clutching hands now.

"Of course!" Bonnie yelled. Water streamed off the pizza-shop awning and rippled across Third Street in waving curtains. "I went to an AA meeting! And lo and behold, this sweetheart sat down right next to me! The crazy thing is," she went on, shouting over the rain, moving her look between Jude and Caleb, "I thought to myself, She seems like the sort of person Judy would be friends with—wouldn't Judy just happen to know her? Isn't that just—"

How baffling, Jude thought. How awful. Caleb's "friend," revealed. She tried to catch his eye, but he was looking away, over his shoulder, across the street. "Well, I for one am already soaked," Jude said, her call for their dispersal, but she was drowned out by the surround-sound pummeling.

"What?" Bonnie screamed. Pedestrians ran with raised arms, trying to make the light. Umbrellas flipped up like prop flowers. A line of people shoved through their sidewalk foursome, separating them, pushing Jude and Caleb out into the tempest. "Is there somewhere we can go?" Bonnie wailed. "Somewhere *dry*?"

A HOSTESS with orange lipstick made a fuss at first about the rope (*I'm not sure we can accommodate . . .*) but eventually gave up her tiny share of power when Caleb smiled at her. The décor was French-farmhouse rustic, rural dungeon chic; she led them to a sizable table near the back, mumbling that it was usually for sixes, a planked bench for Caleb and Jude and stiff-looking chairs for Bonnie and Hannah. It was early still, before the dinner rush; waiters in unnecessary leather aprons went around with long lighters, clicking flames into votives. Outside the paned windows, the deluge continued. Rivers flowed in the gutters.

Jude shivered in the air-conditioning. The rope was heavy with sog, her feet swampy in her sandals, and her blouse, of vintage navy silk, stayed plastered to her chest. She patted her face and arms with her napkin, then offered it to Caleb—determined not to be mad, to show him she wasn't mad. But he shook his head without looking at her. With rigid concentration he was studying the menu; defensive, she saw, annoyed, probably, that he was here at all, about to eat an overpriced, mediocre meal in the company of his current girlfriend, his alcoholic ex, and her new, unlikely friend, his girlfriend's also-alcoholic mother. She put her hand on his leg but he twitched, and she retreated. *It was all your idea, remember? The movie with Hannah. You made us!* This was her punishment. She would be on her own.

*

THE MENU WAS A SORT OF TEST BONNIE HADN'T STUDIED FOR, between its impossible words and filigreed font. Staring at the heavy paper, foreign meats or maybe cheeses, a medley of adjectives and nouns blended together and eluded her like paragraphs of wet print. The prices were through the roof.

"So, you really did go to a meeting then?" Judy was saying. The subdued rainstorm light, the flickering candle, opalized her skin, made it shimmery as makeup. "How was it?" But her voice was somewhat hopeless. Expectant, already, of Bonnie's next failure.

"It was wonderful, actually. Very inspiring. Very *sobering*, as a matter of fact." Someone filled their water glasses, and Bonnie drank thirstily, smiling against Judy's challenge. She swallowed. "And I'm going to go through the steps again, you'll be happy to know," though she found herself addressing the table more generally, more safely, Hannah and Caleb, too. "The whole kit and caboodle." She pointed at Judy. "Prepare yourself for a thorough apology." It came out jokey and weird. No, Bonnie, thought, wrong. She steadied herself. Her heart cleared its throat. "I'm sorry, Judy. About last night. I really, truly am. Your old mother." She returned her eyes to the illegible menu, before she embarrassed herself further with tears.

The waiter came over with a notepad. In the time it took for the specials to be prattled, Bonnie noticed that the tension between Judy and Caleb was also a tension between Judy and Hannah. You could see it in their distracted glances, their too-formal postures, their fidgets and their frowns. Judy was doing that thing she'd done since childhood, pursing her lips in endurance of a tumultuous inner question.

"Did he say *awful*?" Bonnie asked, when the waiter had left. "I think he said *braised awful meat*."

"It's offal," Caleb said. "O-f-a-l."

"O-f-*f*-a-l," Judy corrected. "As in entrails. Organs. As in the parts that *fall off* when you slaughter an animal. It's Dutch."

Caleb cleared his throat. "Jude works in restaurants, in case no one knew."

The waiter returned with their drinks—three club sodas and a cocktail for Caleb the color of Mars—and Bonnie took the opportunity to tell him, "Now, I still don't understand what kind of food this is. Half of it's in another language. Waiter, where are my subtitles!" She laughed, louder than she'd intended.

"Mom . . ."

Bonnie waved her hand and scowled. "Oh I'm joking." She smiled up at the man's tolerant face, pale after a close shave. "We just came from a foreign film." She liked the way this sounded. A New York sort of phrase.

Caleb ordered everything to share, his voice already bored by the prospect of eating. Bonnie nearly stopped him—she saw the tab tallying up, an endless, exorbitant receipt, but Judy, as if reading her thoughts, met her eyes and shook her head: *Don't worry*. She mouthed, *We're getting this*, by which she must mean Caleb. Last night at the bar, before she was too far gone, Bonnie had gawked to glimpse the contents of his wallet—thick, padded, *flush*.

Hannah tapped the table with her palm, like calling a kind of order. She looked at Judy with her creaturely eyes and let her country accent purr. "So, Jude—or Judy? Which do you prefer? How long have you lived in New York, then?" and again Bonnie sensed the awkwardness. They spoke like they hardly knew each other; Hannah inquired politely about Judy's restaurant and the magazine, Judy's college—and Judy responded with brief, one-sentence answers, then volleyed the same questions back, one for one, albeit with greater disinterest, just-perceptible judgment. And how was *her* job, her modeling? How much touching up did they do, Judy had always wanted to know . . . and how was her—what was it, acoustic guitar? It was nowhere near the acrobatic conversing Bonnie knew Judy to be capable of. How interested she could become, when the subject was a book she loved or some political idea—a skill she must've learned at the Geisens' kitchen table, over homey, nutritious cooking.

Bonnie felt some need to help. "Judy—Judy is a writer, too, you know," she said to Hannah now. When she touched Judy's forearm on the table, it was chilly as a bone.

"Oh, what do you write?" Hannah asked brightly. "Like . . . poetry?"

"Lately? Emails," Judy said dryly. "And text messages. Mostly."

Bonnie smacked the arm. "Oh, Judy, come on. Don't be—here—here—" and before Bonnie could stop herself, she had her bag off the chair and was rummaging. Retrieving the journal, she saw the cover had a sticky spot on one corner, tequila spill or burger juice from that bar, the beginning of yesterday's catastrophe. She licked her thumb and rubbed at it. "She's—Judy writes *fiction*. She has a story in here. A wonderful story. She's too humble."

Judy looked tense in the jaw, but Bonnie went on. "I thought it was just . . . so *vivid*," she stumbled, recalling what she'd really felt, her surprise and disturbance. "I loved it, Judy, I really did," she said finally, honestly. Because she loved *Judy*, and Judy had written it. "It was better than . . . well, it was definitely better than that film!"

Caleb asked, "What story?"

Stoically, Judy said to Bonnie, "Thank you. It won a prize."

"I never—when?"

She turned to Caleb. Mad, Bonnie saw. "You never asked," she said to him.

"Well you never—you never told me—"

Hannah cleared her throat. "That's wonderful. What's it about?"

There was a pause; Judy was signaling the waiter for a drink now, after all, and so Bonnie began, "It's about a girl who . . . well, she's an orphan, apparently, and she goes off to find her real mother. She hitchhikes way out into the desert . . . it's almost like a fairy tale, sort of, but modern . . ."

Bonnie went on, synopsizing as best she could while Caleb flipped through the magazine, then passed it across to Hannah, who nodded and smiled. But Judy looked upset, distraught, her eyes turned toward the window, away from the group. As Bonnie spoke, her heart tumefied, to remember the story's characters and the way she herself matched, too distinctly, the profile of that awful mother. "Anyway, I did . . . especially by the end . . . I did find the mother to be . . . I guess she's a good example of . . ." but she could only finish by saying it to Hannah. "The kind of mother, the kind of *person*, I don't want to be."

"Anymore," Judy finished. She said the word as if speaking to someone else, to her own face in the window across the room. As if Bonnie hadn't heard, she repeated, "The kind of person you don't want to be *anymore*."

The waiter came over with a large, white dish. "Grilled octopus meze with harissa, charmoula, and blackened scapes." Caleb unfolded his napkin while Judy went to work professionally, cutting the exotic tentacles into shareable portions. Hannah's hand found Bonnie's beneath the table and squeezed. Her smile, when Bonnie looked, ached with sympathy.

"Lift your plate, Mom," Judy instructed. Bonnie did as she was told.

"So, you didn't like the movie, then," said Caleb.

"It was fine," Bonnie said, distracted. There were other women her age in the restaurant, in smart trousers and coiffed bobs, miraculously unmussed by the rain, silk scarves dry as LA, accompanied by gentlemen peers. Their husbands, Bonnie guessed. Maybe the trouble was that Bonnie had never imagined herself old. She'd wasted all that time not preparing for it. The primal parts of her younger self had assumed she'd be dead before it set in, this long degeneration. "It was . . ." but no smart-sounding descriptor would come. "I liked the black and white."

"And did Caleb tell you," Hannah was saying to Judy, trying to draw her out again, as if nothing sour had happened, "about *Persona* in college? How he *embarrassed me* in this class, calling me out in front of our professor and everything—"

"Okay, all right," Caleb interjected.

"Well, and he was so much *older*, you know, than everyone else—he was a senior and I was a freshman, plus he started late—"

"Come on," Caleb moaned, "it was ten years ago—"

"No, you're right," Hannah conceded, smiling. "It's silly old history."

"I'm sorry, okay?" Caleb said. "I'm truly sorry for being so—"

"Man*splaining*," Hannah said to Judy.

"Well, sometimes men can't help it," Bonnie said absently.

"Excuse me?" Judy said.

"Sometimes men can't . . . control their . . ."—feeling her face heat up, unprepared to defend what she'd only let slip carelessly. She looked from Caleb to Hannah to Caleb then, putting something together. "So, you two know each other from college?"

Judy said, "They're old friends, Mom. They used to date. That's how we all know each other."

Bonnie could feel her mouth smiling; she'd put on lipstick at a makeup counter in Union Square, and now she saw its pink print on the rim of her water glass. It confused her, struck her as self-punishing and stupid, to go to movies with your exes, to stay friends or pretend to. She remembered how jealous it used to make Rick, the mention of any man with whom Bonnie had had sex. As if he could retain some illusion she'd been a virgin until him! As if he, himself, wasn't ruled by the impulses in his pants. "Well that's nice," she said now, pushing away the thought of Rick. "That you can all be friends and not . . . feel uncomfortable, or things like that." She cleared her throat in the quiet that followed, afraid she'd said, again, the wrong thing.

Hannah's eyes were focused down toward her lap, and tiny twitches in her neck revealed that she was tap-tapping on her phone but trying to seem discreet. When she glanced up, their eyes caught; she looked frightened as a little rabbit, Bonnie saw, before she looked away again quickly, raised her glass and bit her straw. A thought took shape in Bonnie's brain . . . a repellent thought she'd rather not be forming. The ex-boyfriend Hannah had mentioned that morning . . . and here was an ex, just across the table, still bound, absurdly, to her own daughter. Bonnie pushed herself to remember even as she recoiled from it. Had Hannah said *wanted to sleep*, a fantasy, safe as long as it stayed locked up inside her? Or had she said, as Bonnie feared, *sleeping with*, actively, in the present? And then there'd been the mention of the new girlfriend. Pretty and smart . . . *I can't stop sleeping with my ex* . . .

Another dish came. "Hen-of-the-woods, blood orange, fiore sardo, and spelt cracker."

But girls like Hannah would've had lots of boyfriends, surely, a whole slew of past lovers. It must be a different ex. There could be no other option.

Hannah excused herself for the bathroom, but when she stood up, her chair, weighted by her purse, toppled backward in terrible slow motion. A bus boy dove to catch it. Hannah looked around, blushing, smoothing down the front of a frilly, cantaloupe-colored onesie that couldn't be so different, Bonnie thought for the first time, from the lingerie she modeled. A vacancy rushed up where her feelings for this stranger had been. It was as if, having discovered a cute top at a store, you got it home to find it different in the bad light of your room: the shoulders unflattering, a button loose, deodorant stains from somebody else's pits.

*

WHEN HANNAH RETURNED, CALEB AND JUDE WERE LISTENING TO Bonnie with the same placid, suffering expressions on their faces—looks Bonnie must've thought she could break through, though she seemed to be making no headway. For a moment, Hannah imagined picking up her bag, claiming an emergency at home, her cat loose on the fire escape—but Bonnie turned to her and flapped an anxious hand. "Listen, listen, listen, I'm just telling about El Compadre, an old Mexican place on Sunset Jeff and I used to go to. Jeff is my brother, he passed a long time ago, but anyway, Jeff loved this place, and we'd go down there sometimes for margaritas and chimichangas. Anyway—"

Hannah must've missed some crucial segue while in the bathroom, but the gist of the anecdote seemed to be that down at this Mexican place, a little man would come around—a *midget*—in a mariachi outfit and an enormous plastic sombrero that doubled as a kind of serving platter for chips and salsa. "And he'd scoot up to your table and say, *Buenas noches, people!* and then stand there very still so you could take a chip and dip it!" She threw her hands up in amazement. "And I don't think he was even Mexican! It was an ongoing debate Jeff and I had. Was he *Mexican*, or just a very tan midget who knew a little Spanish?"

A silence ensued in which Hannah felt she'd become, unwittingly, the person at the table Bonnie was most performing for. She did her best to react—"That's—" fumbling for delight. "What a funny thing to have in a restaurant." She turned to Jude. "Did you ever go there, Jude?"

But Bonnie cut in again. "Oh no, by the time Judy was born there wasn't money for restaurants. Although later, actually, Judy's stepfather and I went. But the midget wasn't there. Maybe it was his day off, or maybe he had died. Rick was disappointed, I can tell you."

Caleb was on his third Negroni (not that Hannah was counting), and Jude had one too now; they looked delicious in the candlelight. She watched Jude pick out the twist and drink until there was only ice.

"You can't say midget, Mom. It's *little person* now."

Bonnie snorted. "Oh I can't, can I? I don't see any midgets in this room to—"

A voice said, "Burrata, muskmelon, guanciale, and torn mint."

Jude ordered another drink. Something mean sparked up in her eyes. Hannah had noticed this the first time they'd met in the spring, on the train. The new couple was en route to the Noguchi Museum while Hannah was on her way to meet a friend at PS1, and they'd suffered three immensely awkward stops together, awkward because, in addition to Caleb making no effort to facilitate small talk, just that morning he'd burrowed under the covers of Hannah's own bed, licked her until she came, then fucked her without a condom in the wet and blissful nonstate of her orgasm's aftermath. He'd showered in her bathroom. He'd used her towel. He'd brushed his teeth with her toothbrush, presumably to freshen his breath for *this*—what she was seeing now—a museum date with someone he'd mentioned so easily, so *by the way*, not three hours before. *I'm hanging out with someone. Just so you know.* Then, on the train, Jude had been hardly able to hide her snobbishness (they talked about the PS1 show, Jude so anxious to outknow Hannah, but coolly, as if she could care less) and yet Hannah had felt, too, a pull—a perplexing attraction to this girl, whom she found herself wanting to be liked by, against all reason, even while Jude intimidated her. It wasn't the same with Caleb. What she felt for him was a by-now-shameful need, an old, leftover sense of ownership and of having been happily owned that stubbornly refused to ebb. Since Jude moved in with him, their meet-ups had hardly stopped. She was at the restaurant plenty of evenings; often when Caleb came to Hannah's, he'd either just been there for a meal or would be headed there afterward.

Hannah looked at her plate now, the uneaten cheese browning by the second, the leaking orange and limp sea creature's tentacle. Worry twisted behind her sternum—what, exactly, had she said to Bonnie earlier? She hadn't used Caleb's name, she knew that much (she'd lived in New York long enough to know that *everyone* knew *someone*; you didn't use names unless you were trying to use a name). But what if Bonnie put the pieces together anyway? What if Bonnie repeated, later, to Jude, everything she suspected? What if she could read it, if they could all read it, in Hannah's awkwardness, Hannah's silent sitting, not touching the food, not participating in the table talk? If Hannah was accused, she would deny, deny, deny. And she knew Caleb well enough; he was incapable, actually, of telling the truth.

"I just think," Jude was saying now, "that since this story is such a staple in your repertoire, Mother, that maybe you'd want to, you know, update the terminology from time to time. Make it relevant. Since you so love telling it, and no one has any idea why."

Bonnie's eyes flitted around the table, puzzled, looking for some clue to her misstep. "Well I—I'm sorry, I didn't realize I'd told you about the midge—the *little person*—before."

Jude was beside herself. "Bonnie!" she shrieked. "I've been hearing about the little tan man since I was—god—six years old! And probably before that, I just don't remember or didn't understand language yet! It's the same stories, the same references, for literal decades now. It's like your own personal *mythology* that doesn't relate to anyone—to any*thing*—else! But it's not even the irrelevance that gets me, it's the *romanticizing*, the making funny. Jeff, okay, fine; I never knew the guy, you can romanticize Jeff until your hair falls out. But Rick was terrible! How can you even bring him up? All casual? He was *abusive*, obviously! How can you be in such denial, *still*?"

Outside, the rain had stopped, leaving the sky a spooky, moony green. The color of bad oysters, gluey in the shell. Of early summer hurricanes.

Bonnie looked at a point near the center of the table. "You know, you're very lucky, little miss, to have the life you have. Do you know that? To live here, to have lots of friends, to have your good looks and your smarts. Your writing to keep you occupied." Some of the bitterness drained from her voice. "Do you know how lucky you are?"

Jude snorted. "Oh, thank you for noticing, Bonnie. I do know I'm lucky, yes. And none of it's thanks to you."

The air seemed to stutter. A large party came in and settled across the room. Hannah was awash with shame, to be sitting here at all. Her own mother, in Bonnie's position, would have slapped her. Hannah would never dare. But maybe this was routine for Bonnie and Jude, saying cruel, cutting things. Maybe they enjoyed it.

Finally, Bonnie raised her eyes. Her face looked different—recomposed, without the faintest trace of upset. As if something hard to accept had at last been absorbed.

"I was thinking of something yesterday," she said. Her voice was gentle. "When I was up at the Statue of Liberty, looking out at the city, I was thinking how amazing it would be, how incredible, to live here, to be in Judy's shoes, to live Judy's life for a day . . . I was wondering to myself, *Now, how did my Judy figure it out?* Where did she get this . . . *idea*, this brilliant Judy idea, to leave her sad childhood behind, her dumb old mother, and make her life in New York?"

Another dish was set down, by a woman in kitchen whites, but this time silently. No one spoke. No one moved.

Bonnie said again, "Why did you, Judy, move? Here, I mean. Of all the places. How did you—how did you *know*?"

Jude was caught off guard; her brow furrowed, and she stared into her drink. She'd been prepared for a fight, Hannah saw, but her opponent had set down her weapon.

"I read about New York in another girl's diary." She looked up at Bonnie. "Remember Meghan?"

"Of course," Bonnie said. "She gained all that weight."

"So, Meghan and I"—but before she continued, she turned to Hannah. "Meghan was this mean girl I was friends with in middle school. I thought she was so cool, and pretty, and—well, you get it."

So Jude didn't hate her after all. It was the smallest indication, but Hannah was grateful.

"Meghan and I—I've never told you this before, Mom. Meghan and I met this high-school girl in a chat room—or who we thought was a high-school girl. One weekend we snuck out and took the train to San Luis Obispo. We told you we were going on some school trip, I remember . . . I wish I could remember more. Anyway, this was the summer after you and Rick got married, and you were . . . let's just say you were in love jail . . . and when we got there, to this girl's house, to Cassie's house . . . she wasn't there."

The story continued. It was a strange tale, dreamlike and unbelievable— writers tended to embellish, Hannah thought, for dramatic effect—and yet the way Jude's voice lapped on, hypnotically, describing, Hannah knew it couldn't be a lie—why would it be? She looked at Caleb across the table. His eyes were nowhere in particular. He seemed to be listening, or at least trying to appear listening, but Hannah saw through it, had long understood what narcissism—what buried fear—kept him always detached. Jude, of course, would know nothing of that episode, more than a decade ago, when he'd been caught. Their first Christmas together, he'd brought Hannah to the family's "cottage," a property several times the size of her own childhood home, perched on a sand dune overlooking Lake Michigan. While Caleb and his father were out shopping, Hannah had been left behind, stranded at the kitchen table with his mother, Lena, who shaped pie crust while Hannah fiddled awkwardly on her laptop, sensing she should be more useful, though she knew nothing about baking. For two days, she'd felt as if she were auditioning for the role of

Caleb's girlfriend, and his mother was the casting director: how many *questions* she asked, about Hannah's major and where she was from and *what it was like, growing up in the South*—so that the amount Lena knew about her grew exponentially on this visit, while Hannah continued to know very little about Lena except that she was an excellent cook who, at every meal, served Caleb first. Because she was nervous, and conversation had stalled; because Lena had begun humming along to Vince Guaraldi; because the tab was already open on Hannah's laptop, and the site appeared when she clicked her email closed—Hannah found herself asking, *Did Caleb tell you about the interview he did last month? That his painting teacher helped set up?*—not *forgetting*, exactly, what the interview included (the questions that appeared, now, on Hannah's screen as she scrolled) but not really thinking about it, either. Or thinking it wouldn't matter. This was his mother, after all, who of course knew everything already.

Interviewer: So, when did you start writing graffiti?

Interviewer: You memorialize your brother, now, in your paintings. He was your partner, right?

Interviewer: I hope this isn't too personal, but how did he pass?

Lena stopped with the rolling pin and scrunched her brow, injured. *An interview? He didn't tell me.* But her smile bounced back quickly. *I'd love to see it.*

Hannah pivoted the laptop. She didn't have to pee, but she excused herself to the bathroom.

CL: He developed a lot of health problems after this assault. This isn't really— it's not something I talk about a lot, but he was held at gunpoint in Detroit, writing graffiti, in 1997. Detroit is no joke, man; you're out there and, you know, you're exposed to the elements, violence included. These dudes rolled up on us one night. Another crew, tough guys, who had beef with someone we painted with. We were in this old house, just fucking around, nothing major—but they showed up out of nowhere and pulled a gun. Told us to strip, took our paint, and then, just, coated us. Painted us like we were furniture. People say these things happen really fast, you know, but for me it was slow motion. Silver is super toxic—whatever's in it that makes it metallic, and my brother got it bad. I recovered pretty quickly, but Miles was never the same. Lung issues and a bunch of other stuff. He was only nineteen when he died. I miss him every day.

Interviewer: Wow. That's so terrible. So, you were both attacked. I had no idea.

CL: Yeah, I mean, it's totally surreal. Part of me feels like it happened to someone else. Maybe that's a thing, right, with trauma?

Interviewer: I think so, yes. You disassociate.

CL: I would trade places with him if I could. My baby brother.

When Hannah returned, it was clear that something had gone very wrong. Lena's face, so impressive all that holiday in its happy elasticity, even at sixty-something, even having lost a son—looked bony, colorless, drained of life. She didn't look at Hannah. Her eyes were fixed to the screen in a kind of hypnosis, as if she were reading and rereading her own obituary, and Hannah knew she'd made a grave mistake.

But, it turned out as the truth unfolded, not as grave as Caleb's. An hour later, sobs having reddened her face and graveled her voice, his mother intercepted him halfway down the sloping drive. Caleb and Brian were opening the car doors, hauling groceries. In her mounting guilt, Hannah had trailed Lena almost loyally until, sensing the intensity of the coming family storm, she stopped on the salted steps, unsure of whether to stay or go back inside. She was learning as Lena wailed: he had lied in the interview—inserted himself into a tragedy that was not his, a true episode that had claimed a real life—and the depth of the offense began to clarify. If he'd lied in the interview he'd lied to her, too. When she'd first read the blog and so tentatively asked, *How come you never told me about that?*, and his voice had quivered as the tears rolled—*I'm sorry, I'm sorry*—she'd been confused; his apology had so outsized the crime. Now, this stranger in front of her, the bags weighing down his posture, had his head turned aside, his eyes closed, while a woman screamed accusations.

I forgave you for not going in there—I really did, of course I did; they had a gun, we forgave you! But to say it happened to you? Why? Why would you—

It just slipped out, Caleb said to the pavement.

No. No. Something like that doesn't just 'slip out.' What was happening in your head to—

Caleb's father facilitated a move into the house, while Hannah (she might as well have been invisible by then) slipped into the car to wait (thank god they'd thought to rent one, she'd think later: a torturous ride to the airport, at least, had been averted). After an eternity, Caleb appeared: threw their things in the trunk, bags still holding the presents they'd brought for his parents, then peeled down the steep drive so fast Hannah was sure they'd sail off the edge, down into the spindles of trees that met the ice-sculptural beach. But no, they drove, and they didn't talk; Caleb fuming and furious, doing eighty, ninety, on the forested Michigan back roads. They spent the night in a Red Roof Inn, got plastered watching television, fucked like devils (she'd taught him, of course, everything he knew). When they woke up, it was Christmas morning. They shared a curious, hungover numbness. They were still young and beautiful, the full-length mirror revealed, naked among white sheets, Caleb talented and going to be successful, Hannah grateful to be adjacent. What a relief to find them so: as if their survival of yesterday's revelations had somehow sealed the couple together overnight, dried the glue of an unspoken pact that they would, so simply, *look the other way.*

I have lied, but you'll still love me, Caleb's embrace wagered. *I have chosen one thing over another thing.* His hands were sweaty, clutching at her stomach from behind. She was only twenty!

But Caleb—Caleb had been twenty-six. *Mature,* as she'd imagined him. The possibility of righting the record was never suggested by either of them, just as neither worried (aloud, at least) over the lie's eerie permanence: it would stay on that website ostensibly forever, indelible information in the public ether, and soon enough it was reiterated. After Caleb's first solo show, the lie manifested again and again, in articles, reviews, other interviews, and on social media; in gossip exchanged at openings. *Why?* Lena's voice resounded. *Why would you lie about that?* Almost laughing, choking on the wrongness. Was it a coincidence, Hannah wondered now, that, shortly after, *WHY NOT* appeared in ink across Caleb's thighs? A philosophy of evasion, of inconsequentiality?

Hannah had given her hot beloved the benefit of the doubt: a blithe mistake, a weird fib, gathering unintended momentum. *He isn't a bad person!* Hannah had thought, even as her sense of him shifted, dimmed, so slowly it was hard to track.

A year into dating, away from him for even an afternoon, she grew irritable, despondent; the world had no color, and she did not like herself. She became suspicious he was cheating (the way he leaned in too close, to whisper into the ears of Justine or Amelia; his Nokia always on silent, facedown, within inches of his person). But when she sussed out his password easily enough and began checking his email (a habit that grew regular—compulsive, almost—over the course of their relationship), it wasn't missives to other girls she found but terse ultimatums from Brian LeBlanc—*All we're asking is that you acknowledge the mistake and correct it*—and long plaints from Lena: *Please call. I can't stand the thought of losing you, too.* One of these messages included a forward from someone named Taylor (a cousin? a family friend?)—an almost formal update that puzzled Hannah. *Dear Mr. and Mrs. Leblanc, I am doing good, I am screen printing a lot these days and working on T shirt designs. I'm making one for Miles, like a tribute, I will send you some when those are done. My health has been fine, no complaints. Thank you again for all your help with my doctor bills, I can never thank you enough for that. My grandpa is also doing good. He is in his shop every day still and has more energy then me. I'll send you those shirts soon. I hope you are both well.* It frustrated her that she couldn't ask Caleb directly—but she guessed this was another ghost from Caleb's old life. She'd written down his email address for future reference, on a slip of paper long since lost. Clicks into Caleb's Sent box showed that such messages remained perennially unanswered.

Finding no concrete evidence of infidelity relieved her, at least superficially (it would be years before Hannah could accept that Caleb was far from loyal; he merely preferred phone-based and in-person modes of deception, one of which eventually spelled their end). But awareness of a different precariousness took its place: if Caleb found her out, the snooping would be unforgivable; he'd leave her instantly. To compensate for her crime, to quell her guilt, she clung even more desperately to the ideal *him* she'd first fallen for—the handsome, talented, funny half whose whispered love, late at night, she still believed in. Any further insight into who Caleb was, engendered by the email-reading, became, instead, the ignored byproduct of her more urgent project of *keeping him*—of keeping the him she wanted intact.

If Caleb was a liar, then what had ever made Hannah, tirelessly devoted to a liar, any better? All these years, even after their dissolution, she'd returned to him—a kind of mirage-person that had maybe never existed—with the distorted belief that she was not quite real, not quite herself, without his obscure blessing.

Though she'd eaten almost nothing, acid moved north in her body. Across the table, he was draining the last of one drink and picking up the next as Jude continued to speak. He'd *tied* this woman to him! His faith in himself astounded her. She was afraid to move—to sip, even, her water—for fear she would scream everything, a manic confession before running outside and over the bridge, back to the safety of Brooklyn, where she'd never again leave the shelter of her eight-by-ten bedroom. His eyes moved to the ceiling as he tipped back the glass, but on their descent they met Hannah's. He looked worn down: the immense task of keeping up appearances, and of finding new people to fool. But then his stare composed itself in that old, familiar look that sought to dissolve her.

You are nothing, the look said.

No, you are nothing, she said back. Someone she knew, the roommate of her friend Gabriella, was a hostess at Jude's restaurant. It would be easy enough to get Jude's number. She thought she might throw up.

Jude was saying, "She'd written all about it in her diary," her tone morose, though Hannah had lost the thread of the story. "It was—I mean, she'd been assaulted like that, and I was . . . only because of these strange circumstances, the only other person who knew. A total stranger. Me and Meghan. Though Meghan didn't have much sympathy."

Hannah saw that Bonnie, too, had not touched her plate. "It reminds me of your story," Bonnie said to her water glass.

"Yeah," Jude said. She blinked very slowly. "I was thinking of Cassie—of where she might have been, of what she had been through—when I wrote Kiki."

"That ending," Bonnie said. Her voice bent down like a string while tuning. "Oh, Judy, that *ending*. I—how *awful*."

Jude smiled sadly, her lips closed. "But things like that happen all the time."

Bonnie cleared her throat. "Rick"—her voice trembled, then paused. "And were you thinking of Rick, with the Jed person?"

The name rhymed in Hannah's head as it had that morning, which seemed, now, years before. "Mom," Jude began, speaking into her drink, "do you remember when I told you that Rick walked in on me? And the things he said? It was—I told you right after that trip. We were in the car, on the way to Vons." She raised her eyes to Bonnie then. It was clear that Hannah, and Caleb, and the rest of the restaurant, the city, the world had disappeared. "I—I finally told you, I worked up the courage to tell you, and you didn't believe me. You said it was just an accident, and that you never wanted to hear another thing like that come out of my mouth, and that I should be ashamed of myself for making such an accusation. You sided with Rick. A guy you'd known six months. You went into the store to shop, and I stayed there in the car, and we never broached the subject again."

Close beside her, Hannah could feel Bonnie's radiant pain. She couldn't look. An alarm went off, and she jumped. Caleb raised his phone, frowning. It was time, he announced, for a photo.

*

WHEN SHE WAS A LITTLE GIRL, BONNIE HAD GONE ALONG WITH her mother sometimes, on weekends or breaks from school, to her cleaning engagements in Glendale mansions and Pasadena villas, rotundaed Spanish-styles and big, dark, leaded-windowed Craftsmans. Her mother would set her some time-consuming task: polish all the silver in the butler's pantry, or iron the spare sheet sets with the starch sprayer, without scorching. But there was one house belonging to an elderly couple, an old woman and her even older husband, who wouldn't hear of it—when she helped her mother haul in the mops and dusting caddies, the woman told Bonnie she could play anywhere in the house she liked, to make herself at home, to treat their furniture as her own, to eat the cookies in the cookie jar. Her mother hated this, of course, and wanted Bonnie to wait in the car—but Bonnie delighted in the woman's generosity and did just as she'd been invited to, knowing her mother was too fake-polite, too concerned with how others saw her, to undermine the offer. At the back of the house there was a small room with bookshelves all around and a collection of horns in cases, black metal music stands and chairs with embroidered seat cushions, a metronome she set to ticking, and French doors that opened onto a patio paved in slate, where flowers drooped in urns. Bonnie had seen fancy rooms before, in other mansions, but this one felt like *hers*, as private in its stillness as an organ in her body. She was outgrowing the age of make-believe and dolls, but she was not too old to imagine going back in time or being someone else. She moved around the room in circles, removing a flute and pretending to play, picking an old, clothbound book off the shelf and flipping through its dusty pages as if she were reading, as if she enjoyed reading, as if she were a woman who passed the time reading while her husband was off doing something brave. Lifting the figurines of small porcelain dogs from a dark-wood shelf one at a time, naming them, petting their shiny, hard coats, then reprimanding them, *Now, you have to wait here, Patchy, until my husband comes home at lunchtime.* But then one of the dogs had slipped from her hand and broken on the floor, its hind legs dislodging in a clean, pretty line, and she'd seen the blue cavity of an object revealed to be hollow, when Bonnie had assumed the dogs solid, almost living. Her mother rushed in and gasped. The old woman was kind about it, but Bonnie hid her face. Shame gripped her more mercilessly than any feeling she'd ever known. She could not find the strength to look up, let alone apologize. Somehow, it seemed, in the pit of her heart, that the woman, the dog, should apologize to *her*. On the car ride home, her mother was furious. She hoped Bonnie had enjoyed herself that day, because now she'd lost the privilege to come along cleaning, for good. Shortly thereafter—a week, a month, Bonnie couldn't be sure—her father threw her across the kitchen for not the first time, though *that* time she landed on the tile and lost consciousness. When she came to, they were sewing stitches in the back of her head, twelve, enough that it was hard to hide them later with her hair. Jeff had gotten a bracelet of cigarette burns.

She *didn't* remember it—in the car, before grocery shopping; maybe she'd been drunk, distracted and scared and eager to shove Judy's experience into the black space where so much else had gone. Still, she was supposed to respond now. Something crucial was required of her, as the seconds slipped and the camera was returned, but Bonnie had frozen inside herself. "Running away, all of it—it does sound very scary," she trembled. "And Rick—it turns my stomach. To hear that. But I'm—in all honesty, honey, I don't remember you telling me."

The restaurant, Bonnie noticed, was unnervingly musicless suddenly.

"Can you just say, *I believe you now*? Can you please just say, *I'm sorry*?"

She sipped her water cautiously and made her face impenetrable. Judy wanted an apology, but who had ever apologized to Bonnie? Something urged, *Tell her. Tell her she was right. Tell her you were wrong.*

When she looked up again, her daughter's eyes were on her. Bonnie felt gutted, her offal parts spilling out. "I—Judy—I'm—I simply don't *remember*."

How nasty Rick had looked, in that picture the girl had posted. And yet Bonnie wasn't Rick. She still had goodness in her and, attached to this, pride, however shredded, which she clung to with all her might. How else could she survive?

Judy sounded far away. "*I'm sorry, Petunia, that that happened and that I wasn't there to stop it and that I didn't do anything after you—*"

"I believe you now," Bonnie said stiffly. Like the last mother alive on earth, she'd finally been hunted down. "I believe you, and it makes me feel just . . ."

"I was terrified," Judy said. "That he might—"

Her heart rushed her throat. "But that was all, right? Just the peeping?"

Judy's voice was bitter. "It was enough."

SOMETHING was different around the table. Caleb and Judy were still there, Judy with her hands in her lap, her face tilted down, the restaurant glowy and sad in its candlelight, trying too hard. But the space on Bonnie's right was empty. With a start, she said, "Where's Hannah?"

Caleb sucked on ice. "I think she left," he said.

"She did," Judy said thinly.

They had frightened her away. The waiter came over and cleared all of their plates in one coordinated go. The woman they were with, he informed them, had seen to the check.

5. Tuesday

IT TOOK JUDE SEVERAL SECONDS TO REALIZE THE PINGING wasn't Caleb's alarm. He'd decided to forgo tonight's pictures; the dinner had exhausted all three of them, and he'd downed an Ambien, against her protestations, on top of all the drinks. His face beside hers was as placid as death. The sound came from her own phone, a text, glowing on the nightstand.

The message was long; the first wordy capsule filled the whole length of the screen. *Hi Jude, it's Hannah*—and her heart began to drum. *I have to tell you that Caleb and I*—she was entirely alert now. *It's been many times, not just once.* The typing went on and on, the messages appearing more rapidly than Jude could read. *I am disgusted with myself and don't expect your forgiveness . . . But I'm telling you anyway because you deserve to know.* She scrolled back to the top and read again, struggling to breathe, until each revelation clarified, and truth began its descent. *He's also used a story to get ahead in the art world. I'm sure he told you how he was attacked . . .*

Jude looked down at the sleeping man, as if for evidence of change, but he looked freakishly identical to someone she'd known mere hours ago. His inscrutable sameness made her stomach flip. His bottom lip hung open. He snored just gently enough that his nostrils flared, then contracted. In the filtered streetlight, his face was as stubbornly handsome as ever. It all seemed to prove what Jude already knew: that love was more honest than people.

Like the rest of the world, she was a fool.

She thought she might scream from claustrophobia. Every molecule of her skin cried for release. She gripped the rope, frayed and prickly, but rather than go at the knot, which was fused and hard as bone now, she concentrated on wriggling. She kicked down the sheet and lifted her pelvis, careful not to disturb the mattress, shimmying up as she pushed the bondage down. Her heartbeat filled her ears. Her hands were slick with sweat. *Shrink*, she willed herself. Become one compact, concentrated, manageable length of being. If there were any grace in the universe, let this, at least, be possible. She jerked down, scraping skin. The pain was fierce but she cleared her hips. She scooted and bent her knees. And then, as if by magic, she was free.

*

BONNIE WASN'T ABLE TO SLEEP, AND NOW SHE HEARD MOVEMENT in the bedroom. The squeak of a floorboard and the door cautious on the hinges. When Judy appeared in the dark, she was alone. Bonnie sat up and turned on the lamp. Her daughter came into view just standing there, in a T-shirt and underwear, gripping her phone. The look—the forehead-creasing worry—made a battlefield of her face. "Mom?"

They moved quickly and in silence. *Shhh*, she said, when Judy stuttered to explain. Bonnie knew. She put Judy in a pair of her own pants, then zipped up her suitcase and lifted it; rolling would be too noisy. They left like that, without turning in the couch or going back for Judy's bag.

Out on the street, the air was gummy and tropical. They waited at the intersection beside a garbage pile, Judy holding her shoulders and peering oddly down into it, while Bonnie flung herself into the bike lane, hailing anything, even cars that were not taxis, just to up her chances. She was good in crises— *Bonnie to the rescue*—except when she wasn't. A black sedan stopped. She flung open the door, and Judy, catatonically, climbed inside.

"We need a hotel," Bonnie said to the driver's head, hefting the suitcase in after her. "A decent one."

Judy roused herself. "Not Times Square." She gave cross streets and the name of a neighborhood, that lovely word, *Flatiron*.

Bonnie was so proud of her. "Oh, honey," she said, weepily but not about to let herself cry. "You sound like an aristocrat."

"It's near the restaurant we were at tonight." Judy was almost serene, looking ahead at the quiet streets, the whole neighborhood shiny as oil. "I know people who work there. They can probably get us a discount."

In three-quarters profile, etched at the cheekbones and framed by frizzing hair, Judy was a painting. They had half the same genes, mother and daughter, but Bonnie was certain she'd never looked like a painting, not once in all her life. Bonnie was more of a Polaroid. She hazarded to smooth a wisp back from Judy's temple. "It's good, whatever you're moisturizing with. You'll have to give me the name."

The car shuttled them fast. Judy turned toward the window. "I'm sorry for earlier," she said. "I know I can be terrible."

Something dislodged in Bonnie's chest, and she thought, it must happen now—it must happen before it doesn't. "I have to tell you something, Petunia. It's—you were right about Rick. I must've known it but I didn't—*let* myself know it." Was this true? It was as close to the truth as Bonnie could get. "He—I found out he raped—raped—he raped someone." The word contained so little, and yet it left her without blood. Her helplessness was immeasurable. "Right after we got married. A girl on his volleyball team."

For the first time, Bonnie really felt it. That girl. Just a teenager. The physical pain and then its memory, the long, long aftermath. Hating yourself, not knowing yourself, afraid of yourself. How long suffering could go on, Bonnie knew. Forever, if it had its way.

Judy kept her eyes out the window. She didn't gasp or yell. She exhaled deeply through her nose. "He should go off and die."

Bonnie let out a puff of laugh. She picked up Judy's hand and squeezed. "He should, shouldn't he. And leave his money to us."

"Or to her," Judy said. "How did you—"

"Oh, the internet," Bonnie said casually.

And then my mother and I rode over the majestic bridge, holding hands in the backseat. When we came into the city we were on a wide boulevard, at five o'clock in the morning, Judy might one day write.

Bonnie unzipped her suitcase and rifled—Judy had no purse, no supplies, and she was desperate, suddenly, to provision her daughter. She stuffed a few sad sundries into the crumpled bag from the museum, then found her coin purse, what little cash she had.

Beside her, Judy was staring down at a phone screen gone black. "Here— here—take mine," said Bonnie, digging for her charger.

But Judy shook her head. "It's okay. It's probably better if—"

"For now, it's probably better," Bonnie agreed. She clutched her hand again. Their time was draining away. Already they were in Manhattan, passing gated storefronts, fast food and clothes and twenty-four-hour pharmacies that turned corners fluorescent. At an intersection, two girls tottered and bent, clutching each other like just-born giraffes or the barely escaped. Figures took shelter in dark cubbies, and men in hard hats exited a chain convenience store.

Too soon, the car was slowing, pulling to the dreaded curb. Bonnie asked the driver if he could take her on to LaGuardia, but when he nodded, *No problem*, utterly bored, she couldn't help herself. "But just—not quite yet. Can you wait just a minute?"

Judy wiped her face on Caleb's T-shirt. "Or you could delay your flight? Stay a few more days, if . . ." Her voice trailed, second-guessing its hope.

Bonnie understood. "Oh, there'd be change fees and all that." She forced a smile. Greg was due to pick her up, and she couldn't ask the store for any more time off. Her life, modest as it was, was hers alone to tend to. "And you'll come to California soon, right?"

Judy's tears were back. She pressed her palms into her eyes, then brought them away, blinking, and when she looked at her mother she was smiling again. "Of course. Or you'll come back here whenever you can. Next time will be better." She laughed, and Bonnie laughed, for no reason and for every reason, and their laughs were similar, in pitch and volume and breath.

Just a little longer . . . A pang, and she missed her sharply—the daughter who kissed her mother on the cheek and was climbing out of the car, now, the ratty gift bag held against her chest, disappearing inside the revolving doors.

*

THE MENTION OF MAYA'S NAME AND THE DISASTER OF JUDE'S FACE were enough for the guy behind the desk to hand her a key to a comped room. She was speechless with gratitude. "You're good for tonight and tomorrow night," he said. It seemed, to Jude, like the rest of her life.

The room was on the sixteenth floor, with windows like a floor-to-ceiling dare and furniture so sleek and simple that the space seemed linked, somehow, to an early-life state of aloneness she hardly remembered. Jude took off her sandals, poured a glass of water, and climbed onto the big, starched bed. The human-sized air pulsed beside her. Caleb was gone. Her mother was gone. But the bag from Bonnie slumped on the nightstand like an afterthought, tearing at the handle. One at a time she removed a folded pair of underwear, a travel-sized Secret, a half-used tube of toothpaste, nine damp dollars. And something heavy. She unwrapped the tissue and stared. Even in the plastic case, the scissors were beautiful, substantial, with rose-gold handles discreetly engraved *MoMA* above the hinge. There was no note, but Bonnie's voice came wryly in: *Terrible timing, I know . . .*

She'd be at LaGuardia by now, enacting small braveries: walking barefoot through security; waiting for a dirty bathroom stall; panicking to buy coffee, find her gate, check her boarding pass—but smiling, always smiling, casting her goodwill upon anyone who would have it. Would Jude's heart always be half-broken for her mother? Of course it would; it was her own small bravery to know it.

Instinctively—as if Bonnie hadn't yet slipped entirely away, as if Jude might still catch her and wave, send off love—she went over to the windows. The view sucked her heart back. Down below, cars crawled in the grainy beginnings of morning—the rain-washed tops of trucks and buses, the shiny shells of cabs. The day's first workers hurried over damp concrete, swinging their arms and looking at phones, emerging from underground or sinking down the station steps, people the size of past-people, memory-people, when they've become very small and faceless, their points and purposes gone and yet there they remain, after all these years, stubbornly a part of you. When Jude looked up, the panorama was just awakening. New light crept up build-ings, blazed windows, turned corners and spread, painting walls, rooftops, billboards, everything. Her breath stopped—to catch the eye of her own impossible luck. She *was* very lucky. Beside a city plated gold, her problems were so earthly. The regret of yesterday; the ache of tomorrow. She watched the sky above Queens until a west-traveling plane lifted, rising into the fade, and then she pulled the curtains closed, hoping to sleep.

Acknowledgments

I'm filled with gratitude for the intelligence and warmth of my editor, Caroline Zancan, who understood the spirit of this project from the very beginning and helped make it so much better. Thank you to Lori Kusatzky, Molly Bloom, Molly Lindley Pisani, and everyone at Henry Holt, for all of your expertise and attention. The keen editorial insights of Henry Dunow were instrumental in making this book what it is. Thank you, Henry, for taking a chance on a new author during a global pandemic, and for the care with which you've treated my work.

Several residency programs gave me the gift of time away from the world to write. Thank you to the Wassaic Project, the Ox-Bow School of Art, the Studios of Key West, Marble House Project, and the Lighthouse Works, where the seed of this story was first planted. I'm especially indebted to the Helene Wurlitzer Foundation in Taos, where everything became sentences.

Thank you to Maia Asshaq, Dana Cohen, Alexis Georgopoulos, Suki Gershenhorn, Kathryn Mueller, Matt Polzin, Sheila Prelle, David Richardson, Kayla Romberger, Helen Betya Rubinstein, Walker Rutter-Bowman, Orion Shepherd, Stephen Somple, Sofia Theodore-Pierce, and Alisha Wessler, who each inspired and encouraged me at different times, in different ways, throughout this project. Special thanks to Nick, my oldest friend in Detroit, for first showing me the city and all its signs of life. Thank you, Paul Wackers; I'm a better artist because of you. Thank you to my dear Soumeya Bendimerad Roberts, this book's first reader and cheerleader, for your very big brain and even bigger heart.

Thank you, Tyler, for the enormity of your faith in me, and for sticking with me in this weird creative life.

Thank you, Alex, Mom, and Dad, for your unflagging love and support, through the writing of this book and always.

About the Author

Leigh N. Gallagher's work has been published in *American Short Fiction, Beloit Fiction Journal, Salt Hill*, and the *Reading Room* anthology, and in non-traditional formats through collaborations with artists and musicians. She holds an MFA from the University of Michigan, and her writing has received support from many organizations, including the Helene Wurlitzer Foundation of New Mexico, the Vermont Studio Center, and Marble House Project. Originally from California, she lives in Philadelphia. *Who You Might Be* is her first novel.